DIAMONDS OF DECEPTION

H.C. Hannah

ISBN: 9781795339254

For you mum and dad, with love
Thank you for always believing in me

ONE

10:17 pm, Sunday, September 3, 1995
Rock Palm Resort Hotel, Antigua

'And now, ladies and gentlemen, for my final illusion of the evening. Everything you've observed on stage tonight has followed certain laws: the laws of physics, the irrefutable natural laws of our world. I know that. *You* know that. Magic is merely an art form. It makes the impossible appear possible, the illogical appear plausible. The aim of a magician is to take the laws of nature and convince his audience that these laws are being broken. It's about smoke and mirrors, sleight-of-hand, misdirection, perceptual manipulation.

'Or is it...? Permit me tonight to challenge the laws of our physical world, to achieve the impossible. What you are about to see, ladies and gentlemen, is an illusion which has thrilled live audiences in theatres and fairgrounds since the late eighteen hundreds. It is an illusion which will astound and astonish, a deception which will delight and disturb!'

Seated somewhere in the middle of the fifth row from the front, fifteen year old Alicia Clayton fixed her gaze, through a pair of large, black-rimmed spectacles, on the magician. He was dressed in a flowing, black velvet cape with black trousers and a white shirt. He wore black gloves and his dark brown hair was scraped back from his pale face, onto which even paler makeup had been generously applied. Alicia sat mesmerised, scrutinising the magician's every move, not to be entertained, but to figure out how each trick was done. Of course she didn't believe in magic, or the supernatural — it was all nonsense as far as she was concerned, even if the magician's tricks *had* been impressive and his accompanying patter persuasive — but she did believe in hidden trapdoors, concealed compartments, smoke and mirrors, and the ability to deflect an audience's attention away from what was really happening.

The small auditorium was full, every seat was taken, yet an audible hush of tense anticipation hung over the spellbound audience seated in a wide arc around the stage. They had been amazed and enthralled throughout the evening with close-up magic, sleight-of-hand, card tricks and mental magic. In spite of the air conditioning, the theatre was hot and clammy. The sickly scent of dry ice, with a faint aroma of body odour, hung in the air. As the magician, alone on the stage, continued his monologue, synthesised chords in a minor key increased in volume. The suspense was building and Alicia tried hard to contain her excitement while remaining focused on the magician. She shot a swift glance at her parents who sat either side of her. Her mother gave a brief smile before redirecting her attention to the stage on which an elaborate set design had been constructed. It resembled a cemetery with an array of Gothic tombs, gravestones and fake, ivy-strewn wrought iron gates on each side; not exactly the kind of thing one would expect to see on vacation in the Caribbean, Alicia thought with amusement. It was a little too macabre and overdone; a far cry from the flamboyant Caribo Dancers and energetic steel drum band who had captivated hotel guests by the pool the previous evening.

In the centre of the stage stood a large, open-sided cabinet on a platform with a set of four steps leading up to it from the right hand side. The cabinet, about twelve feet high and made of dark wood, was elevated so the audience could see the stage behind and beneath it, and right through the cabinet itself. It was empty.

As the stage darkened, purple-coloured lights pirouetted across the ghostly set and the music grew louder. The magician fell silent and Alicia held her breath. Still alone on the stage, the magician walked slowly around the back of the cabinet with flourishing gestures of his gloved hands to show the audience that it was empty. On reaching the right hand side of the cabinet, he climbed the steps and onto the base of the platform inside to demonstrate beyond all doubt that the cabinet was, indeed, empty.

Alicia noticed that further to the right of the stage a large coffin, illuminated by the glow of a red light, was positioned, side on, with the foot end pointing towards the cabinet. Wisps of dry ice drifted around the coffin, garnished with cobwebs. Alicia's eyes darted back to the magician as he came back down the steps to greet one of his assistants who had entered from stage left. She was dressed in an elaborate ballgown — black in colour — with a tight bodice and a wide, hooped skirt with ruffles, down to the floor. Her long blonde hair, which held a soft wave, was partially scooped back from her face with a black velvet ribbon. She joined the magician who took one of her hands and kissed it delicately.

The magician's assistant gracefully ascended the steps into the cabinet where the wide, hooped skirt completely filled the platform on which she stood. She looked out towards the audience, a faint smile playing on her lips. Three more assistants in sequin-covered playsuits and knee-high boots joined the magician and took their places: two at each side of the front of the cabinet and one behind the steps. The purple lights danced in time with the music as the magician, standing in front of the cabinet, reached up and grabbed a cord which hung from the top of it. The two assistants standing next to him did the same with cords hanging at each side of the cabinet. The girl in the ballgown continued to smile at the audience. Alicia wondered who she should be watching. Who held the secret to this trick? The girl in the cabinet? The magician? Or maybe the assistant standing behind the steps with apparently nothing to do.

It became clear that the three cords controlled three shades which could be lowered at the front and sides of the cabinet. The magician let down his shade at the same time as the two assistants lowered the shades at the sides, but not all the way; each shade was lowered to just two-thirds down, leaving the ballgown visible in the bottom third of the cabinet. It swayed gently from side to side. Alicia watched intently, fearful that if she blinked she would miss a vital moment of the trick. *So far so good,* she thought. *The girl's still in there and so is her dress.*

As the magician demonstrated the girl's continued presence with more flourishing hand gestures, the assistant standing behind the steps neatly wheeled them to the side of the stage, leaving the cabinet with the girl standing inside, alone. The audience watched with intrigue — none so attentively as Alicia — as the magician strolled casually around the back of the cabinet behind the girl in the ballgown, clearly visible in the lower third of the cabinet not covered by the shades. *She's still there*, Alicia thought to herself.

Back at centre stage, the magician took hold of the shade at the front of the cabinet and fully lowered it at the same time as his assistants lowered the shades at the sides. Perfectly synchronised. All three shades were lowered to the floor of the cabinet, now completely obscuring the girl and her dress. Alicia watched carefully, but within seconds the magician and his two assistants released the three shades, sending them rapidly back up to the top of the cabinet. The girl and the wide, hooped ballgown had vanished. The audience gasped in surprise.

Suddenly, the beam of the white stage light which was focused on the now empty cabinet swung across to the right of the stage, illuminating the coffin. As the music and lights reached a dramatic crescendo, the lid of the coffin slowly began to open away from the audience. Still wearing the ornate hooped ballgown, the magician's assistant emerged from the coffin, immaculate and serene, as she had appeared in the cabinet just seconds before, the faint, all-knowing but never-revealing smile still on her lips. To a rapturous applause from the delighted audience, she walked gracefully towards the magician who extended his arm to her and bowed modestly to the auditorium.

With a standing ovation the audience continued to clap and cheer, but the magician and his assistants barely had time to acknowledge the accolade before the house lights came up and the music was all but muted. The cast of the magic team was suddenly joined on stage by the general manager of the hotel, a man in his early forties, dressed in a white, short-sleeved shirt and pale green trousers. He was holding a microphone with a lead trailing behind. The magician and his assistants looked momentarily confused before stepping aside as the man nodded apologetically at them. The applause faded rapidly, with the echo of a few lone claps around the auditorium from over-enthusiastic spectators. The latest arrival onto the stage began speaking into his microphone.

'Good evening ladies and gentlemen, I hope you enjoyed the show. It looks as though it was a great success! We're very grateful to have such talented performers here at Rock Palm.' He beamed at the small group to his right before returning to the audience with a more solemn expression. 'Please everyone, if you'd just take a seat for a moment...' He paused and waited patiently while the surprised audience obediently reseated themselves. When the momentary commotion had subsided, he began speaking again.

'As most of you know, my name's Leon Fayer. I'm the general manager here at Rock Palm Resort. I'm sorry to have to put a damper on such a wonderful evening — and, of course, the night is still young and the cocktail bar still open — but, as you're all aware, since last night we've had a number of serious weather warnings about an approaching hurricane from the Atlantic. Hurricane Luis. My team and I have been in continual contact with government officials and weather experts and have received regular updates on the path of the hurricane in order to keep you, our guests, as informed as possible. Your safety and that of our staff here is of paramount importance. To that end, I know you've all been aware of the possibility of evacuating the resort and, sadly for you and for us, shortening your vacation here in Antigua. Most of you, I know, already have travel arrangements in place for an early departure, and, with the help of your holiday reps and the airlines, have secured flights home tomorrow. I'm aware that most airlines have laid on extra flights in response to the hurricane warnings.'

Alicia glanced at her father with a raised eyebrow; he nodded confirmation that their premature flight home was booked. Under the heat from the stage lights, beads of sweat glistened on Leon's forehead. He dabbed his face with a handkerchief and continued.

'While we've all been hoping and praying that Hurricane Luis would bypass the Caribbean Islands, unfortunately I have some bad news. The very worst news, in fact. After weather forecasters informed us yesterday that Hurricane Luis became a Category Four hurricane — that's one where catastrophic damage can be expected — they've been tracking its path closely. It has since taken a definite westerly course and appears to be heading right for us.'

He paused. This time the gasp from the audience was one of alarm. Leon swallowed and ploughed on with his hastily rehearsed address.

'Please don't be concerned unduly; according to the forecasters the hurricane is moving in slow motion and is still between five to six hundred miles away from Antigua, which gives us time to prepare and evacuate and take all necessary precautions to ensure everyone's safety. Unfortunately, however, the hurricane is due to make landfall sooner than originally anticipated. As from tomorrow afternoon, the hotel management has taken the decision to close the hotel and therefore asks that if any guests have not yet finalised their departure plans that they speak immediately with our reception team or their holiday representative. We would, however, ask you to pack your cases this evening and be prepared for a more expeditious departure should circumstances change. Of course, my team and I will keep you fully informed of any developments.

'I'd like to thank you all for staying with us at Rock Palm and appreciate your understanding and cooperation in this matter. I wish you all a safe journey home and look forward to welcoming you back in the very near future. Thank you.' Leon gave a small nod to the audience and another to the magician and his assistants before stepping down off the stage and making his way to the rear of the auditorium. There was suddenly a low buzz of nervous chatter. The mood of excitement generated by the final stage illusion had been extinguished and replaced by concerned discussions about packing and flights and airport transfers.

'Come on you two,' Alicia's father said, the base of his seat springing up as he stood, 'we'd better get ourselves packed for the morning.'

'How d'you think they pulled off that last illusion dad?' Alicia asked as she followed her father along the narrow row between the seats to the aisle.

'I've no idea Alicia,' Paul Clayton replied. 'Probably had two girls in identical dresses or something. Now, I'm thinking we should meet for breakfast at eight o'clock sharp tomorrow morning. Do you agree Bryony?'

'That sounds sensible,' Alicia's mother replied.

'What time's our ride to the airport tomorrow?' Alicia asked, still thinking about the illusion.

'Eleven o'clock,' her father replied over his shoulder. 'You need to be ready for ten-thirty Alicia. I suggest we head back to our rooms now. Tomorrow's going to be a busy day.'

TWO

11:58 pm, Sunday, September 3, 1995

Alicia couldn't sleep. She tossed and turned and listened to the sound of the waves lapping on the beach a short distance from her room. The ceiling fan hummed quietly as she lay on her bed staring up at the gently rotating blades. It reminded her of the hurricane, far out over the Atlantic Ocean, its strong winds and thunderstorms spiralling around a central, clear eye, whipping up waves and preparing to ravage everything in its path as it spun relentlessly towards Antigua and the nearby islands lying helplessly in its track.

She wasn't sure whether her wakefulness was due to her contemplating the endless possibilities of how the magician's final stage illusion had been executed, or if she was excited about the prospect of being stranded on a tropical island when a hurricane hit, however unlikely that was. Regardless, Alicia decided that this, the last night of the holiday, surely shouldn't be wasted in a hotel room. Lost sleep could be restored during the flight home. She sat up and reached for her spectacles on the bedside table. Sliding out of bed, she padded across the room to the slatted doors which led to the terrace outside. She pushed them open and breathed in the warm night air. A half moon shone brightly and stars shimmered in the deep indigo sky. Tall palm trees swayed in the gentle breeze. Crickets and tree frogs chirruped pleasantly. Alicia slid her feet into her flip-flops, grabbed her little flashlight and stepped outside.

Dressed only in a vest top and pyjama shorts, she relished the feeling of the warm tropical heat which instantly engulfed her. Quietly pushing the doors closed behind her, she set off on the path to the beach. It was illuminated by low-level lights and flanked by palm trees, bougainvillea, hibiscus and tropical foliage, which displayed vibrant shades of pinks, purples and reds by day. Alicia breathed in their delicate floral scent, mingled with the sea air, as she made her way down a set of shallow stone steps which led to the beach: a wide stretch of soft white sand. Taking off her flip-flops, Alicia walked barefoot a little way towards the sea, enjoying the feeling of the velvety sand between her toes, still warm from the heat of the day.

She glanced momentarily back towards the hotel, brightly lit against the dark sky. She could hear muffled voices and the soft clink of glasses as guests, making the most of their last night of vacation, enjoyed late night cocktails at the pool bar overlooking the beach. To the right of the pool bar was the open-sided restaurant with its spectacular sea view, now closed but with a handful of waiting staff placing cutlery on tables in preparation for breakfast. They appeared solemn and subdued, Alicia observed, in contrast to their usual laidback, cheerful demeanour. Hardly surprising, she thought to herself. The tourists were leaving — some had already left and the rest would be departing in the morning — but the properties and livelihood of the inhabitants of the island were under the threat of a looming cloud of devastation.

She gazed back out to sea. All was calm and quiet with nothing but the sound of the waves and tree frogs, a typical Caribbean night, relaxed and carefree, which made it hard to imagine that five hundred miles away, across the ocean, an angry, raging hurricane was heading straight for them. The calm before the storm, just like the buildup to the final stage illusion in the magic show. Just like the magician's assistant, gliding serenely across the stage in her elaborate hooped dress, preparing for the action that would take place inside the cabinet. Which still had to be figured out.

How did they pull it off? Alicia's mind explored countless possibilities, most of which were flawed in some way. Was there a second girl in the coffin, dressed to look exactly the same as the first, as her father had suggested? But where did the first girl go? The cabinet was open-sided; you could see right through it and underneath it. There was nowhere for her to vanish. Trapdoors under the stage? The girl could have climbed down through one trapdoor and then up into the coffin through another. Again, that wasn't feasible because the audience had had an unobstructed view beneath the cabinet, through to the back of the stage, the whole time. And there was still the question of how the girl had managed to disappear from the see-through cabinet and reappear within seconds. It just wasn't possible. But it had to be, Alicia thought. Because it had really happened. She had seen it with her own eyes.

She was suddenly aware of raised voices coming from the direction of the hotel. Turning, she noticed the silhouettes of three figures in the restaurant. Most of the staff had disappeared, having finished their preparations for the morning. Alicia recognised the three figures as Leon Fayer, the general manager of the hotel, and two guests whom she had observed from time to time during her stay. They behaved as if they were an extravagantly wealthy couple. For a start they were staying at Rock Palm Resort, which certainly wasn't the cheapest on the island. A classy but low key hotel, set in a magnificent beach location overlooking a crescent-shaped bay with a vivid turquoise sea and dazzling white sand, it was one of the most exclusive, not to mention expensive, places to stay. There were only two reasons her father would agree to the family returning to such a resort year after year. Somehow, his line of work in property development had forged connections with Carlos Jaxen, the owner of the hotel. They had become firm friends and business associates over the years and, as a result, Mr and Mrs Clayton had only to pay for their flights. Their rooms — always the luxury suites — came with the unreserved compliments of Carlos. The second reason was that Bryony, his wife, loved Antigua and wouldn't consider staying anywhere else.

But the couple in the restaurant with Leon, who looked to be in their early forties, seemed to exude wealth to Alicia, from the expensive-looking luggage set they had arrived with, to the endless supply of somewhat dubious outfits, jewellery and shoes the woman styled herself in. They also displayed an entitled, condescending attitude to the hotel staff and most of the other guests which Alicia disliked immensely. The only person she had seen the woman interact amiably — perhaps even flirtatiously — with was Owen Rapley, the tennis coach and sports reception manager.

The trio in the restaurant seemed to be having an intense discussion which was careering rapidly towards a heated argument, although Alicia was too far away to hear anything other than raised voices. From his body language, Leon looked as though he was attempting to pacify the woman, who seemed to be distraught about something. Intrigued as to the nature of the argument, Alicia decided to take a stroll up from the beach and along the path just in front of the restaurant. Blessed — or cursed — with an inquisitive nature (sometimes she wasn't sure which), it had been Alicia's childhood dream to become an investigative journalist. Always one who wanted to be where the action was, she could make a compelling story out of the most mundane state of affairs.

As she returned to the path, a young couple approached her. They were making their way to the beach, preoccupied with each other. Alicia glanced casually at them as they passed her. They were laughing together, oblivious to her presence. Suddenly, she stopped and her eyes locked onto the couple in surprise. She recognised the handsome, well-built frame of the man and the slim figure and long, blonde hair of the woman: it was the tennis coach, Owen Rapley, and the magician's assistant — the girl in the black ballgown — whom Alicia knew only as Anastasia, her stage name.

They walked hand in hand towards the sea as Alicia stared back at them, blinking through her spectacles. She was tempted to run over to Anastasia and ask her the secret of the illusion. Then again, if the young woman was staying in the hotel, perhaps Alicia could accost her at breakfast. Satisfied with this idea, she turned back to the restaurant where the heated discussion had intensified and was now within earshot.

'I'm terribly sorry about this, Mr and Mrs Karleman. Really, I am.' Leon Fayer sounded flustered. He patted his forehead with a crumpled handkerchief.

'*Sorry*?!' Mrs Karleman replied sharply, in a clipped British accent. She was wearing a fuchsia-pink chiffon gown which served only to accentuate the lobster-red of severely sunburned skin. 'I'll need more than a *sorry* from you, Mr Fayers. I'll need a full explanation as to the whereabouts of a diamond necklace worth nearly ten million dollars.'

'Believe me, Mrs Karleman, I have my guest relations team looking into this urgent matter as we speak.'

'Vivienne darling, I'm sure it will show up soon enough,' Mr Karleman said, bravely. He was deeply tanned and gym-honed with close-cropped dark hair and piercing blue eyes. The angry glare of his wife stifled any further offers of reassurance he may have been about to make.

'Exactly whose side are you on, Charles?' came the furious retort.

'Well, we don't know for sure that it's been stolen…'

Vivienne Karleman's face, crimson from sunburn, began to turn almost purple with rage.

'Of *course* we do Charles. What're you implying? That I've just *lost* it or something? Dropped it in the pool?'

'No darling, I merely said…'

'It's quite obvious that one of your staff has *stolen* it, Mr Fayers.' The wrath of Vivienne had redirected itself to the general manager, who looked like a frightened rabbit paralysed by the headlights of a monster truck. Alicia was slightly irritated by the way Vivienne insisted on adding an "s" to the end of his surname.

'It's *Fayer*, you ignorant woman,' she said under her breath. She leaned against a palm tree with her back to the restaurant, gazing out to sea, as she listened to the heated conversation with curiosity.

'Mrs Karleman, I can assure you that none of my staff have stolen your diamond necklace,' Leon said firmly. 'They're an entirely honest and trustworthy team of people; they're like family and I have the utmost confidence in them. We've never had any items go missing from the hotel safe in the twenty-seven years I've been general manager here.'

'Until now,' Vivienne Karleman cut in sharply.

Alicia knew of the diamond necklace Vivienne was referring to. It was hard to miss. In fact, it was the most incredible piece of jewellery she'd ever seen. Vivienne had worn it on a number of occasions during her vacation, mostly at dinner or in the cocktail bar, keen to flaunt it at any opportunity. Alicia didn't know much about diamonds, but from the way it sparkled and shimmered in the light, she knew the necklace was something special, almost mesmerising. A circle of glittering, colourless diamonds with a dazzling pear-shaped, pink diamond in the centre, it was a stunning piece of jewellery and captivating to the eye. To learn it was worth nearly ten million dollars came as no surprise, although the idea of wearing something so valuable seemed overwhelming to Alicia.

'Now Mr Fayers,' Vivienne continued in a condescending tone, 'you'll be needing a full description of my necklace.'

'That won't be necessary, Mrs Karleman. My reception team made a comprehensive note when they checked it into…'

'It consists of forty-eight flawless, round brilliant cut diamonds on a single circular thread. The pear-shaped, pink diamond in the centre…'

'Vivienne darling, Leon's just told you, he knows what the necklace looks like,' her husband interjected wearily. He turned to the general manager and, with a desperate expression, almost pleaded with him. 'If you could, you know, get your team to try a bit harder to find the necklace. I'm sure it's here somewhere, but, well what with the hurricane on the way and the hotel being evacuated, time is of the essence.'

'I'm not leaving until my diamond necklace has been found — hurricane or no hurricane — and neither are you or any of your staff, Mr Fayers,' Vivienne snapped. Both men looked startled and finally Leon's patience and calm exterior also snapped.

'*Mrs* Karleman,' he said forcefully. 'We are doing everything we can to locate your diamond necklace, but right now we are also dealing with the very real threat of a Category Four hurricane. While your necklace is important to us, in the grand scheme of things, the safety of the hotel staff and guests is my top priority. I'm afraid that whether we find your necklace or not by tomorrow afternoon, you and your husband, along with the other guests and the hotel staff, *will* be leaving this hotel. Is that clear?'

Unable to compose a quick-fire response, Vivienne stood open-mouthed and speechless.

'I'll be in touch if we have any news on your necklace,' Leon said curtly, adding, 'goodnight Mr and Mrs Karleman,' with an air of finality before he turned and made his way out through to the pool deck behind them.

Alicia was suddenly excited at the prospect of a missing diamond necklace, especially one so magnificent and with such a price tag. She debated whether or not to conduct her own search but the time on her watch showed it was just after one am and there was a place she meant to explore.

As she approached the now darkened entrance to the auditorium, located on the east side of the resort, she glanced behind her. The hotel was all but deserted with most of the guests having retired to their rooms, some not sleeping as peacefully as they might have hoped, the looming threat of a hurricane turning the most pleasant dream into a disturbing nightmare. The subconscious could be a powerful thing, Alicia mused, gently pushing the unlocked, wooden-slatted door open. She stepped inside and switched on her flashlight, shining it around in front of her. The foyer was long and narrow with a white-tiled floor. To the left and right it led to a pair of wooden, saloon-style doors at each end, which opened out into the auditorium. The only sounds were the sway of the palm trees catching a lift in the breeze outside and the slapping of Alicia's flip-flops as she turned right and walked to the end of the foyer, retracing her steps from earlier in the evening. As she slid through the doors, they swung shut noiselessly behind her, and she stepped into the auditorium.

The place stood dark, silent and empty, a far cry from the bright lights, dramatic music and rapturous applause of a few hours before. Alicia shone her flashlight in a wide arc across the rows of red velvet seats which sloped gently down towards the stage. The exit lights in the aisle stairs between the seats emitted a faint golden glow. Standing still at the top of the auditorium, part of which must have been built underground, Alicia shone her flashlight towards the stage and inhaled sharply. The wooden cabinet was still there, right where it had been at the end of the show, along with the graveyard props and the coffin. Surely the magician and his team should have packed everything away by now, in order to make a swift exit from the hotel in the morning? Alicia wondered why it was all still here, with not so much as a frond of ivy or a cobweb cleared away.

The temptation was too great for the inquisitive fifteen year old to leave without first inspecting the props. Shining her torch slowly from side to side, she descended the stairs towards the stage. A faint smell of dry ice and body odour still hung in the hazy air. She reached the bottom and walked to where a small set of stairs led onto the stage. Gingerly she climbed them and, as she stepped onto the stage, turned and shone her flashlight out into the auditorium across the vacant seats flanked by the two aisles. The place looked smaller from here.

Swinging the beam of her torch back towards the stage she approached the props, reaching the coffin first. The lid was open and, apart from the fact that the side facing the rear of the stage was open — this detail not being visible to the audience — it had no secret compartments or trapdoors beneath. Alicia tapped at the crude wood from which it was made and carefully inspected the nearby props and surrounding area, but there was nothing perceptible to reveal how the trick was done.

Disappointed, she shone her flashlight towards the cabinet, now with the shades fully up and the sides open. She walked across the stage and examined it more closely. There had to be something here, some clue as to where the girl in the ornate, hooped dress had disappeared. She shone the light upwards and along each side of the cabinet to where the shades were fixed to the wooden frame at the top. Here she spotted something which surprised and faintly puzzled her: the cabinet had no ceiling. She peered under the base of the wooden frame and stopped suddenly, her lips curling into a small smile. As she straightened up, she noticed the steps the magician's assistant had used to climb into the cabinet were still pushed away to the side of the stage near the coffin.

She perched on the side of the cabinet and swung her legs up into it before shining her flashlight around inside the wooden structure, above her and below, onto the metal base on which she stood. She stamped firmly with one of her feet sending an echo around the auditorium; it seemed solid to her. She began to inspect each corner carefully when suddenly she heard a noise from the direction of the foyer. She stood still and listened. It was the sound of soft but audible footsteps. She clicked off her flashlight and climbed silently down from the cabinet. Carrying her flip-flops, she walked barefoot to the stairs at the edge of the stage, just visible from the light of the exit sign above.

As the slatted door at the top of the aisle stairs began to open, Alicia dropped to her knees and crawled between the front two rows of seats. Trying to control her breathing, she listened quietly as someone entered the auditorium. She saw the beam of a powerful flashlight and heard footsteps descending the aisle stairs towards the stage. Was it the magician returning to pack away his props? Surely not at this hour of the morning? Why hadn't he switched on the house lights? Was he alone?

The footsteps came closer as the unexpected visitor neared the stage. Alicia crouched low in the shadows, between the two rows of seats, as a pair of man's brown leather shoes stepped into view, behind the beam of the flashlight. They stood still on the bottom stair, just in front of Alicia. She slid her gaze upwards from the shoes. The man wore a pair of dark grey cotton trousers and a white linen shirt, open at the neck. As she looked up at the back of the man's head and the side of his face, Alicia caught her breath in surprise. It wasn't the magician. It was someone who surely had as little business in the auditorium as she did that night. It was Charles Karleman.

THREE

Charles remained standing on the bottom step of the aisle stairs for a few minutes, casting anxious glances at his watch and occasionally looking back towards the door at the top of the stairs. He was nervous and agitated and appeared to be waiting for someone. Finally, after another check of his watch, he pulled down one of the front row seats to the right of the stage and sat on it. Alicia suppressed a frustrated sigh. She was trapped. She knew she'd be in trouble if she was found sneaking around the auditorium in the middle of the night. An explanation would be required for her parents as well as the hotel manager. The lesser of the two evils which presented themselves at that moment was to wait it out. Charles stood up and walked towards the stage.

'Megan? You there?' he called uneasily into the darkness. His voice echoed slightly and was followed by silence.

'Megan?' he called again. He looked at his watch and swore under his breath before walking to the side stairs and climbing onto the stage. Through the gap between the front row seats Alicia watched as he navigated his way cautiously between the stage props, the beam of his flashlight casting ghostly shadows from the gravestones and wrought iron gates. The cabinet seemed to take on the form of a giant gallows.

'Megan?' Charles spoke a little more intensely.

She's not here Charles, Alicia wanted to say. *No one's here but me.* She wondered who Megan was. One of the other guests? What on earth was he doing here, of all places, in the middle of the night, meeting with another woman? What was wrong with the beach like everyone else? And what would his obnoxious wife Vivienne say if she found out? Then again, she was probably too obsessed with the hunt for her missing diamond necklace to care about... Alicia's train of thought stopped abruptly as a terrifying scenario crossed

21

her mind. What if Charles was secretly meeting one of the female guests for a sordid last night stand? A quickie on the stage between the gallows and the coffin. A last chance saloon before the end of the vacation. Alicia didn't need this. It was the very last thing she wanted to have to witness. She had to get out of there. She peered through the gap in the seats at Charles who had sat down on the front of the stage with his legs dangling over the edge, flashlight beside him. He'd obviously been stood up, although his face bore more of a look of desperation than of disappointment.

As the minutes ticked by, Charles grew more impatient and Alicia more uncomfortable. She was almost at the point of breaking her cover when Charles, apparently deciding he couldn't wait any longer, slid off the stage and made his way slowly back up the aisle stairs. Alicia heard the door at the top of the auditorium open and swing shut followed by footsteps in the foyer and the entrance door opening and closing. After two more minutes of silence, she decided it was safe to emerge from her hiding place. With one final glance at the stage, she headed back up the stairs to the foyer, conscious of the possibility of running into Megan — whoever she was — late for her secret rendezvous with Charles.

Once outside, Alicia breathed a sigh of relief and made her way back to the hotel. The moonlight and glow from the low-level path lights was enough to see without the need for her flashlight. The tree frogs and crickets continued their enthusiastic chorus in spite of the late hour, along with the gentle sound of the waves on the beach. The hotel was dimly lit and Alicia could see the small reception area was empty as she approached, save for the lone receptionist, engrossed in paperwork. Alicia walked confidently past, nodding politely. The receptionist nodded back before returning to the papers on the desk in front of her.

The pool bar was deserted and Alicia circled the edge of the swimming pool where the moonlight reflected on the still, silent water. On the opposite side was a set of small steps down to a pathway which led back to her room. She was surprised to see one of the hotel waiters hurrying up the steps carrying a tray covered with a white cloth. She remembered his name — Anton — from when he had waited at their table a couple of nights ago. He was particularly memorable because her mother had commented on how rude and inattentive he'd been towards the guests throughout dinner that evening. As Alicia was well aware, manners were important to her mother, who had been close to complaining about Anton's.

'He never smiles either,' Bryony had said. 'Not once have I seen that man make an effort with the guests. The other waiting staff are so polite and friendly. What on earth is he doing in a job serving customers? He obviously hates it.'

As they passed each other, Alicia smiled at Anton but, as usual, he appeared preoccupied and barely noticed her. Probably busy with late-night room service, Alicia thought. Apparently the most suitable shift for him. She jogged down the steps onto the manicured grass which stretched from the guest rooms to the beach and was interspersed with beds of tropical plants and tall, swaying palm trees. As she headed for the path, Alicia wondered whether the light breeze from earlier in the evening felt a little stronger. She glanced out to sea, searching for signs of an approaching hurricane, when suddenly she spotted a lone figure walking up the steps from the beach. She assumed it might be Owen Rapley, the tennis coach, but to her surprise it was the magician. He was dressed in black and although he no longer wore the pale stage makeup, his face took on a deathly pallor in the moonlight. He walked with his hands in his pockets and his gaze directed downward. To Alicia's relief, when he reached the path, he turned east, towards the main hotel, in the opposite direction.

She walked a little faster, glancing over her shoulder to check he was still walking away from her, but he had disappeared. Even his stage name, *Mallory Mortimer, Master of Deception*, sent shivers down her spine after her father had pointed out that "Mallory" was derived from a French word which meant unfortunate or ill-fated and the first part of the word "Mortimer" was *mort*, a French word meaning death. But she didn't need to ask the magician how his grand stage illusion with the vanishing girl had been executed; by the time she reached her room, the final workings of the trick were clear in her mind.

As she fell into bed and drifted to sleep, she dreamed of being a magician's assistant, of the dramatic music, the swirling stage lights and the cheering audience. But the music quickly became dark and haunting; the cheers of the audience, chilling screams. The purple-coloured lights began to turn a shade of deep crimson, like blood, illuminating the eerie shape of a coffin and the wooden cabinet, which contorted into a gallows. A rope hung from the top of the frame. It was looped around the neck of a body which swung gently to and fro. The face of the body was pale, like the magician's. But as it swung on its rope, it abruptly changed to that of Charles Karleman, and then Vivienne Karleman, wearing the glittering diamond necklace on her sunburned décolletage, and then Anastasia, the magician's assistant in the hooped dress.

Alicia awoke with a start and sat up in bed. The air conditioning was set on high but she was sweating and clammy. She oriented herself and checked the time on her bedside clock; it was nearly four am and still dark outside. She thought she had heard a noise or a cry, a scream perhaps. She wasn't sure whether it was a man's or a woman's voice. Was that what had woken her? Then again, maybe it was all just in her dream. She took a sip of water and settled back into bed, listening to the sound of the waves as she drifted back to sleep once more.

Alicia and her parents were seated for breakfast in the restaurant overlooking the bay at a few minutes past eight that morning savouring warm croissants, crispy bacon and fresh fruit from the buffet. In spite of the dining room staff attempting to keep up the holiday mood for the last remaining guests, the atmosphere was far from casual; it was tense and uneasy with an air of apprehension. The dark clouds obscuring the azure blue of the Caribbean sky and the strong breeze which had picked up overnight did little to assuage the concerns of both staff and guests. Hurricane Luis was moving closer. Unusually for this time of the morning, there was a chill in the air and the aquamarine of the sea in the bay, which was notably rougher than usual, had turned an angry shade of grey.

The main topic of conversation between the guests over breakfast was the approaching hurricane and the staff did their utmost to provide updates and reassurance. Leon and his guest relations team were on hand, armed with clipboards, weather reports and travel information, ensuring the evacuation arrangements for everyone were on track. As she spooned yoghurt over her fruit, Alicia felt sad for the staff who were doing their best to appear understanding and sympathetic towards disappointed guests. Sure, holidays were being cut short, wedding and honeymoon plans were cancelled and day-trips aborted, but nobody's homes or livelihood were under threat. She watched with a tinge of heartache as members of the resort grounds team shimmied up tall palm trees to cut down larger branches, which fell forlornly to waiting groundsmen below and were thrown into a small trailer. Other staff members were boarding up windows and doors, stacking tables and chairs, taking down parasols and piling up sandbags, in an attempt to secure the property as best they could. There was activity everywhere, but not the usual cheerful hustle and bustle of the resort that the staff and guests were accustomed to.

Most of the guests were either British or American and would be piling into a variety of taxis and minivans for the ride to the airport later that morning. Every hotel porter appeared to be on duty, wheeling luggage on trolleys in one direction, through to the entrance area for the mass checkout.

'How did you sleep Alicia?' Bryony asked her daughter.

'Er, good, thanks mum.' Alicia suppressed a yawn and felt her cheeks flush. Was it a leading question? Did her parents know about her night time escapade? To her relief, her mother moved the conversation along.

'I wish I could say the same. I didn't sleep at all well. I suppose it's from worry about this hurricane. I do hope they'll all be safe here.' She broke off as Anton stopped by their table to refill their coffee mugs.

'So you're all leaving us today?' he said unexpectedly, with a downcast expression which Alicia was sure he was faking. He looked at each of them without so much as a knowing glance in Alicia's direction.

'Yes, we're sorry to be cutting our holiday short, but even more sorry at the thought of the hurricane heading straight towards this beautiful island,' Bryony replied.

'Hopefully we won't suffer too much damage and then you can come back and finish your vacation,' Anton said, in an attempt at cheerfulness.

'Oh — well, of course, we'd like that,' Bryony said, slightly taken aback at Anton's cordiality, 'wouldn't we, Alicia?'

'Absolutely,' Alicia replied quickly.

'I'll be here waiting for you!' Anton joked awkwardly as he turned towards the next table to offer a refill of coffee to an elderly couple.

'What's got into him this morning?' Bryony asked suspiciously.

'He's probably thrilled all the guests are leaving,' Alicia volunteered.

'It's a little strange,' her mother said. There was a pause before she continued. 'I just hope they'll all be okay here. I feel so sorry for the people who live here, their homes, their livelihoods.'

'I'm sure they're doing everything they can to keep themselves safe,' Alicia's father interjected. 'They know they have to be prepared for this kind of thing. Alicia, you are all packed, aren't you? The porters are collecting our cases at nine.'

Alicia nodded at her father.

'Good,' he said, taking a gulp of coffee and attacking a slice of bacon with his fork.

If one casually observed the Clayton family from a nearby table, it would almost certainly be noted that while Paul and Bryony Clayton were fair skinned with blonde hair, Alicia's skin took on an olive tone and her hair was dark brown. Alicia's surname had not always been Clayton, although she had no idea what it was originally because she had been found abandoned on a street in the East End of London as a baby. She never knew her biological parents and, in her view, there was little point in trying to find out. She spent her early years as Alicia Jones in a variety of foster homes before being adopted just before her fifth birthday. Nobody actually knew when this was, but the medical team who assessed her when she was taken to a hospital as a baby, suggested it was roughly around the beginning of July. Since that time, her official birthday became July the first.

Paul and Bryony Clayton were a wealthy couple who had everything they could wish for, except the one thing that they longed for the most: a child. To their immense sadness, all interventions and attempts to have a family had failed, for no identifiable reason. By the time they made the decision to adopt they were in their mid-forties and the hope of a biological family was all but gone. The adoption agency had a small number of children whom they recommended to the Claytons as possible matches. Alicia wasn't one of them. It was during a meeting with Tammy, a member of the adoption team, that Bryony noticed Alicia's photograph, which had slid out of a confidential file on the desk.

'Who's that little girl?' she had asked, captivated by the dark eyes and inquisitive smile.

'Erm, let's see...' Tammy had picked up the thin file, opened it and scanned the front page. 'Her name's Alicia Jones. She's four years old. We're looking for a foster family to place her with at the moment. She's not getting on too well with her current foster parents.'

'Could we meet her?' Bryony had asked, glancing at her husband who had nodded his agreement.

'Er, sure. I guess I could get something set up.' Tammy had appeared slightly taken aback. 'I thought you were interested in a child of a slightly younger age, but of course, I'll make some enquiries and get back to you. In the meantime, would you like to ask any questions about any of the other children here?'

'No thank you,' Bryony had said firmly, 'we'll wait to meet Alicia.'

The loose photograph changed their lives forever and Alicia Jones, a girl who had drifted from one foster home to another with no real identity, became Alicia Clayton, loved and adored by parents who had wanted her and chosen her to be theirs.

'Alicia, have you finished your breakfast?' her father was asking. 'I need to go to reception and confirm the time of our airport transfer; we might be leaving a little earlier than originally planned.'

In a flurry of pastry flakes, Alicia hastily shovelled the last chunk of a croissant into her mouth, ignoring the disapproving look from her mother.

'Alicia, really…' Bryony began, but Alicia had caught sight of someone approaching Leon on the other side of the restaurant.

'Isn't that the magician from last night?' she asked with her mouth full.

'*Alicia*!' her mother said sternly.

'It *is* the magician,' Alicia said. 'By the way, I worked out how he did that stage illusion last night. Anyone want to know?'

'Yes, of course, but we ought to be going,' her father replied, getting up from the table.

'He seems upset about something,' Bryony observed with a frown as she turned in the direction Alicia was pointing.

'He does,' Alicia agreed. 'I wonder what's happened.' She briefly recalled his pale face as he walked up the beach path in the darkness a few hours before.

'I'll meet you two back at our rooms,' Paul was saying. 'I'm going via reception.' As Alicia and her mother got up from the table and passed close to where the magician and Leon were standing, Alicia strained her ears.

'You haven't seen her this morning then?' The magician sounded anxious.

'I'm sorry Mallory, I haven't,' Leon replied, patting his forehead with his handkerchief. He turned to a guest. 'Yes, Mrs Fisher, the porters will take care of your cases.'

'She was supposed to meet me and the other assistants at the pool bar at eight this morning. We need all hands on deck to dismantle the stage props. It's not like her to be late.'

'I'm sorry, but I haven't seen her at all today.' Another guest interrupted the conversation and Leon broke off to reply. 'Of course Mr Terrill, let me check for you… yes, here we are, your airport pickup time is ten-thirty. No problem at all.'

'So you've no idea as to her whereabouts?' the magician asked. Leon's reply was silenced by a familiar female voice.

'Mr Fayers. I need to speak to you immediately.'

As Alicia and her mother made their way through to the pool deck area from the restaurant, Vivienne Karleman entered with Charles in tow, close behind. Alicia glanced briefly at Charles, wondering if he'd managed to locate Megan, whoever she was. From the wearied look on his face she guessed not. But then again, a mere few minutes in the company of his wife would probably sour even the freshest of faces.

'I hope you have some good news for me this morning Mr Fayers,' Vivienne began in a threatening tone. The troubled look on Leon's face suggested that he had nothing of the sort.

'Leon,' Mallory interjected, 'I really need to be getting back to the auditorium. You will let me know if Anastasia reappears, won't you?'

It sounded almost comical coming from a magician.

'Yes, yes of course I…'

'*Mr* Fayers, I am *speaking* to you and I dislike being interrupted *very* much. It's the height of rudeness.' Vivienne stepped forward. Leon took a deep breath. In spite of the cooler temperature of the morning, he pulled out his handkerchief. A bead of sweat from his brow trickled down the side of his face.

'*Now*,' Vivienne went on, 'about my diamond necklace…'

FOUR

09:24 am, Monday, September 4, 1995

'For anyone booked on the British Airways flight leaving Antigua at four pm this afternoon, your luggage is over here by minivan two.' A sweating, flustered-looking holiday rep, dressed in a white shirt and navy skirt, both of which were at least two sizes too small, stood in the covered area outside the hotel reception. With one arm she pointed and waved, while balancing a black, leather-bound folder bursting with papers and documents in the other. The animated expressions on her face vacillated between radiant smiles at guests to intensely troubled looks at her folder, to the frustrated rolling of her eyes when nobody appeared to be paying attention to her instructions.

'Is there anybody here booked on the British Airways flight at four o'clock?' she asked again, her voice an octave higher.

'Is that us, dad?' Alicia looked up at her father who was scanning a newspaper he had picked up from the restaurant at breakfast.

'We're on that flight, yes,' Paul Clayton nodded, 'but we're not going in the minivan; we've got a private transfer to the airport at ten-thirty.'

'Why do we have to get there so early if our flight's not till four?' Alicia asked.

'Well, sweetie, because of the hurricane the airport's going to be packed. They need to fly every last tourist off the island today, so check-in and security and everything are going to get very busy and will take a lot longer.'

'So we've still got an hour until our taxi leaves here?' Alicia asked. She looked at the chaos around her: the array of suitcases, the confused, anxious guests, the harried hotel staff and holiday reps trying to appear calm, the porters struggling to wheel luggage trolleys through the mass of people gathered outside the hotel entrance, and the taxi and minivan drivers, patiently waiting to load their vehicles with tourists and luggage, all destined for the airport.

'Something like that,' her father replied, glancing at his watch.

'In that case, can I go and take a last look at the beach?' Alicia asked tentatively.

'I don't see why not, as long as you're back by ten-thirty.'

'We'd better say ten-fifteen.' Her mother interrupted the conversation. 'Just in case the taxi gets here early.'

'All right, ten-fifteen,' her father agreed. 'We've got a long day ahead of us so go and stretch your legs and enjoy the scenery, but make sure you're back on time.'

'I promise,' Alicia smiled at her parents. 'Ten-fifteen.' She squeezed her way through the throng of bodies back into the hotel, through the reception area where the reception staff were settling final bills and checking out the last guests in a turmoil of paperwork and whirring printers. She continued along the covered walkway which led to the pool deck area. Her parents knew their daughter's inquisitive, energetic nature too well to insist she stood and waited with them for an hour in the crowded hotel entrance. From the time of her adoption at the age of five, she had insisted on knowing everything there was to know and understand — from the point of view of a five year old — about her adoption, including the reasons why her new parents had chosen her. Even as a young child, she had been remarkably matter-of-fact and accepting and had adjusted well to her new family.

Passing a couple who were wresting with their suitcases on the steps to the pool deck, apparently having missed the instructions to leave all luggage in their room for the porters to collect, Alicia took a circuitous route around the pool bar, back to the restaurant where she could hear the formidable voice of Vivienne Karleman in another heated discourse with Leon.

Towards the beach and out to sea Alicia observed menacing grey clouds which hung in the darkened sky, heavy with moisture and a portentous sense of foreboding. Hurricane Luis was on its way, beating a path to the island. Nothing could stand in its wake. Palm trees bent and swayed in the wind, stronger now, which whistled eerily through the covered passageway between the pool deck and the restaurant, temporarily drowning out Vivienne's shrill voice. Alicia shivered; the air temperature seemed to have cooled even since breakfast. She was wearing a cotton blouse underneath a short, denim pinafore dress — the clothes she'd elected to travel in — but had left her cardigan with her luggage.

Suddenly, there was a low rumble of thunder, far out across the ocean. Alicia scoured the horizon and wondered exactly how close Hurricane Luis was. Would their flight take off in time, before the storm hit the island? Her thoughts were interrupted by a high-pitched scream coming from the beach. She turned sharply to see one of the female guests, a middle-aged woman in a long, flowing dress, emerge from the direction of the beach path. She looked pale and shocked and was panting, breathless from running.

'Help!' she screamed, catching sight of Alicia and a young couple nearby. 'Help! There's a body down there, on the beach. It's a young woman... I think she's... There's blood everywhere...' Too short of breath to finish her sentence, she jabbed a finger frantically in the direction of the beach path, her dress flapping wildly around her ankles in the breeze.

'Someone help!' the woman shrieked again, as Leon appeared at the entrance to the walkway with Vivienne and Charles close behind.

'Is everything all right out here?' he asked. He looked past Alicia, who stepped back into the shadows, and caught sight of the female guest approaching, wide-eyed with fright and gesturing wildly towards the beach.

'Mrs Sheehan, what's happened? You look like you've seen a ghost.'

'There's a body... On the beach...' Mrs Sheehan gasped, before bursting into tears. 'Oh gosh, it's awful...' Her voice quivered and she put her hand to her mouth.

'A *body?*' Leon asked in disbelief.

'A woman's body,' Mrs Sheehan continued, 'covered in blood... it looks like she's been... *stabbed.*'

'Is she — moving?'

'No,' came the reply through fits of sobbing, 'I mean, I don't know, but I think she... I think she's *dead.*'

As Leon reached Mrs Sheehan, she collapsed into his arms with an agonising wail as he tried awkwardly to console her, still with a clipboard under one arm. Charles and Vivienne remained where they were, close to where Alicia was standing. Vivienne was silent. At that moment, Owen Rapley appeared from the opposite side of the pool deck. Spotting him, Leon motioned to him to come over.

'Everything all right, Leon?' Owen asked, looking with concern at the trembling Mrs Sheehan.

'I'm not sure,' Leon replied, unable to extricate himself from the frightened guest. 'Mrs Sheehan was walking on the beach this morning and says she saw a woman's body...'

'She's just down there, lying there on the beach...' Mrs Sheehan interrupted, turning to point in the direction of the beach once more, 'covered in blood. She's been — you know — stabbed.' She descended into another episode of inconsolable sobbing into Leon's chest.

'Right. Okay.' Owen began composing himself, 'We'd better take a look.' He pulled his radio from his belt and spoke into it. Alicia heard him request assistance from security and a staff member with first aid skills. The muffled reply from the radio was inaudible, but Alicia guessed from Owen's acknowledgement that help was on the way.

'Anyone else on the beach, Mrs Sheehan?' Owen asked.

'I — I don't know.'

'That's okay,' Owen said, a little more gently. 'D'you think you'd be able to show us where the body is?'

'I... yes, I think so.'

'Let's go then. The other staff will catch us up.'

A body. On the beach. Alicia was already imagining the cover story she would write for the school newspaper on her return home. It could be her big break for a part time job with the local newspaper. Of course, she needed to *see* the body — just briefly — in order to write an accurate description. Leon, Owen and Mrs Sheehan had already started back down the beach path, and there wasn't much time. Alicia hurried through to the restaurant, passing Vivienne and Charles, who remained where they were, unsure of what to do. From the restaurant, Alicia stepped through the open side which led onto a grass lawn area, before making her way towards a small grove of palm trees interspersed with foliage, between the hotel and the beach. The trees were more thinly planted here, to allow guests a sea view while they dined.

The last part of the way down to the beach was a little steeper, before the grass gave way to soft, white sand. Alicia scanned the immediate area around her, wondering where the body was. There was an elderly couple further along to her right, who seemed oblivious to Mrs Sheehan's discovery. The beach was otherwise deserted, with most guests choosing to remain in the reception area to await their airport taxis. Alicia glanced to her left and suddenly spotted it. A few feet away, there was a woman's body lying face up on the sand, with what looked like deep gashes across her chest and neck, now covered in congealed, dark red blood. She was wearing a short black dress which was twisted around her torso.

Breathing hard, Alicia steadied herself against a palm tree. She heard voices from her right and knew that Leon and company would be there in less than a minute. She needed a good, first-hand description for the school newspaper. She couldn't let her own fear or squeamishness stand in the way. Swallowing hard, she took a step towards the body, followed by another. As she walked closer, she noticed the woman had bare feet with red-painted toenails and slim, toned legs, as if she was some kind of performer, perhaps a dancer. Alicia forced a brief glance at the mangled chest area and then at the woman's face, partially covered by her long blonde hair, damp and matted.

Suddenly Alicia noticed something familiar, loosely attached to the woman's hair: a black velvet ribbon. She remembered it from the previous night when she had seen it twice before. The first time was on the stage in the auditorium, the second as she had walked up from the beach on the path towards the hotel. Mesmerised, Alicia walked slowly towards the body. She knew she shouldn't touch anything, or even leave footprints in the sand surrounding the scene of a crime, but she had to know for sure if it was her. A few steps closer and Alicia was two feet away. She could see the deep stab wounds, so apparently ferocious that the ones across the woman's neck had almost completely decapitated her. As the feeling of nausea arose in Alicia's throat, she looked straight at the woman's face, and with a small cry, closed her eyes and looked away. It was her. It was Anastasia, the magician's assistant. Her glazed, bloodshot eyes were open, but with a fixed, vacant stare; a stare of one for whom attempts at resuscitation would be futile. Her skin was mottled, pale and bloodless. Her mouth was partially open, as if she'd been about to cry out. Her lips were cyanosed and cracked, and brushed with a thin layer of sand.

There was a crack of thunder far out to sea and Alicia heard voices behind her. It was time to leave before someone spotted her. She took one last glance at Anastasia before hastily retracing her steps back through the palm trees and foliage. Remaining in earshot, she turned to see the small band of hotel staff — closely followed by a couple of curious hotel guests — led by Mrs Sheehan, Leon Fayer and Owen Rapley, as they approached the body of the magician's assistant. Alicia tried to process the image she had just seen: the mutilated body lying in the sand, the red-painted toe nails, the deep stab wounds, the fixed, vacant stare and the matted blonde hair with the black velvet ribbon. A few seconds in time would be etched on her memory forever.

Owen, the first to reach the body — now partially obscured by foliage from Alicia's vantage point — knelt down in the sand. Even though it was clear to everyone that the young woman was beyond reviving, he gingerly reached out a hand and placed it tentatively on a small piece of skin on her neck, bloodied but still intact, in the region of the carotid artery. It was a token move at best. He looked up at Leon with a small shake of his head.

'Isn't that... yes, I think it's her. I think it's Anastasia, one of Mallory's assistants,' Leon said quietly, peering over Owen's shoulder, a troubled look in his eyes. 'He was searching for her this morning, said it wasn't like her not to show up to help with dismantling the stage props. I told him I hadn't seen her, and now I'm going to have to tell him that she's — she's been found...'

'I'm sorry Leon,' Owen said standing up, brushing his hands on his shorts. Alicia noticed they were trembling slightly. 'Yes, you could be right. It could be her. I don't know her personally I'm afraid — not well enough to be sure she's one of the magic people — but she does look a little familiar.'

Alicia frowned. *I don't know her personally I'm afraid…* What was Owen on about? He and Anastasia had certainly been more than merely acquainted on the beach path the previous evening. How could he now deny knowing her? Alicia watched him carefully. In spite of his shaking hands, he appeared detached and emotionless, almost completely unaffected at the sight of the murdered girl.

As four other members of staff from the hotel joined them, Leon, visibly upset, attempted to take charge, giving instructions.

'Er, Violet, could you — would you — please take Mrs Sheehan back to the hotel and get her a cup of tea. Or a brandy. Whatever you think. And Roslyn, the police; can you ask one of the receptionists to call them? Tell them to come as soon as they can. What else… Eddy, are you okay to stand guard by the body? Don't let anyone come within five yards, no, make that ten; I suppose this is a crime scene now. Henroy, if I'm right, and this is Anastasia, one of Mallory's assistants, would you ask him to come down to the beach? You know, just to confirm it's… the body… it's her. He's dismantling props in the auditorium. At least that's where he said he'd be. And on your way back can you cordon off the beach path? With some rope or tape or something? We can't allow anyone on the beach until the police get here…'

Alicia watched the commotion but with particular attention to Owen, who had quietly retreated to the edge of the group. Why had he not admitted to knowing Anastasia? They had clearly been close in one sense or another. Did he have something to hide? He had quite possibly been one of the last people to see Anastasia alive. Perhaps he *was* the last person. Had he murdered her?

Suddenly remembering she'd promised to rejoin her parents outside the hotel reception at ten-fifteen, Alicia checked her watch. She realised with horror that it was nearly ten-thirty. She desperately wanted to stay and observe the events unfolding on the beach, but her parents' disapproval if she delayed the airport transfer was far less appealing and so, with reluctance, she retreated to the restaurant. By this time a small group of staff and guests, eager to know what was going on, had gathered just in front of the restaurant, trying to catch a glimpse of the excitement on the beach below. Charles and Vivienne were not among them, although Anton, the waiter, was watching the developments with interest. Avoiding the onlookers, Alicia stepped up into the restaurant further along and hurried to the hotel entrance where she was greeted by her parents, displeased at her late arrival.

'Where have you been?' her mother asked with annoyance. 'It's ten-thirty Alicia, our taxi's been waiting for five minutes.'

As Alicia reached them, her mother's voice changed to one of concern. 'Are you all right? You look very pale. What's happened?'

'I'm sorry mum,' Alicia said. She knew she was shaking and tried to steady her voice. 'I've got something to tell you both. There's a body. On the beach.'

'You can tell us on the way to the airport,' her father replied briskly. Alicia wondered if he'd even heard what she'd just said.

'A body, dad. A woman's been murdered.'

'A body? Murdered?' Her mother looked at Alicia, shocked. 'What d'you mean? Has it been washed up on the shore or something?'

'No, she was murdered on the beach,' Alicia said.

'Oh my goodness, what's happened?'

'Let's finish this conversation in the taxi,' Paul said firmly, pointing to a black minivan with darkly tinted windows. 'If there's actually been a murder then it's a matter for the police, not for us and definitely not for you Alicia. There's nothing we can do and I don't want to be delayed a minute more.'

Mr Clayton ushered his wife and daughter through a small band of guests towards the minivan, where the taxi driver stood by the door waiting for them. To her right, Alicia noticed Charles and Vivienne standing next to a mountain of expensive-looking suitcases piled high on a luggage trolley, most of it Vivienne's probably, Alicia thought to herself. Standing silently, side by side, the Karlemans appeared pale and subdued. They neither looked at nor spoke to each other. The loss of the diamond necklace had obviously hit them hard.

'Look mum, it's that couple,' Alicia said under her breath.

'You didn't actually *see* the body, did you?' her mother asked.

'Come on you two,' Paul said impatiently behind them. 'I don't want to keep our driver waiting any longer.'

'Sorry we're late, it's my fault,' Alicia said apologetically as they reached the minivan.

'No problem,' the taxi driver replied with a wide smile revealing a gold tooth, 'we still got lots of time, but the hurricane's on its way. We need you all to stay safe.'

'Thank you,' Alicia said, climbing into the van and settling into a single seat towards the rear.

'Don't you want to sit with us darling?' Bryony asked, sliding along the front row of seats.

'I'm fine here,' Alicia replied shortly. After the events of the morning she wanted to sit alone and replay the beach scene again in her mind. She watched Charles and Vivienne as they stood waiting for their own ride to the airport. They looked straight ahead without even acknowledging each other. From Alicia's perspective, they appeared agitated and uncomfortable. *They're probably just all shook up after losing the diamond necklace*, she thought to herself. She pictured the necklace in her mind and wondered where it was. Perhaps it had been found and was safely stowed away in one of the suitcases. But Vivienne's solemn expression said not. So then where was it? Had it really been stolen by one of the staff, as Vivienne suspected? Or perhaps one of the guests had broken into the hotel safe, or bribed one of the staff for access, and taken it.

The cogs in Alicia's imagination whirred with possibilities as her father, the last to get in, moved across the seat next to his wife. The driver slid the door shut before clambering into the driver's seat. He started the engine with a roar, scribbled something on a notepad before placing it in the pocket beside him, and began a slow turn around the circular, tarmac driveway which opened out onto a single track road leading away from the hotel. Fifteen year old Alicia gazed out of the window through her large, black-rimmed spectacles towards the chaotic entrance of the hotel. As the minivan rounded a corner and the hotel temporarily disappeared from view, Alicia's thoughts shifted from Charles and Vivienne and the missing diamond necklace to Anastasia's body on the beach. She longed to know what was going on down there as more questions flooded her mind, along with the image of the bloodied body. It would be a long time before she could forget it. The scene would be imprinted in her memory, perhaps forever. It would play on her mind, along with the torrent of questions.

Why had Owen behaved as if he didn't know Anastasia? They'd been together the previous night. Had he murdered her? Why? Alicia realised she herself must also have been one of the last to see Anastasia alive. Would the Antigua police track her down to question her and find out what she'd seen? But what *had* she seen? She tried to remember events as they had occurred the previous night and decided she'd write them down as methodically and objectively as she could at the airport. She wished she'd paid more attention to Owen and Anastasia instead of heading to the auditorium. Perhaps if she'd followed them to the beach she might know what had happened to Anastasia. She could have been the star witness in a murder trial.

As the minivan continued its slow-moving journey along the narrow road, winding its way up a hill through a palm tree-studded golf course, Alicia looked back at the hotel, growing smaller in the distance. Beyond the beach and the bay, the sea, with its white-tipped waves, was wild and black. A stark reflection of the angry grey clouds above. Alicia wondered if the body on the beach, so viciously hacked to death, was even real. Had it actually been there at all? Was it Anastasia, beyond all doubt? The words from the magic show, delivered by Mallory Mortimer, the Master of Deception himself, drifted into Alicia's mind. *Magic is merely an art form. It makes the impossible appear possible, the illogical appear plausible… It's about smoke and mirrors, sleight-of-hand, misdirection, perceptual manipulation. What you are about to see, ladies and gentlemen, is an illusion….* Was Anastasia really dead or, in the words of the magician, was it merely an illusion?

The minivan reached the end of the track leading from the hotel and turned onto the main road. Alicia gazed back towards the bay. It was to be her final glimpse of Rock Palm Resort for twenty-three years.

FIVE

A few hours later, a black van which held a woman's body covered with a plastic sheet and strapped to a gurney, sped along a narrow road flanked by a high-rising bank on one side and a steep drop on the other. Both sides were covered in trees and thick, overgrown foliage. The driver of the van was Dr Daryn Miller, a medical examiner who was accompanied by his assistant, Tyrell Green. They were on their way back to a hospital mortuary in St. John's, the capital of Antigua. Daryn stepped on the gas pedal as he accelerated out of a sharp bend, red-lining the needle on the tachometer gauge.

'Dr Miller, would you mind slowing down a bit?' Tyrell ventured nervously. 'This ain't no race y'know.'

'A hundred mile hour winds about to whip the hell out of this island and you tell me to slow down,' Daryn replied scornfully. He crunched the gears, hunting for second. 'You an' me are gettin' back to the hospital as fast as we can. Last place we wanna be right now is stuck out here, trust me.'

'Hurricane Luis's not gonna reach us before nightfall,' Tyrell replied, adding, 'my Aunt Tamila say we ain't gon' get no hurricane anyway. She say it's gonna go right by us to the north.'

'Your Aunt Tamila know better than the weather experts, does she?' Daryn stepped hard on the gas pedal again and swung violently into a corner. Tyrell grabbed hold of the handle on the door of the van. Convinced they were on two wheels, he cast a terrified look at the gurney in the back, its flimsy caster wheels secured to the floor of the van which rattled and bumped over the uneven tarmac as Daryn braked and accelerated, swerving to avoid potholes and traffic.

'Dr Miller. Slow down,' Tyrell said again. '*Please.*'

'Chill out Tyrell,' Daryn replied, 'you'll thank me later.'

'Not when I'm lyin' in a hospital bed in a plaster cast.'

'What're you sayin' 'bout my driving?' Daryn looked indignantly at his companion who suddenly threw his hands on the dash.

'DR MILLER! WATCH OUT!' Tyrell screamed.

Daryn turned back to the road in alarm to see a large, black SUV heading straight towards them. With the steep drop falling away from their side of the road, there was nowhere to go. Daryn pressed on the horn, but the SUV kept coming. No time to react. There was a loud bang as it rammed the side of the van, which slewed violently to the edge of the road with the force from the SUV. In spite of his attempts to hold the wheel, Daryn lost control. They hit a pothole and careered over the edge of the road, hurtling down the steep drop below. As the van bounced and crashed through foliage, one side struck a large rock, tipping it into a roll. It turned over and over, gaining momentum as the doors flung open and the occupants, including the gurney, were thrown clear. It finally came to rest against two palm trees in the thick undergrowth, on its roof. The chassis was twisted and contorted, the windows were smashed and one of the doors had been ripped off. A few feet away, a weak voice cried out helplessly, 'Dr Miller? You okay? Oh man, I think my leg's broken, I can't get up. Dr Miller? Daryn? You hear me?'

Tyrell waited, but there was no reply. From the road at the top there was the roar of an engine as a vehicle drove quickly away, and then there was silence.

Throughout the day of Monday, September the fourth, Hurricane Luis maintained its relentless track towards Antigua and the nearby Leeward Islands in the Caribbean Sea. Distended grey clouds boiled and churned their way across the sky and the strength of the wind increased by the hour as the Category Four hurricane approached. By late afternoon the last of the flights evacuating tourists from the island had safely taken off from V. C. Bird International and the remaining staff and officials set about shutting down the airport in anticipation of the imminent storm.

The temperature continued to drop and a heavy rainfall began. There was no sunset that evening, just a dark, angry sky heralding the arrival of Hurricane Luis. Shops, offices, hotels, bars, restaurants, and homes were barricaded and boarded up. From St. John's, the capital, in the north of the island, with its usually crowded streets throbbing with reggae music and traffic, to Rock Palm Resort in the south, now empty, with all staff and guests evacuated, Antigua resembled a ghost town, with every resident taking shelter, watching and waiting.

During the early hours of Tuesday, September the fifth, Hurricane Luis made landfall in Antigua. Rock Palm Resort, in the southeast of the island, was one of the first places to be hit by winds approaching one hundred and forty miles an hour. The sound of the wind and the lashing rain, falling in sheets, was deafening. Waves crashed on the beach and rose higher, the tide swelling over the lawned area in front of the hotel. The sandbags, piled in front of the bay side of the hotel, did little to stop the waves from smashing into the restaurant and guest rooms which faced the beach. Seawater swirled over the tiled floors, washing over them and receding briefly before yet another wave, stronger than the previous one, rolled in, covering everything in its wake. Tables and chairs, stacked neatly in a corner of the restaurant were toppled and scattered by a giant wave, and were left lying on their sides, swept to and fro by the current.

More waves blasted over the top of the pool deck area, depositing sand and broken palm branches into the swimming pool. Roof tiles, flying debris, loose palm leaves, sea spray and sand whirled in the air, caught up in the force of the wind and driving rain. Tall palm trees bent over, almost completely touching the ground, while the tropical plants and foliage on the beach path were battered and beaten. With a deafening crash, but barely audible over the sound of the wind and rain, the covered entrance of Rock Palm Resort collapsed in front of the reception area.

At around eight o'clock that morning, after skimming Antigua, the eye wall of the hurricane passed directly over Barbuda, a small island to the north, leaving a further trail of devastation. Although the strength of the storm had lessened slightly, the wind remained strong and, along with the rain, thrashed the two islands with unrelenting force throughout the day. Neighbourhoods were transformed into kaleidoscopic junkyards of debris as the wooden dwellings of the poor and the palatial residences of the rich were flattened. Swimming pools were murky with mud, sand and rubble. Cars and trucks were upended and thrown on their sides. The marinas at English and Falmouth Harbours, with their multimillion dollar yachts half-submerged in the dark water or haphazardly flung on top of each other, resembled a scene of utter chaos. There were power outages and, in some areas, almost total disruption to infrastructure, sewage and water systems. Every building had suffered damage or had been completely destroyed by one of the strongest and deadliest hurricanes of nineteen ninety-five. Hurricane Luis had left its calling card.

By Wednesday, September the sixth, the worst of the storm had passed. The grand, luxurious Rock Palm Resort was still standing, but it had suffered catastrophic damage. Like many other hotels on the island, it stood ravaged, empty and silent, mercilessly battered by the wind and rain. A pitiful scene of utter carnage and devastation. But amongst the ruin, a dark secret had been buried, concealed within the rubble of the hotel. The only person who had known the secret lay strapped to a gurney buried in undergrowth, halfway down a steep hillside. And she was dead.

SIX

7:20 am, Monday, August 20, 2018
Bow Street Station, London, England

Spencer Warne took a sip of his morning cappuccino, a daily purchase from the mobile coffee vendor outside Bow Street underground station, and joined the throng of City commuters heading into the station. He took the covered walkway over the platform and jogged down the steps to where a westbound District line train rumbled into the station, braking sharply with an earsplitting screech of metal on metal. Along with the familiar faces of his fellow commuters, all of whom recognised but rarely acknowledged each other, Spencer stepped onto the train and sat down. At this time of the morning you could always get a seat. In addition, it was the summer holidays which meant that the trains were quieter than usual.

London was basking in an August heatwave and already the mercury was approaching seventy degrees. Spencer folded the grey jacket of his suit over his arm, carefully holding the cappuccino with his other hand. The suit was one of only two that he possessed and the cost of dry cleaning was extortionate. He tried to hold his arms a little way from his body, conscious that the clean white shirt he had put on that morning was already beginning to show circular patches of sweat. He took another sip of the cappuccino. It wasn't doing a lot to cool him down, but he needed the caffeine.

He'd never been a fan of early mornings, although two months as an inpatient in a private rehab centre had helped to instil some kind of ante meridian routine into him. It had been tough but he'd been determined. When he'd first walked into the centre, a discreet five-star establishment set in acres of parkland in Hampshire, a county on the south coast of England, Spencer had been an emaciated specimen of a human being, addicted to heroin and alcohol. When he walked out, after sixty days of an intense rehabilitation programme, he was a changed man.

Thanks to the healthy eating plan and regular gym sessions, he'd gained nearly forty-five pounds. Sure, he still looked scrawny and was never going to be mistaken for the Incredible Hulk, but he was proud of what he'd achieved in such a short time. Thanks to the morning group sessions led by Marie, the counsellor, and the afternoon behavioural sessions conducted on a one-to-one basis by Celeste, his therapist, Spencer was now living a life free of drugs and alcohol. Sure, he was aware of the risks of relapse, especially during the first six months following treatment, but Celeste had taught him how to understand his triggers — things which might tempt him to begin using again — and ways to overcome them. He had also enrolled in a local support group and was due to return to the rehab centre for a check-up with Celeste in a couple of weeks, for her to ensure he was staying the course.

Upon his "release," as he liked to call it, from the rehab centre, he'd had a few more hurdles to overcome. The first had been finding a place to live. Prior to his spell in rehab, he'd been living on the streets in the East End of London, squatting in abandoned buildings and migrating from one hostel to another, his sojourns at these temporary residences punctuated with frequent admissions to the emergency departments of various east London hospitals. Returning to this way of life would mean a swift regression into his old habits — something Spencer was adamant would never happen — and so he had contacted a friend for help. The friend happened to know a landlord with a small studio apartment to rent in Bow. The friend had given him a solid reference and had paid the deposit and the first three months' rent for Spencer. He promised he'd pay her back. When he'd got a job and earned a bit of money. The second hurdle. Who in the world was going to employ a former alcoholic and heroin addict, fresh out of rehab with no reliable track record? And that was only part of it. Spencer had also done time inside for burglary and possession of drugs. Any prospects of gainful employment were about as realistic as unicorns and Father Christmas.

Although he had grown up in a wealthy family, had been privately educated and had once enjoyed the favour of business and social connections, the youngest child of four had descended into a wayward life of alcohol and drug addiction, breaking his mother's heart and causing the rest of his family to disown him. Already strained relationships between them were severed completely after Spencer served time in jail in his late twenties. On the cusp of forty, it was over ten years since Spencer had communicated with any member of his family. Prior to his time in rehab, his only concern had been where and when he was next going to get high. But now, as a result of the group discussions, the therapy sessions with Celeste and the early morning yoga classes he had religiously attended, Spencer had a renewed desire to rebuild broken bridges and reconnect with his long lost family.

But first he needed a job. And once again, his resourceful friend had a plan. It was an outrageous plan but as his new employer, Tobias Moncler, the owner of a prestigious Hatton Garden jewellery store, had remarked, Spencer had already passed the interview process with flying colours. One of Spencer's attributes was that he was nosy. Spencer preferred to use the term inquisitive, or perhaps curious, but whatever he chose to call it, Spencer had always been interested in his surroundings. He watched people, he noticed things and he remembered them. In contrast, as a homeless man on the street, buried in a filthy sleeping bag, people generally didn't notice him. Or at least they tried not to. Which is precisely what happened in the early hours of a misty September morning three years before, when Spencer was hunkered down in the doorway of a small coffee shop opposite a jewellery store in Hatton Garden. Tobias Moncler's jewellery store.

High from drugs and swigging from a half-empty bottle of vodka, apparently minding his own business, Spencer had watched from the shadows as four men broke into the jewellery store and stole over two million pounds' worth of gems. He was the sole witness of the robbery and instantly dismissed by the police as a reliable one: he was homeless, a known drug user and probably high or drunk at the time, or both. Hardly trustworthy. True, he'd been all of those things, but when a reporter investigating the crime spotted him, bought him coffee and a bagel and asked him if he'd noticed anything, he'd surprised even himself with the details. And anyway, this reporter, probably in her early thirties and with a killer body, was seriously hot. He would never normally have considered being a snitch — rules of the street and all that — but there was free coffee and bagels on offer and an exclusive audience with a complete stunner who obviously wanted him. It was worth it just for that.

When the conversation was over, Spencer had supposed that this was the last he'd be seeing of her. But unknown to him, she validated his evidence, passed along the intelligence to the police — without revealing her source, which Spencer was grateful for — and ran a story on the front page of the national broadsheet she was writing for at the time. Thanks to Spencer's testimony, all four perpetrators were caught and almost all of the stolen gems recovered.

And then there was the fifty-thousand pound reward offered by Tobias Moncler for anyone providing information leading to a conviction. The cute reporter had claimed the reward on Spencer's behalf, tracked him down, and revealed his identity to Tobias who had asked to meet him to thank him personally. It was decided that although — even by his own admission — Spencer could not be trusted with the money, and indeed no longer had a bank account in which to put it, the reporter would open a new trust account in his name with her credentials. Tobias had duly transferred the reward money into the account for which the reporter was an authorised signatory. No funds could be withdrawn without her approval and consent. And there the money had sat until one chilly November evening the previous year, when Spencer decided it was finally time to check into rehab and get clean. The reporter authorised the bank transfers and, before he could change his mind, Spencer found himself embarking on a sixty-day detox programme at a private rehab centre. It was one of the best in the country according to Orla, his long-suffering drugs worker. In addition, there had been enough money at the end of the rehab stint to pay for some extensive dental work, Spencer's decaying, rotten teeth having been ravaged by the prolonged drug use.

Prior to his time in rehab, while he was still living on the streets, the organisation of Spencer's reward and bank account had led to regular meetings with his new reporter friend. She would treat him to a slap-up lunch at a diner in Whitechapel, Spencer's stamping ground in the East End of London. It was during these reunions that Spencer's talent for noticing things was increasingly employed. He soon became an unofficial informant for the reporter. A number of potentially baffling crimes were solved as a result of the information passed from Spencer to the reporter to her sources in the Metropolitan police. Spencer never revealed anything directly to the police, but he would provide the reporter with every scrap of information he could glean relating to various crimes across London, in exchange for the coveted lunch dates.

It was an unusual relationship which, in spite of the reporter's frustration at Spencer's ongoing drug use, began to develop into more of a friendship. They built up a trust, of sorts. They shared a similar sense of humour and the last case Spencer had been instrumental in solving had cemented their alliance. And now, thanks to his journalist friend, Spencer Warne, reformed alcoholic and drug user, ready to prove himself to the world, was offered a job as a trainee sales assistant at Tobias Moncler Jewels.

'You honestly trust me to handle diamonds and precious stones and shit?' Spencer had said to Tobias during an informal meeting at which his loyal journalist friend had also been present.

'I trust you Spencer,' the jewellery store owner had replied, looking him straight in the eye. 'You earned my trust when you helped catch those four men who robbed my store two years ago. Our mutual friend here has kept me updated with your ongoing work, which I understand has helped solve numerous crimes throughout the City. She's also told me about your successful spell in rehab. Business has been doing well and I could do with another member of the team on the shop floor. I and my staff will provide you with any training and support that you need if you're prepared to work hard and give it your all. This is Hatton Garden remember, the centre of the UK diamond trade and London's jewellery district. Competition is fierce. I expect the best from my people. But, in turn, I reward them well.'

'I don't know what to say,' Spencer had beamed with delight, revealing an impressive set of dazzling white teeth. 'Yeah man, I'll do my best, I promise. I won't let you down.'

'That's all I ask of any of my employees,' Tobias had replied kindly. 'Now we've discussed your starting salary, I'd also like to give you a little bit extra this month so you can buy yourself a couple of smart suits to wear for work. You'll need to look presentable on the shop floor.'

'Oh right. Yeah, I hadn't thought of that.' A horrified look had come into Spencer's eyes.

'I'm sure your friend here will be able to accompany you on a little shopping expedition,' Tobias had said, with a glance and a raised eyebrow at the reporter. She had nodded confirmation.

'No problem at all Tobias,' she had replied, adding with a grin, 'I know just the place. We'll get Sales Assistant Warne here measured up for the perfect pair of suit pants in no time.'

'I don't like the sound of that,' Spencer had said dubiously. 'Can't we just go to a normal high street shop and get something off the rack? I'm not really into all that snooty measuring shit.'

'Trust me Spencer, you'll be fine,' his friend had said reassuringly. 'We need to work on your language too. The customers of Tobias Moncler Jewels will not appreciate swear words with every other sentence.'

'No. Course not.' Spencer had spoken like a chastised child. 'Sorry about that. It won't happen again.'

'I'm sure it won't,' Tobias had replied. 'Congratulations on your new job, Spencer and welcome to the team. I'm happy to have you on-board.'

It had been one of the greatest days of Spencer's adult life. Now, six months later, he was still as enthusiastic as his first day on the job. Sure, it hadn't all been good and at times he'd found himself under considerable pressure, but he'd been given a second chance in life, and he wasn't going to blow it. From the start, he'd made up his mind that he'd make a success of things. He'd be Tobias Moncler's most conscientious employee, his most dedicated store assistant. He'd learn his trade and read up on everything he could about diamonds and precious stones. Maybe one day he'd even study for that diamond diploma course he'd read about on the internet.

The District line train shrieked to a stop at Mile End station and, along with most of the other passengers, Spencer got out and crossed the platform to where a Central line train was slowing to a halt. The doors snapped open and he stepped into the carriage. There were fewer seats this time, so he stood at one end and pulled a small, dog-eared booklet out of his backpack entitled *The Four Cs of Diamonds*. He'd read it at least twenty times, but he needed to know it off by heart, back to front, word for word, cover to cover. The jewellery store customers expected him to know what he was selling. He started at the beginning: *A good, basic understanding of the four Cs is essential for anyone in the jewellery business from bespoke designers to diamond traders. Each of the four Cs of a diamond can be graded in order to help determine its quality and value.* Spencer scanned the rest of the blurb to where the four Cs were listed. He held the booklet down for a few seconds and closed his eyes, frowning as he tried to recall what they were: *cut, colour, clarity and carat weight*, he said quietly to himself, before bringing the booklet back up to continue reading.

Some days all this learning was hard going. Some days he'd rather stick his headphones in his ears and zone out with the Metro news or Timeout, but he needed to stay focused and learn as much as he could about his new passion. He wanted to impress his stunning reporter friend with his extensive knowledge of diamonds. In addition, he'd recently signed up to an online dating site. He was nervous about the whole dating scene and wasn't sure if it was a bit soon for him, but he'd decided to throw himself in at the deep end and give it a shot. If he could astound women with a detailed monologue on crown and pavilion angles of diamonds, while steering clear of his shady past, surely they'd be all over him. What woman didn't want to talk about diamonds?

It was early days, however, and he had yet to find anyone more beautiful, charming and intelligent than the hot reporter. Unfortunately, his love remained unrequited as she had a boyfriend, although Spencer made no secret of the fact that he hoped one day she'd see the light. His mind briefly drifted from the Gemological Institute of America's diamond colour gradings to his reporter friend. Actually, she didn't call herself a reporter anymore. She was a freelance investigative journalist or something. She still wrote stuff for newspapers and magazines though. Spencer wasn't exactly sure what the difference was, but as long as he got to see her from time to time he didn't care what she did. Speaking of which, a lunch date between the two of them was long overdue. He pulled his cell phone out of his trouser pocket and tapped on the screen. He had few friends and her name was never far from the top of his WhatsApp conversations. Alicia Clayton. He smiled to himself as he typed the word "lunch?" and pressed send.

SEVEN

It had been an uncommonly slow morning at Tobias Moncler Jewels. Although Spencer appreciated the downtime, there was still work to be done. As usual, his day had begun with the removal of the showroom contents from the night safe, along with what was known as a case-count. This happened every morning, before the store opened. Spencer and his co-workers had to count every single item of jewellery in the showroom. On his first day in the job, Tobias had explained to Spencer that everything had to be accounted for whether it was sold, returned, held for a customer, or even stolen. Tobias had pointed out that employee theft at some jewellery stores was rife, but he prided himself on hiring people with honesty and integrity. Spencer had nodded soberly at this comment and had uttered a few words of agreement.

Once the jewellery had been set out in the glass display cases and the store opened, it was time to sell as much as possible. Spencer was aware — along with the rest of the team — that they had a daily sales quota of a few thousand pounds to meet and a weekly quota of jewellery care plans to sell. He sometimes despaired of the quotas; you couldn't control who came into the store and on which days, and you certainly couldn't force them to spend thousands instead of a few hundred. Some days it was impossible to meet the quotas. Today looked like it was going to be one of them. Spencer guessed most people would rather be outside in the sunshine, lazing in the park, or sipping a frosé at a rooftop bar than shopping for jewellery. He shivered and decided he needed his jacket on after all. For some reason Tobias insisted on having the air conditioning cranked up to temperatures suitable only for industrial meat lockers. Surely there were health and safety rules about hypothermia in the workplace.

Aside from the lack of customers and Arctic working conditions, Spencer's morning was moving slowly for another reason: the store supervisor, Camilla Johnson. Camilla was a gaunt-looking woman in her fifties with pinched cheeks and thin lips which never smiled, especially not at Spencer. She had worked at Tobias Moncler Jewels for longer than Tobias himself as far as Spencer could work out, and was something of an authority on gems and precious stones. She also possessed a number of qualifications which had been bestowed upon her by both the Gemmological Association of Great Britain, or Gem-A as it was known, and the Gemological Institute of America, or GIA.

In spite of Tobias's reassurances that no one knew of Spencer's shady past, Camilla was somehow aware of it and didn't like him for it. She made no apologies for the fact that she was suspicious of his motives for employment at a jewellery store. As far as possible, Spencer ignored her. He reminded himself that her prejudices were nothing compared to the hostility he'd faced as a drug-addled homeless man on the streets of London.

The morning dragged on, the minute hand of the large, antique clock on the wall seemed to have stopped and the only customers Spencer managed to sell anything to were a middle-aged man shopping for a birthday present for his wife and an American couple hoping to return home with a Hatton Garden souvenir. Spencer knew that Camilla, busy with her own clients, was watching him with a disapproving eye.

'Why did you suggest white-sapphire studs instead of diamond ones to that man looking at earrings?' she asked when they were alone in the showroom.

'He said he couldn't afford diamonds,' Spencer replied, carefully folding a gem polishing cloth. 'I thought it was better to sell the sapphire studs than nothing at all.'

'How many times do I have to tell you? It doesn't matter whether the customer can afford it or not, that's what the financing options are for. In this business you've just got to get on and sell the stuff. And if the customer has to spread the cost with a payment plan, even better, because we get extra commission on that too.'

'But he said he couldn't afford the diamonds,' Spencer protested. 'I know what it's like to have money worries. I didn't want him to…'

'That's not the point,' Camilla snapped. 'You are here to se[ll] jewellery, is that clear? We have sales quotas, targets and deadlines t[o] meet. I don't care what the customers can afford. That's irrelevant. The important thing is that they spend money — lots of it — in this store. Do you understand?'

'Yeah I get that,' Spencer said with resign.

'And you're folding that polishing cloth wrong. *Again*,' Camilla added frostily. 'How many times have you been shown, Spencer? Fold it *lengthways*, not *endways*.'

'But it's a square cloth,' Spencer replied with a confused look. 'It doesn't matter which way you fold it. It's a *square*.' He emphasised the word "square" as if he was teaching a mathematics class to primary school children.

'Of course it matters and you're doing it wrong.' Camilla reached across the glass counter to snatch the cloth away from Spencer.

'*Don't touch me*,' Spencer said angrily, pulling the cloth towards him. He could feel the heat rising in his cheeks in spite of the air conditioning.

'Give me the cloth,' Camilla barked. 'You're folding it wrong.'

Spencer didn't notice Tobias Moncler, disturbed by their raised voices, enter from a small door behind him.

'I'm not folding it wrong,' Spencer retorted. 'The cloth's a square you stupid bitch. You can't fold a square cloth the wrong way. Why don't you just...'

Spencer stopped. He didn't know why, but he had the sudden feeling that they were no longer alone in the room. Perhaps it was the startled look in Camilla's widened eyes which were now focused on something — someone — immediately behind him. He stopped just short of saying two words he knew he would later regret, and which had no place in a respectable jewellery store, and turned slowly to face his employer.

'What's going on?' Tobias asked quietly.

'Sorry Dr Moncler,' Spencer replied. He felt suddenly ashamed of himself for getting into a dispute over a polishing cloth, and annoyed at the way he had allowed himself to become exasperated by Camilla.

'Is there a problem between you two that I should know about?' Tobias asked, removing a pair of thin-rimmed spectacles and massaging his forehead.

'No, not at all,' Spencer said quickly. As much as he detested Camilla and wanted to complain about the way she nit-picked and bullied, he knew she was worth far more to Tobias than he was. If he wanted to keep his job, he had to keep the peace with everyone, including Camilla, no matter what.

'Sorry Dr Moncler, I think I misunderstood something Camilla was trying to tell me.'

'I see,' Tobias replied. 'Camilla?'

'Er, yes,' Camilla said quickly, slightly taken aback at Spencer's apology.

'So it's safe to leave you two on the shop floor together?' Tobias asked.

'Absolutely, Dr Moncler.'

'Yes, of course it is.'

'Good, because in case you'd forgotten, I'll be away for a couple of days on business. I'm leaving in a few minutes. Camilla, you'll be in charge. If I feel you can't manage the team appropriately, we'll need to have a little talk.'

'But it was...' Camilla stopped herself. 'Right. I understand. There won't be any more problems.'

'Pleased to hear it,' Tobias replied, adding, 'and that includes any friction with Ronan as well.' He was referring to Ronan Elliott, another employee at the jewellery store. Spencer didn't much care for him either, although he had an impressive sales record and always reached his targets. Ronan was good looking, intelligent, knew a lot about diamonds and had the gift of the gab. In Spencer's mind these were all things which Spencer did not have. At times Ronan could be overconfident and often arrogant, which meant that skirmishes with Camilla were not infrequent. Ronan was notably jealous of Camilla's role as the store supervisor and deeply resented the fact that, even as senior sales assistant, he was still accountable to her.

Of all the employees at Tobias Moncler Jewels, Spencer, naturally, was at the bottom of the pile and to be looked down on, from Ronan's point of view. There was an advantage to this however, in that if Ronan was in a particularly patronising frame of mind and the showroom was quiet, he would engage Spencer in an in-depth teaching session. Although Spencer realised Ronan's motive was wholly to impress Tobias, annoy Camilla, get out of cleaning duties and least of all to educate a fledgling sales assistant, the ad hoc teaching sessions were usually interesting and informative and Spencer learned a lot from them.

Tobias often had Ronan work on various assignments in one of the back offices. Spencer wasn't sure what these assignments involved, although Ronan would usually be surrounded by an impressive collection of the tools of the trade, from a simple pair of tweezers to complex grading kits and diamond gauges, most of which still baffled Spencer. Today was one such day when Ronan was hidden away in some secret, windowless office at the back of the store. The other two sales assistants working that day were Otto and Keeley. They were pleasant enough, if a little lazy at times, and were apparently unaware of or indifferent to Spencer's past.

Tobias looked at his Rolex watch, then at the antique clock on the wall and then at Spencer.

'It must be time for your coffee break Spencer. Why don't you go now? Otto and Keeley can man the store while I brief Camilla before I head off.'

In need of caffeine, Spencer agreed wholeheartedly with the idea and elected to take his gemology books to the coffee shop across the street, out of reach of Camilla. Over a latte macchiato with an extra shot of espresso, Spencer revised the ten most common diamond shapes as outlined in *The Four Cs of Diamonds*. He had just finished drawing and labelling a marquise-shaped diamond on a little notepad, when his cell phone vibrated in his pocket. He pulled it out and glanced at the screen. Trying to disguise his delight, he opened the message. It was from one Alicia Clayton: *Can't do lunch. How about dinner after work? Meet at Mullrose Grill, Covent Garden, 7pm?*

Spencer typed a reply: *Love to. See you then!* He pressed send and grinned to himself. A dinner date with Alicia Clayton in — he checked his watch — eight hours and counting. He drained the last of the macchiato and tossed the disposable cup in the recycling bin, before straightening his jacket and heading back across the street. As he entered the store, Ronan was busy showing an elderly man a jewellery tray containing a selection of gold bracelets. Otto and Keeley were also serving customers. A sudden flurry of activity. Spencer hovered in the background with one eye on the antique clock. The countdown to dinner with Alicia was now seven hours and fifty minutes.

Tobias was nowhere to be seen; he'd either left the store already for his business trip or had retreated to his office to finish up some paperwork. Sometimes he would make an appearance in the showroom if it was particularly busy or if there was a customer who wanted to buy something unusual or expensive. Aside from that, Spencer wasn't sure what his employer did back there in his darkened office all day. Perhaps he studied rare diamonds or had a secret black market racket going on. Or maybe it was just simple, honest business accounts.

Spencer assumed his finest store assistant's pose: shoulders back, back straight, hands clasped loosely together in front of him and legs slightly apart. He watched Ronan carefully remove various bracelets from the tray for his customer and listened intently to his sales pitch, cleverly disguised as informative explanations. He may be arrogant and egotistic, but Spencer knew Ronan's persuasive patter could almost hypnotise customers into parting with their money.

EIGHT

It was late in the afternoon and Spencer, by now bored, tired and anxious about leaving on time for dinner with Alicia, was reluctantly polishing one of the glass display cabinets. There were few things about his job that he really didn't take pleasure in. But this was one of them. It was never-ending. And probably the most thankless task known to man. No sooner had he cleaned the glass of smears and smudges, there would be a customer, "just browsing," but who would manage to touch every display case in the showroom, leaving a fresh trail of fingerprints. And Spencer was back to cleaning the glass again.

Camilla was showing a female customer a tray of Gucci watches while Otto and Keeley were multitasking: completing sales paperwork while deep in conversation about a nightclub which had recently opened in east London. The paperwork was another aspect of the job that Spencer wasn't keen on. A sale was only the beginning of a lengthy paperwork exercise. After that, you had to process the transaction at the till, take the deposit, complete the warranties, maybe arrange the payment plan and hopefully throw in a service plan amongst a whole bunch of other stuff. Six months in, he was still discovering new forms and documents which he had no idea how to fill out. There were forms for returned items, forms for exchanges, forms for repairs, forms for cleaning, forms for held items, forms for appraisals, forms for restored items… Like cleaning the glass, it was never-ending. But at least wiping a cloth over the display cabinets didn't require much brain activity. Perhaps this last job of the day wasn't such a bad deal after all.

Except it wasn't the last job of the day. To Spencer's dismay the tinted glass entrance doors slid open with a pleasant rush of heat, and a lady walked in. She was wearing a fitted, navy, mid-length dress which hugged her slim figure, and tan court shoes. Her bare legs and arms were gently bronzed and she looked to be a little older than Spencer, probably in her late forties. Her short, dark hair and heavily made-up face were immaculate. She glanced around the showroom for a few seconds before noticing Spencer. He cast a hopeful look in Camilla's direction but, irritatingly, she was still busy with her customer. Otto and Keeley buried their heads deeper into their paperwork and Ronan was in his mysterious room in the back of the store. It was five minutes to closing time, dammit, and then they had all the display trays to remove from the window followed by the end of day case-count, before packing everything into the night safe. Why did people choose the very last moment to come into a store when they'd had all day? He huffed crossly under his breath and stepped towards her with a gracious smile. If she made him late for his dinner date with Alicia, he wouldn't be amused.

'Good afternoon madam,' he said in his carefully practiced sales assistant's voice. 'Can I help you?'

'I hope so,' the woman replied with a smile. She placed her bag on one of the glass countertops. It was an expensive-looking, medium-sized shoulder bag in tan leather, which matched the shoes. An alluring scent encompassed her like an aura; it was a luxurious bouquet from some exquisite perfume. Neatly manicured hands with glossy red fingernails slid a square box covered in black velvet out of the bag. It was roughly ten by ten inches, and one inch deep. She placed the box on the counter and, without a word, opened it towards Spencer. He peered in curiously. Its contents caused him to gasp in awe and surprise. The velvet box contained the most spectacular diamond necklace he had ever seen. Set against a black satin lining, it glittered and dazzled and sparkled in the spotlights overhead. Mesmerised, Spencer gave a low whistle.

'That's a beautiful necklace madam,' he remarked, suddenly forgetting the lateness of the day.

'Thank you,' she said with a more serious expression. 'I always thought so.'

Spencer gazed at it for a long moment, awestruck. It was a perfect circle, approximately fifteen inches long from end to end, and consisted of what appeared to be forty or fifty glittering, colourless diamonds. Even to Spencer's untrained eye they looked to be something special. But it was the stone in the centre which made him take a sharp breath in and held his gaze for the longest moment. It was a large pear-shaped diamond in a striking pink colour, which surely weighed no less than ten carats.

'It's, um, it's yours?' Spencer was lost for words. He had never seen a piece of jewellery quite like it. Certainly Tobias Moncler Jewels handled some exquisite articles but this was surely out of the league even of Tobias himself.

'It is mine,' the lady replied solemnly, 'although sadly not for much longer I fear.'

Unsure of how to respond, Spencer waited for her to elaborate.

'My husband and I are divorcing. He's moved out — or should I say moved in, with his new girlfriend, twenty years his junior — and I'm left with the house. I'd like to stay but I can't afford to without selling some of my jewellery. I love this beautiful necklace, but right now I need the money. Can you help me?'

'Er, yes, of course madam, I'm sure we can help. And I'm sorry to hear about the divorce and everything.' Spencer was momentarily taken aback. He was torn between gazing at the necklace, wondering who on earth in their right mind would divorce such an attractive woman, and trying to work out what to do next. A brief glance in Camilla's direction confirmed that she was still busy with her customer.

'Well, er, first of all we'll need to examine your necklace and get it appraised. And valued,' Spencer said hesitantly to the lady.

'Oh, of course, I appreciate that,' she nodded. 'I really just want a quick sale, without any fuss. I need the money, you see.'

'Yes, madam,' Spencer replied. 'I understand. Both my co-workers are highly trained gemologists. They can certainly give you a detailed assessment and description of your jewellery, with an official valuation certificate.'

'That's wonderful. How long will it take?'

'We aim to complete valuations within twenty-four hours. Single pieces can sometimes take as little as three or four hours to value, but with a necklace of this... calibre, it might take a bit longer. I can assure you we'll work as fast as we can though.' He had a sudden thought. 'Do you have a grading report for this necklace at all, madam? You know, like a certificate that tells you about the stones?'

'Oh yes, I forgot about that. I have it with me.' The lady unzipped her bag again and pulled out a brown envelope. She placed it on the glass counter in front of Spencer. 'I have the one for the necklace, which is the identification and origin report for the pink diamond, but I also have grading reports for the other diamonds.' She reached into her bag and pulled out a second brown envelope, thicker and heavier than the first. 'There's one for every stone. There are forty-nine in total. The smaller diamonds were loose stones before they were hand-crafted into this necklace. Oh, and please call me Vivienne.'

'Certainly... Vivienne.' Trying to steady his hands, Spencer opened the first envelope and pulled out a single sheet of water-marked paper.

'I'm Spencer.'

'Nice to meet you Spencer,' Vivienne replied, watching him carefully as he examined the report. On one side it was headed: GIA COLORED DIAMOND REPORT. Underneath, the report number was listed, along with the shape and cut of the large pink, pear-shaped diamond. Its measurements were listed, along with the carat weight: an impressive 10.02 carats.

'A ten-carat diamond?' Spencer said incredulously, looking from the report to the diamond.

'Correct,' Vivienne replied. 'Ten-point-oh-two carats to be precise.'

'I've never seen anything quite like this necklace before,' Spencer said, almost reverently. He placed the report on the countertop and picked up the second envelope from which he pulled out a small bundle of around fifty sheets of the same, water-marked paper, secured with a clip. As he read the top page, Vivienne spoke softly: 'Each of the colourless diamonds weighs around two carats...'

'And they're flawless, according to these reports,' Spencer said, leafing through them.

'That's also correct,' Vivienne acknowledged. They were silent for a few moments as Spencer detached the clip from the bundle of papers and spread them out in front of him. He was familiar with diamond grading reports and fluent in reading and understanding them. Every Tobias Moncler Jewels diamond that was sold was accompanied by a grading report issued by the GIA, the Gemological Institute of America. Spencer was aware of other grading laboratories although Tobias always insisted that the GIA was the benchmark of diamond grading, observing the most rigorous standards. Each grading report included an assessment of the four Cs of a diamond: colour, clarity, cut and carat weight. It also contained a plotted diagram of the diamond's clarity characteristics — the surface irregularities, or blemishes, and internal features, or inclusions, of a polished diamond — and a graphic representation of the diamond's proportions.

He examined one of the grading reports for one of the colourless diamonds which was dated March 4, 1994. It confirmed that the diamond weighed 2.02 carats and had a colour grade of D. Spencer knew that diamonds were graded from D, a colourless stone, to Z, a light yellow or brown. The less colour in a diamond, the higher the grade. Even the slightest hint of colour could make a dramatic difference to the diamond's value. The immaculate colour purity of a D-coloured diamond justified the high prices that they commanded.

The report stated that the clarity grade of the diamond was FL, which meant that the diamond was flawless, without any inclusions or blemishes. Flawless and internally flawless diamonds were extremely rare and difficult to find. In fact, some jewellers spent an entire lifetime in the trade without ever seeing one. Spencer knew that a flawless, two-carat, round brilliant diamond could fetch around fifty-thousand pounds, and that was just for starters.

According to the report, the diamond was perfectly proportioned and its cut, polish and symmetry were all graded as excellent. He glanced at the string of glittering gemstones and wondered which diamond this particular report referred to. He knew that the unique GIA report number, listed at the top of the page, would be inscribed by a laser on the corresponding diamond's girdle — the narrow section between the crown, at the top of the stone, and the pavilion at the bottom — in order to match it to the relevant report and identify it.

Aware that Vivienne was watching him, and feeling slightly nervous, he briefly glanced through some of the other reports, all dated in the spring of nineteen ninety-four. They looked almost identical. Each diamond listed was round with a flawless clarity, a colour grade of D and an excellent cut. Without exception, each diamond was perfectly proportioned and weighed just over two carats. Spencer reminded himself that while the reports were useful, the only way to prove for certain that the diamonds were what the reports said they were, was to remove each individual stone from the necklace and examine it as a loose stone under a microscope. He knew that it was impossible to accurately judge the clarity and colour, and indeed to ascertain the inscribed GIA serial number of a diamond, while it was placed in a setting. Flaws could easily be hidden under prongs and the colour could be obscured by reflections from the setting itself. Tobias had always maintained that, as a general rule, a diamond worth over two thousand pounds should never be purchased without first seeing it loose under a microscope.

Spencer also knew that the GIA did not grade complete pieces of jewellery and only issued reports for individual gemstones. Although the pink diamond report noted that the stone was part of a necklace, the details it contained on the colourless diamonds were scant, merely stating that there were "forty-nine colorless, round brilliant cuts set in a white metal necklace". Even though the other forty-nine diamonds would be of significant value too, and had their own reports, the coloured diamond report did not acknowledge this.

Almost unable to take his eyes off the necklace, which glittered radiantly against the satin lining of the box, Spencer returned to the original report Vivienne had produced; the one for the coloured diamond, dated June 29, 1994. He could hardly believe the words in front of him. He read for the second time that the magnificent pear-shaped stone was 10.02 carats. In contrast, the average purchased carat weight for Tobias Moncler Jewels was around 0.90 carats. Perhaps it was the colour which attracted the most attention to the stone. Spencer had read about pink diamonds in one of his study books. They were some of the rarest and most highly prized jewels due to a limited number of sources around the world from which pink diamonds could be mined. These included places like South Africa, Brazil and India, although the largest cache was located in a mine in Western Australia.

Spencer had read that with the exception of red diamonds, high-quality pinks were the most expensive natural diamond colour available on the market. He reread the colour grade a few times, allowing it to sink in. The report declared the pink stone to be Fancy Vivid, with a natural colour origin and even distribution.

Spencer didn't know a lot about coloured diamonds, partly because they were so rare and priced accordingly, and partly because most people shopped for traditional colourless diamonds. He had therefore focused his learning on these more popular gemstones. He'd learned, however, that coloured diamonds retained a uniform colour throughout the entire diamond that was constant, regardless of whether it was being tilted in the light or not. They were known as "fancy coloured" diamonds in the trade and were graded by the intensity of their colour. He noted the GIA grading scale for fancy coloured gemstones on the report; the intensity levels ranged from Faint to Fancy Vivid.

In addition to its natural hue, a pink diamond could also have a secondary colour or overtone, such as purple, brown or orange. He knew that the colour and carat weight of a pink diamond had the greatest impact on its price; pink diamonds skyrocketed in value along with their size and colour intensity.

Spencer carefully placed the report for the pink diamond back on the countertop. He handled it almost as delicately as if it was the diamond itself. He tried to process what was in the black velvet box in front of him, but he couldn't quite get his head around the numbers. Even without the pink diamond, he guessed the market price of the necklace could be well over two million pounds. But the pink diamond itself would be worth more than all of the other diamonds together. Much more. He didn't even dare to imagine the total value of the whole necklace. He guessed it was approaching something in the region of ten million pounds. Maybe even more.

'This is… quite a valuable necklace,' he found himself saying.

'Yes, it is,' Vivienne replied sombrely. 'It was a gift from my husband, many years ago. I love it, but not the memories attached to it, and now I need the money. Is it possible for you to get it valued for me Spencer and then perhaps we can come to some kind of arrangement…?'

'Well, yes, of course, but this is just a regular jewellery store,' Spencer replied. 'I mean, we appraise valuable stuff — sorry, jewellery — but this might be a bit out of our league. Have you thought about going to an auction house like Sotheby's or Christie's? They'd probably be more…'

'What's out of our league?'

Spencer turned to see Camilla peering over his shoulder. Her own customer had just left, bag in hand, and she was intrigued as to whom Spencer might be serving. It was past closing time and Otto and Keeley had begun removing the display trays from the window on the far side of the showroom.

'Oh my, what a stunning piece of jewellery,' Camilla said, spotting the necklace and turning the box towards her. She pulled some white gloves out of her pocket and put them on. Reaching for the necklace, she addressed Vivienne.

'May I…?'

'Oh yes, please, go ahead.' Vivienne nodded, looking directly at Camilla. Her voice was smooth, silky and well modulated. Her perfume was luxurious and enticing. There was something about her. She continued speaking. 'I was just saying to Spencer that every diamond in this necklace is a flawless stone. The pink diamond is from a mine in Western Australia. These diamonds are beautiful but, as you know, incredibly rare.'

'Of course,' Camilla agreed as she carefully lifted the necklace out of the box and held it in her gloved hands, tilting it gently in the light. Spencer looked on in awe, longing to hold the prize for himself. Just to touch one of those gemstones would be enough. Fifty resplendent diamonds, worth millions, almost radiated light as they shimmered and twinkled with each twist and turn of Camilla's wrists.

'Stunning,' Camilla said in a low voice. 'Remarkable.' She turned to Spencer. 'Get Ronan out here. He should take a look at this.'

As Spencer obediently disappeared through the door to the back of the store, he heard Vivienne begin to say something to Camilla about the cut grade of the pink diamond. On his return to the showroom with Ronan, he found himself jostled into the background as his co-workers marvelled at the necklace with repeated exclamations of admiration, each secretly vying for Vivienne's attention. Between them they had a combined total of several decades in the jewellery trade and, apparently, neither of them had seen anything quite like it. Ronan, although still in his early thirties, had travelled the world working within the diamond industry. Camilla had attended numerous conferences, courses, masterclasses and study days, but nothing either of them had ever seen came close to the diamond necklace that was now in front of them.

Spencer was ordered to make Vivienne a cup of coffee as she was ushered to a private room, like royalty. Keeley and Otto were ordered to finish removing the display trays and commence the nightly case-count before packing the night safe. Every item, every ring, pendant, watch, necklace, bracelet and charm had to be placed in the safe every night. With one person, this took the best part of an hour. With two, they would probably be done in thirty minutes.

Placing the coffee on the table next to Vivienne, Spencer hovered to one side as Camilla pored over the necklace and grading reports as if they were the Holy Grail, and Ronan fawned over Vivienne. Both of them ignored Spencer who was beginning to feel like a spare part. He wondered if he should stay or return to the showroom to help Otto and Keeley with the case-count. Suddenly, Vivienne glanced up at him and, making deliberate eye contact, flashed him a radiant smile. Returning the smile with a wide beam, Spencer decided he'd stick around for a few more minutes. As Camilla examined the necklace, Ronan plied Vivienne with gushing compliments and an enthusiastic sales pitch.

'You've made the perfect choice in consulting us here at Tobias Moncler, Ms...'

'Karlsson. But please call me Vivienne,' she replied, touching Ronan's arm lightly.

'Vivienne. Yes, of course.' Ronan nodded eagerly and his cheeks flushed a tinge of pink. 'Camilla and I are the in-house gemologists here at Tobias Moncler. I'm sure you're familiar with the Gemological Institute of America? Highly esteemed, the world's leading authority on precious stones...'

'Yes, the diamonds in my necklace have been individually graded by the GIA.' The smooth, silky voice, carefully inflected, was like the harmony of a beautiful tune.

'Oh yes, of course they have.' Ronan's cheeks flushed to scarlet. 'As I was saying, Camilla and I have both been trained — extensively — by the GIA. Between us we've years of experience in the business and we'll be able to conduct a quick and accurate appraisal of your necklace to ensure you receive the best possible price...'

'Good, because to be frank Ronan, I need the money. If you're able to provide me with a swift valuation and...'

'Yes, yes of course. Happy to. We're trained experts, you know, once we've appraised your necklace, which won't take long at all...'

'I'm sure it won't Ronan. You seem like a man of your word. How long?'

'Ohhh we normally say a few hours, but I'm sure we can keep the valuation time to a minimum. The grading reports all seem to be in order, we'll just need to do a few checks with the GIA and...'

Hang on Ronan, you haven't even looked at them yet, Spencer thought to himself.

'Camilla and I will be able to calculate an offer *very* quickly and can ensure same-day payment if required. *So* glad you came to us Vivienne. Wise move on your part. Did you know that auction houses often charge up to twenty-five percent of the selling price in commission? Yes, that's right, *twenty-five percent!* And then there are the cataloguing charges. All *so* expensive. Not to mention time-consuming. No, you made an excellent choice in coming to us.'

Ronan was rambling now. Spencer wasn't sure whether he was dazzled more by Vivienne or her jewellery. At least Camilla would have the sense to conduct a proper appraisal of the necklace and grading reports and prevent Ronan from rushing into making some kind of foolish offer. At any rate, Spencer knew that nothing could be done without Tobias's approval.

It was now twenty minutes past the time Spencer was supposed to have left for the day, but his managers appeared to have forgotten that he was still there. Spencer knew he would have to leave soon, in order to arrive on time at the restaurant where he was due to meet Alicia for dinner, but the necklace was captivating. He felt as though he could stare at it all night as it shimmered and sparkled in the overhead lights. It appeared almost fluid in nature. And then there was Vivienne. She was enchanting, almost bewitching. Ronan certainly seemed to be enthralled by her. Normally composed and hardened for business deals such as this, he seemed to have been reduced to a rambling fool, fumbling over his words and giving all manner of reassurances and promises that Tobias would surely never approve. Perhaps more astounding was that Camilla was not opposing a single one of them. At times, she even appeared to be in agreement. It was a bizarre scene to watch. Spencer could only imagine the necklace really was something special. Then again, he was almost mesmerised by Vivienne himself. There was something about her…

As he observed the proceedings in front of him, his eye caught one of the grading reports which Ronan had pushed to the side. He absentmindedly slid it towards him. It was for one of the round diamonds. He'd briefly glanced at a handful of the reports in the showroom, but now he examined this one more carefully. As he did so, he thought with puzzlement about the question he had put to Vivienne before Camilla had joined them. Why had she not taken the necklace to an auction house? He knew the pros and cons, but surely for such a rare, valuable item of jewellery, an auction house would still have been the most suitable choice.

Suddenly, he frowned. There was something slightly odd with the report. He looked at it more closely. The document looked genuine but something bothered him. He studied the wording and the lettering, the diagrams and the printed grading scales. What was wrong? The GIA hologram on the bottom right of the report caught his eye. It looked strange somehow. In a rare moment of cordiality, Camilla had once explained to Spencer that although there were counterfeit GIA reports in circulation, the genuine reports contained security features that were difficult to fake including microprint lines, watermarks, a two-dimensional barcode and a hologram, amongst others. These measures were taken in order to prevent a report from being forged or duplicated. But Camilla had also emphasised that the jewellery industry was built on trust, integrity and good reputation. It would be a foolish diamond trader indeed who would fake a grading report and risk losing his business and livelihood.

The GIA also had an online Report Check service which could verify whether the information contained in the report matched the information on the gemstone in the GIA database. Again, a diamond could only be properly graded as an unmounted stone. For any customers asking for their diamond to be graded, a jeweller would first have to remove it from its setting.

Although the rest of the report Spencer was looking at appeared entirely genuine, there was something about the hologram which bothered him. He surreptitiously slid another report towards him and inspected the hologram on that. Once again, something was definitely wrong. He shot a glance at Vivienne who sat perfectly upright, watching Camilla closely as she examined the necklace. If the grading reports were fakes, was it possible that the diamonds which made up the necklace were also fake? On first impressions, everything had seemed legitimate, but now, Spencer wasn't so sure. Was the necklace just a little *too* perfect? Which led to a thousand other questions. Was Vivienne really who she said she was? And what of her background story? Was she telling the truth about the divorce and the need to sell her jewellery quickly and quietly?

'*Spencer, are you listening to me?*' It was Ronan. Startled out of his reverie, Spencer jumped to attention.

'Yes?'

'Get me a pen and a fresh cup of coffee for Vivienne.'

'Certainly, your highness,' Spencer muttered under his breath as he moved to the door. Ronan appeared not to have noticed and had already redirected his attention to Vivienne.

A few minutes later, Spencer was back with the coffee for Vivienne and the pen for Ronan which he placed ceremoniously on the table with a curt 'Here we are.'

'Thank you,' Vivienne smiled warmly at Spencer. Camilla was still preoccupied with the necklace, but Ronan gave Spencer a look of disdain before saying: 'That's all Spencer. You can go home now. Camilla and I will carry on here.'

'Gee thanks Ronan,' Spencer mumbled.

'What was that?' Ronan asked sharply.

'Thanks, I'll be off now,' Spencer said loudly, pronouncing his words as if he was speaking to someone hard of hearing. Ronan scowled at him before picking up the pen and pulling a client detail form from a drawer under the table.

'So Vivienne, is that *Mrs* Karlsson or, er, *Miss*?' He was all smiles again.

'It's *Ms*.'

'Ah *Ms*, of course.' Ronan's cheeks were back to scarlet.

'And it's Karlsson with two Ss.'

He threw his backpack into the corner of the office and moved behind the desk. He tapped a key on the keyboard and waited for the computer screen to come alive, listening for any sounds in the corridor outside. There were none. The office was at the other side of the store to the private room in which Vivienne was currently being entertained; Ronan and Camilla were a safe distance away and sufficiently busy eyeing their potential new prize. They would have expected Spencer to have left the store after Ronan's dismissal. He was sure there would be no interruptions as he logged onto the GIA website and typed the report number, which he had memorised, into the box on the screen.

Without inspecting the corresponding loose stone under magnification, there was no way anyone could confirm that the details in the report matched those of the diamond in the GIA database. Spencer could at least check to see if the report existed however, and if it did, he could confirm that the information in the database was the same as that on the report Vivienne had produced. He reminded himself that a GIA report would be very difficult — almost impossible in fact — to fake.

In the even less likely event that the reports were genuine and the diamonds were fake, Vivienne would have needed a laser inscription machine to inscribe the unique GIA serial number listed on the report onto each gemstone, to ensure they matched the reports. Not all diamonds had serial numbers; only those graded by the GIA or other grading laboratories. The serial number was engraved onto the girdle of the diamond as part of the reporting process and matched the corresponding report number. And the fake diamond would have to exactly match the information on the report. Again, almost impossible. Perhaps Spencer really had been mistaken and the hologram on the report was entirely genuine.

The GIA report was displayed on the computer screen and Spencer examined it carefully. He had tried his best to memorise the physical report that Vivienne had produced. As far as he could tell, the information on Vivienne's report exactly matched the report in the GIA database. It was dated March 4, 1994 and gave the diamond's weight as 2.02 carats. The colour grade of the diamond was D and the clarity grade FL, or flawless. The cut, polish and symmetry were graded as excellent, just as in the physical report. Everything checked out. Yet Spencer felt a small sense of niggling doubt in his mind. What was it about the hologram? He wished he could look at it one more time. As he shut down the computer, he tried to persuade himself that Vivienne was a legitimate customer with genuine diamonds and genuine GIA reports. And if she wasn't, he tried to persuade himself that Camilla and Ronan were highly trained gemologists who were smart enough to know when they were being deceived.

NINE

'Spencer, you look terrible, are you all right?' Alicia looked up from her laptop as Spencer approached the table and sat down heavily in the chair opposite her. He was hot, sweating, out of breath and, at that moment, deeply regretting the years he had chain-smoked his way through an extensive smorgasbord of illegal substances.

'I'm okay,' Spencer wheezed as a waitress handed him a menu and filled his water glass.

'Busy day?' Alicia shut her laptop.

'Slow. Until the end when I had to stay late.' Spencer paused to inhale more oxygen and took a gulp of water. 'How was yours?'

'Not bad. I'm working on a couple of stories at the moment.'

'Anything interesting?'

'One's about an online banking scam. The other's about a property developer who started digging up a site to build some houses, only to uncover the remains of five bodies.'

'Damn, that's awful,' Spencer said with a horrified expression.

'It's pretty grim. They're still in the process of identifying the bodies, but it looks as though one of them belongs to a young girl who disappeared nearly forty years ago. It's possible the site may have been a burial ground for a serial killer.'

'Awful,' Spencer said again.

They spent a few minutes in silence perusing the menus, although Alicia had already made her choice and anything with the word "burger" in the description attracted Spencer's attention. The waitress returned to take their order: crab linguine for Alicia and the mushroom stuffed cheeseburger with all the toppings for Spencer. They opted for iced water to drink. Alcohol was firmly off the menu for Spencer and Alicia was anxious about keeping him on track. The waitress disappeared and Spencer reached for a bread roll.

'I do like this place,' he said, attempting to spread hardened chunks of butter straight out of the refrigerator onto his bread.

'Not bad, is it?' Alicia replied.

'It's nearly as good as Chicken Shop.' Spencer was referring to Chicken Shop and Dirty Burger, the Whitechapel diner where he and Alicia used to meet regularly for lunch, initially as reporter and informant, later as firm friends.

'I've moved up in the world now though,' Spencer added, with a mouth full of bread roll and butter chunks. 'I'm dining in Covent Garden now.'

'There's nothing wrong with Whitechapel, Spencer,' Alicia laughed. She watched him with amusement and a small feeling of pride. He'd come a long way since his time in rehab. Even Orla, his drugs worker, had been amazed at his progress. He'd stayed clean since being discharged from the private clinic, had held down a job for six months, took care of his new teeth and paid his rent on time. He was a far cry from the Spencer Warne Alicia had known a year ago. Even so, she kept a watchful eye on him; no one was immune from tumbling off the wagon.

They made small talk and enjoyed the relaxed atmosphere of the restaurant while they waited for their entrées to arrive. Mullrose Grill was a bustling Covent Garden hotspot with a trendy website boasting a "seasonal, sustainable menu" and "signature cocktails". The decor leaned towards Spanish Mission style: white stucco walls and dark wood furnishings. Seating was on two levels, with leaded glass doors opening onto the street for al fresco dining. From business breakfasts to post-theatre dining, Mullrose Grill was always fully booked. Tonight was no exception and, had Alicia not been personally acquainted with the executive chef, the waiting time for a table would have been most of the evening.

'So what kept you at work tonight Spencer?' Alicia asked. 'Did Tobias call you into his office to give you a promotion?'

'I wish,' Spencer replied. 'As long as that bitch Camilla's there, there won't be any promotions coming my way.'

'It's not up to her,' Alicia said. 'She's not your boss. Tobias is.'

'Actually, she *is* the one in charge right now,' Spencer said dolefully. 'Dr Moncler is away for a couple of days.'

'Don't let her bully you,' Alicia said firmly. 'Now, how *did* your day go?'

'As I said: slow. Until around five o'clock when this lady came in.'

'To buy something?'

'No, to sell something actually: the most amazing diamond necklace I've ever seen.'

'Better than the one I borrowed from Tobias for my undercover work at Club Maiiva last year?'

'Way better. Like millions of pounds better.'

'And she's selling it?'

'Getting it valued so she can sell it.'

'Why?'

'She said her husband's left her and they're getting divorced. She wants to keep her house but can't afford to unless she sells some of her jewellery. I reckon her place is a bit posher than my flat, don't you?'

'Sounds like it. How much is her necklace worth then?'

'It hasn't been officially valued yet. The other sales assistants, Ronan and Camilla, were looking at it when I left the store, but if it's the real deal I'd guess it's worth something like ten million pounds.'

'*Ten million*?' Alicia's eyes widened.

'You should see the diamonds,' Spencer said as the waitress arrived with the crab linguine and cheeseburger. When she had supplied Spencer with extra helpings of ketchup, mayonnaise and spicy brown sauce, as requested, she refilled their water glasses and disappeared. Leaving his knife and fork untouched, Spencer picked up the cheeseburger with both hands and took a large bite.

'Delicious,' he said, with his mouth full. Carefully spiralling a delicate helping of the linguine onto her spoon with the aid of a fork, Alicia made a mental note to speak to Spencer about his old habit of talking with a mouthful of food. Although intrigued with the story of the diamond necklace, she decided to refrain from questioning Spencer further, to allow him to eat without having to talk at the same time. She didn't have to wait long for him to be able to resume the conversation however; the cheeseburger was devoured at breakneck speed and Spencer leaned back contentedly in his chair watching Alicia.

'How's the linguine?' he asked.

'Very nice.'

'Need some help with that?'

'No thanks, I'm just taking my time. Tell me about the ten million pound necklace.'

'Oh the necklace, well, as I said, I've never seen anything like it in my life. Don't think I've even seen anything like it on TV or in the movies. Seriously impressive piece of jewellery.'

'I've seen some pretty valuable necklaces in my time, especially as a crime journalist. What was it like?'

'Well...' Spencer thought for a moment, trying to recall the necklace as accurately as he could. 'It was made up of a perfect circle of pure, colourless diamonds — quite large ones, about two carats each — with this incredible pink diamond in the centre, a huge pear-shaped stone which weighed a whopping ten carats. You've never seen anything sparkle as much. Looked like the Crown Jewels. If I could afford something like that, I'd buy it for you Alicia, show you how I feel about you. I know you always say I'm...'

'Describe the necklace to me again Spencer,' Alicia said suddenly. She had a strange look in her eyes. Spencer stopped talking.

'What?'

'Tell me what the necklace was like again.'

'Uhh, okay. It was a circular thread of round diamonds — colourless ones, forty-nine of them in total — with a huge pear-shaped, pink diamond in the middle. The round diamonds were a flawless clarity, excellent cut... Stop me if I'm getting too technical...'

Alicia waved him on and Spencer obediently continued, secretly thrilled he'd been able to squeeze the last sentence in.

'The whole lot — including the pink diamond — probably weighed close to one hundred carats. Pretty awesome piece of jewellery. Like I said, if I had the money to...'

'Why did the lady bring the necklace to Tobias Moncler?' Alicia asked. She pushed her fork and spoon to one side of the plate.

Spencer eyed the linguine that she had left but decided he probably shouldn't eat anything else.

'I already told you, she was getting divorced and couldn't afford to keep the hou...'

'No, Spencer, why did she bring the necklace to a *jewellery store*?'

'What d'you mean?'

'Surely it would be better to take a piece of jewellery as valuable as that to an auction house. Why didn't she go to Christie's or Sotheby's?'

'Oh right, I see, yes, that's exactly what I asked her. She said she just wanted a quick sale without any fuss.'

'That sounds a little strange,' Alicia said, with a puzzled look.

'It does a bit,' Spencer replied. 'I thought that too. But some people can be intimidated by those big auction houses. Plus they can take ages to sell your stuff because they don't hold auctions that often. And then there are the costs involved that you don't get with a jeweller; auction houses can take a fat percentage of your earnings from the sale, and that's assuming they sell your item at all, which is never guaranteed.'

'Sure,' Alicia said doubtfully. 'But if you own a necklace worth that much, it's hard to imagine being intimidated, even by a major auction house. And if it's a rare piece of jewellery, surely an auction house is by far the better option?'

'Maybe. There was something slightly odd though,' Spencer said suddenly.

'Yes?'

'The grading reports.'

'The what?'

'You know, when you buy a diamond it should always come with a grading report. Some people call them certificates but they're actually reports. They're sort of a detailed description of the diamond's characteristics; its proportions, colour, the way it's been cut, how much it weighs, stuff like that...'

'I know what you mean.'

'Right. They're there to confirm the diamond is what you say it is.'

'So what about the grading report for the necklace?'

'There was more than one report. One for every diamond actually. The lady said the diamonds had been loose stones before they were made into the necklace so each one had its own report.'

'So there were what, fifty reports?'

'Yeah, must've been. But there was something about them that just didn't seem right.'

'With *all* of them?'

'I only looked closely at a couple, but...'

'Something about them, like what?'

'I'm not sure, but I don't think they were genuine. On first glance they *looked* genuine, but there was just... maybe it was the hologram, or the watermark, or... oh I don't know, I can't put my finger on it. It was probably just in my imagination.'

'Or perhaps it wasn't. You know how I feel about gut instincts. What's yours?'

'I think the reports might be fake,' Spencer said slowly.

'And the diamonds themselves?'

'At first glance, they looked genuine too. And if they were genuine then that necklace *is* worth a fortune,' Spencer continued. 'I mean, the diamonds looked pretty perfect to me. Almost *too* perfect. But if the reports said they were flawless, maybe they really were. So they *would* look perfect. I've never seen diamonds like that before so who am I to say they're not real?'

'What about the setting?' Alicia asked. 'If the diamonds were real, surely they'd be mounted in a decent metal like — I don't know — white gold or platinum or something?'

'I didn't really get close enough to look properly,' Spencer replied. 'The whole necklace sort of exuded quality, with a price tag to go with it, but I can't be certain what the setting was made of. It was the reports that bothered me more, but why have fake grading reports for genuine diamonds? It doesn't make sense. That would be the most stupid thing ever. It would instantly cast doubt over whether the diamonds were real or not. Why would anyone want to do that?'

'How about if they were stolen?'

'You'd sell 'em on the black market, wouldn't you? You definitely wouldn't take them to a reputable jewellery store with a bunch of phoney grading reports. Even I wouldn't be that stupid. But anyway, the reports can't be fake because I checked the details of one of them in the GIA database. You know the GIA? The Gemological Institute of America? It's the gold standard of diamond grading labs according to Dr Moncler.'

'I've heard of it.'

'Right, well the GIA supposedly issued the reports the lady brought to the store with her. Each diamond in that necklace should have its own unique GIA report number, which is registered in the GIA database. The number itself would be inscribed on the girdle of the diamond and is only visible through a loupe or a microscope. Anyway, I memorised a report number for one of the round diamonds. Before I left work I looked it up in the database.'

'And?'

'It was there all right. As far as I could tell it matched the report the customer brought in. If it matches one of the diamonds too then everything's genuine. You can't always trust your instincts, I guess.'

'How easy would it be to fake a report?'

'Not very. They have all sorts of security features: watermarks, holograms, microprint lines, stuff like that. Actually I'd say they'd be almost impossible to fake.'

'What did Camilla and Ronan think? Were they suspicious of the reports or the diamonds?'

'No.' Spencer shook his head. 'At least they hadn't noticed anything out of the ordinary by the time I left the store this evening. They were acting pretty weird to be honest. Camilla was poring over the necklace like a kid in Hamleys at Christmas, and Ronan was all over the customer like a leech. They're probably still there now. I must be wrong though. With all their experience and qualifications they'd spot a fake immediately.'

'Unless they were so captivated by such a stunning piece of jewellery and its potential value that they were blinded to any thought that it could be a fake?' Alicia suggested. 'Sometimes we only choose what we *want* to see, rather than what's actually in front of us. Can you physically compare each report with the relevant diamond to check for authenticity?'

'There are basic tests you can do to see if a diamond is real or not,' Spencer replied, 'but to match it to a report you'd have to take it out of the necklace and examine it properly under a microscope, check for serial numbers, characteristics of the stone, all that. Which is definitely not something I'd be able to do. That would be a job for Camilla or Ronan. Or Tobias. I guess I could have another look at the reports though — assuming Camilla and Ronan haven't locked them away somewhere — and compare them with a couple of genuine ones. I would've paid more attention, but it was closing time and I wanted to leave. If only the lady'd come to the store earlier in the day…'

'Have you considered that she may have come in when she did for a reason?' Alicia left the question hanging in the air as the waitress returned to clear their plates and offer the dessert menu. They declined and ordered two large cappuccinos each.

'Want to know a simple test to tell if a diamond is a fake?' Spencer asked suddenly, when the waitress had gone. He continued before Alicia had a chance to reply.

'You fill a drinking glass like this one with water,' he lifted up his own glass, 'about two-thirds to the top. Then you drop the stone into the glass. If it sinks, it's a real diamond. If it floats underneath or at the surface of the water, it's a fake. Want to know why?'

Alicia, gazing at her own glass of water, didn't respond.

'A real diamond has a high density, so the water test…' Spencer began, but Alicia interrupted.

'Spencer, that diamond necklace. Describe it to me one more time.'

Slightly irritated that she had cut his explanation short, Spencer took a defiant sip of his iced water.

'Okay, but I've already told you what it was like. Twice,' he said, in a grudging voice.

'I know,' Alicia replied. 'It's just that, it sounds familiar somehow, as if I've seen it before, but I just can't think when or where. Tell me one more time.'

'All right then.' Spencer exaggerated a frustrated sigh. He spoke in a singsong voice, as if reading from a textbook. 'It was a single circular thread, roughly fifteen inches from one end to the other. There were forty-nine flawless, round brilliant cut diamonds, around two carats each, that's about eight millimetres in diameter. And then there was the stone in the centre: a large pear-shaped diamond, just over ten carats in weight. It was a Fancy Vivid pink diamond, at the top end of the GIA colour intensity scale. A diamond of this size with this colour is pretty much unreal. Which means it's expensive. With coloured diamonds, the price increases with the intensity of the colour. That diamond alone is probably worth eight or nine million pounds. More probably. Assuming it's genuine, of course…'

But Alicia wasn't listening. Her mind was in another place. The door to a memory which had closed many years before was slowly being opened. It led to a time over twenty years ago and a place over four thousand miles away. It was a starlit night and she stood, a fifteen year old teenager, leaning against a palm tree. She could feel the warmth of the Caribbean breeze and hear the sound of the waves gently lapping on the beach. And the sound of a heated discussion between three people drifting down to her from the restaurant of the hotel. She heard one voice in particular — a woman's voice, feverish, angry — as the words came tumbling back to her in jumbled fragments: *I'll need a full explanation as to the whereabouts of a diamond necklace worth nearly ten million dollars.* And then a man's voice, calmer and quieter: *We don't know for sure that it's been stolen.* The woman's voice again: *It consists of … flawless, round brilliant cut diamonds … a single circular thread … the pear-shaped, pink diamond in the centre…*

TEN

'Two cappuccinos?' It was one of the waiters. Alicia was startled out of her thoughts.

'Thanks,' she said as the waiter placed the over-sized cups and saucers in front of them.

'Spencer, the necklace, I think it *is* real. It *does* exist,' Alicia said suddenly. Spencer took a sip of his cappuccino and looked at her over the rim of his cup before placing it noisily back onto the saucer. He licked the milk foam from his top lip.

'How d'you know that?' he asked.

'At least, it *did* exist once upon a time, a long time ago, but it was stolen.'

'Stolen? The customer told me her husband had given it to her as a gift.'

'Tell me about her. How old was she? What did she look like?'

'She was quite slim, attractive — not like you, but she was alright-looking — dark hair cut in a shortish style, sort of like a pixie but with a long fringe over one side.'

'Age?'

'Ohhhh, I don't know.' Spencer looked uncomfortable. 'I'm not very good with women's ages, I wouldn't like to…'

'Take an educated guess. Was she a teenager? A pensioner?'

'Somewhere in between probably.'

'Well, that narrows it down,' Alicia said sarcastically. 'Come on Spencer, you can do better than that. Don't tell me you're losing your people-watching skills. Give me a ball-park. Was she in her sixties, for example?'

'Noooo, she was a lot younger.' Spencer deliberated for a moment. 'She was probably a bit older than you though. Forty-something I'd say, but that's just a guess.'

'You sure she was as young as that?' Alicia asked. She cast her mind back to the sunburned woman who sashayed around the swimming pool deck wearing little more than a beach cover-up and an expensive diamond necklace. She must have been at least forty in nineteen ninety-five, although when you're fifteen everyone over the age of twenty seems old.

'Yeah, she couldn't have been much older than that,' Spencer said decisively. 'I'm sure of it.'

Alicia felt a wave of disappointment, although she didn't know why. Even with the help of extensive surgery and clever make-up, it was highly doubtful that the woman in the jewellery store was the same woman who had stayed as a guest at the Antiguan resort over twenty years ago. She'd be in her sixties, at least, by now. The ages didn't match. The necklace, which could have changed hands many times since the nineties, sounded the same, but the women were different. Alicia tried to recall the name of the woman who had stayed at the hotel in Antigua, but for now, her memory failed her.

'You remember anything else about the woman?' she asked.

'Not really. She was wearing nice perfume.'

'What was her name?'

'It was… oh what was it now… it began with a V… I think it was Vivienne. Vivienne Karlsson.'

Alicia tried to remember the name of the woman from the hotel in Antigua who had once owned the diamond necklace. Perhaps the name Vivienne Karlsson sounded familiar. She couldn't be certain. The memories of a vacation taken over twenty years ago had faded.

'Vivienne Karlsson,' she said thoughtfully.

'Yeah, that was definitely it,' Spencer replied. 'Why? D'you know her?'

Alicia shook her head. Throughout the time he had been her informant on the streets of London, watching and listening, he had rarely been mistaken with names, faces and important details, even when he was high. Spencer had earned his reputation for noticing things and people and particulars, and accurately interpreting situations. Alicia trusted his descriptions. She trusted his gut instincts and his intuition. If the customer's name was Vivienne Karlsson, then that's what it was. If his gut told him the grading reports were fake, then they probably were.

'Did you say you'd seen the necklace before?' Spencer asked.

'Yes, and the one I saw *was* the real thing,' Alicia replied. No woman would make that much fuss over a string of fake diamonds.

'When? And where?'

'It was a long time ago. I was fifteen years old. The necklace was owned by a wealthy lady. I can't remember her name though. It might've been Vivienne. She was a guest at a hotel called Rock Palm Resort on the island of Antigua, in the Caribbean. All the guests were evacuated from the hotel because of a hurricane which was heading towards Antigua and the nearby islands: Hurricane Luis, back in ninety-five. The night before we were evacuated the lady claimed that her necklace had been stolen.'

'*Had* it?' Spencer asked curiously.

'I've no idea what happened to it in the end,' Alicia said with a shrug. 'Like I said, we had to leave the hotel. I don't know if the necklace ever showed up.'

'Wow, that's... Perhaps the one I saw earlier today *was* the real thing,' Spencer said. 'Perhaps it *was* stolen, which would explain why the grading reports were faked. The original ones are probably still with the genuine owner.'

'It's remotely possible,' Alicia agreed, 'but my memories are from over twenty years ago. It's unlikely the two necklaces *are* connected. Your customer's necklace just sounded similar to the one I remember from my vacation at Rock Palm, that's all.'

'I ought to get back to the store,' Spencer said, suddenly excited. 'I should tell Camilla and Ronan that the necklace is stolen. Whoever that lady is, she's trying to get rid of it on the quiet. I need to...' He pushed back his chair and began to stand up.

'Sit down Spencer,' Alicia said sharply. 'You can't just waltz back into the store and accuse a customer of being a thief. For all you know, she could have purchased the necklace legitimately and been fooled by the grading reports herself. Or it might not have anything at all to do with the necklace I remember from Antigua. I'm not even sure that necklace *was* stolen; it's only what I overheard at the time. You'll need more to go on than my teenage memories before you start accusing people of theft.'

Spencer hovered in midair for a few seconds considering this, before sinking back down into his seat.

'You're right,' he said, looking slightly disappointed.

Alicia thought for a moment before asking: 'Does the GIA database give information on the ownership of gemstones submitted for grading?'

'They'd obviously have a name for the person who submitted the stones, which can always be falsified, of course. In many cases, it's the name of a jeweller rather than an individual though, so it still wouldn't prove ownership; the jeweller could be submitting a gemstone on behalf of a client. But I doubt the GIA would give out confidential information just like that anyway.'

'So in the *very* unlikely event that your customer's necklace is connected in any way to the one I remember from Antigua, there's no hope of tracing those diamonds back over the years anyway.'

'No. Not really. I'm pretty sure that would be almost impossible.'

Alicia didn't reply. She had a distant look in her eyes.

'Alicia?'

'Yes?'

'What're you thinking?'

'It's funny. I'd forgotten all about it.'

'About what?'

'Something else happened that night too.' Another chilling memory, long forgotten, had drifted into Alicia's mind.

'What?' Spencer asked.

'There was a murder. A young woman's body was found on the beach.'

'What happened to her?'

'She'd been stabbed to death. And after that, I don't know. We were all evacuated from the hotel and flown off the island before Hurricane Luis made landfall. The hotel was badly damaged by the storm. Dad was friends with the owner, Carlos. After the hurricane, Carlos had some kind of legal dispute with some planning officials when he tried to go about repairing and restoring the place.'

'Is it back to being a hotel now?'

'No.' Alicia shook her head sadly. 'As far as I know the disagreement was never resolved. And Rock Palm Resort remains abandoned to this day.'

ELEVEN

Alicia and Spencer finished their cappuccinos in silence and Alicia motioned to the waitress for the bill, which she would pay, as usual. It almost felt like old times again, with Spencer as her informant and she listening intently to his narrative, making mental notes and feeling the adrenaline surge at the beginnings of a story. Except this story was personal. Twenty-three years ago, the most incredible diamond necklace she had ever seen in her life was reported stolen from the very hotel at which she had been staying. Over the years, she had occasionally wondered what had become of it, and sometimes she had puzzled over the true identity of the murderer of Anastasia, the magician's assistant. But those memories had faded over time, forgotten and abandoned, like Rock Palm Resort, the setting for the opening scene of the story. Until now.

'Thanks for dinner,' Spencer said as they stood to leave.

'You're welcome,' Alicia said, nodding at Spencer's chair as a prompt to remind him to tuck it under the table. Sometimes her relentless insistence on him displaying proper manners irritated him. It was tiresome, but he knew she was only trying to help and he reluctantly obeyed.

'What's Antigua like?' he asked as they made their way to the door. 'I've never been.'

'A typical tropical island. You know, blue sky, turquoise sea, white sandy beaches stretching for miles, palm trees…' Her voice lacked its usual enthusiasm. Instead, she sounded detached and aloof.

'Have you been to any of the other Caribbean islands?' Spencer was asking, but for the second time that evening, or the third or fourth, Alicia wasn't listening. As they left the restaurant, she caught the gaze of a middle-aged gentleman. He was dining alone at a corner table. As she glanced across absentmindedly at him, he instantly looked down at a folded newspaper on the table alongside his plate of food. He had thick grey hair, cut in a short style, and was clean-shaven. He wore a pale blue shirt and peered at his newspaper through a pair of black-rimmed, retro square-framed spectacles. They reminded Alicia of the specs she had worn as a teenager, before her eyesight had been successfully corrected by laser treatment in her twenties. Frowning, she gazed at the man for a moment more, before turning towards the door, with Spencer close behind her. She didn't recognise the man and he hadn't appeared to recognise her. She dismissed the glance as one of those casual moments when one briefly catches the eye of a stranger, and nothing more.

'Perhaps you and I could, you know, go to that hotel in Antigua one day,' Spencer suggested as they stepped outside into the warmth of the August evening. The cobbled street was filled with a lively crowd, some dining al fresco, others out for an evening stroll taking in the relaxed, convivial atmosphere.

'Perhaps. One day,' Alicia replied offhandedly. She turned to Spencer. 'I want you to do something for me first.'

Anything, Alicia. Anything at all, Spencer almost burst out loud, before stopping himself. He was already imagining the two of them alone together on a white sand beach, walking hand in hand… He reeled his thoughts back to the present.

'Spencer? I want you to do something for me,' Alicia said again.

'Er — what might that be?' he asked casually. He could guess what was coming and it wasn't a request to accompany her on a month-long Caribbean vacation. He knew her too well by now and was beginning to regret mentioning the diamond necklace and its dubious grading reports. Still, at least it might mean regular lunches and dinners with her again. They had been woefully lacking of late.

'When you go into work tomorrow, just out of interest, can you find out for me exactly how the meeting went between your customer — Vivienne Karlsson — and your co-workers?'

Spencer nodded obediently.

'Find out what Ronan's and Camilla's conclusion was as to the authenticity of the diamonds and grading reports. I'm curious to know if they detected anything unusual or suspicious,' Alicia continued.

'If *I* managed to spot something was up with the reports, *they* definitely will have,' Spencer said.

'Let's hope so,' Alicia replied, 'but even if they don't and were planning on making an offer for the diamonds, I doubt they'd have the authority to do anything without Tobias's approval. They'll have to wait for him to get back to sign and seal a deal.'

'Yeah, that's true. They might be a spiteful pair, but they know their trade. They wouldn't just rush into making an offer without a proper appraisal first, especially for a piece of jewellery like that. And formal checks take time. We've got that on our side.'

'Keep your ears to the ground, all the same.'

'I'll do my best. I'm not usually privy to high-end business deals in the store though. They're above my pay grade. *Well* above.'

'You've never admitted defeat before.'

'I'll see what I can do.' He looked across at Alicia. 'Shall we go for a little walk? It's a gorgeous evening.'

Alicia checked her watch. It was nearly nine pm and dusk was falling. She could be at her parents' home, on the north side of Hampstead Heath, within the hour.

'Sorry Spencer, I'd love to but I've got an errand to run.' Noticing his forlorn expression, she added apologetically: 'But we'll meet again for dinner soon, I promise.'

'Tomorrow?' came the hopeful reply.

'Wednesday,' Alicia said firmly. They'd been walking in the direction of Covent Garden station. Alicia stopped outside the entrance, beneath the large arched windows and awnings.

'I'll see you soon,' she said.

'But it's still early,' Spencer protested, with a note of disappointment.

'I need to visit my parents. And you have work tomorrow.' Alicia squeezed his arm as she turned towards the entrance. 'We'll meet again. Wednesday night.'

'But Alicia…'

'Wednesday night Spencer, don't be late,' Alicia called over her shoulder as she disappeared into the station.

'Alicia *wait*!' he called out after her, pushing past a group of tourists, but she was gone, immersed in a sea of commuters and early evening revellers.

TWELVE

The Piccadilly line and the Northern line are two deep-level London Underground lines with elevators and steep escalators taking passengers to and from the station platforms. As Alicia stepped into one of the elevators, she knew her cell phone reception would diminish to nothing. She began typing a WhatsApp message to her mother which she hoped would send at a surface section of one of the lines or when she changed from the Piccadilly to the Northern line, one stop over at Leicester Square.

Hi mum. On my way over. Quick visit. Be with you and dad by 10. What do you remember about Rock Palm? See you soon xx

Within twenty minutes, the underground train clattered into Archway station, slowing rapidly to a halt before the doors slid open. Alicia stepped out of the carriage onto the platform and took the escalator to the exit at street level. As she made the short walk to the bus stop outside she checked her cell. There was a reply from her mother: *Hello darling, looking forward to your unexpected visit. Is everything all right? Do you want dinner? I'll have some for you just in case. Rock Palm brings back memories! I'll ask dad. Love you xx*

Alicia slid her phone back in her pocket as the bus arrived. There were plenty of seats on the lower deck and she settled into one near the middle of the double decker for the remainder of the journey, which would take as long again as the underground. Dusk was almost over and the last few rays of the vivid orange sun streamed through the tinted glass of the windscreen of the bus as it traveled in a westerly direction. Alicia was reminded of the Caribbean sunsets she had admired from the beach at Rock Palm Resort and at the Sunday night barbecue parties from a place called The Lookout, at Shirley Heights, a restored military lookout and gun battery on the southern tip of Antigua.

With arguably the finest views on the island, the spectacular setting looked west to English and Falmouth Harbours. Best known for Nelson's Dockyard in the eighteenth century, English Harbour was a former British Navy base once commanded by Horatio Nelson. Alicia had enjoyed many a Sunday afternoon with her parents exploring the restored eighteenth and nineteenth century buildings from the colonial period of the dockyard. They would then make their way to Shirley Heights to admire the breathtaking sunsets, soak up the atmosphere and the live music, and savour the barbecued jerk chicken and ribs. On clear days, the views from The Lookout extended to the neighbouring islands of Montserrat and Guadeloupe. Daylight, as it always does in those places closer to the equator, would fade fast. Alicia and her parents loved to gaze from The Lookout towards English Harbour, which had become a popular marina with bars, restaurants and expensive yachts. When darkness fell, the harbour lights twinkled brightly, reflecting on the water. To Alicia it was a magical sight.

She was jolted from her teenage memories as the bus began to slow and she realised she should have got off at the previous stop. She thanked the driver and alighted, only slightly annoyed at herself for not being more attentive; it was little more than a short walk back and then on to her parents' home and the evening was still warm. She could use the extra time to ponder the questions she would put to her parents. To her shame, she realised it had been a few weeks since she had last visited her mother and father, now in their seventies, although she kept in contact with her mother almost every day. Even tonight, the visit was not entirely a social one and she hoped they would indulge her with their memories of Antigua, in particular, Rock Palm Resort. Although they had taken vacations to other Caribbean islands since that time, they had never returned to Antigua and had never spoken much of their last visit there as a family.

Alicia reached the tall oak gates to the driveway of her parents' home and punched in the security code on a brick pillar to one side. The gates slid open revealing the circular, block-paved driveway which led to the home she had grown up in since her adoption at the age of five. Before she reached the front door it was already open and her mother stood in front of her, open-armed and with a beaming smile. It was the greatest welcome in the world to Alicia; she had always vowed she would never take it for granted.

'This is a wonderful surprise!' Bryony Clayton exclaimed.

'Good to see you Alicia!' Paul Clayton appeared at his wife's shoulder and they parted to allow their daughter through the front door.

'Thanks mum, thanks dad!' Alicia said, hugging each of them tightly. 'Good to see you both too. Sorry it's been a while.' She placed her handbag on the hall table.

'Don't worry darling, we know how busy you are,' Bryony replied warmly. 'But we're always thrilled to see you whenever you can make it. How about dinner? I've got some…'

'Thanks mum, but I've already eaten out earlier this evening, so I really don't…'

'Oh good! Where did you go? Was it with that handsome man of yours? Graymond? How is he? You know, we haven't seen *him* for a while either. I'm sure he's busy with his aviation business and so on, but you *must* bring him for lunch one of these days.' Bryony ushered Alicia through into the large, open-plan kitchen with Paul following behind.

'No, not with Gray, and yes he's very well thanks mum,' Alicia replied. 'It was actually with Spencer. Spencer Warne. D'you remember me telling you about him?'

Bryony frowned briefly as she filled the kettle and set it back on the work surface before removing three large mugs from a cupboard. There was a sudden glimmer of recognition in her eyes.

'Spencer Warne, yes, of course I remember you mentioning him. Wasn't he the homeless man who helped you find a murderer?'

'That's him.'

'And then he went to a rehab clinic for a drugs problem. So sad these young people getting all mixed up with drugs and ending up on the streets.'

'It is sad, but Spencer's been a bit of a success story,' Alicia said, sliding out one of the bar stools at the kitchen island and sitting down. 'He's got a nice little place to live and has held a job down for, what, must be nearly six months now.'

'Oh good for him,' Bryony said as she bustled around with the kettle and mugs, tea bags and milk.

'What job's that?' Paul asked with interest, taking a seat beside Alicia.

'Believe it or not, he works in a jewellery store in Hatton Garden,' Alicia said with a wry smile.

'Really?' Paul raised his eyebrows with a touch of amusement.

'Yes, really,' Alicia replied. Bryony had finished making the tea and three identical mugs were placed on the work surface in front of them before she took a seat herself.

'In fact,' Alicia continued, pulling one of the mugs towards her, 'Spencer is the reason for my visit.'

'Oh?' Bryony sounded intrigued. 'How's that darling? I thought you wanted to talk about Rock Palm…'

'I do,' Alicia replied, 'but first, let me tell you about Spencer. This afternoon a lady brought a diamond necklace into the jewellery store where he works…'

Her parents listened patiently and attentively as Alicia continued.

'It was a fairly unusual and exquisite piece of jewellery; there were forty-nine round, colourless diamonds on a circular thread with a large pear-shaped diamond in the centre, a vivid pink colour. The diamonds were flawless and the whole necklace weighed almost one hundred carats.' She watched the faces of her parents closely but her description of the necklace returned only blank looks, albeit with a hint of fascination.

'That's quite a necklace if it weighs nearly a hundred carats,' Paul commented.

'A bit heavy to wear though,' added Bryony.

'I'm sure it must be,' Alicia added helpfully. She detected no sense of recollection from her parents. Then again, it was over twenty years ago. She was probably asking too much to expect them to remember something they would have seen only a few times or, in her father's case, may have paid no attention to at all.

'You'd think it'd be quite a memorable piece of jewellery if you ever saw it, wouldn't you?' she ventured.

'I'm sure it would,' Bryony nodded. 'It doesn't sound like any ordinary necklace to me.'

'Sounds like something you'd find at a Sotheby's auction,' Paul remarked.

'Or at a high-end resort in the Caribbean perhaps,' Alicia suggested.

'Quite possibly,' Paul agreed.

'It's the kind of necklace you'd want to lock firmly in a safe if you were staying in a hotel,' Alicia continued. 'What a nightmare it would be if a piece of jewellery like that should go missing…'

Suddenly her mother's eyes lit up.

'Is this why you were asking me about Rock Palm? You're talking about that lady's necklace, aren't you?' Bryony asked slowly. 'The diamond necklace that was stolen the night before we were evacuated.'

'Yes, I am.'

'I do remember it,' Bryony replied. 'It was quite a piece of jewellery, although far too excessive for my liking. I wasn't very keen on the lady who owned it though,' she added with a frown, 'or her husband. Thankfully, they mostly kept themselves to themselves and always gave the impression they thought they were better than everyone else. And as for the way they treated the staff… that was appalling…'

'So are you saying the same necklace that was supposedly stolen at Rock Palm Resort, what, twenty-odd years ago now, has suddenly resurfaced at the jewellery shop where your friend Spencer works?' Paul asked Alicia, redirecting the conversation.

'To be honest dad, it's pretty unlikely.'

'I'll say it is.'

'But I was just wondering if either of you could recall the name of the lady who wore it at Rock Palm?'

'Oh goodness Alicia, that was such a long time ago now, I'm sure I can't…' began Bryony, but Paul interrupted: 'As a matter of fact, I think I can. Wasn't their surname Karleman or something?'

'Karleman? Or Karl*sson*?' Alicia asked.

'Karleman I think,' her father replied. 'Charles and Vivienne Karleman. I've no idea how, or why, I remember their names but I'm pretty sure that's what they were. Not a couple you'd want to get to know though.'

'I'm glad you remember, dad,' Alicia said slowly, 'because the name of the lady who brought the necklace into the jewellery store was Vivienne Karlsson.'

'That's a bit of a coincidence,' Bryony remarked.

'It wasn't *the* Vivienne Karleman was it, and Spencer just got the name wrong?' Paul asked.

'No,' Alicia said shaking her head, 'it definitely wasn't Vivienne Karleman from Rock Palm. I got Spencer to describe the customer, Vivienne Karl*sson*; she was way too young. As far as I can tell, they're two different women.'

'But with the same necklace and very similar names,' her father added.

'Possibly,' Alicia said. 'What d'you think? Is this just a very far-fetched coincidence or has the Rock Palm necklace, supposedly stolen, just resurfaced?'

'Maybe it was found at Rock Palm after all,' Bryony said. 'If it was stolen, what are the chances that it would reappear again, twenty years later, in the very store where Spencer works? Where's it been all this time?'

'Good question,' Alicia replied, 'always assuming it *is* the genuine necklace.'

'Any reason to suggest it isn't?' Paul asked.

'Spencer mentioned something about the grading reports that the customer brought in with the necklace, said there was something that didn't look right about them.'

'His personal opinion or was there something tangible to go on?'

'Nothing tangible really. Just his gut feeling. Admittedly he's only been doing the job for six months, but I trust him. He never let me down as a street informant. The Metropolitan Police solved a number of crimes thanks to information provided by him.'

'What about the woman who brought the necklace into the store?' Paul asked. 'If she's not the original Vivienne Karleman from Rock Palm, then who is she? Why's she calling herself by an almost identical name?'

'I don't know dad. It's just, I don't know, it's all a bit strange, isn't it?'

'What's strange is that she's approached a high street jewellery store to sell a multimillion pound diamond necklace. An auction house would be a far more sensible — not to mention profitable — way of going about it. But it's interesting you should mention Rock Palm, Alicia. I had drinks with the owner, Carlos, only a couple of months or so ago.'

'Carlos Jaxen? I didn't know you were still friends with him.'

'We've stayed in touch through the years, off and on. I hadn't spoken to him in, oh probably a couple of years now, but he's over from the States sorting out some business here in London and gave me a call. Sad really, what's become of Rock Palm.'

'Did Carlos ever resolve the legal disputes he had with the planning officials about rebuilding the place?' Alicia asked.

'Apparently not,' Paul replied. Alicia and Bryony waited for him to elaborate but he wasn't forthcoming with any further information.

'So what's going to happen to it?' Alicia asked.

'I'm not sure. To be honest, it barely came up in conversation. We mentioned it briefly but we had other business to discuss and, as far as Carlos is concerned, there's little to talk about with Rock Palm anymore.'

In spite of the fact that Paul Clayton was in his seventies, he was far from retired and enjoyed as much energy and enthusiasm as a man half his age. He still ran his successful property development company with the same tenacity and drive as when he had first started the business. Alicia wondered what mutual venture her father and the owner of Rock Palm might have been discussing.

'I find it very sad,' her mother was saying. 'A stunning resort like that, right on the beach, prime location, just left to ruin. It's heartbreaking. And all because of a bunch of lawyers who can't agree on something. That's what it comes down to at the end of the day: money.'

'I got the impression Carlos has all but given up on the place now,' Paul went on, 'and I don't blame him. His wife Sophia died last year and she was really the driving force behind Rock Palm. Her family set up the resort in the fifties and for decades it was the ultimate resort playground for their international Jetset clientele. They had all kinds of celebrities and dignitaries stay there; according to Carlos, it was once one of the most sought-after vacation destinations in the Caribbean.'

'We were lucky to stay there,' Alicia said.

'We were, thanks to Carlos and Sophia, but no one could have predicted — or prevented — the damage caused by Hurricane Luis.'

'Such a shame,' Bryony lamented sadly.

'Yes, but dad, why didn't they just get on and rebuild the place?' Alicia asked. 'Other resorts and hotels had to pick up the pieces and get themselves back together in the aftermath. Why couldn't the Jaxens?'

'I honestly can't tell you why. The property world is a strange one. You know yourself, sometimes things just rumble along from one legal dispute to the next and are never finally resolved. I fear that's what happened to the Jaxens.'

'I'd buy it and restore it myself if I had the money,' Alicia said with determination.

'I think you might change your mind if you saw it now. Carlos had a few recent pictures with him; the place is a wreck. It's been neglected for over twenty years and now the property is pretty much derelict and abandoned. If you bought it you'd need the same money again and then some to demolish it and start over.'

'It's so sad to hear,' Bryony said. 'At least we have our lovely memories. I dug out a few old photo albums if you wanted to have a look through Alicia?'

'I was hoping you'd preempt me with that mum.'

'I'll go and get them.' Bryony slid off the bar stool and disappeared.

'Did Carlos ever mention the missing diamond necklace to you dad?' Alicia asked suddenly.

'No, we never discussed anything like that. He wouldn't have had much to do with it anyway. Leon Fayer, his general manager — remember him? — he was handling it I believe. Back then we only talked about business-related stuff and, of course, Carlos always wanted feedback on our vacation time at Rock Palm, but that was about it.'

'What about the Karlemans? Did Carlos ever talk about them, even just generally?'

Paul thought for a minute before replying.

'Yes, I do seem to think they were mentioned a couple of times although I've no idea why. Perhaps it's why I remember their name: Karleman. But Carlos didn't talk about them when we met a couple of months ago.'

'Did Carlos ever say what line of business Charles Karleman was in? Was it property, like you dad?'

'I know they weren't short of cash, that's for sure, but I've no idea what Charles did. I don't think he was in property, but I couldn't say for certain.'

Bryony returned with two large photograph albums and placed them on the work surface.

'Here we are, Clayton vacations in the late eighties and early nineties, almost all of them at Rock Palm Resort.'

'We were an adventurous family back then, weren't we mum?' Alicia said with good-natured sarcasm. 'Always going to new places, trying new things…'

'Very funny Alicia,' Bryony smiled. 'I realise your childhood holidays were somewhat limited where the destinations were concerned, but I personally feel you'd have been the first to complain if we'd announced we were going anywhere else.'

'You're probably right mum,' Alicia grinned. 'It *was* a stunning place. I loved it there; the people, the hotel, the beach. We were incredibly lucky to go every year. I'm not ungrateful really!'

'I'm glad to hear it,' Bryony replied. She opened one of the albums, bulky, leather-bound and of encyclopaedic proportions, to the first two pages where eight carefully positioned photographs were displayed. 'Now, what exactly are you looking for Alicia?'

Alicia took a sip of tea which she had previously ignored and leaned over to examine the pictures.

'I remember that day!' she said with a laugh. She pointed to a picture of a young girl — a much younger version of herself — wearing a matching red t-shirt and shorts, kneeling on a beach with a red bucket and spade. 'Didn't we do crab racing on the beach that evening? I remember collecting my crabs in that little red bucket before tipping them back into the rock pools later that night. It was so much fun.'

'I took those pictures!' Paul remarked. 'How old were you there Alicia?'

Alicia looked at the date at the top of the page where Bryony had written in faded letters: Rock Palm Resort, Antigua, May 1988.

'I was eight,' Alicia replied.

'Oh you did look sweet in that t-shirt and shorts ensemble,' Bryony cooed.

Alicia turned a few more pages and they examined the collection of photographs with exclamations of delight, laughter and fond reminising. It was many years since they'd pored over their old family photo albums together.

'I could look at these all night,' Alicia said, 'and as much as I'd love to, the ones I'd really like to see are the pictures from our ninety-five vacation; the one which was cut short, when we were evacuated. Where are those mum?'

Bryony pulled the second album towards her and, opening it, flipped the thick cardboard pages towards the back.

'Ninety-three, ninety-four… Ah. Here we are. Rock Palm, nineteen ninety-five.' She slid the album across to Alicia. The eight landscape photographs were displayed across two pages in a similar fashion to those in the first album. The matte-finish holiday snaps had been taken with the same camera, which had long been replaced by iPhones and her father's digital camera. Alicia examined the pictures, in almost all of which she featured, now as a tall and fairly inelegant-looking teenager with long, dark hair and her trademark dark-rimmed spectacles.

'I will never forgive you for making me wear those specs,' she said with a playful smile at her mother.

'They were fashionable at the time,' Bryony replied, 'and anyway, you chose them yourself.'

'I may not have been the most discerning of teenagers, but I definitely did *not* choose those spectacles,' Alicia said. She looked at her father. 'Come on dad, back me up here, mum *made* me wear those terrible things. No wonder I didn't have a boyfriend until I was in my twenties.'

'Alicia, I learned a long time ago not to get in the middle of a debate between you and your mother,' Paul said with a chuckle, 'and I'm firmly sticking to that resolution.'

'Dad, you disappoint me,' Alicia said shaking her head, 'but anyway, ignoring my *incredibly unfashionable* eyewear, chosen by my *mother*, let's look at these pictures from ninety-five. We didn't know it then, but it was to be the last vacation we'd ever have at Rock Palm. Oh look, there's one of the pool bar, it really hadn't changed much since the eighties, had it? Perhaps a fresh lick of paint, but that's about all. Who's that in the background?' Alicia squinted at one of the pictures before removing it from its sleeve in order to examine it more closely.

'It looks like one of the staff,' Paul said, peering at it over her shoulder.

'Oh I remember him, he was that very rude waiter,' Bryony remarked. 'He wasn't one of the regular staff that we knew well, in fact, I don't remember him being there for the other years. I think he'd only started working at the resort that summer. Goodness knows what possessed the general manager to hire him. They can't have been that desperate for staff.'

'Anyone remember his name?' Alicia asked, still scrutinising the picture.

'Can't say I do. It's not one I'd go out of my way to memorise,' Bryony retorted, 'other than to make a complaint.'

Alicia placed the photograph to one side and turned the page. The next four photos were of her parents in sportswear playing a game of tennis on one of the courts.

'Nice backhand action shot there dad.' Alicia uttered the comment before removing the photograph and subjecting it to the same careful examination as the previous one.

'Who's that in the background behind mum?'

Once again, the three of them looked closely at the picture. In one corner was a young, well-built man who looked to be in his early twenties. He was tall, handsome and muscular.

'I believe he was the tennis coach and manager of the sports reception,' Bryony said. 'Fancied himself. A lot. I didn't like him much but I remember that lady with the necklace used to give him plenty of attention. She was always having tennis lessons and hanging around the sports reception. He seemed to lap it up, but then I suppose it was part of the job and he had to whether he liked it or not. He can't really have been attracted to a woman like her.'

'D'you remember his name?' Alicia asked.

'Again, not one I'd bother to memorise, but I think it was Rapper… something like that…'

'Rapley,' Paul interjected quickly. 'His name was Owen Rapley.'

'Oh yes, that's it. Owen Rapley,' Bryony said.

'Owen Rapley,' Alicia repeated slowly, almost to herself. Owen Rapley. She looked closely at the picture; it was a little blurred but there was something familiar about that face. Suddenly, she remembered. It was the same face she'd seen at the beach that night, the night Anastasia had been murdered. They'd been together, walking hand in hand, carefree, laughing. But then another memory clouded the smiling faces. This time it was of Owen kneeling in the sand beside the body. *Her* body. There was a cold, hard, emotionless expression on his face as he turned to the general manager of the hotel. *I don't know her personally I'm afraid*, he was saying.

'Funny you should remember him so well Paul,' Bryony remarked, 'I didn't think you had much to do with the man; *I* was always the one who had to book the tennis courts.'

'Some names just stick, I suppose,' her husband replied coolly.

'Never mind,' Alicia said, although she too was intrigued as to why her father had remembered Owen's name so readily. She took a sip of tea and began to remove the photograph. 'Can I take this one too mum?'

'Yes, of course, but I'm not sure what all these pictures have to do with that necklace reappearing after all this time.'

'Neither am I. There's probably no connection at all, but it's still nice to look through these old photos again.'

Alicia turned another page and stopped. It was a double page spread of the pool deck area, including the pool bar. On one of the photographs Alicia was leaning against the bar on one elbow. She was sipping an elaborate-looking cocktail from a pineapple through a straw and smiling for the camera. Behind her, the barman was serving a couple who looked to be in their early forties. The woman, whose skin was an alarming shade of red, either due to the lighting or an extreme case of sunburn, wore a bright green sarong and an oversized straw sunhat with a matching green ribbon. The man standing just behind her was bare-chested. Their lower bodies were obscured by Alicia's pose. But there was one item in the photograph which caught her attention: the piece of jewellery around the woman's neck. It was the diamond necklace.

'Mum, dad,' Alicia said softly, 'there it is; the necklace.' She slid the photograph out of the page and held it up to the light. Her parents leaned in towards her.

'You were spot-on with the description,' Paul remarked. 'The necklace you described from Spencer's jewellery store, it's exactly like the necklace Vivienne Karleman is wearing in that photograph. There can't be two necklaces like that, surely? It has to be a one-off.'

Alicia examined the photograph. There was no mistaking it: the necklace which Spencer had described exactly matched the one she was looking at on the matte photographic paper. She pulled her cell phone out of her pocket and took a snapshot of the necklace around Vivienne Karleman's neck. Zooming in on the diamonds, she cropped the picture and sent it to Spencer with the caption: "Is this it?"

'It is an exquisite piece of jewellery,' Bryony remarked. 'But what on earth's she doing wearing it by the pool?'

'Showing off probably,' Paul said.

'No wonder she lost it.'

'Lost? Or stolen?' Alicia interjected.

'*She* said it was stolen,' Bryony replied. 'Accused poor old Leon of having one of his staff take it. What a thing to say to such a sweet, kind man. I do wonder what became of all the staff at that place. I felt so sorry for them with all the guests leaving. I suppose they all got jobs elsewhere once the island got itself back on its feet.'

'I can think of someone who *would* know,' Alicia ventured, looking at her father.

'I can put you in touch with Carlos if you like,' Paul replied, reading his daughter's mind. 'He's still here in London for another couple of weeks I believe, although I don't think he'll be able to help much. Remember it was over twenty years ago now. He's hardly likely to be in touch with the resort's old tennis coach, or even the GM, and I'm certain any communications with former guests would have petered out years ago.'

'Even so...'

'All right, I'll give you his number and you can ask him if he still has any contact with anyone or remembers anything. Tread carefully though and be tactful as to how you broach the subject of Rock Palm; the endless legal wrangling has taken its toll on him over the years, along with a few other challenges he's had with his property enterprises. Poor old Carlos hasn't had an easy ride of it and Rock Palm was really his late wife's project, so the whole topic is a pretty sensitive one for him at the best of times. He never really got over her death.'

'I'll be gentle, I promise,' Alicia said, 'but I'd appreciate his number.'

They were suddenly interrupted by the bleep of her cell phone. She picked it up and checked the screen. It was a reply from Spencer.

'He says the necklace in the picture I sent him looks exactly the same as the one he saw in the store this afternoon,' Alicia said.

'Perhaps there's more than one necklace after all,' Paul said. 'It's the only feasible explanation I suppose.'

'And the names?' Alicia asked. 'Karlsson and Karleman?'

'Who knows?' Paul shrugged. 'But I'd suggest there's nothing to it.'

'You're probably right,' Alicia replied. She knew she could become excited over the smallest of coincidences. She would imagine all kinds of stories developing, which would often come to nothing.

'And just as an aside, if you're going to be asking Carlos about Rock Palm, there's something else you should perhaps be aware of, which I doubt you'll recall,' Paul continued.

'Yes?' Alicia replied.

'As well as the hurricane devastation and failure to rebuild, Rock Palm has another dark cloud hanging over it,' her father said warily, almost reluctantly.

'I think I already know…' Alicia said. 'The murder…'

'Yes.'

'I'd forgotten about that.' Bryony brought her hand to her mouth. 'That was an awful thing. For everyone. For the staff and… Didn't one of the guests find the body on the beach?'

'Yes,' Paul nodded. 'When I met up with Carlos a few months afterwards he told me about it. He was pretty cut up about the whole thing, as well as all the damage to Rock Palm from the hurricane. D'you remember the magician who used to perform in the underground auditorium there? Mortimer, or whatever he called himself. Apparently the murdered woman was one of his assistants…'

'Anastasia…' Alicia said softly.

'Yes, Anastasia, that was her name. Her body was found on the beach by one of the guests the morning we were evacuated from the hotel. She'd been…'

'Stabbed…'

Paul looked at Alicia with a frown.

'How d'you know so much about this?'

'I — I'm not sure.' Alicia hesitated. 'Probably just what I heard at the time, when we left the hotel.'

She had never revealed to her parents exactly what she had been doing just prior to their departure from Rock Palm. Fearing the potential repercussions of admitting to anyone that she had stood in the sand less than two feet away from Anastasia's mutilated body, she had spoken of it to no one. She had been so close to the body, she could have reached out and touched it. She had stared directly into the vacant, bloodshot eyes of the dead woman. The nightmares had faded over time, but the recollection of that haunting gaze had never left her. It had been a closely guarded secret for twenty-three years and for now, at least, would remain as one.

'Sorry dad, I'll try not to interrupt again,' she said. 'You were saying what Carlos told you about the murder.'

'It's only what he said to me in the aftermath, and that was a few months later. I've probably forgotten most of it anyway.'

'What *do* you remember?' Alicia coaxed. Her father looked at her suspiciously.

'You are *not* to bring this up with Carlos under any circumstances, is that clear?'

'No dad, of course not. I wouldn't dream of it. I'm just interested, that's all.'

'That's what worries me Alicia.'

'Dad,' Alicia said firmly, placing a hand on his arm, 'I won't mention any of this to Carlos. Sure, I'm curious, I'd be lying if I said I wasn't. I'm interested to ask him about the Karlemans and the diamond necklace and it'll be good to reminisce about old times, but I won't talk about the murder. I'm sure that's been case-closed for years anyway.'

'As a matter of fact, it hasn't,' Paul said, watching his daughter's reaction carefully. He knew this would attract her attention like a moth to a flame and he was right. Suppressing a surge of adrenaline at an unsolved murder, Alicia feigned a look of nonchalance.

'Oh?' she asked casually.

'*Alicia...*' Paul said in a warning tone.

'I promise dad. I won't speak to Carlos about this.'

'I'll tell you what I remember, but it isn't much. It *was* over twenty years ago. According to Carlos, the body was identified at the scene by the magician and the other magic assistants.

Apparently they were pretty distraught about her death, or appeared to be. Then the police arrived, along with the medical examiner and his assistant. I think they were from a hospital in St. John's. The police cordoned off the area and the ME and his man did their thing, concluded a time of death and all that. According to Carlos, after they'd finished up on the beach, they set off for the hospital mortuary with the body while the police carried on processing the scene, interviewing suspects and taking statements and so on. Obviously it was a difficult job for them and time was running out because of the approaching hurricane. Most of the guests had already left for the airport, or were in the process of leaving; it was a mandatory evacuation so the police couldn't do anything to keep them at the hotel. They couldn't conduct a proper investigation and question everyone, and then, as you know, their crime scene was completely demolished by Hurricane Luis. Any remaining evidence was washed out to sea or swept away by the wind, gone for good.'

'The knife that Anastasia was stabbed with?' Alicia asked.

'Never found.' Paul shook his head. 'The murderer certainly picked the right night for the crime.'

'Who *was* the murderer?'

Paul paused for a few moments, debating how to reply. Finally, he said: 'They were never certain.'

Alicia raised her eyebrows.

'Who did they *think* it could be?' Bryony asked curiously.

'There was one man who was always thought to have been guilty of Anastasia's murder. He was in some kind of romantic relationship with her and was one of the last people to have been seen with her on the night she was killed. According to a couple of witnesses — guests, no members of staff interestingly — he was spotted on the beach alone with her that night.'

'Who was it?' Bryony asked.

'Owen Rapley,' Paul replied.

'Owen? The tennis coach?' Bryony said with surprise.

Paul nodded. He glanced at Alicia who had a distant look on her face. Her mind was in turmoil. *It could be her. I don't know her personally I'm afraid…* His words. His lies. Why did people lie? To hide the truth. But what *was* the truth?

'Was he charged?' Bryony asked.

'No, he wasn't. Even though he was one of the last people to be seen with her when she was alive — perhaps *the* last — and he had no alibi for the time of death, there was insufficient evidence for a conviction.'

'But what about the police investigation? Surely they were able to prove if he did it or not?'

Paul shook his head firmly.

'Don't ask me for details. All I know is that the police didn't have enough evidence to convict him. They had to let him go. The story goes that even though he was seen walking hand in hand with Anastasia along the beach on the night she was murdered, he initially lied to the police and said he only knew her as an acquaintance. After further questioning, he finally admitted the truth, that they'd been romantically involved and had been secretly seeing each other for a few months.

'According to Carlos, the lies, together with the guests' witness statements, sent him straight to the top of the list of suspects. After that, Owen Rapley's name was tarnished forever. He'd been a prime suspect in a murder case, he couldn't prove his innocence and he never quite recovered from that. As far as Carlos knew — and admittedly this was a long time ago — Owen's blackened reputation preceded him wherever he went and he was never able to clear his name and move on. He couldn't get another job and eventually became homeless, living on the streets.'

'What a waste, an accomplished tennis pro like him. But maybe that's exactly what he deserved,' Bryony said.

'Perhaps. Or perhaps not. The staff at the hotel and even the magic team were wholly on his side and unanimously in support of his innocence.'

'Really?' Bryony asked. 'How could they have been so certain when there were witnesses who saw him with the girl on the night she was murdered?'

'I can't answer that. I don't think Carlos could either. Something didn't add up and that's what the police couldn't get their heads round. Owen had the means and the opportunity, but what was his motive? It didn't help matters either that the investigation was severely hampered by the hurricane. And then there was the absence of the murder weapon and the body.'

'The *body*?' Alicia looked shocked. This was one piece of information she had never heard about.

'I thought the ME took it to the hospital mortuary.' Bryony spoke.

'They never made it,' Paul replied.

'But… what happened? Where did they go?'

'Nobody knows,' Paul said with a shrug.

'Wait a second dad, back up,' Alicia said. 'A medical examiner's van complete with an assistant and a body on a gurney can't suddenly vanish into thin air. Someone must know what happened to it. Antigua's hardly a big place to hide something like that. Didn't the police search for it?'

'Alicia, less than twenty-four hours after this all took place, the island was hit by a Category Four hurricane and subjected to severe devastation. By the time the police were informed that the ME's van had gone missing, it was too late to even think of sending out a search party. After the hurricane had moved away from Antigua, leaving a trail of utter destruction in its wake, there were power outages, telephone lines were down preventing all forms of communication, and many of the major roads were completely impassable for days. An extensive cleanup operation took priority over anything else and the law enforcement officials had other problems to deal with like looting and plundering of shops and businesses. Hundreds of people were left homeless, many were simply struggling to survive, and the scale of devastation was so severe that the Antiguan government even sought international aid for help with basic shelter, food and medical supplies, and fresh water.'

'Okay, I get your point. It's just that… the van had to be *somewhere*.'

'Yes, of course, unless you believe in aliens or spontaneous combustion,' Paul agreed. 'The police felt the same and did everything they could, but it was days later before they were even able to attempt to conduct any kind of search for the van. For sure, it left Rock Palm, but it never arrived at the hospital mortuary. After the hurricane, the medical examiner, his assistant and their van, and Anastasia's body, were never seen again. What made the search even more challenging was that Rock Palm and the hospital are at opposite ends of the island. There were a number of routes the van could have taken back to St. John's. You know what the roads are like in Antigua; some of those inland roads are pretty winding and undulating with steep drops and thick foliage on either side. No one could be certain of exactly which route the ME took on his return journey to the hospital. As well as the devastation across the island, there was a complete lack of knowledge of where to look. It was almost impossible to narrow the search to a specific area, and people didn't carry cell phones back then so there was no means of tracking their location.'

'But what do they *think* happened? There must've been some speculation at the time?'

'I think the most likely possibility bandied about was that the van broke down somewhere, possibly along a coastal road. The ME and his assistant couldn't get help or sort the problem before the hurricane made landfall and they were caught up in it and swept out to sea.'

'That's one explanation I suppose.' Alicia sounded less than convinced. 'Except you wouldn't take a coastal road to get to St. John's from Rock Palm. The quickest way would be to go inland.'

'I agree, but it was the most feasible, and perhaps only explanation as far as the police were concerned. There were no reported accidents or sightings of the van — which was apparently fairly nondescript and unremarkable to look at — and extensive searches came up with nothing. The obvious conclusion was that it was no longer on the island.'

'And it never washed up on another shore someplace else?'

'Nope.'

'So if all attempts to track it down were to no avail…'

'It meant that in the absence of a body, and indeed, an ME's report, it was very difficult to continue with the murder investigation,' Paul went on. 'Any evidence, DNA, fingerprints, sperm, hair, things like that, which may have pointed to Rapley — or someone else perhaps — had been lost. And there was nothing anyone could do about it.'

'So the case was never closed…'

'I don't think so.' Paul shook his head. 'Unless there've been further developments that I don't know about. If there were, Carlos has never spoken of them to me.'

There was silence for a few minutes as his words sunk in.

'I wish I could go back in time, twenty-three years ago, and investigate for myself,' Alicia said out loud.

'I doubt you'd have had much more success than the police,' Paul said. 'I know you pride yourself in solving mysteries Alicia, and you're a very effective investigative journalist, but trying to conduct a murder investigation on an island devastated by a Category Four hurricane is a whole different ballgame altogether.'

'Sure, I get that,' Alicia agreed, 'and you're probably right dad. But has anything been done since? Anything at all to close the case? Or locate the ME's van?'

'Not to my knowledge,' her father replied. 'I'm sure Carlos would've let me know if there were any significant updates in the investigation. As far as I'm aware the case went cold years ago and has remained unsolved ever since with no fresh evidence or information coming to light. And Carlos had his own battles to fight; he had neither the time, the money, nor the energy to set about solving a murder with his own legal team and private investigators.'

'So Anastasia's murderer — whoever that person might be — walks free to this day.'

'Yes. Although if it was who the police thought it was — the Rapley guy — then he's hardly been living it up. Perhaps it would've been better if he'd been found guilty. He could've served his time, been let out early for good behaviour, and now he'd be free to get on with his life again, instead of having drifted from one street doorway to the next for the last twenty years.' He paused before adding: 'But I know how you feel about people serving a life sentence for a crime they didn't commit, Alicia.'

Paul was right. The subject was close to home for his daughter; the man she had been dating for the last two years, Graymond Sharkey, or Gray as he was known by his friends, had once been wrongly convicted of a double murder that he hadn't committed. He was sent to prison to serve a life sentence at the age of twenty-three. Seventeen years later, he was released on parole and decided to set about finding the real killer, the person who had walked free. Alicia had taken an interest in his case; she'd been a junior reporter covering the original murder trial and had always had her doubts about his culpability for the crime. Aware of his release from prison and believing in his innocence, she offered her assistance in tracking down the real killer. Together, they succeeded. And at the same time, fell in love.

'It's always better to get the right person,' Alicia said firmly, feeling a brief moment of regret for the lost years of Gray's twenties and thirties spent behind prison bars.

'I still feel you should avoid speaking to Carlos about the murder,' Paul said.

'What if *he* brings it up?' Alicia asked.

'That's his call,' Paul replied. 'Just be careful Alicia. Be sensitive. Carlos isn't the tough business tycoon he used to be. He's a man who's been beaten down and wearied from the world. A murder, a theft and total hurricane devastation at his most lucrative and prestigious Caribbean resort, all within twenty-four hours, left him destitute, fighting for his reputation and embroiled in bitter legal disputes all over the place. Sure, he recovered himself to a point, but the legal wrangling over Rock Palm has dragged on and on over years and years. I think Sophia's death last year was the final straw for him and he's ready to give up the fight for Rock Palm now.'

'I'll be gentle dad,' Alicia promised. She yawned.

'Alicia darling, you look tired,' Bryony said glancing at her watch, 'and it's gone midnight. What time would you like breakfast in the morning?'

'Eight should be fine,' Alicia replied, yawning again. 'I've got an appointment at ten-thirty in Shoreditch tomorrow so I'll have plenty of time. I'm interviewing a property developer.'

'A property developer?' her father asked with interest. 'Anyone I know?'

'I don't think so dad. It's a story I'm working on. This guy started digging up an old derelict site to put some houses on it and ended up stumbling across the remains of five bodies.'

'Ohhhh that's a property developer's worst nightmare,' Paul said rolling his eyes. 'He won't be building anything on that site for months, maybe years. It'll cost him an absolute fortune while the investigations get underway. Poor guy. He has my sympathies.'

'*Dad*, don't be so heartless,' Alicia said, shocked, 'Those bodies belonged to five people who may even have been murdered. One of the bodies is close to being identified as a young girl who went missing nearly forty years ago. Imagine it was *your* family buried down there.'

'Sorry, I didn't mean to sound callous, I was just looking at it from the developer's point of view; that sort of thing is an absolute disaster for business. I remember the time I'd acquired a site for a new-build property and the archaeologists — they have to inspect the site before you can get started — found evidence of an old Roman settlement. It set me back about six months and cost tens of thousands of pounds. Not what you need when you've got contractors waiting to get started. But yes, sorry, a few old pots and coins is a nuisance but it's a different story altogether if it's a mass grave.'

'Yes, it is,' Alicia said firmly, 'and a little bit of inconvenience with money and time is nothing compared to the anguish those relatives must've felt when their loved ones didn't come home. When the bodies have been officially identified I hope in time the investigations can provide closure for the families involved, and I want to be a part of that, which is why I do what I do.'

'And you're absolutely right,' Paul said. He gave his daughter a proud smile before adding: 'I stand humbled and corrected as usual!'

'On that note I think it's time we got some sleep,' Bryony announced gathering up the empty tea mugs. Alicia collected the little pile of photographs she had removed from the second album and kissed her parents goodnight before making her way upstairs to her childhood bedroom. It was a large space occupying most of the second floor of the house and hadn't changed much since she'd officially left home to attend university at the age of eighteen. It was decorated in neutral colours with a wall of slatted oak doors, Rock Palm style, at one end, which led to a large walk-in wardrobe. It was this part of the room that Alicia made her way to now.

Switching on the lights, she went to the far side of the wardrobe and pulled a basket off the top shelf. She sat on a stool and placed the basket beside her. Inside was a bundle of papers, cards, scrappy notes, mementoes and other keepsake items from years gone by. Between two bundles of notes was a small rectangular box. She pulled it out and opened it. It contained the large, black-rimmed spectacles she'd worn as a teenager. What on earth had possessed her to keep them she wondered with amusement as she replaced them in their box.

She continued to sift through the contents until she found what she was looking for: an A4-sized notebook. She took it out and flipped through the pages to somewhere in the middle. The heading at the top of the page, written in bold capitals in her teenage handwriting read: MURDER AT ROCK PALM RESORT, SEPTEMBER 1995. Brushing a dead spider from the edge of the page, she began to read. It was an article she had written twenty-three years before, never intended for publication. She'd submitted two other articles for the school newspaper that September: a generalised one on Antigua and another on stage illusions and magic shows and how an audience's perception of what is happening in front of them can be quite different to what is actually taking place. The murder article, however, was only ever for her eyes. She wasn't exactly sure why she'd written it. For posterity perhaps? Or maybe it was to provide clarity to her mind of the things that she'd observed. Whatever the reason, it was a detailed account of the last twenty-four hours of their vacation in Antigua, along with a few other notes relating to Rock Palm: names and descriptions, her own thoughts and feelings and fifteen-year-old memories, journal-style.

Perched on the stool, Alicia pulled her knees up to her chest, balancing the notebook on top of them, and leafed through the pages. The memories came flooding back: the pleasant sounds of the ocean, the crickets and tree frogs, the warm humidity of the tropics, the aroma of fresh coffee from the beachfront restaurant, the salty sea air, and the sickly scent of dry ice and stale body odour in the auditorium. Finally, she turned back to the first page. The article began with words which seemed vaguely familiar, words which had been held deep in her subconscious mind. Dark and haunting, ill-fated perhaps, they were uttered during the magic show just before the cabinet illusion, the final act of the night. It was the last magic show that would ever take place at Rock Palm Resort. The stage curtains would never reopen. And Anastasia would never perform again. Alicia began to read. *Magic is merely an art form. It makes the impossible appear possible, the illogical appear implausible... It's about smoke and mirrors, sleight-of-hand, misdirection, perceptual manipulation. What you are about to see, ladies and gentlemen, is an illusion...*

THIRTEEN

10:57 am, Tuesday, August 21
Hatton Garden, London

It was another day of blue sky, bright sunshine and searing heat as Spencer drained the dregs of his morning cappuccino and tossed the disposable cup in a recycling bin. He wasn't due to start work until eleven that morning and although he appreciated the lie-in which came with starting work later, he found it hard to catch up with what was happening in the showroom when he got there.

A double decker bus rumbled its way past sending a cloud of dust into the air. Spencer stepped into a shop doorway to take refuge from the street filth drifting towards his white shirt, clean on that morning. He glanced down to see a homeless man slumped against the wall with his eyes closed. The man wore a dirty, blue checked shirt and grey trousers a few sizes too large for him. A navy baseball cap was pulled down low over his eyes and the lower part of his face was mostly obscured by a scruffy beard. A small backpack lay beside him and in one hand he clutched a large bottle containing a clear liquid. He smelt strongly of sweat and alcohol and appeared not to have noticed Spencer. But Spencer knew only too well the feelings of hopelessness and desperation that went with life on the street. He glanced at his watch; he didn't want to be late for work, but this was important too. He knelt down next to the homeless man and spoke softly.

'Hey man, you had breakfast this morning?'

There was no response. Spencer touched his arm gently.

'Mate, are you okay?'

The man stirred slightly and tried to sit up before descending into an episode of violent coughing. Spencer waited patiently and, when the man had recovered himself, spoke again.

'Are you okay? That cough sounds bad.'

'Whadda you want?' the man said nastily, slurring his words. 'Go away. Leave me alone.'

Spencer was undeterred.

'Can I get you anything? How 'bout a coffee?'

'Get lost,' the man replied, 'I don't want nuffink from you.'

How many times had he himself muttered those words to kind passers-by, Spencer thought, feeling slightly ashamed. He stood up and made his way to the coffee shop a few doors down.

'Morning Zoey,' he said brightly to one of the servers who recognised him immediately.

'Morning Spencer, you're in late today,' Zoey replied. She was a platinum blonde college graduate filling in time while she looked for a meaningful job with prospects. 'I've been here since five-thirty. Think I need a job where you work.'

'I'll put in a good word for you.'

'Your usual, is it?' Zoey asked, reaching for a disposable cup.

'Actually no, although I could do with another shot of caffeine to get me through the morning. Nah, there's a homeless guy a couple of doors down. Did you see him this morning? I thought I'd get him a coffee.'

'Can't say I did see him, no.'

Typical, Spencer thought. The homeless were invisible to the majority of people walking along the streets. Still, Zoey was a kind person with a generous heart; perhaps the guy really hadn't been there when she'd opened up the coffee shop at five-thirty that morning.

'What's he having then?' Zoey asked.

'I'll get a large Americano and one of those blueberry muffins to go,' Spencer replied, eyeing the selection of freshly baked cakes and pastries in the display cabinet.

'Coming right up.' Zoey poked a long fingernail at the touchscreen on the cash register before starting on his order.

'Another scorcher of a day out there,' she said as she worked. 'Bit hot for me though. I prefer it cooler. Can't bear the underground in this weather. I'm just not keen on being stuck with all those sweaty people in a stuffy carriage.' Spencer listened politely, willing her to hurry; the clock on the wall said the time was ten fifty-nine.

'Here we are.' Zoey placed the items on the counter top. 'One large Americano and a blueberry muffin to go. That's four pounds and five pence.'

Spencer pulled out a five pound note from his wallet and handed it to her before picking up the coffee and brown paper bag containing the muffin.

'Thanks. Here's your change.' Zoey produced a handful of coins from the till. Spencer looked at his own hands in consternation; in his right he held the coffee and in his left, the bag with the muffin.

'Keep it,' he replied, before hurrying out of the shop. Two doors down, the homeless man was still there, slumped against the wall as he had been minutes earlier.

'Here's breakfast,' Spencer said as he bent down and placed the large cup and brown paper bag beside the man. 'Coffee and a blueberry muffin.'

He stood up and was about to walk away, conscious of the time, when the man glanced up at him.

'For me?'

'Yeah mate. For you.'

'God bless you. Have a good day.' The homeless man reached for the coffee.

'You too,' Spencer replied before turning away. As he crossed the street to the jewellery store a puzzled expression came over his face. In the brief moment when the homeless man had glanced up at Spencer, there had been something familiar about him. Spencer wasn't sure what it was, or even if it was just his imagination, but he was certain he'd seen the man before. Then again, he'd spent so many years living rough on the streets of London himself, he may well have encountered the man at some point in his former life, perhaps at a hostel or homeless shelter. He pushed open the door to Tobias Moncler Jewels and instantly received an icy blast of air conditioning. It was like stepping from the Caribbean straight into the Arctic. The large, antique clock on the wall showed the time as five minutes past eleven. Keeley, who was polishing the glass of a display cabinet containing trays of glittering diamond rings, smiled at Spencer as he walked in.

'Morning,' she said pleasantly.

'Hi Keeley.' Spencer looked around. 'You here by yourself?'

'No, Otto's about somewhere and Camilla and Ronan just got back from the bank. Said they had some important business to finish up in the back office. Don't know what that could be, do you?'

'No idea,' Spencer said quickly. 'But they went to the bank?'

'Yeah. They both had to go apparently. Needed two signatures or something.'

The news that Ronan and Camilla had made a joint visit to the bank was alarming.

'Did they say what it was about?' Spencer asked.

'Nah, just that it was important and that they both had to be there together. So it's been Otto and me on the shop floor. Thankfully it hasn't been busy. Not supposed to leave the store in the hands of the juniors though, are they?'

'Take it as a compliment they thought they could trust you,' Spencer said. 'I'll throw my bag in the coffee room and be right back.'

'Sure. See you in a minute,' Keeley replied, returning to the display cabinet.

As he punched in the four-digit code on the keypad beside the door at the rear of the showroom, Spencer wondered if it would be possible to avoid Ronan and Camilla and make it back out before they noticed he was late. Tobias was strict about time-keeping, but would surely have shown understanding for arriving a few minutes late after helping a homeless man. It certainly wouldn't pass on the list of excuses in Camilla's eyes, however. An LED glowed green and there was a faint click as the door unlocked. Access granted. Spencer headed for the staff break room to drop off his backpack.

In the corner of the break room was a small flatscreen TV. It was divided into four quarters and displayed live footage from four closed circuit security cameras positioned discreetly around the showroom. Spencer hoped that Camilla was still busy in the back office with Ronan and unaware that he had only just arrived. As he entered the room, however, his heart sank. She was sitting at a table to one side of the room, near the TV, finishing off what looked to be a slice of a Honeydew melon. She glanced up as he walked in.

'Good morning Spencer,' she said with a smile. Spencer opened his mouth to reply, but no words came out. Was she smiling at him? He threw his backpack on the floor and hung his jacket on a hook above it.

'How are you this morning?' Camilla asked airily, almost cheerfully.

'Fine thanks,' Spencer replied.

'All ready for another profitable day's work?'

'Er, I think so.'

'Good to hear Spencer.' Camilla managed another disconcerting smile.

'I'd better get…' Spencer began, but before he could finish, the door opened behind him and Ronan walked in.

'Morning rookie!' he beamed. 'I trust you had a wonderful evening last night?'

'Yeah, thanks.' Spencer felt suddenly uneasy.

'Good, good,' Ronan went on. 'Has Camilla filled you in on the news yet?'

'What news?' Spencer asked cautiously, looking from one to the other.

'You remember Vivienne, the charming customer who came into our showroom just before closing last night?' Ronan asked.

'Yes.'

'Then you'll also remember the incredibly valuable diamond necklace she brought with her?'

Before Spencer could reply, Ronan continued.

'Obviously Vivienne was herself in a rather sad predicament financially, but I'm pleased to say that we were able to come to a *very satisfactory* arrangement for both her and us.'

'An arrangement?'

'How much would you say that diamond necklace was worth, Spencer? I know you're still very new to this game, but you saw it; give me a rough ballpark.'

Spencer wasn't sure he wanted to give any kind of opinion as to the value of the necklace, but Ronan and Camilla were both looking at him from opposite sides of the room. Sharks circling their prey, ready for the kill. It was sure to be a trick. He swallowed hard. He was trapped.

'Well, there were forty-nine of those round diamonds, the flawless ones, and they were about two carats each, if I remember,' he stammered uncertainly, 'so that's what, nearly a hundred carats. So you're looking at maybe two million pounds or something...'

'Two point five million to be precise, but not bad,' Ronan said in a patronising tone. 'And how about the pink diamond? What price would you put on that?'

Spencer inflated his cheeks and blew out air through his mouth.

'I guess I'd say that thing was worth, oh I don't know, probably a lot more than all the other diamonds put together.'

'Correct,' Ronan replied. 'Well done, rookie. A diamond as rare and as large as that is worth around fifteen million pounds. That's what Camilla and I valued it as and we're normally spot on with our numbers, aren't we Camilla?'

Camilla agreed enthusiastically. Spencer was beginning to wonder whether the Honeydew was laced with amphetamine.

'Now then, here's your big arithmetic challenge Spencer,' Ronan went on, as if he were addressing a class of five year olds. 'How much would you say the *entire necklace* is worth?'

The question was almost too easy and again, Spencer wondered if there was a catch.

'If you're asking me to add fifteen to two point five, it's seventeen point five,' he said warily.

'Congratulations rookie! Gold star for you!' Ronan said in a mocking tone.

'But wait,' Spencer said suddenly. He couldn't help himself. 'How did you get the whole necklace valued so fast? You must've been working all night. Surely you didn't... How did you appraise each stone? Did you take the necklace apart already?'

'Oh Spencer, you've so much to learn,' Ronan said. 'A little word: when you've as much experience in the trade as Camilla and me, you don't need to be doing things like that.'

'But what about Dr Moncler's rule that any diamond worth over two grand should never be purchased without looking at it loose under a microscope first? What about that?' Spencer asked.

'What about it?' Ronan shrugged.

'If Dr Moncler thinks that's important…'

'Dr Moncler's not here, is he?' Ronan said. 'Vivienne wanted a quick sale and Camilla and I were happy to oblige.'

Ronan kept talking. He liked to talk.

'Of course, we haggled back and forth, but as you know Spencer, the primary advantage that *we* can offer over *other* channels is *time*. If you want a quick, easy sale without a fuss, then you go to a jeweller, a diamond dealer or a pawnbroker. Our reputation for getting things done in a timely manner preceded us apparently. According to Vivienne, she chose us over all the other Hatton Garden jewellery stores specifically for that reason. We couldn't let her down now, could we?'

'So you made her an offer without properly appraising the diamonds?' Spencer asked.

'The diamonds *were* appraised properly,' Ronan said with an irritated frown. 'How dare you suggest otherwise?'

'But they…' Spencer stopped himself.

'To answer your question, and following a *thorough appraisal* of the diamonds, we reached a mutually acceptable price within a fairly short time and yes, we made her an offer. In fact, Vivienne was so happy with it, she didn't even want to go away and think about it.'

'I'm assuming you ran that past Dr Moncler?' Spencer asked.

'Excuse me?' Camilla snapped. Spencer jumped at the slightly ferocious interruption from the other side of the room. 'Who d'you think you are, undermining my authority like that? *I'm* in charge when Tobias is away, which means *I* have the final say as to what goes on here.'

'We get your point Camilla,' Ronan interrupted, annoyed that her sudden flare-up had interrupted the flow of conversation. He looked directly at Spencer and said: 'What number do you think we agreed on?'

'I've no idea,' Spencer replied.

'Take an educated guess. You're an intelligent man.'

Not what you told me yesterday, Spencer thought to himself.

'Come on, give me a number.' Ronan was goading him. Spencer felt trapped again.

'Um, well if you valued the necklace at seventeen point five million pounds, then maybe you offered her, I don't know, seventeen point five million?'

'What are you on about?' Ronan said, sounding appalled. 'Don't you understand the term *business deal?* If something's worth a certain amount but the vendor wants a quick sale, the whole point is that you go as low as possible with your offer. The customer wants a snappy deal, they pay for it. Try again. How much?'

The only "business deal" Spencer had experience of which involved haggling over the price, was with his dealer, for the purchase of a few grams of white powder. Clearly the world of high-end jewellery was in a different league.

'Sixteen million pounds?' he ventured hesitantly.

'Go lower!' Ronan said excitedly, a glint in his dark eyes.

'Errr - fourteen million?'

'*Lower!*'

'Thirteen?'

Ronan smiled.

'Lower still?' Spencer sounded incredulous.

A nod from Ronan.

'Ten? Surely not less than ten? Nine?' Spencer gulped. '*Eight?*'

'That's right rookie, *eight million pounds!*' Ronan said jubilantly. 'For a necklace worth seventeen point five million! Not bad for a day's work, is it?'

'But… if the necklace is genuine you've totally ripped her off,' Spencer said in disbelief.

'What d'you mean *if the necklace is genuine?*' Ronan shot back. 'Of course it's genuine. Do you honestly believe Camilla and me, with all our knowledge and expertise, can't tell a real diamond from a fake? How do you think we've got where we are today?'

'But how can you properly grade a diamond when it's still in its setting?'

'Stop going on about appraising the diamonds,' Ronan said angrily. 'They're genuine, all right? Bona fide. The real deal. So are the reports. You'll be telling us the GIA database is lying next.'

'I know the database can't lie, but now you mention them, there *was* something about those reports yesterday that looked a bit odd.' The words were out before Spencer could stop himself. But hadn't Ronan and Camilla noticed? Surely if something was wrong they'd have spotted it too?

'The GIA reports were all in order,' Ronan insisted. 'Every one matched the records in the database.'

Spencer couldn't disagree with that. He'd checked one of the reports himself. How could the GIA database be wrong? There was no way around that argument. He must've been mistaken after all.

'I still think you should've consulted with Dr Moncler first,' Spencer said. 'It's his business and his money. He's only away for a couple of days. Surely the customer could've waited till then?'

'Shut up Spencer,' Ronan retorted. He was now red-faced with indignation. 'Why don't you go back to the street doorways where you belong?'

In spite of the vicious air conditioning, Spencer could feel the heat beginning to rise in his own cheeks.

'Like I said, you're the rookie here,' Ronan went on, breathing hard. 'Camilla and I know what we're about in this business. That's why Tobias puts us in charge when he's away. The reports and the diamonds are genuine. We've been through everything. You've got to when you're dealing with gemstones of this calibre. I signed the official documentation with my own hand last night.'

Spencer was shocked at the speed with which Ronan and Camilla had sealed the deal. Even if everything *was* genuine, a hasty agreement to purchase an item of jewellery supposedly worth millions was surely not the wisest move. There were a multitude of things which might have been overlooked, such as the obvious question of whether the necklace was stolen. He opened his mouth to speak but was cut off by Camilla.

'We've heard enough from you,' she snapped, 'and it didn't escape my notice that you were ten minutes late this morning, so you can forget your lunch break and work straight through until the end of the day.'

'That's hardly fair,' Spencer protested, but Camilla wasn't listening. Her eye had caught a movement in the top right hand corner of the TV screen. Spencer followed her gaze. The camera facing the showroom doorway showed Vivienne Karlsson entering. She was dressed in a black, tight-fitting blouse with tan-coloured trousers and, from the image on the screen, looked as immaculately styled as she had the previous evening.

'Ah good, she's right on time,' Ronan said. He sounded calmer. 'We've certainly got some wonderful news for Ms Karlsson this morning, although I'm sure she's already been in touch with her financial people.' Turning to Spencer, he said: 'Bring three cappuccinos and a plate of cookies — the posh ones — straight to the private client room, the one we were in yesterday.'

Spencer hesitated.

'Well hurry up then,' Ronan barked. 'Get on with it.'

'Your visit to the bank this morning,' Spencer said quickly, his voice trembling, 'you've already transferred the eight million, haven't you?'

'Since you ask, yes, we have,' Ronan replied. 'Camilla and I don't hang around when it comes to a shrewd business deal. You've got to strike while the iron's hot.'

'Well, the iron hasn't exactly had much of a chance to cool. It's less than twenty-four hours since that necklace was brought in,' Spencer said. 'But you're sure about the diamonds? That they're real, I mean. And the reports?'

'What's your problem with all this?' Ronan asked, screwing up his face with annoyance. 'So what if Camilla and I are decisive and efficient and good at what we do? Vivienne wanted a quick sale and we were able to facilitate that. It's how we do business here, Spencer. It's why Tobias Moncler Jewels is a successful company.'

'You know what Ronan?' Spencer muttered as he turned to the coffee machine and pulled three mugs from the cupboard above.

'I don't know if the diamonds or the reports are real or not — I'm just the rookie here, as you're so hell-bent on reminding me — but I think you've been conned, both of you. There's something very wrong with this whole thing. I'll bet you anything you like Vivienne Karlsson's not trying to raise cash because of a divorce at all. She's a con artist out to rip you off. And she's done it, hasn't she?'

'And you know this how?' Ronan said in a low voice, trying to control another surge of anger.

'Because, as you frequently remind me, I was a homeless drug addict on the streets. You get to know when someone's out to dupe you.'

'Why don't you just crawl back to your little homeless dump, you wretched, pitiful lowlife?' Ronan said savagely.

'There's no way you can prove any of that Spencer,' Camilla added.

'You're right, I can't. And I'm not even going to try. But you'll see.'

'Leave him alone Camilla,' Ronan said, exasperated. 'We're wasting our time. He doesn't have a clue about any of this. Leave him to sell the cubic zirconia to the thirteen year olds with their mommies while we take care of the big stuff.'

'Why didn't you wait for Dr Moncler to get back?' Spencer asked as he punched buttons on the coffee machine. 'Vivienne Karlsson's a random customer off the street. Someone you've never even met before. How could you just trust her like that?'

'Enough from you, Spencer,' Camilla said sharply. 'Hurry up with the coffees and then get out to the showroom.'

'And don't forget there's no lunch break for you today Cinderella,' Ronan called over his shoulder as he and Camilla left the room, slamming the door behind them.

FOURTEEN

Spencer stood by the coffee machine which was noisily spurting out a combination of coffee and frothed milk into three large coffee mugs. He realised it was too late. The deal had already been done. The contract of the sale had been signed. And Camilla and Ronan had transferred eight million pounds to Vivienne's account.

As he waited for the cappuccinos, Spencer began to regret speaking out about his hunch. What evidence did he actually have that the diamonds and reports were fake? He had seen both for no more than a few minutes; Ronan and Camilla had clearly spent most of the night poring over them. Spencer had no more than a few months' experience in the jewellery trade; Ronan and Camilla had decades behind them. The odds would be on Ronan and Camilla's opinions and expertise. Of course Dr Moncler would trust them rather than him; they were highly respected gemologists, he was a reformed drug addict. He began to wish he'd never said anything to anyone; not to Alicia, nor Ronan and Camilla. If his co-workers were correct and the diamonds and reports were genuine, then this was indeed the bargain of the century. Tobias would return in two days' time and congratulate his esteemed employees for closing the deal, while berating Spencer for insubordination. Maybe he'd even lose his job over the whole thing.

And yet in spite of his lack of knowledge and experience, and proper evaluation of the diamonds and grading reports, the uneasy feeling that something was wrong wouldn't go away. There was nothing he could do. Ronan and Camilla would never listen to the "rookie". He hoped he was mistaken, that his suspicions were unfounded. If they weren't, then it was entirely possible that Tobias Moncler Jewels, a prestigious Hatton Garden store with a reputation for quality and integrity, had just exchanged eight million pounds for nothing more than some impressive-looking costume jewellery.

Holding a tray containing three mugs of cappuccinos and a plate of haphazardly arranged cookies, Spencer stood outside the door of the private client room. Inside, he heard the silky tones of Vivienne's alluring voice.

'I trust everything was in order with the diamonds and the reports Ronan?'

'Yes, all in order, as we expected,' came Ronan's reply.

In the absence of any free hands to knock, Spencer pushed the door open with his foot and entered. He immediately noticed the sweet aroma of the mildly intoxicating perfume that Vivienne had worn the previous day.

'Come on in, Spencer.' Ronan beckoned to him. Seated at the glass-topped table between Camilla and Vivienne Karlsson, he was all smiles again. The satin-lined box containing the diamond necklace was open in front of them next to a small pile of grading reports which Ronan pushed to one side to make room for the tray. As Spencer placed it on the table, the necklace, glittering and sparkling against the black satin, caught his eye. He gazed at it for a long moment. *Was* it the real thing? His eyes slid across to the grading reports and to the hologram on the bottom right hand corner of the top one. It looked genuine. Didn't it? What was it that had caught his eye the day before? There was a sheet of paper on the far right of the table next to Ronan. It contained the contact details for a Ms Vivienne Karlsson. Fussing over the mugs, taking extra time to place them on the table with the handles facing the right way, a thought came into Spencer's mind and he casually took note of the address and cell phone number on the form.

'Thank you Spencer, that's all for now, you can leave the cappuccinos where they are,' Ronan said.

Spencer stood up hastily, almost to attention. He cast a suspicious glance at Vivienne, who flashed him a wide smile with perfect teeth, before he turned and left the room with a token nod, repeating the address and phone number over in his mind. When he reached the coffee room, he typed a message to Alicia and pressed send. By now it was almost eleven-thirty and he headed to the showroom where Otto and Keeley were busy serving customers.

Picking up a polishing cloth, Spencer made an unenthusiastic attempt to wipe the glass of one of the display cabinets. Twenty minutes later, Camilla and Ronan emerged with Vivienne, their new best friend, all smiles and pleasantries.

'Such a pleasure doing business with you,' Ronan was saying.

'Likewise Ronan,' Vivienne replied graciously, placing a hand on his arm.

'And if you should ever need any future assistance,' Camilla added.

'Oh Camilla, I wouldn't dream of going anywhere else,' Vivienne said in her signature silky tone, with an obliging pat on Camilla's hand. 'You've all been wonderful.' She glanced in Spencer's direction as she spoke. 'Spencer, I'm glad you're here. I wanted to thank you for your help yesterday, and for your kind words to me. Such a comfort at such a difficult time. And your knowledge of diamonds is astounding. What a fabulous team you have here at Tobias Moncler.'

'Er, thanks,' Spencer spluttered. He wasn't sure what to say. The woman was a con artist. He couldn't prove it but he knew it. He'd spent long enough on the streets to know when he was being taken for a ride. This was one of those times. Ronan and Camilla, two experienced professionals, had been spectacularly deceived. He was caught in a tension between a strong feeling that all was not as it should be and the fact that his senior co-workers had enough expertise between them to determine if a bunch of diamonds in a necklace and their corresponding grading reports were real or not. Art versus science. Art was currently winning. But art would be harder to prove.

Perhaps it was the sixth sense he'd gleaned from the streets, or perhaps it was the scene Alicia had set the previous night: the stolen necklace, the murdered woman. Or perhaps it was the look in Vivienne's eyes; one of mystery and cunning and deceit. It certainly wasn't a look of pain and misery from a broken heart and a bitter divorce. Her story was a lie and Spencer knew it. Perhaps she had even detected that Spencer could see right through her. Yet somehow, Ronan and Camilla had fallen for it completely.

They'd just transferred eight million pounds to where? An offshore account in the Cayman Islands which would most likely be emptied and closed within the hour? And now there was nothing anyone could do to stop that.

Vivienne Karlsson left the store in a flurry of handshakes and thank yous. As the door closed behind her, Ronan sighed with satisfaction.

'Business concluded,' he said with a broad grin. He looked at Camilla. 'Boy do I love my job. That ten-carat whopper of stone is worth way more than the amount we've just paid out for the whole necklace, never mind the rest of the diamonds. And they're worth a couple of mill by themselves!'

'I can't believe she actually agreed to eight million,' Camilla replied, hardly able to contain her excitement. A rare moment, Spencer thought to himself.

'It's unbelievable!' Ronan was laughing now. 'Some people are just so gullible. Pinch me! Yes, it really did happen! Now it's time to see how many millions of profit we can slap onto the resale price. Christmas is coming early this year, Camilla. Tobias is going to love us!'

Spencer watched them, horrified.

'Vivienne's account, was it a UK bank?' he asked suddenly.

Ronan and Camilla looked at him in surprise.

'What's that to you?' Ronan asked nastily. 'Keep believing she's a con woman and the diamonds aren't real if you want to you little street vermin, but you're wrong.'

'Humour me. Where did you send the eight million pounds this morning?'

'It's confidential and absolutely none of your business,' Ronan replied, 'but since I'm in a very good mood, I will humour you. It was to an account in Jersey. That's in the Channel Islands, in case you didn't...'

'I know where it is thanks. Was it in her name?'

'Of course it was,' Camilla snapped. 'Anyway, Ronan and I have some paperwork to fill out. We'll be in the back office. As you're not having a lunch break you can stay here. There are sales targets to meet, remember? And how many service plans have you sold this week?'

Spencer didn't reply.

'I really think we should arrange for Vivienne and Tobias to meet,' Ronan was saying as he disappeared through the back door of the showroom behind Camilla. 'We must set up a lunch date sometime. Yes, I think I'll give her a call and get something organised for when Tobias gets back.'

'Good luck with that,' Spencer muttered under his breath. His instincts told him this was the last they would ever see or hear of Ms Vivienne Karlsson.

FIFTEEN

A tired, hungry and caffeine-depleted Spencer stepped through the glass doors of The Coffee House, the unimaginatively named coffee shop situated opposite Tobias Moncler Jewels. After a quick scan of the room, he made his way to a table where an attractive woman with long, dark hair and a flawless, olive-toned complexion was sitting, her dark brown eyes glued to the screen of her laptop.

'Am I glad to see you,' Spencer said, slumping into a chair opposite and throwing his backpack on the floor under the table.

'Spencer, you look terrible,' Alicia replied, glancing up from the laptop. The greeting was becoming worryingly routine.

'I feel terrible,' Spencer lamented, wiping sweat from his forehead with the back of his hand.

'Tough day?'

'The worst. I need coffee. Urgently. What're you having?'

'Just get me a large Americano,' Alicia said sliding a ten pound note across the table.

'Er — I'll pay for these,' Spencer said, getting up.

Alicia looked at him in surprise.

'Are you sure? You don't have to.'

'I know, but I'd like to.'

'Then that's very kind of you,' Alicia replied. She watched as Spencer made his way to the counter. He'd come a long way since she'd first introduced herself to him, a vagrant slumped in the doorway of the place they now met. Where she had once bought him coffee and plied him for information about the heist in the jewellery store across the street, he was now buying her coffee and working in the jewellery store across the street. Funny how things turned around.

Spencer stood waiting as the barista prepared an Americano for Alicia and a latte macchiato with a double shot of espresso for him. She was probably in her mid-twenties with long blonde hair

132

tied in a low pony-tail. She was tall and slim and, as she turned to reach for a carton of milk from the shelf behind, Spencer noticed the black trousers of her uniform fitted her perfectly. He couldn't recall seeing her in the coffee shop before and was certain that if he had, he would've remembered such an occasion. But then again, there was something vaguely familiar about her.

'You new here?' he asked shyly. He noticed her name badge; it had the name Hattie engraved on it.

'First day,' Hattie replied with a smile.

'Oh. Good,' was all Spencer could manage to say. Had she just smiled at him?

'Here you go.' Hattie placed two large mugs on the countertop.

'Thanks.' Spencer swallowed hard before adding sheepishly: 'I'm Spencer, by the way.'

'Hattie.' The broad smile came again. 'Nice to meet you Spencer. Hope I see you again sometime.'

'Oh yes, you definitely will. I get coffee here every day. I work in that jewellery store across the street.'

'Ooh that's cool,' Hattie replied. 'You must know a lot about diamonds and jewels and things.'

'I know a bit. I can teach you how to tell the difference between a real and a fake diamond if you like?'

'Wow, really? That's so cool,' Hattie said excitedly. 'I'd love to know.'

'And I'd love to order a coffee if you two've finished yakking,' the man behind Spencer interrupted crossly.

'Oops, sorry sir,' Hattie said. She winked at Spencer and said: 'We'll talk soon.'

'I'll see you tomorrow,' Spencer replied, picking up the mugs of coffee. Had she just winked at him? His morning coffee breaks were about to become even more enjoyable.

'New girlfriend Spencer?' Alicia asked casually as he returned to the table and sat down.

'What, that cute barista? I wish,' Spencer replied, taking a sip of the macchiato. In just a few minutes the caffeine would take effect and he'd feel human again. 'She's new here. Apparently. I feel like we've met before though, but I'd definitely remember someone hot like her, wouldn't I? D'you think she's too young for me?'

'Not at all. I think she likes you.'

'You do? Really? Come on Alicia, you're having me on. She's far too pretty for someone like me. But anyway, you said you wanted to meet.'

'Yes, I did, and I'm sorry but I'm not going to be able to make dinner tomorrow night so this is sort of instead of.'

'Oh.' Spencer's face fell.

'I'm having dinner with an old friend of my father's,' Alicia went on. 'His name's Carlos Jaxen. He owns Rock Palm Resort. Remember I told you about that place yesterday? It's the Caribbean resort where I used to go on vacation with my parents; the place where the lady with the diamond necklace stayed with her husband, and where the body of a murdered woman was found on the beach.'

'Yeah, I remember,' Spencer nodded, draining his macchiato at an alarming rate. 'Did you get my message earlier? The one about Vivienne Karlsson's contact details?'

'I did. Good thinking there Spencer.'

'You checked it out, didn't you? Was it, you know, legit?'

'Take a guess.'

'No then?'

'Correct. As you'd taken the trouble to send it, I made a few official and unofficial checks of the address and cell number Vivienne gave your co-workers. The address: thirteen Dornan Mews, London… There is no Dornan Mews anywhere in London, let alone within the WC postcode that she provided which, again, is completely made up. It doesn't exist.'

'And the phone number?'

'An interesting one,' Alicia said with a faint smile. 'It's a sex chatline number.'

'No kidding? But maybe Vivienne's a, you know…'

'I doubt very much she's a phone sex operator. The woman at the end of the line certainly wasn't familiar with the name Vivienne Karlsson. Your customer obviously wasn't intending to be contactable. I think she just used the number as an added insult to your co-workers.'

'So maybe my hunch about the diamonds and the reports being fake isn't so out there after all...'

'Have they appraised the necklace yet?' Alicia asked.

'Define *appraised*,' Spencer replied, 'because if you're going to properly grade a diamond, you need to remove it from its setting first. Ronan and Camilla haven't done that. They've apparently taken the necklace at face value, as it is, without removing any of the stones. And they said they've checked the grading reports and everything is legit. I guess I can't argue with that, although I still think there's something odd about the holograms on the reports.'

Alicia gave a puzzled frown as Spencer continued.

'Anyway, even if my instincts are correct, it's too late to do anything.'

'What d'you mean *too late*?'

'They authorised a bank transfer to an account in the Channel Islands this morning, to the tune of eight million pounds.'

'You're not serious?'

'Afraid I am. The deal's already been done. Tobias Moncler Jewels is now eight million pounds worse off, but the proud owner of what I'm certain is some cleverly made costume jewellery and a bunch of phoney grading reports. And I can't prove any of that, of course.'

'I thought your co-workers were seasoned professionals?'

'So did I. And they are. I can only think they were dazzled by the necklace. Literally. And Vivienne's charms. And they probably got greedy when they realised she was looking for a quick sale and would accept a price far lower than what they believed the necklace was actually worth. They ignored Dr Moncler's rules for appraising diamonds and now... well, who knows what will happen now? Wait for Dr Moncler to get back I guess.'

'By that time Vivienne — and the eight mill — will be long gone,' Alicia said. 'How did they manage to authorise the transaction in Tobias's absence?'

'It seems as long as they're both at the bank to sign at the same time, they have the authority to do that.'

'A bank transfer for eight million pounds?' Alicia asked with surprise. 'I'm amazed to hear Tobias has bestowed them with that amount of power. An oversight on his part, I'd say, but what do I know about running a jewellery business?'

'Then again, they could be right,' Spencer said, taking a final gulp of the macchiato. 'The necklace — and the reports — might be genuine. Those diamonds really could be worth seventeen point five million pounds.'

'There's always that chance,' Alicia admitted, 'but I've been thinking about this. The more I do, the more I'm convinced that there's something we're not getting here. I saw my parents last night and asked them if they remembered who owned that necklace — the one I sent you the picture of — when we stayed at Rock Palm. The name of the lady who wore it was Vivienne Karleman.'

'Really?' Spencer's eyes widened. 'But that's pretty similar to...'

'Exactly. So while Vivienne Karlsson may be nothing more than a clever scam artist who has somehow managed to hoodwink two seasoned gemologists — which is pretty impressive to start with and I'd love to know how she did it — way back in nineteen ninety-five, the genuine version of an identical diamond necklace actually belonged to a woman named Vivienne Karle*man*. It was supposedly stolen the night before the guests of the Caribbean resort where she was staying were evacuated due to an approaching hurricane. On the same night, a woman was murdered — stabbed to death — on the beach near the resort. Her body was discovered the following morning. Whether these two incidents were related remains a mystery, even to this day. But roll on twenty-three years: a diamond necklace, exactly matching the description of the necklace reported stolen, is brought into a jewellery store in Hatton Garden by a woman named *Vivienne Karlsson*. She claims she's going through a divorce and wants a quick sale of her necklace to raise some cash.

'The first question that comes to mind is why Hatton Garden? If the necklace is what she claims it is — an incredibly valuable piece of jewellery — why not take it to an auction house or an international diamond buyer? She'd fetch a much higher price with one of those options. On the other hand, she says she doesn't want to hang about and wants a quick, clean sale. In that case why not go to a pawnbroker or hawk the thing on eBay or craigslist?'

'Even *I* wouldn't try to sell a necklace like that on craigslist, fake or not,' Spencer said wryly.

'Okay,' Alicia went on. 'So she picks Hatton Garden. The second question is out of *all* the jewellers in Hatton Garden — or the whole of London for that matter — *why choose Tobias Moncler Jewels?*'

The question hung in the air as Spencer looked at Alicia with a blank expression.

'Random chance?' he suggested with a shrug. 'Or maybe she didn't *choose* Tobias Moncler Jewels. Maybe she'd already been to a few other stores but they saw through her and sent her on her way. Only Camilla and Ronan were dumb enough to fall for the scam, if that's what it was.'

'Okay, let's go with that for a moment. Let's say it's a scam. Vivienne Karlsson, or whatever her real name is, is a first-rate hustler. This whole thing has been expertly executed, the work of a pro. She's done it before. Many times. Except that when I made a few enquiries with other Hatton Garden stores and contacts a little further afield, no one's ever come across her before.'

Spencer raised his eyebrows with interest.

'Yep, no one's ever heard of her, seen her or had any kind of dealings with her, officially or unofficially. No one's seen the necklace either. She certainly hasn't peddled it around trying to get the best price for it.'

'That's weird. You'd think she'd take it to a few places before agreeing on a sale,' Spencer said with a puzzled expression.

'Exactly,' Alicia agreed. 'But she didn't do that at all. She took it straight to Tobias Moncler. I can back that up further if you like. I've a source who works at the LSTCC.'

'The *what?*'

'The London Streets Traffic Control Centre.'

'Ohhh you mean that place where they have people watching TV screens all day? The ones with a live feed from all the traffic cameras?'

'That's it.'

'Is it true they can change all the traffic lights to green if they want to?' Spencer asked suddenly. 'It'd be cool to watch the screens then.'

'Thanks for that Spencer,' Alicia said, trying to suppress an amused grin. 'You've just made me very grateful I did not recommend you for a job there. And no, I don't believe they can change all the traffic lights to green; I think they can temporarily change the timings on some of the lights to help reduce the build up of too much traffic if there's a lot of congestion in a certain area, but that's it. But back to the traffic and street cameras. I had my source review some of the camera footage around Hatton Garden for a woman matching your description of Vivienne Karlsson, around the time you said she came in to the store. She wasn't easy to spot as it was rush hour and London is bursting with tourists at the moment, especially in this part of town, but my source finally spotted her coming out of Chancery Lane underground station.'

Alicia pulled her cell phone towards her and tapped on the screen before sliding it across to Spencer. It showed a slightly blurry still-shot of Vivienne Karlsson dressed in the navy mid-length dress and tan court shoes, with the tan leather bag over her shoulder, the same outfit she had been wearing on the afternoon of her first visit to the jewellery store.

'That's her,' Spencer nodded.

'Good, I thought she matched your description. My source managed to track her on the street cameras, with timings, all the way from Chancery Lane to Tobias Moncler.'

'Impressive.'

'She made a beeline straight for the store.'

'She what?'

'She never went into any other jeweller in Hatton Garden. Just made her way straight to TMJ.' Alicia nodded to the jewellery store across the street.

'So she knew exactly where she was going…'

'Correct. And so the question, again, is *why*?'

'I couldn't say.'

'You're sure she's never done business at TMJ before? Hadn't previously met Camilla or Ronan? They weren't old friends or anything?'

'No, it seemed like it was her first time in the store,' Spencer replied. 'And unless they were pretending, I'm certain it was the first time she'd met Ronan or Camilla. In fact, she came to me first. Camilla was with a customer and Ronan was in the back somewhere. But even after they'd hijacked her, she still kept looking across at me and smiling. It was a bit weird really, almost as if she *wanted* me to be included, to know what was going on. Or maybe she just felt sorry for me.'

'That's interesting,' Alicia said. She took a sip of her previously untouched Americano while Spencer looked forlornly into the bottom of his empty mug.

'I think Vivienne deliberately targeted Tobias Moncler Jewels,' Alicia said suddenly.

'Why would she do that? Out of all the other Hatton Garden jewellery stores, why target Tobias Moncler?'

'Because of *you*, and your association with *me*.'

'*What?*'

'I think it's about the necklace. And the name, Vivienne Karlsson, which is almost the same, but not quite, as Karleman. It's no coincidence Vivienne went to Tobias Moncler. Out of everyone involved, the only person the necklace *and* that name mean something to, is *me*. Obviously neither meant anything to Ronan or Camilla, because they would've said something. It's clear from what you've told me that they'd never seen the necklace before or heard the name Vivienne Karlsson, or Karleman. And the connection between the necklace, the name, and me, is *you*, Spencer.'

'I don't get it,' Spencer said. Perhaps another macchiato would help, he thought to himself, but Alicia carried on talking.

'I think I do,' she said. 'I think it's a bid for my attention.'

'That's ridiculous. Why would she do that? Why try to get to you through me? Why not just approach you direct? Why go to all the trouble of bringing the necklace to the jewellery store with that made-up divorce story? Even then, how could she be certain I'd tell you about the necklace, or that you'd remember it from all those years ago? And why would she want to get your attention anyway?'

'I realise it's a long shot, but it's not impossible. The fact that you were once my informant on the streets is still a fiercely guarded secret, but it may be that someone, somewhere knows about us and is using that relationship to get to me, by reminding me of something from my past.'

'It still doesn't make sense. I can't believe that in an effort to jog your memory about a necklace from twenty years ago — which she couldn't be certain you'd even remember — Vivienne Karlsson would actually go through with something as daring as that.'

'Yeah, but now she's riding off into the sunset with eight million pounds. *And* she's attracted my attention. It's a win-win for her.'

'If the diamonds aren't real, it's fraud isn't it? So she pulled it off, but it was a huge risk just to get you to notice her. I'm not buying it. I think you've gone a step too far with this, Alicia. You're reading too much into it.'

'Perhaps I'm barking up the wrong tree after all,' Alicia said with a shrug, 'but explain this...'

She reached into her bag and pulled out a guidebook to Antigua and Barbuda along with a faded, dog-eared hotel brochure.

'They were delivered to my mailbox by hand late last night,' she said, holding them up for Spencer to see, 'in a plain white envelope which was given to the night concierge of my apartment block.'

'Delivered by who?'

'An elderly man. I've spoken to the concierge who took the delivery and got the day security staff to run through the CCTV for the reception of the building. There's not much to go on. The man was wearing a navy overcoat with dark blue jeans and a baseball cap pulled down low over his face, which he keeps turned well away from the security cameras. According to the concierge he hardly said a word, just pointed to my name on the front of the envelope and asked for it to be handed to me.'

'That's random,' Spencer said with a frown.

'What's even more random, is *this*…' Alicia opened the guidebook to where a page had been marked with a pink Post-it Note.

'Nice beach,' Spencer said, admiring a picture of a tropical shore with white sand and turquoise sea, spread over two pages. There were two columns of typed information on either side of the picture.

'It's the same beach that Rock Palm Resort overlooked,' Alicia said. 'It's still quite a tourist attraction.' She turned the book towards her and read the caption for the picture: 'The mile-long, white sand beach of the once famous, but now derelict, Rock Palm Resort Hotel, with its crystal clear water protected by a coral reef, was once described as one of the finest beaches in the world.'

'Is that the same place you stayed with your parents when you were younger? Where they found the body of the murdered woman?'

'Yes, it is. I can show you exact…'

'Er, don't worry, no need,' Spencer replied hastily. 'What's that leaflet thing?'

'It's a brochure for Rock Palm Resort. It's got a date on it: nineteen ninety-five.'

'The last year you stayed there?'

'The year of the hurricane, when all the guests were evacuated from the island. The year Vivienne Karleman wore the diamond necklace and claimed it was stolen. The year Anastasia was murdered.'

'Whoever keeps hotel brochures from the nineties?' Spencer asked.

'My mother, for one,' Alicia replied, placing the brochure and the guidebook on the table. 'People hold on to them as mementoes, keepsakes, you know, that kind of thing. What's more interesting is who sent this one to me and why. I think the key thing is the date: nineteen ninety-five. It seems as though it was sent as a sort of backup, just in case I hadn't joined all the dots with Vivienne Karlsson and the necklace. Which I'm certain she was banking on you telling me about, hence why she made sure you were as involved as possible in the first place.'

'Did any of the other pages have Post-it Notes on them?' Spencer asked.

'No, just that one.'

'So okay then, someone's trying to get your attention. But who? And why?'

'I've no idea. But now they have it and, believe me, I intend to find the answers to both of those questions.'

'You haven't exactly got a lot to go on. Maybe the necklace *is* stolen and Vivienne Karlsson is connected in some way. Which would explain why she'd want to remain anonymous.'

'That's one possible explanation,' Alicia replied. 'But why bring it to my attention *now*? Twenty-three years later? She was taking a huge gamble to even *think* I'd put it all together. If that's what this is about…'

'The whole thing's unbelievable,' Spencer said, 'assuming what you're saying has any truth in it.'

'I wish it didn't,' Alicia said, 'but there seem to be a few too many coincidences here. I wonder what Vivienne Karlsson wants from me.'

'I don't like to think about how she knew of your connection to me,' Spencer said uneasily. 'D'you think someone spilled the beans about me being your informant? I thought you said the handful of people who knew about us could be trusted.'

'And they can,' Alicia said firmly. 'It may be that there's another explanation.'

'Such as?'

'She might have been watching me. And subsequently you. It certainly looks that way in light of the fact that the guidebook and brochure were delivered right on cue. Someone knew you'd spoken to me about the necklace already, which was their cue to deliver the brochure and guidebook, as an extra prompt to direct my thoughts to the original necklace and its owner, Vivienne Karleman. If the guidebook and brochure had arrived without your revelations from the jewellery store, I probably wouldn't have thought anymore about it.'

'I don't like that answer,' Spencer said, glancing warily over his shoulder as if at that very moment every set of eyes in the coffee shop was upon him. 'It gives me the creeps. Being watched, from the shadows like that.'

'I'm not overly keen on the idea either. But if that's how she discovered our friendship, she must've been watching for some time. And waiting for the right moment to set her plan into motion.'

They fell into a sober silence. Spencer looked longingly at the serving counter where Hattie was obscured by a line of customers.

'You want another Americano? I might get myself a cappuccino to go.'

'No thanks,' Alicia replied with a shake of her head, 'but you get what you want.'

As Spencer got up from the table and joined the end of the line, Alicia considered the possibility that she was somehow being lured back into the murky past of Rock Palm Resort. Why, or by whom, she didn't know, but someone, somewhere, seemed to be pulling the strings. A mysterious puppet master.

She wondered what had really happened to the genuine diamond necklace worn by Vivienne Karleman at Rock Palm in nineteen ninety-five. Had it really been stolen? Was Vivienne Karlsson's necklace the same one, which had now resurfaced twenty-three years later? Or was it just a cheap replica with fake stones? And what of the unsolved mystery of the murdered girl found brutally stabbed on the beach? Were the two linked somehow? In light of the fact that the murder had never been solved, she couldn't rule it out. Perhaps Carlos Jaxen would have some answers.

In the meantime, the puppet master had her attention. She considered the idea that it was likely to be someone who knew her personally. Someone who knew of her work as an investigative journalist. Someone who knew of her friendship with Spencer and was using him to get to her. But more importantly, it had to be someone who knew her past, who knew she had stayed at Rock Palm Resort as a teenager, who knew she had stayed there in September of ninety-five, the September Hurricane Luis struck Antigua, the September a diamond necklace worth nearly ten million dollars went missing and Anastasia, the magician's assistant was tragically murdered. But, even so, why hide in the shadows and hand deliver anonymous brochures and guidebooks?

Spencer was almost at the front of the line of customers, waiting to order his coffee. Alicia placed her laptop into her bag, got up from the table and walked across to him.

'Spencer, I've got to go. I'll be in touch.'

'Okay, see you soon. Anything you need me to do?'

'Keep on the trail of that necklace. Find out if it's genuine or not. And keep your ears to the ground for anything else that might be useful.'

'No problem. And, what about... you know...' He lowered his voice and cast a wary look over his shoulder.

'You'll be okay,' Alicia said in an attempt to reassure him. 'I may be totally off the mark. There's probably nobody watching you at all. You're perfectly safe.'

'You're certain about that?'

'Ninety-nine percent.'

'I hope you're right.'

'I am. Now, go get Hattie's number,' Alicia said with a wink before turning to leave.

Spencer was at the front of the line. With his brightest smile he ordered a large cappuccino to go. Hattie returned the smile and set about making the drink. Spencer had a feeling his weekly coffee expenditure was about to escalate sharply.

As the door swung shut behind her, Alicia overheard Spencer's words: 'So, er, Hattie, d'you know where blue diamonds are made? They're actually formed four hundred miles down in the Earth. A chemical element called boron mixes with carbon under pressure...'

Hattie was sure to be impressed. Alicia had observed her frequently glancing in Spencer's direction throughout their meeting. He deserved an admirer, if that was all she was...

SIXTEEN

5:20 pm, Wednesday, August 22

It was almost closing time when Tobias Moncler arrived at the store. He acknowledged Otto who was serving a customer, greeted Spencer amiably and peered at one of the recently polished display cabinets with a look of approval.

'How are you Spencer? How've things been here?'

'Er — great thanks, Dr Moncler. I've had quite a few customers today. Reached the sales quota. Sold three sales plans. How was your business trip?'

'Oh, very successful thank you. Very worthwhile. Hopefully we've some new suppliers. I'm looking forward to working with them. What about Ronan and Camilla? Are they about? I really ought to sit down with them for a quick chat.'

'Yes, you should,' Spencer nodded enthusiastically. This was one chat he'd love to be present for. 'I think they're in the back somewhere. Ronan was here a minute ago but said he had some stuff to do as it's quiet.'

'I'll leave you two capably managing the showroom while I go and check in with them,' Tobias said, giving Spencer a firm pat on the back as he disappeared through the door to the back of the store.

At two minutes past six, Spencer and Otto thanked their final customer of the day and locked the front door of the showroom before commencing the nightly routine. As Otto shut down the cash register system, Spencer began removing the display trays from the window.

'I'm exhausted,' Otto said with an exaggerated sigh. 'And the keys to the display cabinets have been irritating me all week. We need new labels for them. I swear I spend most of my time trying to find the right key. It's embarrassing when the customer's just standing there waiting.'

'No arguments from me about that,' Spencer said, carefully handling a tray of diamond rings.

'Doing anything tonight?' Otto asked.

'Maybe a bit of studying in The Coffee House before I head home. You?'

'Meeting friends for drinks. Why don't you join us? Bit more exciting than dry old textbooks.'

'I'm okay thanks. Better keep at it.'

'Suit yourself.'

They loaded the display trays into a trolley and, pushing it through the back door of the showroom, made their way to the night safe. As they passed one of the offices, they could hear raised voices.

'You did *what*?' It was Tobias's, in stark contrast to his usually softly spoken manner of speaking. 'I find this unbelievable. Utterly outrageous. What were you both thinking? To not even carry out a proper appraisal of the stones is absolutely disgraceful. And as for the authorisation of the bank transfer…'

'What's that all about?' Otto asked with a quizzical expression.

'I dunno,' Spencer shrugged.

They reached the night safe and unloaded the contents of the trolley, completing the case-count, entering the figures into an iPad and scribbling signatures across a dozen forms. With the end of day checks complete and keys, paperwork and electronic equipment safely stowed in a secure room next to the night safe, Otto held the door for Spencer.

'I'm off. Are you coming?'

'You go.' Spencer, who was suddenly engrossed in a message on his phone, waved him on. 'I've just got to reply to this.'

'See you tomorrow then,' Otto replied and the door closed behind him.

Spencer waited a few seconds before returning to the hallway where he could hear Tobias, still speaking in an angry tone. He walked slowly towards the staff break room, which was also in the direction of Tobias's voice.

'Did you even bother to *check* any of these grading reports?'

'Yes, of *course*.' It was Camilla's voice. It contained a note of desperation. She sounded tearful and distressed. 'Both Ronan and I completed extensive report checks on the GIA database. Everything was in order. The GIA records matched exactly with the grading reports Vivienne Karlsson gave us.'

'Yeah, honestly Tobias, I don't understand what's going on.' Ronan's panicked voice. 'The online Report Check was working fine on Monday night.'

'It's working fine *now*,' Tobias replied. 'I've just spoken to an associate at the GIA headquarters; there is *nothing wrong* with their website. There never was. It's been working perfectly all week. And anyway, you've just seen for yourselves, these reports for other gemstones here in the store — reports we *know* are genuine — check out fine with the GIA database. It's just your *customer's* reports that don't match up with anything the GIA has on record. They don't exist. *None*, yes that's right, *none* of the serial numbers on the reports are valid.'

'Let's just try one more time,' Spencer heard Ronan suggest timidly. 'Like I said, everything was fine on Monday. I just don't get what's happened here.'

'*I* do. What's happened is that you two've just paid out eight million pounds for a bunch of gemstones with phoney grading reports. Which begs the question, if the reports aren't genuine, what about the stones? Even just looking at that necklace I have a strong suspicion the gems are...'

'I can assure you they're genuine, Tobias,' Camilla interrupted quickly, her voice quivering. Spencer wondered if he could detect a hint of doubt. 'We spent half the night going over them.'

'Took each stone out of its setting did you?' Tobias said. Spencer wasn't sure he'd ever heard his boss sound so angry. 'Examined each one loose under the microscope did you? Observed the protocols I *specifically* put in place to avoid potential disasters like this?'

'Well, no, we didn't exactly do *all* that.' Camilla again.

'Then these stones haven't been properly appraised, have they?'

'But the reports...' Ronan this time.

'*Aren't genuine*,' Tobias said firmly. 'So take a guess at what you'll both be doing this evening.'

'I — I've actually got plans tonight,' Ronan ventured, foolishly in Spencer's opinion. 'Date night with my wife. She won't be very hap…'

'That's too bad, isn't it? I'm sure she won't be very happy when she hears you're about to lose your job either. What about you Camilla? Any plans *you* need to cancel?'

'No Tobias.'

'Good. Once we've removed *all* the stones from the setting, we'll start appraising them properly, examining them carefully under magnification and using the other grading tools that we've been trained to use. You are both highly qualified gemologists; I expect much more than this.'

'I can assure you Tobias, the diamonds are genuine,' Ronan said as confidently as he dare.

'You'd better hope so,' Tobias replied savagely. 'Oh, and get the customer — Vivienne or whatever her name is — get her on the phone too. I want to talk to her about these reports.'

There was a brief silence from behind the closed door with the exception of the rustling of some papers and the sound of a dialling tone on speaker. Ronan was calling the number Vivienne had supplied. Spencer held his breath. His mind was reeling from what he had just overheard. Sure, he'd suspected the grading reports weren't genuine, but the online inquiry he'd made with a serial number from one of them had checked out on the GIA database. It had all seemed authentic. Which is why he'd doubted himself. And if it had worked for him, there was no reason why it wouldn't have worked for Camilla and Ronan. He was sure they would've run the reports through the GIA Report Check at the very least, even if they didn't properly appraise the diamonds. So what was different now? Why did the reports no longer match with the GIA database? It was puzzling.

There was the sound of a phone ringing on speaker. Suddenly, a woman's voice answered. It was low and sultry.

'Hey stud! How're you doing tonight?'

'Oh, er, hello!' Ronan sounded slightly taken aback. 'Is this Vivienne?'

'I can be whoever you want me to be, darlin'.'

'Um, yeah, hi Vivienne, this is Ronan. Ronan Elliott.'

'Ooh, I luurrrrrrve that name. It's so... sensual.'

The voice was smooth and seductive, slightly breathy, and didn't sound like Vivienne Karlsson at all.

'It's Ronan from Tobias Moncler Jewels.' Ronan tried to sound professional. 'It's about the grading reports for the...'

'Are you thinking about it already Ronan?' the voice interrupted, teasingly. 'Are you imagining me there, with you? Thinking about my lips touching yours, caressing you, then down to your neck, kissing you, biting you...'

'Er Vivienne, my boss is here and you're on speaker phone,' Ronan said awkwardly.

'Are you imagining my arms wrapped around you, pulling me tight against...'

'What the *hell* is this Ronan?' Tobias wasn't amused. Spencer stood outside the door, openmouthed. Alicia's research had been spot on. The number Vivienne had given them was indeed the number of a phone sex line. He suppressed a smile and imagined Ronan squirming with embarrassment in front of his boss. There was a click on the line as someone hung up.

'I'll try that number again,' Ronan said, sounding flustered.

A dialling tone. A phone ringing. The sultry female voice.

'Back so soon, mmmm? Let me tell you what I'm gonna do to you tonight...'

'Who is this?' Tobias said loudly.

'I'm your wildest fantasy, you sexy...'

'No. *Stop*,' Tobias almost shouted. 'What is this? Whose number is this?'

There was a brief silence at the end of the line before the woman replied.

'You're through to the Red Hot Fantasy Sex Line.' The voice had lost its seductive tone and was suddenly brusque and businesslike.

'Do you know anyone called Vivienne Karlsson?' Tobias asked.

'Er no. Don't know anyone with that name, real or fantasy,' the woman replied.

'You're certain of that? You haven't given this number to anyone with that name?'

'*No!* Of course not. This is my personal business line number; I don't share it with anyone. Why?'

'Then I apologise,' Tobias said. 'We must have the wrong number. Goodbye.'

A click on the line followed by silence.

'Do you have any other contact details for Vivienne Karlsson?' Tobias said quietly.

There was a rustling of paper again.

'Yes. Yes, we do. Just a minute,' Ronan replied. More rustling. Spencer imagined him frantically rifling through papers trying to locate Vivienne's address which would be as helpful as the phone number.

'Yes, got it. Here we are. Her address: it's number thirteen Dornan Mews, London, WC…'

'Find it on Google Maps,' Tobias snapped.

'What?' Ronan.

'Check it on Google Maps. Where is it?' Tobias.

'Oh. Oh right, yes I see. Well, it's a WC postcode so it should be fairly nearby…. And I'm sure there's an explanation for the phone number. Perhaps I keyed it in wrong when I took her details. Anyway, let me just bring up… yes, here we are. Google Maps. And er… what was the full postcode again?'

Tobias read it out to him, pronouncing every syllable.

'That's weird.' A distinct note of concern in Ronan's voice.

'What's wrong Ronan?' Tobias asked, almost mockingly.

'It says *No Results Found.* Are you sure you…'

'Read out the correct postcode? I'm very sure Ronan. Here it is, read it for yourself. Entered into the customer information field with your own fair hand.'

'I'll try *thirteen Dornan Mews,*' Ronan suggested.

'By all means,' Tobias replied.

A few seconds passed before Ronan spoke again.

'Er, it doesn't seem to be here. There's a Dorman Walk in north west London, but there's no…'

'Dornan Mews? There's a surprise.'

'Perhaps she meant Dorman Walk?' Camilla ventured.

'Perhaps she did,' Tobias agreed. 'Mews and Walk are very similar sounding words. Similar spellings. Both four letter words. Easy to get confused. I'm not holding out much hope that the email address this Vivienne woman gave you is any more genuine than the home address and phone number, but let's have a look at it anyway.'

'I — I don't believe we took an email address from her,' Ronan replied feebly. 'Did you, Camilla?'

'Don't ask me,' Camilla snapped back. '*You* were the one who was supposed to be getting her contact details. Did you even check for ID?'

'Of course I did. What d'you think I was doing while you were *supposed* to be properly appraising the diamonds? All her identification documents were in order, see here, I took photocopies of her driving licence and passport; the name and address matched up and everything.'

'How *can* they have done?' Camilla retorted. 'They were all fake and you never even spotted it!'

'How *dare* you?' Ronan said defensively. 'What about the grading reports? You checked them as well as me. You never noticed there was a problem, did you?'

'Stop it, both of you,' Tobias raised his voice and there was a sudden silence. 'You are equally responsible for this mess and you will now be working all night to try and get us out of it. This is what we're going to do: Camilla, I want you to remove every stone from that necklace and set out each one in readiness for the most thorough appraisals you have ever conducted. Ronan, while Camilla's doing that, I want you to check over the contact details and ID documents Vivienne Karlsson gave you one more time. See what you can make of them, although I doubt very much there's any way of tracing her.'

'Are you going to inform the police?' A nervous question from Camilla.

There was a pause before Tobias replied.

'Not straight away, no.' He sounded calmer now. 'We need to be sure of what we're dealing with here before we get the police involved. We need all the facts, what's real and what's not. Let's keep it to ourselves and focus on those for now.'

Spencer could imagine an inaudible sigh of relief inside the room from both Ronan and Camilla. A thought crossed his mind that it might be more prudent to inform the police sooner rather than later if Vivienne was on the run. On the other hand, the reputation of Tobias Moncler Jewels was at stake. He could understand his boss wanting to get the technicalities in order before an official investigation was launched.

'I'm going to get a coffee and call my wife,' Tobias was saying, 'tell her I won't be coming home tonight. And then I'll give Rob a call, my guy at the GIA HQ. It'll be late morning over in California. I'll scan and email copies of these grading reports across to him and see what he makes of them. Once we've removed all the stones from that necklace, we'll get some pictures and send them to him as well. We'll have to talk to the bank tomorrow about the transfer you two authorised. I'll need all the details of Ms Karlsson's account as well.'

'Yes, of course Tobias.'

'I'll be back in a few minutes.'

Suddenly aware that his boss was about to emerge from the room, Spencer ducked quickly round the corner and into the darkened private client room, the same one in which Ronan and Camilla had entertained Vivienne two evenings ago. It still smelt faintly of her perfume. He heard the office door open and Tobias's footsteps along the corridor to the break room. The coast would be clear for a few minutes. He slid out of the client room and padded quietly along the corridor. There was no one to be seen. Otto had activated the overnight security system for the showroom; Spencer would have to exit through the back door of the store. He passed the office door on his right and the break room door on his left. Further down the corridor, the door to the showroom on his left and, further still, the door to Tobias's office on his right. It was open. A pale pool of light streamed across the floor. Suddenly Tobias emerged and Spencer jumped in surprise.

'Spencer! What on earth are you doing here?' Tobias exclaimed. 'I thought you left half an hour ago with Otto.'

'Dr Moncler! You surprised me!' Spencer's cheeks flushed. 'I was, er, I was doing a bit of study, you know, for that jewellery course thing, and I guess I must've forgot the time…'

'Is that so?' Tobias asked slowly. 'What were you studying?'

'What was I…?' Spencer was taken aback. 'What was I studying? It was — it was about the, er, the, er…'

Once an expert liar, Spencer momentarily appeared to have lost the art of deception.

'Now tell me what you're *really* doing here.'

SEVENTEEN

Spencer stood, frozen to the spot, attempting to regain composure. The previous conversation Tobias had just participated in had been peppered with lies. Perhaps it was time somebody told the truth.

'I couldn't help but overhear a bit of your conversation with Ronan and Camilla,' Spencer replied sheepishly.

It was Tobias's turn to be taken aback. He recovered quickly.

'You were eavesdropping?'

'No! Not exactly. Well, okay yes, I s'pose you could say I was.'

'How much did you hear Spencer?'

'Most of it, actually,' Spencer replied apologetically, 'but see, Dr Moncler, I was here on Monday when that lady — Vivienne — when Vivienne came in with the necklace and the reports and stuff. Ronan and Camilla took her through to the private client room and they sent me home after that, but the next morning when I got here, they'd just come back from the bank. And then Vivienne came to the store to sign the rest of the paperwork. She was here for about twenty minutes and then she left, and Ronan and Camilla were all excited that they'd just paid small change for a diamond necklace worth seventeen point five million.'

'What the hell were they thinking?' Tobias said with a frown. 'That's not how we do things here.'

'No. I realise that, sir, and I'm not here to snitch on Ronan or Camilla, but there is something I — I just noticed on Monday.'

'Yes?'

'The grading reports.'

'What about them?'

'I'm not sure. But when I looked at a couple of them on Monday, they just looked wrong.'

'*Looked* wrong? What d'you mean?'

'I honestly don't know. I couldn't put my finger on it. It might've been the holograms perhaps. Or the watermarks. Hard to tell exactly. But I memorised one of the serial numbers from a report for one of the colourless diamonds and ran a report check on it before I went home.'

'Did you now?'

'This is the thing, sir. It all checked out on the GIA database. The report was valid. Sure, I've no idea which diamond it matched, or even if it was for one of the diamonds in the necklace at all, but it was definitely there, in the database, a report for a round brilliant, colourless diamond weighing just over two carats. As authentic as any report check I've ever done.'

'But the reports don't exist,' Tobias said. 'None of them do. I've checked them all.'

'So I heard,' Spencer nodded, 'but I assure you, sir, at least one of them did on Monday night.'

'Come into my office for a moment.' Tobias beckoned Spencer in as he stepped behind his desk and sat down. He tapped a key on the keyboard and the screen of his computer came to life. Spencer stood behind him and watched as he brought up the GIA database and signed into the Report Check. Pulling out his cell phone, he scrolled to a selection of images on his camera roll: photographs of each grading report for the colourless diamonds and the identification and origin report for the pink stone.

'We'll pick one at random — not that that makes any difference — and see what happens,' Tobias said, enlarging the report number with his thumb and forefinger and typing it into a box on the computer screen. He pressed return and waited. Where they would have expected to see the corresponding Diamond Dossier appear on the screen, instead, a message read: *An unexpected error has occurred. Try clearing your browser history and searching again.*

'That's weird sir,' Spencer said. 'What about entering another of the report numbers?'

'All right, let's try this one,' Tobias replied, returning to the original screen and keying a different number into the search box. 'And you should know by now that you don't need to keep calling me sir. Or Dr Moncler. Tobias is fine. I've told you that multiple times over the last few months Spencer.'

'Sorry sir. I mean Dr Moncler. *Tobias.*'

An unexpected error has occurred. Try clearing your browser history and searching again.

They entered a few of the other report numbers. The same message appeared on the screen every time.

'What about a report for an unrelated diamond that we know checks out?' Spencer suggested.

Tobias pulled a sheet of paper from one of the trays stacked on his desk; it was a grading report for a loose diamond. He ran the number. The Diamond Dossier associated with the gemstone was instantly displayed on the screen.

'What's going on Spencer?' Tobias asked, looking up at his most junior employee.

'I've no idea,' Spencer replied with a puzzled expression, 'but what I *do* know is that one of the reports checked out on this database on Monday night; I saw it with my own eyes. I've no doubt Ronan and Camilla *did* run Report Checks — on a few of the reports, at least — and if mine appeared genuine, then the ones they ran probably did too. But I don't know why it's not working now.'

'Then that's what I need to find out from my associate at the GIA headquarters,' Tobias replied. 'At this rate, I'll be spending the night here. Camilla and Ronan may have made a very serious mistake involving millions of pounds.'

'I'm sorry about that,' Spencer said. 'Is there anything I can do to help?'

'No. Thank you, Spencer. I'm glad you told me about the report you checked though. Go home now. I'll see you in the morning.'

'I hope you don't mind,' Spencer began timidly, 'but I might've mentioned about the necklace to Alicia. I know we're not supposed to talk about clients and work stuff outside of work, but the report thing bothered me a bit.'

'You told Alicia, did you?' Tobias raised an eyebrow. 'On this occasion, Spencer, I don't think that's such a bad idea. What did she make of it?'

Spencer thought for a moment before replying.

'She said she'd get back to me.'

EIGHTEEN

In a small, dimly lit Italian restaurant in the heart of South Kensington, Alicia Clayton sat across a table from an elderly gentleman with greying hair and a deep suntan. Alicia was dressed in a cream sleeveless blouse and navy trousers; her companion wore a white linen shirt with pale blue chinos. Over plates of tagliatelle bolognese accompanied by two large glasses of a Chilean Malbec, they reminisced about old times at Rock Palm Resort: the dawn sunrises across the bay, the crab racing on the beach, the pulsating rhythms of the steel band that played by the pool bar on Friday lunchtimes and the Sunday night barbecue parties at Shirley Heights.

'Such wonderful memories Alicia, my dear,' Carlos Jaxen said quietly in a soft American drawl. His eyes glistened with tears. Alicia reached across the table and held Carlos's hand in hers.

'And we will always have them,' she said.

'Yes, but that's all they are: memories,' Carlos replied sadly. 'After the hurricane in ninety-five — Hurricane Luis — things changed forever.'

'It's so hard to understand why these things happen,' Alicia said gently.

'I did everything I could to try to rebuild that place. I guess it just wasn't to be.'

'Perhaps,' Alicia replied.

'But even if I'd been able to completely restore and refurbish Rock Palm, without all the legal palaver, I'm not sure it would ever have been the same again. You remember, don't you Alicia? You were there in ninety-five. You and your parents were some of the very last guests to check out. You remember what happened?'

'I think so.' Alicia was careful to let Carlos get there in his own time.

'The girl, Alicia. The body on the beach. I know you were only, what, fourteen, fifteen years old then?'

'Fifteen.'

'Fifteen. Well, that's no thing for a fifteen year old girl to know about. But you did know, didn't you?'

'Yes, I did. She was the magician's assistant, wasn't she?'

'That's right. Anastasia, or at least that's what they called her. She was a wonderful girl; kind, generous, full of life and a stunning performer. She can only have been a few years older than you, in her late teens or early twenties perhaps, and yet she seemed… so much older.'

'What d'you mean?'

'Oh it's difficult to say really. I'm not sure I really know what I mean. I've no idea of her background, but I think she'd had a difficult life. She was like you, my dear; she had no idea who her parents were. I remember her telling me once that Mallory, the magician, and the magic team she performed with were like her family. Do you remember the magic shows at Rock Palm?'

'I do! They were a highlight for me,' Alicia replied. 'Is the magician still performing?'

'I honestly couldn't say. But the real tragedy of Anastasia's death of course, was that they never found the murderer.'

'Oh?' Alicia's eyes widened with intrigue, encouraging him to continue.

'You couldn't blame the police back then; they had more than enough going on in the aftermath of that terrible hurricane. It was horrendous, Alicia. I've never seen anything like it before. Or after. Devastation everywhere. Less than twenty-four hours after Anastasia was murdered, the beach where her body was found was covered in debris from the hotel. There were palm branches and rubbish strewn all over the place. There was no way the police would ever find any evidence. And then the medical examiner's van went missing.'

'Missing?'

'Never made it back to the hospital mortuary in St. John's. And it was never found. It just disappeared, with the ME, his assistant and Anastasia's body.'

'But how? And where?'

'Another mystery, Alicia. The only explanation the police could come up with at the time was that it had been washed out to sea, but who takes a coastal road to St. John's from Rock Palm? You know the island. Tell me.'

'I agree. You wouldn't. Unless you were taking a scenic detour or something, which obviously an ME's van, pressed for time and carrying a body would not.'

'Precisely.' Carlos took a long sip of the Malbec before he went on. 'You see, I don't believe it's an accident that the van went missing. Something happened to it. Something calculated and cold-blooded. Premeditated.'

'What makes you think that?' Alicia asked, frowning.

'It's just a feeling, nothing more. I can't prove anything. Somebody once knew, I'm sure of it. Maybe somebody still does. But to this day, Anastasia's murder remains unsolved, her body has never been laid to rest, the case has never been closed, and dear old Rock Palm is forever tarnished with the memory of her tragic and untimely death. Some say Rock Palm is haunted and that she roams the ruins at night, searching for her killer to avenge her death and vindicate Owen, her lover. He was always suspected of murdering her, but never convicted. Of course, the ghost stories are a load of nonsense, even though some people claim to have seen a corpse-like figure wandering through the hotel wearing the black, ruffled dress she wore for her final stage show in the auditorium.'

'Tell me about Owen,' Alicia said. 'Owen Rapley, wasn't it?'

'Oh, poor Owen. Yes, Rapley was his surname. You've got a good memory young lady. I suppose it comes with your job. He was a young Antiguan, in his early twenties at the time, and a very talented tennis player. He worked at the resort as the tennis coach and managed the sports reception too. He was very popular, especially with the women. Sure, he enjoyed the attention, but he only had eyes for Anastasia. And she for him.' Another sip of the Malbec before he continued. 'Those two were very much in love. But when Anastasia's body was found on the beach, two guests came forward who had witnessed them together, walking along the beach in the early hours of that morning.'

I can vouch for that, Alicia thought to herself.

'Of course, I *believe* the guests,' Carlos went on. 'I didn't see Owen and Anastasia myself that night, but they would often go for moonlit walks along the beach after Anastasia had finished a performance. But none of the magic team or the hotel staff would ever have said anything to implicate Owen. They knew he could never have murdered her.'

'Do you agree with them?'

'Without question,' Carlos replied. He emphasised the words as he spoke. 'I knew Owen. He was devoted to the girl. I saw it in his eyes. And I don't believe he was capable of doing such a thing either. He may have enjoyed the attention from the female guests, but he would never have betrayed her and he didn't have a bad bone in his body.'

'People can surprise us though.' Alicia watched Carlos carefully.

'Not Owen,' he said firmly. 'He was innocent. I've always believed that.'

'Then who?'

Carlos held out both hands, palms up and shrugged.

'I can't answer that one. I just know it wasn't him. It's so sad what happened to him afterwards though.'

'What *did* happen?'

'It was all too much for him, poor boy. He didn't help himself to start with when he lied to the police about not being with her, or even knowing her. Understandably, he knew it would look bad for him if they realised he was one of the last people to see her, and in a place very close to where her body was found.'

Which would explain his reaction — that she, herself, had witnessed — when he first saw Anastasia's body lying in the sand, Alicia thought. Perhaps it was as much a shock to him as to anyone else.

'Owen didn't realise he'd been seen with Anastasia that night,' Carlos went on, 'but when there were witnesses with accounts that the police could corroborate, albeit with rather shaky evidence, he became their prime suspect. He had no choice but to own up and tell the truth. Which put him in a very bad light. Why lie to begin with? It makes people instantly suspicious. After that the police homed in on him, assuming he had something to hide. If he'd only told the truth from the beginning things might have worked out differently for him.'

'Where is he now?'

Carlos gazed at his wine glass, deep in thought.

'Carlos?'

He looked up, startled.

'Yes?'

'Where is Owen Rapley now?'

'Where? I've no idea. Haven't a clue. I lost touch with him years ago. I had my own problems to take care of, as you know. Although the police were never able to gather enough evidence to convict him, his name was sullied. After the hurricane I understand he desperately tried to find another job, but no one would employ a man who'd been the prime suspect in a murder case, especially in the tourist industry. The last I heard, he was living on the streets. Homeless. St. John's, I think. Shall we order another bottle of this excellent Malbec?'

'Absolutely,' Alicia agreed. She signalled their request to a waitress.

'Would you know how to locate Owen Rapley if you wanted to find him?' Alicia asked, turning back to Carlos. She had decided to relax caution with the questions; her initial tactics of innocent reminiscing about the old days at Rock Palm had worked. Carlos certainly wasn't reluctant to talk about the past and he hadn't queried her motives for asking. She had merely led him to believe that as he was back in the UK, she wanted to catch up with him as an old friend of the family. He'd been more than delighted.

'Leon might know where Owen is now,' he said, in answer to her question. 'Leon Fayer, my former GM. I suppose you remember him?'

'Of course. What's he doing now?'

'He's the general manager of a five-star resort.'

'Still in Antigua?'

'Yes. I forget the name of the place, but he's doing well. All my staff had to find new jobs after the hurricane, not that there was any work in the tourist industry for a while. There was so much to be done before the island could get itself back on its feet and return to business as usual, but there's one thing about Antiguans: they're a resilient people.'

'Yes, they are,' Alicia agreed. 'It's why I love them.'

'I do too. And I miss the island.'

They broke off from conversation as the waitress arrived with a new bottle of Malbec. With Carlos's approval, she filled their glasses and removed their empty plates. They declined her offer of the dessert menu and she left them to it.

'I'd like to catch up with Leon again,' Alicia said, taking a sip of wine. She savoured the velvety tannins and subtle hints of blackberry and plum. It had been a perfect accompaniment to the tagliatelle.

'He was such a kind man,' she continued. 'We got on very well. Every Friday lunchtime when the steel band were playing, he'd come down to the pool deck and dance with me. He had all the time in the world for the guests at Rock Palm.'

'That doesn't surprise me at all!' Tears briefly filled Carlos's eyes again as he spoke. 'He's a wonderful man. And very loyal. The best GM I've ever employed. The place he works now is very lucky to have him.'

'My boyfriend and I are considering a trip to the Caribbean later this year.' It was a stretch of the truth, but Alicia was sure she could persuade Gray to join her.

'Then I must give you Leon's number and you can give him a call ahead of time,' Carlos said. He picked up his cell phone and began to scroll through the contacts. It was all too easy, Alicia thought to herself. She hadn't even had to ask for it.

'Here we are, I'll send it to you now,' Carlos said. 'He remembers you and your parents with great fondness. I know he'll be delighted to hear from you again. All my staff at Rock Palm had a special place in their hearts for the Clayton family.'

'That's wonderful to know,' Alicia smiled, 'and, of course, the feeling was — *is* — entirely mutual. I'll look forward to seeing Leon again.'

'I wish I could remember which resort he's at now...' Carlos was tapping at the screen of his phone again. 'Let me check... ah yes, that's it. He's the GM of The West Beach Club. It's in the south of the island.'

'Near Rock Palm?'

'It is on the south coast, yes, but a little further west, hence the name. I'd say it's a thirty minute drive from Rock Palm. Not too far away.'

'What is Rock Palm like now, Carlos?' Alicia asked gently. She spoke with caution, wondering if it was a question too far. She watched her companion. A flicker of a smile at the memory of happier times was quickly replaced by a look of sadness and heartache.

'Oh I'm sorry Carlos, I didn't mean to...'

'No, it's all right.' He held up his hand to silence her. 'Please don't apologise. I wish with all my heart things had turned out differently and we'd been able to rebuild. But sometimes fate doesn't give us those choices or those chances, for whatever reason. Rock Palm might be a place of decay and dereliction today, but I want the memories we all have, along with those of the thousands of guests who've darkened the doors of the hotel throughout the decades, to live on.'

'And they will,' Alicia replied softly, taking another sip of wine.

'It's truly abandoned now,' Carlos continued sadly. 'All these years, while all the legal wrangling has been going on, I've been able to do nothing with the place. It's about money and bureaucracy and red tape. I've fought for twenty-three years Alicia, but it's no good. After Sophia died, I lost the will to keep going.'

'I'm so sorry Carlos.'

'Thank you my dear. Your father has been the greatest friend and support to me over the years. It makes me very sad to think I will never again be able to host a Clayton family vacation on the beautiful island of Antigua.'

'Oh Carlos, please don't apologise for that,' Alicia said. 'As you've said, we have the memories — lots of them — and those will be treasured forever.'

'But as to Rock Palm,' Carlos continued. 'You wouldn't recognise the place now. It's a scene of utter devastation. Nature has taken over, as it always does, and the magic has gone now.'

'Speaking of magic,' Alicia said suddenly. 'What's become of the auditorium?'

Carlos paused for a moment.

'You know what? I've no idea,' he replied. 'You're aware half of it was built underground?'

'Yes.'

'And you know the foyer caved in during the hurricane, effectively closing off the entrance and making the place inaccessible?'

'I didn't, no. But wasn't there a stage door?'

'There was, which was also impassable after debris fell on top of and around it during the storm.'

'Has anyone tried to find a way in since then?'

'Not to my knowledge,' Carlos replied, shaking his head. 'Of course, Rock Palm has had its share of vandals, but they'll generally hang out in places which are easy to get to. The entrance to the auditorium was well and truly concealed after Hurricane Luis and, as far as I'm aware, nobody has ever gained access to it since. I'm not sure I'd even know where to find it now myself, the place is so overgrown.'

'That's… interesting.' Alicia contemplated the abandoned resort, untouched for twenty-three years, and the old auditorium, where no one had set foot for over two decades. She finished the last of her wine and decided she would research flights to Antigua, departing within the next few days, on her way home. She hoped she could persuade Gray to join her.

'May I ask why Rock Palm has suddenly attracted your curiosity, aside from the happy reminiscing?' Carlos asked.

'The simple reason I'm interested in Rock Palm again is because of a diamond necklace,' Alicia replied. It was time to find out what he knew.

NINETEEN

Carlos listened carefully as Alicia explained that a necklace resembling one worn by a guest at Rock Palm Resort in nineteen ninety-five — and allegedly stolen from the guest during her stay at the hotel — had reappeared at a Hatton Garden jewellery store earlier in the week. The necklace had been taken to the store to be valued, with the intention of being sold, by a lady calling herself Vivienne Karlsson. The name of the lady who had originally worn the diamond necklace, worth around seventeen million pounds today, was Vivienne Karleman. At the mention of her name, Alicia noticed a flash of recognition in Carlos's eyes.

She went on to explain that the name Vivienne *Karlsson* had been false, along with the contact details the woman had provided. There was also a strong possibility that the necklace and accompanying documentation were also fake. Alicia had attempted to carry out some research on the ownership and provenance of the necklace between September ninety-five and its unexpected reappearance in the Hatton Garden jewellery store on Monday. This had proved unsuccessful. Admittedly, she had neither the contacts, the inside knowledge, nor the resources or expertise to easily track the path of a diamond necklace over the last twenty-three years.

A source with access to a variety of international crime databases had managed to do a small bit of digging for information on her behalf, but this had revealed nothing of interest. According to the research conducted by her source, a diamond necklace matching the description of the one Alicia had provided had never been reported as stolen. The source had added that if a necklace worth over twenty million dollars *had* been flagged up in relation to a theft, it would have undoubtedly been newsworthy in certain circles, yet the search had come up with nothing.

Alicia, slightly puzzled as to why the Karlemans had never reported the necklace as stolen, had subsequently drawn a blank as to how to investigate further. The obvious explanation was that the necklace had been found prior to their evacuation from Rock Palm in ninety-five and was never stolen at all. As to the authenticity of the identical necklace which had surfaced at Tobias Moncler Jewels, Alicia had only Spencer's instincts that the accompanying grading reports were fake, probably backed up by Tobias's inability to confirm otherwise. She hoped they would know more tomorrow. She felt as though she were in the middle of a breaking news story with the customary message to "check back later for more details" spooling across the bottom. Carlos listened with interest as Alicia unraveled her thoughts and the events leading up to them. When she had finished speaking, he took a long sip of wine and placed the glass carefully on the table.

'I remember the necklace,' he began, 'and I also remember the Karlemans: Charles and Vivienne. British couple. Incredibly wealthy. He was a self-made millionaire, a very successful businessman, although how he made his millions I'm not exactly sure. Sometimes it's better not to know. As long as they're spending money in your hotel, you don't ask questions. She was typically spoiled with far too much time and money on her hands. It was their first — and last — vacation at Rock Palm. I remember the luggage she brought with her was ridiculous. The porters sure had their work cut out when the Karlemans arrived.

'My dealings with them were limited, of course. Leon had much more to do with them, being the front-of-house manager. I don't think he particularly warmed to them, but he had a job to do in keeping them happy and that's what he did. For the most part. As I understand it they were quite difficult to please. From what he told me, they weren't well liked among the hotel staff. I don't think Vivienne treated them with a whole lot of respect. As for the necklace, I remember Leon consulting me about it on the morning of the evacuation. Apparently Vivienne was accusing a member of staff of taking it although this was entirely unsubstantiated. I couldn't tell you what the outcome of this unfortunate business was, although to my knowledge the necklace was never found. I believe the Karlemans left Rock Palm without it. And, strangely perhaps, that's the last time I ever saw or spoke to them.'

'So you've no idea where they are now?'

'Sorry,' Carlos said, shaking his head, 'none at all. Leon might. He had a lot more contact with them than I did and probably followed up on the necklace as well. He'll know what happened in the end. I stand by my staff to this day though. None of them would ever have taken anything from a guest. They were the most loyal team of people an employer could wish for. I don't know what happened to the necklace, but it had nothing to do with my staff. Leon will know. Catch up with him and you'll have the puzzle solved, I can assure you. But is this why you're asking me about Rock Palm? You're investigating the mystery of Vivienne Karleman's missing diamond necklace twenty-three years later?'

'I'm not certain exactly,' Alicia replied hesitantly. For the first time, she wondered exactly what she *was* investigating. Sure, it had been the necklace with its suspicious grading reports which had initially seized her attention, along with the assumed name of Vivienne Karlsson. And then the account from her father of Anastasia's unexplained and unsolved murder had intrigued her further. And finally there was the mysterious package, delivered anonymously, containing the guidebook marked with a Post-it Note and the Rock Palm brochure from nineteen ninety-five.

The more she learned and the more she had become reacquainted with the tragic past of Rock Palm Resort, the more she had unwittingly been sucked into an unfinished symphony. A story with no ending. At that moment, in the dim light of the restaurant, as she gazed into the sad, tired eyes of Carlos, Alicia knew it was time for the final movement of the symphony to be written. It was time for the ending of the story to be told and the book to be closed. For Carlos. For his late wife Sophia. And for Anastasia.

TWENTY

A heavy rain had begun to fall as Alicia hurried towards South Kensington underground station. Steam drifted upwards in mystical swirls from the pavement, still warm from the heat of the day, while newly formed puddles of water reflected the hazy orange glow of the street lamps and the lights from the bars and restaurants along the street. Carlos, who had been picked up by a car outside the restaurant, had offered Alicia a ride to the station, but she had declined. It was only a short walk away. Running towards the shelter of the brightly lit entrance she regretted her refusal of the lift, however. She was soaked through and grateful that she was little more than twenty minutes from her Fulham apartment. She entered the station and headed towards the ticket barriers. Although it was nearly ten-thirty, the night was hot and humid and the station was still busy with City workers and groups of tourists.

Stepping through one of the ticket barriers, which snapped shut behind her, Alicia headed for the entrance to the Piccadilly line. Glancing to her left, she had the sudden feeling that she was being watched. She caught the eye of a middle-aged gentleman dressed in a black shirt and dark blue jeans. He immediately looked away, turning towards a map of the underground displayed behind him, but there was something familiar about him. Alicia slowed to a halt, trying to recall how she might know him. Had she recently interviewed him? Was he a friend of Gray's? Where had she seen him before? A group of three well-dressed young couples, laughing and chatting loudly walked between Alicia and the man, and he was obscured from her line of sight. Suddenly she remembered where their paths had crossed: he had been dining alone in Mullrose Grill two nights ago when she had met Spencer for dinner. That night he had been wearing the black-rimmed spectacles which had reminded her of the ones she wore as a teenager. Tonight he didn't have them on, but she was certain it was him. There was something about his gaze. It was intrusive, almost sinister in nature. Was he stalking her? Even at Mullrose Grill, she felt as though she had seen him before, although she couldn't recall where. Had he been in the background somewhere, forming an image in her subconscious mind?

She shivered; she could almost feel a chill in the hot, humid air. The well-dressed party of six clattered down the steps to the District line leaving a gap in the foot traffic. Alicia looked to where the man had been standing, but he was gone. She glanced quickly around, from the entrance to the platforms, to the ticket barriers and the station entrance beyond. There were late night travellers, hurrying through the station with purpose, but the man in the black shirt and dark blue jeans had vanished. Where was he? Annoyed with herself for not being more alert, she scanned the faces of each person heading towards the entrances for the underground lines but there was no sign of him. It would be a pointless exercise to go back through the ticket barriers in order to search the station entrance. He'd realised he'd been made and had made a hasty departure. And now he was gone.

Joining the stream of travellers on the escalator descending towards the platform for the westbound Piccadilly line, Alicia took a swift sideways glance at each person she passed. She arrived on the platform at the same time as the train which rumbled into the station with a screech of brakes. Stepping quickly into the carriage, she sat down, covertly examining each passenger. The doors jerked shut and Alicia stared out of the window as the train pulled away from the empty platform. Suddenly she froze. He was there, standing alone, watching the train intently, as if he was searching for something. Or someone. Their eyes met briefly before Alicia's carriage plunged into the darkness of the tunnel. And he was gone again.

Alicia arrived at her Fulham apartment building a little after eleven pm. She nodded at Dale, the night concierge and security guard, seated behind a desk in his navy uniform. He was in his mid-to-late-fifties and endlessly cheerful. While his hairline was receding, his waistline was expanding and he could probably do with a uniform a couple of sizes up.

'Evening Miss Clayton,' he beamed at her. 'How are you?'

'Fine thanks Dale. How's your night going?'

'Fairly quiet. So far.'

'I hope it stays that way,' Alicia replied. She debated whether to give him a description of the man at the station and ask him whether he had spotted anyone similar hanging around the apartment building but decided against it.

'I signed for a package for you earlier. Are you expecting anything?' Dale asked.

'A package?' Alicia thought for a moment. She shook her head slowly. 'No, I don't think so. Not that I remember, anyway.'

'Oh. Well, I put it in your mailbox,' Dale said with a shrug. 'Enjoy the rest of your evening.'

'Thanks.'

Alicia was tired and eager to get back to her apartment, but as Dale had taken the trouble to mention the delivery, she decided she should make the effort to collect it from the mailroom. She took the elevator to the basement. The mailroom, located next to the underground car park, was typically nondescript with a white marble floor, white-painted walls and rows of aluminium mailboxes from knee to shoulder height. As usual, it was empty. Some residents in the building didn't bother to check their mailboxes for weeks on end. The large recycling bin in the corner filled with Indian takeaway menus and estate agents' leaflets was testament to the fact that the majority of mail most people received was junk.

Opening her own mailbox with a small key, Alicia pulled out two takeaway menus: one for a pizza restaurant round the corner, the other for a newly opened Chinese place two blocks away, and a white A5 envelope with her name and address typed on the front. An official Royal Mail Special Delivery Guaranteed sticker stated that the package had been sent by an Omar R. Prestlock — a name she didn't recognise — from an address in EC1, a central London postcode. She froze as she read the first line of the sender's address:

13 Dornan Mews. She recognised it immediately; it was the same as the one Vivienne Karlsson had provided for Ronan and Camilla, except the postcode she had given them began with WC. This time, the postal code was EC1. Alicia ran through the London postcode districts in her mind. Her knowledge of central London was reasonable; one of the areas within the EC1 postal code was Hatton Garden. Different postcodes, same fictitious address.

Alicia turned the envelope over and examined it carefully. It was blank on the reverse. She was aware of a CCTV camera in one corner of the mailroom and decided to open the package in the privacy of her apartment. Sliding the envelope into her bag, she took the elevator back to ground level where Dale sat alone at the reception desk. He looked up as Alicia approached him.

'Everything okay?' he asked.

'Dale, this package you signed for, did it come with the usual mail delivery?' Alicia asked, holding the envelope out towards him. He took it and looked at it closely before turning it over and handing it back to her.

'Yeah, it did. I had to sign for a few things, as usual. This was just one of them. Why?'

'Did you recognise the postman?'

'Sure. It was Merv. He's been around as long as I have. What's up?'

'No, nothing Dale, just so long as you didn't notice anything unusual with the delivery this evening.'

Dale shook his head with a puzzled look.

'I'm afraid I didn't... *Should* I have?' Dale took matters of security very seriously.

'Not at all,' Alicia replied reassuringly. 'Please don't worry, it was just out of interest really.'

'Oh. Good. Well, you have a great night then, Miss Clayton.'

'Thanks Dale. You too.'

TWENTY-ONE

Alicia took the elevator to the seventh floor and made her way along the carpeted corridor to her apartment. She let herself in and kicked off her shoes as she switched on the lights to the open-plan lounge and kitchen area. Absentmindedly admiring the river views and city lights before closing the curtains, she sat down on the sofa and pulled the envelope out of her bag. She turned it over a few times, examining it carefully. It was a regular envelope. There was nothing unusual about it apart from the sender's address which Alicia knew wasn't real. She peeled open the top with care and peered inside. It contained documents of some kind. She pulled them out and dropped them onto the cushion beside her. There were about four sheets of A4 paper, stapled together and folded in half. Unfolding them, Alicia looked at the top sheet. Her eyes widened in confusion and surprise.

The top sheet of paper was a confirmation letter containing the flight details for two first-class return tickets from London Gatwick to V. C. Bird International Airport, Antigua. One ticket was booked in her name, the other in her boyfriend's name: Graymond Sharkey. The second page outlined accommodation particulars: a beachfront villa for two guests at The West Beach Club. Alicia recalled that this was the resort where Leon Fayer now worked as the general manager. Pages three and four consisted of the usual small-print disclaimer information concerning flight security, seat numbers, passports, and visa and health requirements, along with the itinerary for private transfers to and from the resort. The outbound Virgin Atlantic flight was booked to leave London Gatwick at ten-thirty in the morning on Friday, August 24. The villa at The West Beach Club was booked for fourteen nights with the overnight return flight scheduled for Friday, September 7, arriving at Gatwick at seven thirty-five the following morning. Each page was headed with the logo of a well-known, reputable travel company.

Alicia stared at the documents for a few seconds before checking the envelope once more. It contained another item which she had missed. She slid it out and realised it was a folded map of the Caribbean islands of Antigua and Barbuda. As she opened it up and spread it out she noticed two crosses in black pen had been drawn on it. They were both in the south of Antigua; the first was over to the west of the island, marking the location of The West Beach Club. The other had been drawn next to the bay where the derelict Rock Palm Resort was situated. Alicia frowned in puzzlement. It was too late to call the travel company. She picked up her phone and called Graymond's number.

'Hey Alicia.' He answered after the third ring.

'Hi Gray. How was your day?'

'Busy, but not bad. Only got home half an hour ago. How was yours?'

'It just got interesting. Gray, do you know anything about flights to Antigua?'

Silence at the end of the line.

'Antigua?' he asked. 'What, as in the Caribbean island Antigua?'

Alicia could tell by the tone of his voice that he knew as much about the booking as she did.

'Yes, *that* Antigua,' she replied. 'You haven't planned a surprise trip or anything have you?' It was a wild and unlikely stab in the dark, especially as the package had been sent by someone called Omar Prestlock and the map had a cross next to Rock Palm. Gray wouldn't know anything about that. Alicia wasn't even sure she'd ever told him that she stayed there with her parents as a child.

'Sorry, but no.' He sounded taken aback. 'Why? Did you want me to? I thought you didn't like surprises.'

'I don't,' Alicia said firmly. 'Do you know anyone by the name of Omar Prestlock?'

'Don't think so. Should I?'

'I don't know,' Alicia sighed.

'What's going on Alicia?'

'I'm not sure. Except that I seem to have inadvertently got mixed up in something, although I've no idea how exactly, or why.'

'What d'you mean *mixed up in something*?'

'I wish I knew.'

'Are you okay? It's nothing to do with that bodies-on-the-building-site story you're working on is it? I'm still not happy about you being involved in that.'

'No, it's not. And yes, I'm fine. At least, I think I am. I'm not sure, but I might be being watched. It's a long story Gray, but I've just received a package containing two first-class tickets to Antigua; one for me and one for you. And confirmation of a villa booked for fourteen nights at a resort called The West Beach Club. The flight leaves on Friday.'

'Wait, slow down. What're you on about? You're being watched? By who?'

'It's *whom* Gray, and I don't know. Can you take two weeks off and come with me?'

'What, to Antigua? On Friday? It's less than two days away. No, of course I can't. You know that. I'm extremely busy right now. I've got back-to-back meetings and I'm taking delivery of a new Gulfstream next week. There's no way I can take time off. Who booked these tickets anyway?'

'I think they were booked by someone called Omar Prestlock...'

'Who's that?' Gray interrupted.

'I don't know, Gray,' Alicia said with impatience. 'That's why I asked you. I'll find out, obviously. Look, it's late and it's a long story, but I've got this feeling I should go. I'll call the travel company tomorrow to find out who set this up, and sure, I'd love you to come with me, but I appreciate Friday is very short notice. I'll take someone else and get the tickets changed.'

'Hold on Alicia. How safe is this? You can't just get on a plane and go to some random place in the Caribbean because a stranger sends you a bunch of tickets. How d'you know they're even valid? There'll be a catch somewhere. And how did they get your — *our* — personal details to book the flights?'

'It's not a totally random place,' Alicia replied. 'I used to know the general manager of the resort we've been booked to stay at. And, like I said, I'll call the travel company first thing tomorrow to confirm who arranged the tickets and that they're valid. I might see if Spencer can come instead; he was telling me how much he'd like to visit the Caribbean.'

'What, that homeless drunk you have lunch with? You're not asking him to go with you.'

'He's not homeless and he's not a drunk,' Alicia said defensively. 'And if you don't want to come, then I'll ask whoever I want.'

'All right, sorry, I forgot, he's been to rehab and he's clean. Even so, I'm not sure I like the idea of you sharing a suite, or a villa, or whatever with him. What about one of your girlfriends?'

'I doubt any of them can be free at such short notice, but, okay, I get your point about Spencer. I'll see if I can get him another room. Failing that, I'll go alone.'

'You're not going by yourself Alicia. And just — hold on about Spencer. Let me see what I can do here. I can't promise anything, but I might be able to get Finn to man the fort for the next couple of weeks.'

'Really?' Alicia asked hopefully. The tactic of suggesting that Spencer joined her had worked, as she had suspected. Finn was Gray's right hand man; he was bright, loyal and trustworthy. Alicia knew he would be more than capable of taking care of business in Gray's absence.

'I'm not promising *anything*, but I just don't want you going alone. I'll get back to you tomorrow, as soon as I've been through my diary properly and checked Finn's happy with everything.'

'Thanks Gray, I'll wait to hear from you.'

'And I'd like to know how and where this Prestlock guy got our passport details from,' Gray added. 'That's personal. And if he has our passport information, what else does he have on us?'

'I don't know,' Alicia replied. 'I'm as uneasy about this as you are, believe me. Let me do some digging and we'll talk tomorrow.'

'Just be careful Alicia. Sleep well. I love you.'

'You too, Gray.'

Alicia said goodnight and placed her phone on the table beside her before leafing through the travel documents again. She tried to make sense of the events of the last three days. It looked like the puppet master was at work again, mysteriously pulling the strings behind the scenes.

Who are you? Alicia said out loud. *What do you want? Why are you hiding in the shadows?*

Who was Omar R. Prestlock? Was he the puppet master? Was he the man who'd been watching her in the station and at Mullrose Grill? And who was Vivienne Karlsson? Alicia concluded they had to be working together, but were they her friends or her enemies? What was their connection to the past and how had they come by a replica of the original diamond necklace worn by Vivienne Karleman? If it really was a replica. And what of the original necklace? It was all very well to send her to Antigua, but what was she supposed to *do* there? It was as though she'd been sent the pieces of a jigsaw puzzle without the picture. It was up to her to figure out how to fit them together. She knew that the only way to find the answers to her questions was to go along with the puppet master. The stage had been set and it was time for the performance to begin, wherever it took her. She had a part in the play, but someone had forgotten to give her the script. And now she was more determined than ever to discover the secrets of Rock Palm that had been concealed for twenty-three years.

TWENTY-TWO

7:58 am, Thursday, August 23
Hatton Garden, London

Spencer arrived at Tobias Moncler Jewels the following morning breathless, sweating profusely and already exhausted. Paranoid that he was being watched by every man, woman and child he passed along the street and shared a carriage with on the underground, he had spent the previous evening researching various online articles on how to elude pursuers, evade capture and effortlessly blend into the surroundings. His morning commute had taken twice the usual amount of time due to the circuitous route he had selected, however according to one website, it was essential to vary journeys made regularly such as those to and from work. Another website had stressed the importance of transiting through highly populated areas which would make it more difficult for the pursuer to keep his eyes on the target. Thus Spencer had headed for the crowds, which, in turn, had further slowed his journey.

As he opened the door to the jewellery store he was grateful to have made it to work unscathed and relieved that, for this journey at least, he had successfully managed to avoid being accosted by whoever was out there watching him. For once, he even relished the icy blast he received from the air conditioning. Keeley and Otto, already at work, had begun removing jewellery from the night safe in preparation for the case-count. The mood in the showroom was subdued and Spencer detected a tension in the air.

'Morning!' he said cheerfully, still out of breath.

'Put your stuff in the break room and get back out here as soon as you can,' Otto hissed, without smiling.

'What?'

'Don't ask,' Keeley added. 'We don't know what's happened but I've never seen Tobias so angry. Think Ronan and Camilla made a deal when he was away that's gone sour.'

'Oh?' Spencer asked, feigning surprise.

'We don't know any more than that, other than to steer well clear of Tobias,' Otto went on.

'Thanks for the heads up,' Spencer said. He pushed open the door to the rear of the showroom. As he walked along the corridor to the staff break room, he could hear raised voices from the office where Ronan and Camilla had been with Tobias the previous evening.

'I'm still trying to understand how two seasoned professionals, with decades of experience behind them, can have been so blind.' It was Tobias's voice. Spencer slowed to a halt outside the office door.

'I'm so sorry Tobias.' Camilla was sobbing. 'I just don't know how this happened.'

'But how could you *both* miss the fact that the grading reports were fake? And as for the diamonds… well they're not even diamonds, are they?'

'But on Monday the grading reports checked out on the GIA website.' Ronan was still holding onto his story. 'And those — stones, I just don't know how… It's a vicious trick. She was out to get us.'

'It's too late for excuses Ronan,' Tobias said quietly. 'You've cost my company millions. I doubt I'll ever get it back. I'm not even sure I'll be able to keep trading. You've practically bankrupted me. That woman, Vivienne Karlsson, fooled you both and now she's vanished into the ether and left us with a bunch of phoney contact details and a financial catastrophe. There was more fiction in her divorce story than in a library. And you both fell for it.'

'As soon as the bank opens I'll go and…'

'Ronan, the only place you should think about going right now is the Job Centre.'

There was a brief silence. Outside the door Spencer hardly dared breathe.

'I'm losing my job?' Ronan croaked, almost in a whisper.

'I told you you should have…'

'Oh don't even attempt the blame game Camilla,' Tobias interrupted the female voice. 'You're both summarily dismissed for gross misconduct. You can collect your things and leave now.'

'But Tobias, *please*...' Camilla sounded distraught.

'There's nothing more to say, Camilla,' Tobias said firmly. 'I've a lot of work ahead to try and sort this out. The sooner you both leave, the better.'

'You can't just let us go like this,' Ronan protested.

'I can and I am. Have a read of your contracts.'

'This is — this is absolutely unreasonable. You can't do this. I'm going to appeal.'

'By all means, Ronan, but if I was you I'd leave quietly. Do you think any jeweller around here is going to want to employ someone who paid out eight million pounds for a bunch of imitation diamonds worth far less?'

Spencer stood rooted to the spot, unable to believe what he'd just overheard. The diamonds were fakes. Tobias was firing Ronan and Camilla. Letting them go. With immediate effect. The door opened suddenly and Ronan stood in front of him with Camilla close behind, her eyes red and swollen. Startled, Spencer jumped back.

'*You?*' Ronan snarled in surprise. 'What're *you* doing here? You've been eavesdropping, haven't you, you little snitch?'

'No, I was just passing,' Spencer muttered.

'If there's anyone you should be firing, Tobias, it's him,' Ronan said nastily, jabbing a finger at Spencer. 'Why you ever employed such a vile specimen of humanity, I'll never know. He's a loser and a drug addict who'll never be any good at anything. Spencer was the one Vivienne Karlsson first showed that necklace to when she came into this store. I'll bet you anything he knows her. They're in this together. He told her when you were going to be away so she could fool us. Come on Spencer, own up. You're at the bottom of this whole fraudulent nightmare, aren't you? Where's the eight million you just stole from Tobias?'

It was a step too far on Ronan's part.

'If I'm a loser and a drug addict who'll never be any good at anything, d'you really think I'd be smart enough to cook up a scam like that?' Spencer retaliated hotly. 'You honestly think a waster and a dogsbody like me could fool two *supposedly* experienced gemologists into handing over eight million quid for a bit of crappy costume jewellery, do you? You're more stupid than I thought.'

Ronan stood in the doorway, speechless.

'Anyway, if you don't mind, I've still got a job. *Unlike some people.* I'm going to put my bag in the break room and...'

As Spencer retreated in the direction of the coffee room, Tobias called out from behind him: 'No, you won't Spencer. You'll come back to this office right now. I want to talk to you.'

'Oh — okay sir. I mean Tobias.' Spencer instantly regretted his reaction to Ronan's insults. He could guess what this was about: the company was about to go bust and he was next out the door. He'd listened in to a private and sensitive conversation and had spoken rudely to a senior employee. *Former* senior employee, he corrected himself. He swallowed hard and turned round slowly. He wished he'd heeded Otto and Keeley's urgent instructions to keep his head down and get back out to the showroom. Now he'd have to explain to Alicia that he'd lost his job.

Ronan and Camilla, standing side by side in the corridor, watched Spencer with silent disdain as he passed them, avoiding eye contact. He entered the office timidly. Tobias had reseated himself at a large desk. Apparently there were no more words of farewell for Ronan and Camilla.

'Shut the door and sit down,' Tobias said, without looking up. He was examining a complicated-looking document with rows of numbers on it through glasses perched on the end of his nose. On the desk, he was surrounded by diamond grading equipment, GIA reports and, on a velvet-lined tray, the loose gemstones from Vivienne Karlsson's necklace. Spencer pushed the office door closed and slid uncomfortably into one of the chairs on the opposite side of the desk to Tobias. He placed his backpack on the floor beside him. The chair was still warm from where Ronan or Camilla must have been sitting. After a few minutes of uneasy silence, Tobias spoke.

'So, as you overheard, we now know for certain that the grading reports are fake, as you suspected. I'm also afraid to say that those gemstones started life in a laboratory.'

'I'm sorry,' was all Spencer could think to say.

'So am I,' Tobias said with a heavy sigh, 'but it's only money.'

'A lot of *only money*.'

'Yes. It is. And it's doubtful I'll ever get it back,' Tobias said. 'But that's no one's fault but ours. Mine for giving Camilla and Ronan the authority to make such a transaction, and... you know the rest of the story as well as any of us. I'm insured for certain financial catastrophes, but, like I said, it was *our* mistake so I don't think there's a chance I'm covered for this one.'

'But — it's *millions of pounds*,' Spencer said, almost unable to comprehend the amount of money at stake.

'Yes,' Tobias replied shortly. 'And I'm not sure what I'm going to do about it. I'll have to go to the bank of course, just to find out exactly what happened on Tuesday, although it's too late to do anything now. The police will have to be involved as well. I'm pretty certain of what these stones are, but I suppose I'll still have to get them sent to a lab to be properly analysed.' He glanced at the glittering gems, scattered haphazardly on the large square of black velvet in front of him.

'How did you find out that everything was fake?' Spencer asked.

Tobias massaged his forehead with his hand, a pained expression on his face.

'Very easily actually. Too easily.' He removed the glasses from the end of his nose and placed them on the document in front of him.

'Ever heard of moissanite?' he asked.

'Yeah, I think so. We don't sell it here though, do we?'

'No, we don't. We don't normally buy it here either.'

'We just did though, didn't we?'

'It looks that way.'

An awkward silence followed. It wasn't his fault, but Spencer was already beginning to feel partly responsible for the terrible mistake that Ronan and Camilla had made.

'When the customer... When Vivienne Karlsson brought the necklace into the showroom... Should I have been able to spot that the stones weren't real diamonds?' he asked nervously.

'Not at all Spencer. Don't blame yourself for that,' Tobias said gently. 'It wasn't your mistake. I wouldn't have expected you to have realised what was happening. Ronan and Camilla are responsible for this mess and there's no excuse for them. Moissanite is a different type of gemstone altogether. In the world of fake diamonds, it's perhaps the best imposter of them all. To an untrained, naked eye, sure, it can be difficult to tell the two types of gems apart, but an expert gemologist with specialist equipment should know better; the composition of moissanite is quite different to a diamond and they have distinctly different properties.'

'But, those stones... They sparkle just like real diamonds.'

'They certainly sparkle,' Tobias said with a grimace, 'but don't ever forget Spencer, all that glitters isn't gold. Moissanite has a higher refractive index than diamonds; if you're comparing a diamond with a moissanite gemstone, you might notice a higher level of brilliance and fire exhibited by the moissanite. Remember *brilliance* is the amount of light reflected by a gem; *fire* is a term used when the light, which bounces off the inside surfaces of the gem, is dispersed into the colours of the rainbow when it leaves the stone.'

Spencer nodded intently, trying to keep up.

'The way diamonds reflect light is unique,' Tobias continued. 'With moissanite, the brilliance and fire emitted by the stone creates a sort of mirrorball effect, with flashes of rainbow colours. The larger the moissanite stone, the more obvious this may be. The best way to compare the two is to put a diamond and a moissanite gem side by side, like this...' Tobias reached into an open drawer to his left and took out a colourless stone, roughly a third of an inch in diameter.

'A two-carat diamond,' he said, holding the shimmering stone between his thumb and forefinger, 'and a two-carat moissanite,' he picked up one of the gems from the black velvet, 'although technically, this weighs a little less than two carats because moissanite stones are about fifteen percent lighter than diamonds. Anyway, tell me what you see.'

'You're right, they do look different when they're next to each other,' Spencer said, gazing at the stones. 'The moissanite's more glittery and I can see the rainbow colours. It's got a sort of yellowy, greyish tinge. The diamond has a more natural, bright white colour to it.'

'Exactly,' Tobias nodded. 'They're quite different stones when you compare them close up. And there's another distinct difference between the two.'

From a second desk drawer, Tobias produced a slim, pocket-sized instrument made from silver-coloured plastic with an electronic gauge along one side.

'I've seen Ronan use that,' Spencer said.

'It's a moissanite tester.' Tobias pressed a button on the top of it and the gauge lit up in green, yellow and red. 'It tests a gemstone for both heat and electrical conductivity. The heat test isn't particularly useful because moissanite has a comparable thermal conductivity to a diamond, but the electrical test is a big giveaway. Watch.'

He touched the diamond with the pointed end of the tester. The gauge flickered red and a light next to the letters *DIA* glowed blue. He then placed the sensor onto the moissanite stone. The gauge immediately lit up with red, yellow and green lights. A blue light glowed next to the letters *MOI*.

'A diamond is an electrical insulator; moissanite is an electrical conductor,' Tobias said, placing the tester and the two gemstones carefully on the desk. 'What's more, you don't even have to remove a stone from its setting for this check.'

'So this was all Ronan and Camilla had to do to work out the gems weren't real diamonds?' Spencer asked in horror.

'I'm afraid so,' Tobias said. 'Of course, the results of the test should never be taken as a singular verification of the composition of a stone; there's no substitute for a formal appraisal and proper grading, but, as in this case, a moissanite tester can sometimes be useful to confirm one's suspicions.'

'If *you* immediately suspected that the gems were moissanite and not diamonds, why didn't Ronan and Camilla?' Spencer asked. 'Why didn't they think to use that tester thing?'

Tobias shrugged.

'I wish I knew the answer to that,' he said. 'But they were utterly convinced that the stones were diamonds. Even when it became clear that all we had here was a collection of moissanite stones, they still couldn't quite grasp that they'd been fooled so easily. It's baffling really. They're two of the most discerning gemologists I think I've ever worked with. They're usually so conscientious. So *meticulous*. To think they fell for this simple trick is quite astonishing. And of course, it's going to cost me dearly. There's one other significant difference between a diamond and a moissanite stone…'

Spencer studied each gem, wondering what else he was supposed to be seeing.

'The answer you're looking for is not with the stones,' Tobias said. He held up the document with the rows of numbers. 'It's here.'

Spencer peered at the sheet of paper. It looked like a bank statement.

'The price?' he asked.

'Very much so,' Tobias replied. 'A moissanite gem of similar appearance and size to a diamond can cost one-tenth of the price of a diamond.'

'One-*tenth*? That's way less,' Spencer said with a shocked expression.

'You're not wrong there.'

'So if Ronan and Camilla thought the pink diamond was real and worth fifteen million pounds…'

'Its true value is probably no more than one point five million,' Tobias said.

Spencer swallowed hard.

'What about the other stones?' he asked. 'How much are they worth?'

'Those?' Tobias replied, looking at them with disdain. 'At the very most, probably a quarter of a million pounds.'

'So the whole necklace is worth…' Spencer paused.

'About four million.' Tobias finished the sentence. 'At the very most.'

'If Ronan and Camilla paid *eight* million for the necklace and it was only worth half that…'

'Four million pounds,' Tobias said. 'That's how much trouble I'm in — *we're* in — right now.'

'Damn.'

'But d'you know what makes me even more enraged with this whole thing?'

Spencer wasn't sure he did.

'There was a way, a very *simple* way, to be able to tell that there was a problem.' Tobias spoke in a low voice now, as if in an attempt to avoid exploding with anger. 'Even without the moissanite tester, the only things Ronan and Camilla would have needed to confirm that there was something very wrong with the grading reports and the necklace, and, ergo, that Vivienne Karlsson was little more than a devious con artist, were a keen eye and a loupe. In fact, within a few minutes, even *you* said you had concerns over the reports.'

'Well, I did,' Spencer admitted, 'but then they checked out on the database so…'

'I think if you'd had more time to examine and compare those reports, you wouldn't have even bothered with the Report Check.' Tobias slid a report towards Spencer, turning it one-eighty degrees.

'Take a look. Tell me what you see.'

Spencer leaned forward and peered intently at the document in front of him. On first inspection, it looked like a regular GIA grading report. It was for a round brilliant, colourless diamond with a flawless clarity grade. The weight of the diamond in the report was 2.02 carats. He carefully read through the grading information on the left hand side of the watermarked page before moving to the centre column, where the proportions of the diamond were detailed along with the clarity characteristics. As the diamond was of flawless clarity, there were none. On the right hand side of the page the grading scales were listed for colour, clarity and cut. Underneath was the hologram and a QR code. He focused on the hologram.

'Is there a magnifying glass I could use?' he asked, without glancing up. Tobias had one ready in his hand. He passed it to Spencer.

'Thanks.' Spencer held it over the hologram.

'Could I look at another grading report for a moment? One that's not related to the diamonds from the necklace?'

Without comment, Tobias produced a single sheet of paper and handed it to Spencer who laid the two side by side. They looked almost identical. Spencer hovered from one to the other with the magnifying glass, focusing only on the shimmering holograms of each.

'Do you see it?' Tobias asked.

'I think so.'

'You've got a good eye Spencer.'

'The gemstone and the microscope have been reversed,' Spencer said, 'and the words around the outside of the shield…'

'Yes, the words.'

'What does it mean?'

'I haven't a clue. But now it's definitely a matter for the police.'

'How did you spot it?'

'In very much the same way you did. After you spoke of your concern about the grading reports to me, I took a good look at them all. The ones for the colourless diamonds first attracted my attention. All forty-nine of them. If you look, the grading results for the characteristics of each diamond are *all the same*. They're all for round brilliant diamonds with a D colour grade and flawless clarity. And each one weights two-point-oh-two carats. What are the chances of that?'

Spencer frowned. Tobias continued. 'It's pretty much impossible. I've never seen anything like it. You know as well as I do, not all diamonds are created equal. Every one is unique. They come in different shapes, sizes, colours and with exclusive clarity characteristics. No two diamonds are the same. That's how nature works. And although flawless diamonds don't have any visible inclusions or blemishes when they're examined under a microscope, they are extremely rare, as are D colour diamonds. It's why truly colourless diamonds are valued so highly for their rarity. To have forty-nine natural diamonds *exactly the same*, mounted in a single piece of jewellery is, well, pretty impossible.

'The only differences between these reports are the report numbers. And none of those are valid in the GIA database. There's no record of them whatsoever. They don't exist. Never have done. I've no idea why, or how, they appeared genuine on the database when you, Ronan and Camilla ran your report checks on Monday night. I've a good friend who works at the GIA headquarters in California; he doesn't know either. And then there are the holograms, the most disturbing part of it all, aside from the fact that Ronan and Camilla didn't notice any of this. But it's not just about the wording on the holograms. There's more. If Ronan and Camilla had only done what they should've done the first time around: removed the stones from the necklace and inspected each one under the microscope, we'd be having a different conversation entirely right now.'

Tobias slid the microscope carefully across the table towards Spencer.

'I'm not very good at this appraisal stuff,' Spencer said, suddenly flustered.

'You don't have to be,' Tobias replied. He picked up one of the round, colourless stones with a pair of tweezers and delicately placed it on the stage of the microscope. He handed Spencer the tweezers.

'Adjust the focus for your eyes and take a close look at the gem,' Tobias said gently. 'Take your time.'

'What exactly am I looking for?' Spencer asked, holding the tweezers between his thumb and two shaking, sweaty fingers.

'You'll see.'

Spencer peered awkwardly through the eyepieces of the microscope and, fumbling with the focus knobs on the side, attempted to achieve a clear view of the gem. He picked it up clumsily with the tweezers. The small stone promptly slipped out of their grip and fell back onto the stage of the microscope.

'Take your time,' Tobias said again.

'Yes, sir. I'll try.'

Finally, Spencer held the stone between the tips of the tweezers and steadied his hand as he peered intently through the eyepieces.

'It's — it looks perfect,' he said in awe. The stone sparkled and flashed as he tilted it under the beam of the microscope light.

'Of course,' Tobias replied. 'It was grown in a lab in perfect conditions.'

'Wait a sec,' Spencer suddenly said in a low voice. 'I've got it… What the…?'

'You see it then?' Tobias asked.

'It's just like the hologram,' Spencer went on, his eyes glued to the lenses of the microscope. 'The same words. They're creepy and weird. And you're right. If Ronan and Camilla had only removed the stones from the necklace they would've seen this for themselves.'

'I'm still baffled as to how they could've been so easily taken in by this Vivienne woman,' Tobias said suddenly. 'You met her Spencer. What was she like?'

Spencer thought for a moment.

'She was… very nice. *Very* charming. Smart, well-dressed, nice hair and makeup. Spoke quite poshly. She was quite touchy-feely as well, you know, kept putting her hand on Ronan's and Camilla's arms. But you've got her on the CCTV, right?'

'Yes, I've already checked that. We've only got showroom footage as there's no camera in the private client room, but I'll let the police have it for what it's worth. She's probably wearing a disguise though and there won't be much to go on. As for her contact details, they're a complete waste of time too.'

Remembering Alicia's recollection of the original diamond necklace, a question entered Spencer's mind.

'Is it possible to find out if there's an item of jewellery in the GIA database which *does* match the description of Vivienne Karlsson's necklace?'

'You mean like a replica?'

'Yeah, but with real diamonds.'

'It might be. I'm not sure.'

'If there is, could we ask the GIA people to give us the name of whoever originally submitted it to their lab?'

188

'I don't think they'd be able to reveal that kind of information. There are sure to be confidentiality issues. Why d'you ask?'

'Because there might be an original version, an almost identical necklace to this one here, but made with actual real, mined diamonds.'

'What?' Tobias asked in surprise. 'What makes you think that?'

'Alicia's seen it. The original, I mean.'

'Where? And when?'

'I can't recall the exact details, but you know I told her I thought there was something odd about the grading reports? After I described the necklace to her, she thought she remembered seeing a lady wearing an almost identical one — perhaps the original — when she was on holiday in the Caribbean. It was a long time ago now, back in the nineties. Ninety-five I think she said.'

'Ninety-five? But that's...'

'The date on the holograms of the fake reports. Yeah, I noticed that too. It's partly what reminded me of Alicia's necklace. She did mention something about the original necklace being stolen, but you'd have to ask her if you wanted to know any more than that. Come to think of it, she also said something about a murder... Can we get her on the phone?'

'Of course, but... where are you going with this Spencer?' Tobias picked up his cell phone and scrolled through the contacts. He tapped on the screen and placed the phone on the table. It began to ring.

TWENTY-THREE

'Tobias, good morning!' Alicia's voice was audible through the speaker.

'Morning Alicia, how are you?'

'Very well thanks. You?'

'I've been better. You're on speaker here and Spencer's with me. I understand he's told you about my company's latest acquisition: a necklace, purchased somewhat unwisely and in my absence, by two senior staff members who are no longer employed here.'

'He mentioned it, yes.'

'As it happens, the woman who brought the necklace in on Monday appears to have been a very astute con artist.'

'I gathered.'

'She certainly managed to fool two highly qualified professionals with decades of experience behind them.'

'I guess sometimes people only see what they want to believe, rather than what's actually in front of them.'

'You've got that right,' Tobias said ruefully, 'but anyway, Spencer seems to think you might have encountered a similar necklace to the one that is about to cause me quite a few sleepless nights.'

'I'm so sorry to hear that Tobias,' Alicia replied. 'Yes, I believe that an almost identical necklace exists, or did once upon a time, many years ago. It almost certainly consisted of genuine diamonds and was rumoured to be worth around ten million dollars back in nineteen ninety-five. Unlike the necklace you have at your store, which I presume is worth far less.'

'You're correct, sadly. In fact, the necklace I have here isn't made of diamonds at all. The gemstones are a synthetic form of moissanite. They're made from silicon carbide.'

'Moissanite? I've heard of it. But Tobias, I'm not really much of an authority on precious stones. How can I be of any help to you?'

'Alicia, it's Spencer here.' A voice cut into the conversation.

'Hey Spencer!'

'Remember I told you I thought there was something weird about the grading reports for the diamonds, I mean the stones?'

'I do.'

'There *was* something wrong with the holograms, like I thought. The reports *were* fake.'

'Good work Spencer. See? I told you to go with your instincts. What was it about the hologram in the end?'

'D'you know what the GIA hologram looks like?'

'I can't say I do, no.'

'It's the GIA logo, but displayed as a hologram. The logo is a gold-coloured circle with a sort of decorative border around the outside. Inside the circle is a shield divided into three sections: the upper section shows the top half of a globe, and the lower section is again divided into two. On one side there's a picture of a gemstone. On the other, a little microscope. A bit like clipart-style images.'

'I can picture that.'

'Good. The first thing wrong with Vivienne Karlsson's grading reports is that the gemstone and the microscope are on the wrong sides. The genuine GIA logo always has the gemstone on the *left* and the microscope on the *right*, but the logo on Vivienne's reports has them switched. The *microscope's* on the right and the *gemstone's* on the left.'

'Oh Spencer, you'll be doing me out of a job soon,' Alicia said with a laugh.

'But that's not all, and this bit will really interest you.'

'All right then Miss Marple, carry on.'

'Around the outside of the shield, the GIA logo has three words and a date. It says — in very small letters — knowledge, integrity, excellence.'

'Good words.'

'And the date is nineteen thirty-one, which is when the GIA was established. But you'll never believe what it says on Vivienne Karlsson's reports?'

'Enlighten me.'

'I'm about to. First, the date on the hologram logo is nineteen *ninety-five*. Mean anything to you?'

Alicia was silent.

'And the three words around the shield, they don't say knowledge, integrity and all that; on each of Vivienne's reports they say *who, murdered, anastasia*.'

Spencer paused for effect but still Alicia did not reply.

'You said something about a woman being murdered at the hotel you stayed at when you were a teenager. In the Caribbean. She was found stabbed to death on the beach or something.'

'Yes,' Alicia said quietly.

'Do you know what her name was?'

'Anastasia,' came the reply.

Spencer shot a glance at Tobias who pointed to the diamond under the lens of the microscope.

'There's something else too,' Spencer continued. 'You know when a diamond's graded by the GIA — or any other lab — a unique number, the same as the report number, is laser-inscribed on the diamond's girdle?'

'Yes.'

'The moissanite stones that made up the necklace we've got here *also* have something inscribed on the girdle. Some words.'

'Let me guess. Who. Murdered. Anastasia. Am I right?'

'Yeah. You are. Same as on the holograms.'

'Do all the gemstones have those words inscribed?'

Spencer looked at Tobias who nodded.

'They do,' he replied, taking up the narrative. 'I spent half the night checking and rechecking them. We've got forty-nine identical moissanite stones here, all pretty much exactly the same size, colour, weight and so on. Every one of them has the words *who murdered anastasia* inscribed on its girdle, even the large pink stone. Someone sure wanted to make a statement.'

'This is… unbelievable,' Alicia said.

'What's going on, Alicia?' Tobias asked. 'It's just so strange.'

'I'd love to be able to tell you Tobias. I've a few strange things happening at my end too, but it looks as though the imitation necklace delivered by your Vivienne Karlsson is a message directly for me. I'm the only person those words mean anything to.'

'I'm glad they make sense to someone,' Tobias replied. 'What d'you want me to do? As reluctant as I am about this, I'm going to have to get the police involved. It's fraud. If someone's passing off moissanite stones as diamonds and getting away with it, they need to be stopped.'

'I hear what you're saying and believe me, I couldn't agree more, but are you aware of any other recent incidents similar to this in your line of business Tobias? Have any of your fellow traders encountered Vivienne Karlsson?'

'No and no. Not to my knowledge anyway.'

'Which adds even more weight to the argument that she's not out to fleece every jeweller in Hatton Garden. She's targeted one store with apparently one purpose in mind. The words *who murdered anastasia* are very specific. I've been wondering why on earth someone might be trying to get my attention. Now I think I have an answer. But I need to ask a favour of you Tobias.'

'Sure, what d'you need?'

'Can you hold off any police involvement until I've completed a few investigations of my own?'

Tobias paused. He liked and respected Alicia. With Spencer's help, she'd saved his business once before, with a much lesser amount of money involved. He knew he should trust her again.

'How much time d'you need?' he asked. 'I should speak to the police sooner rather than later.'

'Give me two weeks,' Alicia replied. 'I can't promise anything, but I'm flying to Antigua tomorrow to try and pick up the trail from twenty-three years ago. It's not going to be easy unless Vivienne, or whoever is pulling the strings here, gives me a bit more to go on. Someone, somewhere knows something about the stolen necklace and Anastasia's murder. They must be linked. How much this person knows is another matter. I've no idea who your customer, Vivienne Karlsson, really is or how she's involved, but one thing I do know: you won't be seeing her again. Her job's done. She's captured my interest.'

'I can give you two weeks,' Tobias agreed. 'What about the gems?'

'Keep them somewhere secure. In case we need them.'

'That's no problem.'

'Incidentally, how much is your imitation diamond necklace actually worth?' Alicia asked suddenly. 'It's not totally valueless is it?'

'The stones are worth about four million pounds. And I'd say that's a generous estimate.' Spencer saw the pain in Tobias's face as he answered the question.

'Ah,' Alicia said after a pause. 'So just to be clear, a necklace which was claimed to be worth seventeen point five million pounds and was sold for eight million, is actually worth…'

'Exactly,' Tobias said with a heavy sigh. 'And the nightmare's only just begun. I'll head to the bank as soon as I can, but I don't know how I'll recover from this one. I think I'm finished.'

'I'm so sorry,' Alicia said. 'Spencer, help Tobias in any way you can. Go through everything you remember about Vivienne Karlsson's visits to the store. *Everything*. What have you missed? Is there anything she might have said? The way she said it? What perfume was she wearing? You know, the usual things most people overlook.'

'I'll try,' Spencer replied.

'And one last thing Tobias. Your two most qualified gemologists realised they'd made a terrible mistake, when?'

Tobias paused.

'This is where it really doesn't make sense,' he began hesitantly. 'They only noticed when I told them.'

'*What?*' Alicia asked in disbelief. 'So they had absolutely no idea that the stones in that necklace weren't real diamonds?'

'No,' Tobias said helplessly. 'And even when I pointed it out and had them examine the stones themselves, they still took some convincing. It was just… I can't explain it. When you consider all their experience in the trade, it's as if they were completely blind to the fact that the gems in front of them weren't diamonds at all.'

'Perhaps they *were* blind to that,' Alicia replied slowly. 'Perhaps that's exactly how Vivienne Karlsson executed her perfect crime.'

TWENTY-FOUR

Alicia's second telephone conversation of the morning was with Sandra at Tropical Destinations, a travel company with offices in London and Cheltenham. Alicia read out the confirmation number from the travel documents which had been delivered to her mailbox the previous evening. Within a few seconds, Sandra had the booking displayed on the screen in front of her.

'Can I confirm your name please?' she asked in a crisp, businesslike voice.

'Alicia Clayton.'

'Is that Miss or Mrs?'

'Miss.'

'Thank you. How can I help you today Miss Clayton?'

'I just want to confirm who made this booking.'

'Well — *you* did, Miss Clayton,' Sandra replied after a small pause. 'I managed the booking myself. We spoke on the telephone a couple of days ago.'

'Excuse me?' Alicia asked in shock.

'I believe it was… yes, you called on Tuesday morning. I booked everything for you over the phone, there and then. You completed a bank transfer for the full amount immediately after I confirmed your booking as the holiday was at such short notice.'

'I did?' Alicia asked. This was almost comical.

'Of course.' There was a hint of confusion in Sandra's efficient tone. 'You were most insistent that you and Mr Sharkey stayed at The West Beach Club. If you remember Miss Clayton, you were in luck as the resort had just taken a last minute cancellation for one of their beachfront villas.'

'And the bank transfer went through just fine?'

'Just fine.'

Of course it had. But the money hadn't come from Alicia's own bank account, which she had checked online prior to the call.

There had been no unauthorised transactions. The transfer had been from another account. Someone else had paid for the flights and accommodation.

'And… our passport numbers and contact details…'

'Are all in order.'

How did they…

'And I — I just gave them to you? Just like that?'

'Yes, of course. Is there a problem with the booking Miss Clayton?'

There's a serious problem, Sandra. Where do I start?

'No, no, everything's fine. Thank you. I'm so sorry, I'm really not making much sense. This may sound terribly… confused…'

'Not at all, Miss Clayton.'

You're convincing nobody, Sandra.

'Just one more question. Are you familiar with the name Omar Prestlock?'

'I don't think so, no. Is there anything else I can assist you with this morning Miss Clayton?'

I only wish there was, Sandra.

'No thank you, you've been most helpful.'

'Thank you Miss Clayton. You have a wonderful holiday and if I can be of any further assistance in the meantime, please don't hesitate to call.'

'I won't. Thank you. Goodbye.'

'Goodbye.'

The third telephone conversation was with Gray.

'I've spoken to Finn and he's happy to man the fort for the next two weeks,' he spoke hurriedly, 'so I can come with you on your magical mystery tour to Antigua.'

'Oh Gray, that's good news. Thank you. And thank Finn.'

'I will. We're incredibly busy right now and I really should be here for the delivery of the Gulfstream, but I'm just not happy about you going alone. And I'm even less thrilled with the idea of you going with Spencer. Did you call the travel company by the way?'

'Yeah, I just got off the phone to them.'

'And?'

'Apparently *I* booked the flights and made the hotel reservation on Tuesday morning.'

'*Did* you?'

'No! Of course not, Gray. I left my parents' home at nine that morning and was in Shoreditch by quarter to ten where I interviewed a property developer and was shown around a building site in east London. Like I had all morning to be on the phone booking a last minute vacation!'

'Then who did? What about this Omar Prestlock guy? Did you ask the travel company about him?'

'They'd never heard of him.'

'What's going on Alicia? I really don't like the sound of this. What's the hotel like where we're staying? It's not some dive of a place, is it? Oh, just a minute. Yeah, Finn, what time did the flight engineer say he could make it?'

Alicia waited as Gray briefly broke off to speak with his second-in-command.

'He's here *now*? I'd better join you, I need to speak to him myself. Okay great, give me two seconds.' He returned to the conversation with Alicia. 'Listen, I've got to go. We'll talk later and I'll meet you at the airport tomorrow morning. Send me those flight details when you've got a moment.'

'I'll do it now Gray. Thanks for dropping everything at such short notice. See you tomorrow.'

He hung up before she'd finished the sentence. She took snapshots of the travel documents and sent them to him. She'd have plenty of time to fill him in with the emerging details of the reason for the trip during the eight hour flight to Antigua. In the meantime, there were preparations to be made. In other circumstances, the task of packing for a Caribbean getaway with Gray would have been an exciting one. This time however, as she placed an assortment of clothes into her suitcase, she felt a sense of apprehension about what lay ahead. The words *who murdered anastasia* drifted in and out of her thoughts as she slid the Antigua guidebook, the Rock Palm brochure and a couple of maps of the island into her hand luggage, along with her wallet, passport and the travel documents.

Who. Murdered. Anastasia.

The message was straightforward enough. What was not clear was how the unsolved murder of a young woman in nineteen ninety-five was connected to the mysterious appearance of a counterfeit diamond necklace twenty-three years later, a necklace which exactly matched the description of one made of genuine diamonds, allegedly stolen on the same night of Anastasia's death. In addition, who was the man Alicia had observed at Mullrose Grill and South Kensington station and why was he watching her? Was he Omar Prestlock? And who was Vivienne Karlsson? They were linked in some way to both the present and the past, but how? Who had impersonated Alicia and booked the trip to Antigua? And, alarmingly, how had the woman in question acquired Alicia and Gray's personal information? Who was "the puppet master"? Was it Vivienne or Omar, or was there a third person pulling the strings? The answers to the questions both troubled and intrigued Alicia. She was in the process of retrieving an assortment of American dollars from a small emergency stash she kept in her apartment when her cell phone rang. It was Tobias.

'Alicia, I've just got back from the bank.'

'Oh, Tobias. How did it go?' She spoke cautiously, fearing the worst.

'You won't believe this.' He sounded slightly dazed. 'I — I just don't know what to think. I don't understand what's going on anymore.'

'What d'you mean?'

'I got to the bank soon after they opened and spoke to Richard, a senior account manager. He's a good guy, I know him well. Anyway, my business account records showed that yesterday eight million pounds was transferred to an account in Jersey, as authorised by Ronan and Camilla. One of Richard's colleagues dealt with the transaction. The account to which the funds were transferred was held by a shell company called Prestlock Holdings.'

198

'Stop,' Alicia said suddenly. 'Prestlock Holdings?'

'Yes.'

'Have you ever heard the name Omar Prestlock?'

'No. Don't think so. Not that I remember anyway. I can check my customer and supplier records if you like?'

'Thanks. I'd appreciate it. Is there any way the bank can trace the Prestlock Holdings account?'

'No. Richard spoke to a contact at the bank in Jersey. I suppose really this information is confidential, but his contact confirmed that within an hour of the money landing in the account, all eight million was withdrawn and wired to an account in Bermuda. The Jersey account was then closed.'

'Oh no. Can the money be traced?'

'Again, that's a no. The bank in Bermuda won't disclose any information on the transaction or the account, which they are legally entitled to do.'

'I'm so sorry.'

'But that's not the end of the story.' Tobias suddenly sounded strangely upbeat for a man about to face financial ruin. 'There was one other transaction made. Late last night, just before close of business.'

'You've had even *more* funds transferred from your account?' Alicia asked in horror.

'Not *from*! *To*!'

'I don't understand.'

'Last night, eight million pounds exactly was mysteriously transferred from an account in the Cayman Islands to my business account.'

'What?'

'I couldn't believe it either. I've got hard copies of the account statement; the money's all there.'

'But… the account in the Caymans…'

'Was held by guess which company? Prestlock Holdings!'

'Same shell company. Who are they? And why would they do that? Why sell you a bunch of fake diamonds, passing them off as real ones, taking your money, and then refunding the whole lot the very next day?'

'Search me,' Tobias replied. 'To be honest, I'm just happy to have it back.'

'And you're sure it's legit? The transaction I mean?'

'Totally and utterly. The money's there. Richard's been through it with me. He's slightly bemused by it all actually, but he's only really concerned with the numbers at the end of the day. As am I. The eight million is in my account, although who knows where it's been in the last forty-eight hours. Halfway round the world and back, I suspect. But I'm no longer facing financial ruin and, incidentally, the Prestlock Holdings account in the Caymans has since been closed.'

'And is untraceable? There's a surprise. I'm very pleased for you, Tobias. That's a huge relief.'

'You can say that again. There's just one thing though Alicia, and perhaps you can help with this one: what am I supposed to do with the necklace? I mean, technically, the money's been refunded to my account, and if there's something shady behind the gemstones, I really don't want to be responsible for them. Don't even want them on my property.'

'Is it possible for you to hold on to them for now?' Alicia asked. 'Just very quietly keep them locked at the back of a safe somewhere?'

'I suppose so,' Tobias said uneasily. 'We agreed two weeks though, right?'

'Two weeks,' Alicia confirmed, although in her heart she had no idea how she would uncover the mystery of a murder and a diamond theft — cold cases which had apparently evaded all attempts of being solved for twenty-three years — in the space of two weeks.

They exchanged promises to stay in touch and said goodbye. Alicia pulled her laptop towards her and keyed the words "Prestlock Holdings" into a search box. The results revealed a handful of companies with related names. She quickly scanned the information available on each, but, according to their websites, most were legitimate businesses doing honest trade. There was nothing out of the ordinary. None appeared to be likely candidates for a shell company shrouded in secrecy with potential money laundering operations. In any case, she doubted that the information she sought would be readily available online.

With equal levels of doubt, she looked up the name "Omar R. Prestlock". As she'd suspected, nothing immediately sprang out as a possible lead. She was no further forward in ascertaining who Omar Prestlock was or how he was involved. As an afterthought, she typed in "Vivienne Karlsson". Aside from a few Facebook profiles, none of which remotely resembled the Vivienne Karlsson who had walked into Tobias Moncler Jewels four days previously, she drew another blank. It was frustrating. There was so little to go on. Four thousand miles away, a murder remained unsolved, the body unaccounted for, and the replica of a diamond necklace once reported stolen lay in pieces on the desk of a Hatton Garden jeweller. They had to be related, but how? The puppet master had orchestrated the travel arrangements to Antigua on Alicia's behalf. Someone wanted her back where it had all began, on the distant shores of a Caribbean island.

TWENTY-FIVE

2:00 pm, Friday, August 24
V. C. Bird International Airport, Antigua

The Virgin Atlantic airliner touched down on the runway of V. C. Bird International Airport and taxied to the gate. The Captain wished everyone a pleasant stay and instructed the flight attendants to set the aircraft doors to manual. As the airbridge was manoeuvred into position, Graymond and Alicia prepared to disembark with the other passengers. The airport was busy, but they cleared passport control and customs and collected their baggage from the carousel in good time. As they made their way towards the exit, a line of holiday representatives held signs of various shapes and sizes declaring the names of passengers for whom transfers had been arranged.

'How are we getting to our resort?' Gray asked, attempting to extract his sunglasses from his backpack.

'I think the answer to that question is over there,' Alicia replied, pointing to a young man holding a square of laminated white card with the names Mr Graymond Sharkey and Miss Alicia Clayton printed in large letters. Gray and Alicia introduced themselves to the man who shook their hands enthusiastically, welcomed them to Antigua and informed them his name was Revaldo. Taking Alicia's case from her, he ushered them outside to where two lines of minivans and taxis straddled a covered pavement area. Some of the vehicles were operated privately; others by a variety of tourism companies. Holiday representatives and airport officials with files and clipboards rallied around the latest influx of tourists, directing them with interminable amounts of professionalism and patience.

In the absence of a breeze, the heat of the mid-afternoon sun, still high in the cloudless sky, was warm, enveloping and humid. The hot air rising from the baked tarmac shimmered in a heat haze as it met the cooler air above. Behind them, a small twin-engine turboprop aircraft took off from the runway on the other side of the terminal. Revaldo led Gray and Alicia to a blue Ford Explorer with darkly tinted windows. While he loaded their cases into the trunk of the SUV, a young woman called Maribell checked their paperwork before ushering them into the backseat of the Explorer. She wished them a pleasant holiday and shut the door as Revaldo jumped into the driver's seat. He turned to his passengers with a wide grin and handed them two bottles of water.

'How are you guys doing today?' he asked with a lilting Antiguan accent. 'Did you have a good flight from London?'

'Very good thanks,' Gray replied, taking the water and passing one of the bottles to Alicia.

'I've never been to London,' Revaldo continued. 'I'd like to go one day, but everyone tell me it's cold there.'

'It can get very cold,' Alicia replied. 'Right now it's pretty warm though.'

'Your first time in Antigua?' Revaldo asked, as if from a well-worn script.

'It's a first for me,' Gray replied. 'Alicia's been…' he glanced across at her and she held up five fingers on both hands, 'a few times.'

After more jovial comments from Revaldo about snow, ice and cold weather, he started the engine of the Explorer with a roar and tapped enthusiastically on the screen of his cell phone before placing it in a cradle attached to the dash. He shifted the automatic transmission into drive and pulled smoothly away from the curb, hooting at a small group of tourists who had wandered off the pavement. As they left the airport road and joined the highway, Revaldo chattered cheerfully, offering an abundance of information and advice to his passengers on everything from the best beaches in Antigua — one for each day of the year — to the best restaurants and bars on the island, to a potted history of Nelson's Dockyard and English Harbour.

Gray responded with interest at appropriate intervals while Alicia sat in silence, gazing out of the window at the lush, gently undulating terrain. The last time she had travelled these roads was as a fifteen year old girl with her parents. Having visited the island on numerous occasions over successive years however, the journey south from the airport was a familiar one and, in spite of twenty-three years and a number of hurricanes and tropical storms, little had changed. Distant memories of the past, forgotten over time, came flooding back to her as Revaldo drove. The route began to take them further inland and the occasional glimpses of the deep blue Atlantic ocean on the eastern side of the island became less.

As they travelled through a more densely populated area, one-storey houses and low-rise buildings constructed from wooden boards in bright colours of orange, yellow and turquoise clambered on top of each other. A tangle of cables — phone and electrical wires — on wooden poles, criss-crossed the streets. Locals sat on balustraded verandahs watching the world go by. Stray dogs scavenged for food and small groups of children in uniform chattered excitedly on their way home from school.

Alicia turned her gaze away from the window and leaned towards Revaldo who had just finished telling Gray about Cades Reef, a partially exposed coral reef off the south-west corner of the island which was popular for sailing and snorkelling.

'Revaldo, do you remember a hotel called Rock Palm Resort?' she asked.

'Rock Palm?' Revaldo tilted his eyes into the rear view mirror as he deftly navigated a pothole. 'Sure I do. Used to be the best on the island, back in the nineties. The place was devastated by Hurricane Luis in ninety-five though. The owners had some sort of falling out with planning officials and nothing's been done since. Sad to see a place like that go to ruin.'

'D'you remember anything about a murder there?' Alicia asked.

'Yeah, there was. I remember my mom tellin' me about that.'

It was clear that if he knew any further details, they would not be forthcoming.

'What's Rock Palm like now?' Alicia changed tack.

'Saddest thing you ever saw. All broken down and overgrown. The beach there is still one of the best on the island though and it's usually deserted. There's great snorkelling around the reef and a place just off the beach that serves some of the best food on the island.'

Returning to the subject of food, Revaldo was off again on another well-rehearsed spiel of highly recommended eateries in Antigua. Gray continued the conversation while Alicia returned her gaze to the passing scenery. The meandering route followed the sun to the west. The wooden houses and shanties were slowly replaced by rainforest-covered hills, tall palm trees, and thick foliage and lush vegetation.

Finally the road began an unhurried descent towards the coast and Gray and Alicia caught a glimpse of the glittering turquoise sea. Revaldo took a right turn and a large white sign welcomed them to the exclusive West Beach Club. Past a gatehouse, where Revaldo held a brief, animated conversation with the guard, and through gently sloping landscaped gardens brimming with an oasis of fruit trees and tropical plants, the sweeping drive led to an elegant property. The West Beach Club was a stylish resort with an abundance of wood, white stucco and marble. A neat, wooden-tiled roof extended over a wide archway, which led through to a spacious, open-plan reception area. Revaldo slowed to a halt outside the entrance and jumped out of the Explorer. He jogged around to Alicia's side where he opened the door, before moving to the rear of the SUV. A porter in a tan shirt and matching chinos stepped forward with a luggage trolley. Revaldo popped the trunk and pulled out the two suitcases, thanking Gray for the generous tip and wishing them a pleasant vacation.

'Welcome to The West Beach Club,' the porter said with a smile, lifting the cases onto the luggage trolley. 'If you'd like to…'

'Miss Alicia Clayton! Welcome home!' A voice from the reception area suddenly interrupted them. A man, smartly dressed in a white, short-sleeved shirt and light green trousers hurried out towards them. He looked to be in his early sixties, but was bright-eyed and brimming with energy and enthusiasm. His short, cropped hair was slightly greying at his temples and his athletic physique was toned and muscular.

'So good to see you Miss Clayton!' he said, opening his arms wide and embracing Alicia with a bear hug. 'You're looking as stunning as ever! How are you? Did you have a good flight?'

'Leon! It's good to see you too!' Alicia hugged him back. 'You're looking well. And please call me Alicia.' She gestured to Gray who stood a little way behind her. 'Leon, this is Gray, and Gray, this is Leon Fayer, GM of this resort, which I must say, Leon, is very impressive.'

Gray stepped forward and waited for Leon to extricate himself from Alicia's embrace before shaking his hand warmly.

'Good to meet you Leon.'

In a flurry of pleasantries and excited repartee, Leon ushered Gray and Alicia into the reception area. Under a vaulted wooden ceiling from which hung large, rotating fans, comfortable sofas with bright turquoise cushions were casually positioned around glass-topped tables on driftwood bases, adding a sophisticated, contemporary elegance to the colonial charm of the place.

'I worked it out this morning,' Leon said as he gestured to Alicia and Gray to take a seat on one of the sofas, 'it's twenty-three years to the month that we last saw each other. You would have been, what, sixteen? Seventeen?'

'I was fifteen, actually Leon,' Alicia said with a grin, accepting a hot face towel and a rum punch cocktail from a member of the hotel staff.

'Fifteen! So young! And look at you now!' Leon sat on the sofa opposite. 'How are your parents? Are they well?'

'They're very well thanks Leon. They send their best regards to you.'

'Oh, please send mine back to them. When are they coming to stay at The West Beach Club? There'll always be a very warm welcome for them. You're like family to me.'

'I'll pass that along,' Alicia replied. A receptionist briefly interrupted them with a guest welcome form to complete.

'I'll take care of that,' Gray said, taking the clipboard and a pen from her.

'Thanks Gray,' Alicia said. She turned back to Leon.

'I must say I wasn't expecting this welcome from you,' she said. 'It's a lovely surprise!'

'But I've been looking forward to your arrival all afternoon,' Leon beamed. 'Alicia, we're old friends. We go back a long, long way. When Kaleisha, one of our receptionists, gave me your message to let me know you were coming...'

'Wait Leon.' Alicia stopped him. '*My* message?'

'Yes, Kaleisha said you called last night. You told her you were a regular guest at Rock Palm from years ago and weren't sure if I'd remember you, but of course I...'

'No, Leon, stop,' Alicia said. The smile had vanished from her face. 'I didn't call ahead with any message. It wasn't me.'

'Oh?' A look of surprise came over Leon's face. 'But Kaleisha definitely said...'

Alicia had planned a number of conversations that she might have with Leon on their arrival. This wasn't one of them. Leon was obviously unaware of the circumstances surrounding her visit to The West Beach Club. She glanced across at Gray who was busy completing the welcome form. She decided to be candid about the reason for the trip.

'To be honest Leon, a few days ago, I didn't even know I was coming here.'

'Well, I saw your last minute booking,' Leon said. 'And thankfully, we had a cancellation right out of the blue so it was all very convenient.'

'You can say that again. But — and I know this sounds bizarre — I didn't even make the booking. It was made on my behalf, anonymously.'

'A surprise vacation?' Leon asked, nodding at Gray with a wink.

'A surprise, but not from Gray.'

'Are you sure?'

'I'm certain.' Alicia glanced around the reception area. Aside from a young couple in beach coverups talking to a receptionist, the place was deserted. She leaned forward slightly and lowered her voice.

'Leon, what I'm about to tell you should probably go no further for now.'

207

'Of course,' Leon replied with a puzzled frown.

A member of staff returned with three fresh rum punches. Alicia waited for the empty glasses and hot towels to be cleared away before she continued.

'Leon, do the words *who murdered Anastasia* mean anything to you?'

Leon hesitated before replying. He pulled a white handkerchief out of his pocket and dabbed his forehead.

'Yes, they do,' he said quietly. 'That's a long time ago Alicia. The distant past. Why do you ask?'

'It is a long time ago. Twenty-three years. Almost to the day. What do you remember from that time?'

'It was at Rock Palm. The night before Hurricane Luis struck the island back in ninety-five. One of the guests found her body — Anastasia's body — stabbed to death on the beach.'

'Go on.'

'She was one of Mallory's — the magician's — assistants. I was with a couple of other guests at the time her body was discovered, but I was one of the first on the scene, with Owen — he was the manager of the sports reception, if you recall — and soon afterwards a few other members of staff, along with the guest who found the body. It was chaos that morning with the evacuation of all the guests from the hotel and the staff boarding up the property, preparing for the hurricane as best they could. And then the body was discovered.'

Leon suddenly looked straight at Alicia.

'You know, don't you? Because you were there, on the beach that morning. I remember now.'

'What?' Alicia asked, shocked.

'As we reached the body, I saw you there, standing over it. When you realised we were close, you disappeared into the foliage, back towards the hotel. I saw you standing under a palm tree, watching us. I've never said anything to anyone. Until now.'

'Leon, I had no idea I'd been seen,' Alicia said, flushing a deep shade of pink. 'I never… I was being inquisitive… I was…'

'I gathered,' Leon said with a faint smile. 'Don't worry, your secret's safe with me. It's been a secret for over twenty years and will remain that way. There were so many footprints around the body by the time the police arrived, there was little point trying to identify any of them. The police did the best they could with the forensics but it was a hopeless task; the wind was getting up and once the rain began falling, every shred of evidence they might've hoped to find was washed away. But that was the least of their worries. Did you know the medical examiner and his assistant never made it to the hospital mortuary with the body?'

'Yeah, I heard that. What happened?'

'Nobody knows.'

'The ME's van and its occupants were never found?'

'No.' Leon shook his head. 'To this day we don't know what became of that van. The police searched all over for it, but their efforts were obviously hampered in the aftermath of the hurricane. We were hit hard, Alicia. I've lived here my entire life; it was one of the worst storms I remember. Of course we bounced back, Antiguans always do. We're resilient, but it took time.'

'I'm so sorry Leon.'

'And you know, they never found Anastasia's killer,' Leon went on.

'Were there any suspects?' Alicia asked hesitantly.

'Sure, but they'd got it all wrong, and they knew it, which is why they never charged anybody.'

'Who was the main suspect?' Alicia already knew the answer to her question.

'Owen. Owen Rapley. But it wasn't him.'

'And you know this how, Leon?'

'The evidence didn't add up. He might have been in the wrong place at the wrong time, but it wasn't him.'

Not the most convincing argument, Alicia thought to herself.

'Were there any other suspects?'

'Can't remember now,' Leon shook his head slowly, 'Owen didn't do it though, I can tell you that for certain. But I'm curious about your interest in all this Alicia…'

'Actually, so am I Leon,' Alicia replied. 'It's a long story, which I'll tell you later. I'm not sure what to make of it myself. I'm a freelance investigative journalist and someone — I've no idea who — has... *appointed* me to look into Anastasia's murder.'

'After all this time? But why?'

'I don't know Leon. I only wish I did. I haven't got much to go on, and if the police didn't manage to solve the murder at the time, I'm not exactly brimming with confidence about my chances of success either.'

'You said you didn't know who'd booked this vacation for you here at The West Beach...'

'The flights and hotel reservation were made by a UK travel agency called Tropical Destinations, but the person who made the booking with the company impersonated me,' Alicia replied. 'It's a little unnerving; someone had my personal details — and Gray's — at their fingertips to secure the booking. Dates of birth, middle names, passport numbers and so on.'

'That is very worrying,' Leon said with a look of concern. 'Rest assured, Alicia, my team and I take the safety and security and privacy of our guests very seriously. No harm will come to you.'

'Thanks Leon.'

'But do you believe that the person who booked your stay here is the same person who wants you to investigate the murder?'

'That's a fairly safe bet, yes. Leon, the subject of Anastasia's murder hasn't come up recently for any other reason, has it? You haven't been asked anything about it or heard anyone mention it?'

'Not at all,' Leon replied firmly. 'You're the first to speak of it for a very long time.'

'You haven't even been reminded of it, perhaps by something seemingly unrelated?'

The handkerchief was retrieved from his pocket as Leon considered the question and patted his brow.

'Not that I can think of, but I'll give it some thought. It was such a long time ago.'

'I know. Which is what makes this so hard. I could really do with speaking to some of the staff who worked at Rock Palm at the time. Can you put me in touch with any of them?'

'Yes, I can help with that, certainly,' Leon nodded eagerly. 'As a matter of fact, Violet and Roslyn work here as maître d'hotels; I recruited them myself. Do you remember them?'

'I do. Very well.'

'Violet will be on duty at breakfast tomorrow morning so you'll be able to talk to her then. Roslyn's working tomorrow night so I'll ask her to speak with you at dinner. I'm not sure how much help they'll be to you though. We were all questioned at the time, obviously, but none of us knew anything useful or relevant.'

'That's understood. But I need to start somewhere.'

'Of course.'

'And what about any of the other staff?'

'Let's see. Eddy — remember him? He works at a large resort in the north of the island and Henroy is based at a boutique hotel on the west coast. I can put you in touch with both of them while you're here. They were the staff who came with me onto the beach and were directly involved with the events immediately after the body was discovered.'

'And what about Owen Rapley? Do you know where I might find him?'

'Somewhere on the streets of St. John's at a guess,' Leon replied. A sad expression came into his eyes. 'It should never have been. He was full of youth and talent. And he was in l...' Leon stopped himself suddenly.

'He was what?' Alicia asked, watching him closely.

'Nothing. He was an incredible tennis player.' Leon hastily corrected himself.

A memory slid into Alicia's mind. The memory of a starlit night and a young couple walking hand in hand on the path to the beach.

'He was in *love* with her, wasn't he?' she said.

Leon looked down and then back up at Alicia.

'Yes. He was. And she was in love with him,' he said with a sigh.

'But...' Another memory: Owen's own words. *It could be her. I don't know her personally I'm afraid.*

'If he was in love with her, why did he deny even knowing her after she was murdered?'

'That's exactly what the police wanted to know,' Leon replied, 'and sadly, it was this lie which ultimately led to his demise. Oh I understand why he did it; he was one of the last to see her alive. He feared he'd have instantly been at the top of the list of prime suspects if he admitted to walking on the beach with her in the early hours of the morning. Only a few of us knew about Owen and Anastasia back then. He thought he could get away with the lie. The shock of seeing her body on the beach like that, covered in blood, lifeless, I can't imagine what went through his mind at that moment. I think he panicked. And said the first thing he could think of to protect himself: he denied knowing her. Even I couldn't believe what I was hearing, but of course I couldn't say anything. How did you know about the two of them, Alicia?'

'I saw them together on the beach the night Anastasia was murdered.'

'*You* saw them? *You* were on the beach too?'

'Yes, so I guess I was also one of the last to see Anastasia alive.'

'Did you ever speak to the police?'

'No. We'd already left for the airport before the police arrived. But I understand a couple of guests *did* get their witness statements in before they were evacuated?'

'Yes, they did, sadly. And it was these which led the police to bring Owen in for questioning, plunging him into his never-ending bête noire. You've been researching Alicia, I can tell.'

'Oh not really,' Alicia replied, shaking her head. 'I had dinner with Carlos Jaxen a couple of nights ago — he's on an extended business trip in London, as you probably know — he told me what he could remember from that time, but with Sophia's death and his unsuccessful efforts to restore Rock Palm, it wasn't easy for him. He gave me your number and I was planning to contact you, little knowing that I would actually see you again so soon.'

'It's funny how fate takes us on these unexpected journeys sometimes,' Leon said with a sudden smile. 'How is Carlos? We keep in touch but it's a while since I've seen him. So sad to hear of Sophia's death last year. I believe that was the last time we spoke.'

'He's doing okay. But I think his hopes and dreams for rebuilding Rock Palm have finally unravelled.'

'I guess no one can blame him for giving up the fight.'

'The couple you were talking to on the morning Anastasia's body was discovered,' Alicia said suddenly. 'Do you remember who they were?'

It was another question to which Alicia was fully aware of the answer, but she wanted to hear it from Leon.

'Yes, I do,' he replied. In spite of the lapse of time, his memory of the events that took place seemed to be relatively fresh and untainted. Alicia guessed he'd been through the details many times in his mind over the years. When a symphony remains unfinished and the final chapter of a story never written, the human mind has a habit of revisiting the door that is never fully closed.

'Charles and Vivienne Karleman,' Leon said. His face remained emotionless. 'Do you remember them?'

'Yes, I do. I remember you were talking to them the night before we were evacuated and then again, the next morning. You were in the restaurant...'

'The discussion was about a diamond necklace. Vivienne's necklace.'

'I remember her wearing it.'

'The night before everyone left Rock Palm, Vivienne Karleman came to me with her husband, Charles, claiming — no, *insisting* — that her diamond necklace had been stolen.'

'*Had* it?'

Leon shrugged.

'Like many things about that night, to this day I've no idea. She was emphatic that one of my staff had stolen the necklace from the hotel safe. Back then the guest rooms didn't have their own safe as they do now. If guests had a particularly valuable item that they wanted kept securely during their vacation, like an expensive piece of jewellery, it would be locked in the safe in the office just behind the reception area. Everything was logged by the duty receptionist, and signed in and out of the safe. The named guest would also countersign.'

'And the necklace?'

'Was worn by Mrs Karleman during lunch on the day before she left Rock Palm. It was signed back into the safe by herself and the duty receptionist later that afternoon. She signed another much less valuable necklace out to wear for dinner that evening.'

'And?'

'And that's it. There were no further entries in the log. When Mrs Karleman went to retrieve the diamond necklace and the remaining items of her jewellery from the safe later that evening, the necklace wasn't there.'

'Wasn't in the safe?'

'No.'

'And the rest of the jewellery?'

'All present and correct.'

'So what'd happened to the diamond necklace?'

'One can only assume it *was* signed out to her at some point and the receptionist accidentally forgot to record it. The thing was, Alicia, Vivienne Karleman was forever signing her jewellery in and out. She became an absolute nightmare for the receptionists. Often four or five times a day she'd be back and forth exchanging one item of jewellery for another. And she'd always demand to be served immediately, no matter how busy the reception team were. You can imagine how hectic things were for them the night before the hotel was evacuated; settling bills with guests, dealing with all sorts of queries about the hurricane, fielding calls from holiday reps and so on. I asked extra staff to come in for the late shift and then again the next morning, just to keep up with it all, which confused things even more when it came to Mrs Karleman's necklace. Nobody remembered signing it out, but it could quite easily have been overlooked when you consider everything else that was going on.

'It was the very last thing we needed though. As if I had any staff to spare to go looking for that necklace. After it was somehow "signed out" of the safe *without* being signed out, she must've lost it. It's the only explanation. But of course, it was never going to be *her* fault, was it? She blamed it all on my staff. Between you and me, Alicia, she was a piece of work. I don't think I've ever met such a spoiled, self-indulged woman in all my career, and I've met some characters, believe me.'

'There's absolutely no chance that the necklace *could* have been stolen then?'

'I'd say it's highly unlikely,' Leon said firmly. 'My staff were entirely trustworthy. There's no way any of them would have taken it.'

'One of the guests perhaps?'

'Not possible. The safe was locked with a combination known only to myself, Carlos and the reception team. Not that Carlos ever used it.'

'Was there any way a guest could've found out the code to the safe?'

'Well, no, because that would involve one of my staff revealing the code to the guest, which would never have happened.'

'Not even for an obscene amount of money?'

'No. I could trust my staff. All of them. I stand by that.'

'I believe you Leon. It's just, I need to be sure.'

'Of course. But I thought you were here to look into Anastasia's murder?'

'I am. And I've no doubt that your team were entirely trustworthy. They always took the greatest care of my parents and me. I remember Vivienne Karleman's necklace though. *Was* it made of real diamonds?'

'According to her it was and, judging by the fuss she made about it, I'm sure she was telling the truth. She was very fond of describing it: forty-eight flawless diamonds and a large pink diamond which was…'

'Forty-eight?' Alicia asked suddenly.

'I know. That's a lot of diamonds. Each stone was two carats or something, except for the…'

'You're sure forty-eight?'

'Yes.'

'Not forty-nine?'

'No. Definitely forty-eight. Even now, over twenty years later, I remember that because I always thought it was a bit of an odd number. You know, you'd *expect* there to be forty-nine, right? And the large pink diamond in the centre would be the fiftieth stone.

But Mrs Karleman was most insistent about the number of the smaller diamonds being forty-eight. And, of course, the details had to be accurate for our records.'

'Did you actually see the physical record for the necklace yourself?'

'Probably, at some point. I wouldn't be able to accurately recall it now, but I know what Mrs Karleman said to me. It was definitely forty-*eight* flawless diamonds, not forty-nine.'

'I guess the signing-out book for the guests' jewellery is long gone?' Alicia asked.

'I'd say so. I haven't seen it since the morning we evacuated.'

'And the necklace was never recovered?'

'No.' Leon shook his head. 'Not to my knowledge anyway. And I never did find out what happened to it, but things got so busy with all the guests leaving and the preparations being made for the hurricane, and Anastasia's body being found, of course. My attention was obviously directed to what was going on there. After that, I don't believe I spoke to the Karlemans at all before they left Rock Palm. I just assumed they found the necklace in the end but were too embarrassed to admit it and come and apologise to me after all the fuss that woman made. I expect that's what happened. They had so much luggage, they probably found it when they were packing.'

'Did you ever hear from them again?'

'Not a word. Which is what makes me think they found it, either before they left Rock Palm, or when they got home. To be honest, after Anastasia was found and Hurricane Luis devastated the island, the Karlemans and their necklace were the least of my concerns.'

There was a sudden flurry of activity at the entrance of the hotel as four new guests arrived. Porters began loading suitcases onto luggage trolleys as hotel staff greeted the latest arrivals with hot towels and rum punches.

'I'd better go and do my welcome spiel,' Leon said, getting up.

'Of course Leon. I've kept you for far too long.'

'Not at all, it's been my pleasure Alicia. I'm sure we'll have more time to reminisce about the good old days during your stay. Oh, before I go, it's the manager's cocktail party tonight before dinner. Six-thirty. You'll be there won't you?'

'Absolutely.'

'There'll be champagne and canapés and a steel band playing. Do you remember we used to dance by the pool to the steel band at Rock Palm?'

'With fondness!'

'That brings back happy memories.'

Alicia had a sudden thought.

'Leon, one last thing, have you ever heard of someone called Omar Prestlock?'

'Don't think so, no. Who is he?'

'A member of staff who worked at Rock Palm perhaps? A guest?'

'He's definitely not anyone from Rock Palm; I remember the name of every person I've ever worked with. He could've been a guest, I suppose.'

'No matter. Thanks for your time Leon.'

'Alicia, I have all the time for you. I always have done. I'll make arrangements for you to meet with the Rock Palm staff and if there's anything else you need just let me know. And I hope you have a chance to relax and make the most of your stay here at The West Beach Club as well.'

'I'm sure I will,' Alicia beamed. They hugged once more before Leon turned and made his way to the group of latest arrivals. Alicia glanced to where Gray had been sitting. He was nowhere to be seen.

TWENTY-SIX

By the time Alicia found him on the beach, Gray was reclining on a sun lounger in the shade of a palm tree. Far out to sea, the sun was beginning to dip below the horizon, the crests of the waves glinting in the hazy orange light. The lively chorus of early evening crickets and tree frogs could be heard, along with the faint drone of a jet ski further out in the bay.

'Get bored did you?' Alicia asked with a grin, perching on the edge of the sun lounger.

'I hope you don't mind,' Gray said, pulling himself upright, 'I thought I'd check out our villa and the beach and leave you two to reminisce. How did it go with Leon? Was he much help?'

'Not really,' Alicia replied. 'It was the same with Carlos, the owner of Rock Palm; they both have a lot of strong feelings about what happened back then, but nothing tangible to back them up with.'

'Such as?'

'Oh I don't know. They're both adamant that Owen Rapley is innocent of Anastasia's murder because he was in love with her, even though he's apparently the only obvious suspect and was one of the last people to see her that night. And then there's the missing diamond necklace. Leon is very insistent that none of his staff could have stolen it, yet I find it hard to believe that someone conveniently forgot to record a behemoth of a piece of jewellery like that being removed from the safe. It's all *feelings* and nothing concrete. There's barely any evidence at all to be honest, not even a body. I can't believe no one knows anything. Someone's been keeping a secret very carefully all these years.'

'Perhaps one of the other staff who worked at Rock Palm will be helpful.'

'I hope so. It's just that it's such a long time ago. Memories fade or become distorted. And as for any evidence from the crime scene, clearly that's long gone too.'

'How about we forget it all for tonight?' Gray suggested, reaching for her hand. 'It's been a tiring day. Let's just relax for a few hours and enjoy the evening. It's a pretty nice place here.' He glanced at the villa behind them, a little further up the beach. It was a compact wooden structure with a sloping tiled roof and patio doors spanning the entire front of the villa. 'Whoever booked this on your behalf certainly has taste when it comes to classy resorts.'

'Don't relax too much Gray, we've got work to do,' Alicia said tensely. 'We only have two weeks. We need to make every second count.'

'Yeah, I know that, and I'm here for you. Whatever you need. Whatever you want me to do.' He leaned forward and pulled her close, kissing the top of her forehead before whispering in her ear: 'but I hope we also have some time to forget why we're here. It's such a beautiful place. Let's take a tour of the island, explore, go sailing, snorkelling, rent a Jeep, have some fun.'

'We will Gray,' Alicia replied. She held his face in her hands. 'Thanks for coming with me. It means a lot to have you here.'

They held each other for a few moments before Gray pulled back gently.

'Why don't we go for a swim in the sea before dinner?'

'Did the porters deliver our cases yet?'

'Hours ago,' Gray laughed.

'I'll get changed. See you in a few minutes,' Alicia said, standing up.

As she made her way towards the villa behind them, she spotted a man raking the sand a little further along the beach. He glanced up and instantly looked away. Alicia smiled at him but he continued fervently raking the sand without acknowledging her. She shrugged and walked the final few steps to the villa.

Gray and Alicia woke early the following morning to a clear, bright day. The sun was already high in the cloudless sky and, as Gray opened the patio doors, the room was infused with the pleasant warmth of a gentle tropical breeze. It was a short stroll to the restaurant for breakfast. The cabin-style timber construction was surrounded by tropical gardens and overlooked the beach. Leon, armed with a leather-bound folder and dabbing his forehead with his handkerchief, broke off from a discussion with another staff member to welcome them. In a flurry of animated questions, he guided them to a table.

'How did you sleep? Is your villa comfortable? Do you have everything you need? I insist you let me know if there's anything I can do to make your stay here more enjoyable. I know you're familiar with the island, Alicia, but if I can recommend a few trips while you're here... That's if you've time, of course...'

'Thanks Leon. And yes, we're very happy with everything,' Alicia replied.

'I've informed Violet that you're here,' Leon went on as he turned their coffee mugs the right way up. 'She remembers you and your parents well Alicia. In fact, yes, she's on her way over with the coffee. I'll leave you with her, there's a party of six just arrived, I'd better go and say hello, they arrived yesterday as well.'

Leon hurried off to meet a group of six people who had just been seated. As he left Gray and Alicia, a member of the restaurant staff in a brightly coloured blouse and a smart beige skirt approached their table with a large cafetière balanced on a silver tray. She was in her early sixties with short, thick black hair. She smiled broadly.

'Miss Clayton! Welcome back to the island!' she said with a strong Antiguan accent. As she placed the cafetière on the table, Alicia pushed back her chair, stood up and threw her arms around the woman, hugging her tightly.

'Violet! It's so good to see you again!' she said excitedly. 'After all this time! And you haven't forgotten me.'

'Of course I haven't forgotten you,' Violet replied laughing, 'although you're a lot more grownup than when I last saw you. And didn't you used to wear spectacles? Don't think I would've recognised you if Leon hadn't told me you were here.'

'Well you haven't changed a bit Violet,' Alicia said, 'and yes, thankfully I don't wear those awful specs anymore.' She gestured towards Gray and introduced him. He stood up and more pleasantries were exchanged, with Violet complimenting Alicia on her choice of man and asking if they were planning a beach wedding any time soon.

'Not to my knowledge,' Alicia replied with a playful smile at Gray as they reseated themselves, 'but Violet, you'll be the first to know if we are.' Alicia's remark was received with more amused laughter.

'So what do you two have planned for today?' Violet asked. 'A little relaxing? Exploring the island?'

'I'm hoping to show Gray a bit of the island, but unfortunately this trip isn't exclusively a vacation,' Alicia replied.

'Leon tells me you're back in Antigua because you're looking into what happened at Rock Palm…' Violet was suddenly serious.

'Yes, I am.'

'Over twenty years ago now,' Violet said reverently. 'That's a long time.'

'Do you remember much about that morning Violet?'

Violet placed a hand on her hip and frowned in thought.

'Only the state of that poor girl they found on the beach. Terrible sight. Could never get it out of my mind. It's haunted me day and night.'

'I'm sorry to ask you about it now,' Alicia said gently.

'No, it's all right darlin'. Have they reopened the case or something?'

'Not exactly, no. I'm an investigative journalist now. I've been…' Alicia paused. 'I've been instructed to look into the case one more time.'

'Oh, have you?' Violet raised her eyebrows with interest. 'Well, good luck with it.'

'Do you think Owen Rapley was involved?' Alicia asked.

Violet's response was immediate: a firm shake of the head.

'No, they got that all wrong. I've known him since he was a kid. Went to school with his mom. He didn't have it in him to murder nobody. Tennis was his life. That's all he wanted to do. And the girl. He was in love with her. No way he murdered her.'

'Then who, Violet?' Alicia asked. 'Who else should I be looking at?'

'I don't know. It could've been someone off the beach or... I don't know. Too long ago now.'

An elderly couple stood waiting to be seated at the entrance to the restaurant.

'I'd better let you go,' Alicia said. 'If you remember anything from Rock Palm, anything at all...'

'I'll let you know,' Violet said, 'of course. And it's wonderful to have you back in Antigua, Miss Clayton. Help yourself to the buffet and enjoy your day.'

She bustled over to the latest arrivals and Alicia reached for the cafetière.

'Notice the recurring theme?' she asked Gray as she poured the coffee.

'Yeah. It doesn't matter who you speak to, your friend Carlos, Leon and now Violet, they're all adamant that Owen didn't do it.'

'But no one's got any idea of who else it could have been. Who were the other suspects?'

'Perhaps it really was just some drug-crazed maniac who happened to run into her on the beach and ended up stabbing her.'

'That's a bit far-fetched,' Alicia said, taking a sip of coffee. 'What was Anastasia doing down there alone? Especially as she'd already been for a walk with Owen — I saw them together myself — it's not like she was waiting to meet him or anything.'

'Perhaps she was waiting to meet someone else?' Gray suggested. 'Owen might've been in love with her but maybe it was one-sided. What was she really like? Maybe she was sleeping with half the male guests or resort staff. Perhaps one of them saw her with Owen that night and got jealous. Arranged to meet her afterwards and things got out of hand.'

'That's one theory...' Alicia glanced up as Leon approached their table.

'How's your breakfast so far? Oh you know the buffet's just over there,' he made a gesture with his hand. 'Help yourselves whenever you're ready. Alicia, did you catch up with Violet?'

'I did thanks Leon. Wonderful to see her again. It's like a big family reunion. One question comes to mind...'

'Yes?'

'Anastasia, the magician's assistant. What was she like?'

'An absolute darling,' Leon replied warmly, without hesitation. 'We all loved her. Such a sweet girl. It's tragic what happened, you know. She didn't deserve to die like that.'

'Do you think Owen's feelings for her were mutual?'

'For sure,' Leon nodded. 'Yes, Owen and Anastasia were dedicated to each other. There's no way she was involved with anyone else if that's what you're asking.'

'It is. And thanks Leon.'

'Of course. Any time.' He hurried off to chat with the guests on the next table, effortlessly working the room.

'You think they'll all tell us that?' Gray asked.

'I guess so,' Alicia replied. 'They're persuasive enough, but not entirely conclusive. You know, sometimes I think about the necklace that was brought into the jewellery store. Spencer's co-workers *wanted* to believe that the gemstones were real diamonds, and that's what they saw, despite being seasoned professionals. It's possible that in the case of Owen and Anastasia people only saw what they *wanted* to believe, a couple in love, a fairytale romance: he, a tennis pro, she a talented performer, a dancer and magician's assistant. Both young and attractive. You feel like you *want* everything to be perfect between them. You turn a blind eye to anything which doesn't fit with this flawless, idealistic image you have of them. And yet, in the cold light of day, does it really and truly fit with the facts?'

'You think Owen's guilty?'

'I don't think anything right now. Everything we've heard so far is hearsay though. Subjective opinions. Testimonials of faded, biased memories from over twenty years ago.'

'And I think that's all you're going to get. You've set yourself a nearly impossible task here. What concrete evidence have you got to work with?'

'I've got...' Alicia paused. 'Okay, I've got nothing. It's hopeless.'

'Except that someone seems to think otherwise,' Gray replied. 'Someone believes that there's sufficient evidence out there to uncover Anastasia's killer, whether it's Owen Rapley, a random stranger off the beach, or somebody else. Someone believes that enough to bring you back out here to conduct your own investigations.'

'But why *me*?' Alicia asked. 'Why send *me*? Why not hire a professional? Why not a private detective, who'd do a much better job? I'm a journalist. Solving murders isn't one of my specialities.'

'Somebody thinks otherwise,' Gray said, refilling their coffee mugs. 'Let's just follow the plan you've made for the next couple of days and see what happens.'

'Then what?'

'We'll work it out as we go along. And if you're successful...'

'But how will I know if I've been successful?' Alicia interrupted. 'This is ridiculous, Gray. I don't know how I ever thought I could do this. I'm sorry for dragging you all the way out here. It's a waste of time. Let's go home.'

'What and throw away an all-expenses-paid fortnight in a place like this? I don't think so!' Gray replied. 'And anyway, I'm just beginning to get myself into holiday mode. Alicia, I believe in you. If anyone can solve this, it's you. And you've got the greatest advantage over any private detective: you were there that night. Let's go visit the two former Rock Palm employees this morning. What were their names?'

'Eddy and Henroy.'

'Let's rent a Jeep and visit each of them at the resorts they work at. And this afternoon let's take a trip back to the place where it all happened. I've heard so much about Rock Palm Resort, I want to see it for myself.'

'All right then,' Alicia replied reluctantly, 'but I still think it's all pretty hopeless.'

'One day at a time Alicia,' Gray replied. 'Anyway, I'm starving. Let's get some breakfast.'

As Gray piled his plate with pancakes, bacon, eggs, sausages and a generous helping of tomato Ketchup, Alicia's plate resembled a more health-conscious approach to the most important meal of the day with yoghurt, fresh fruit and a blueberry muffin.

'You're disgusting,' she commented, raising one eyebrow at Gray as he balanced a chocolate croissant on the edge of his plate.

'I'm on holiday!' Gray protested.

'It's a *working* holiday; you've just set today's itinerary yourself.'

'If I'm supposed to be chauffeuring you around all day, I need the energy.'

'I'd have to go and lie down for the rest of the morning if I ate all that.' Alicia broke off as she caught the eye of one of the groundsmen in the gardens in front of the restaurant. She smiled as she recognised him; he was the man who'd been raking the sand the night before. He glanced away without acknowledging her smile. Probably shy, she thought to herself as she returned to their table where Gray was attacking the stack of pancakes on his plate.

'I've ordered more coffee, by the way,' he said as Alicia joined him. 'It's a working holiday. We need the caffeine.'

TWENTY-SEVEN

The first destination of the morning was a sprawling one-storey beach resort in the north of Antigua where Eddy, a former employee of Rock Palm Resort, worked as a waiter. Gray drove their rental vehicle, a convertible Jeep Wrangler with a sun-damaged roof stretched across the roll-bar, barely connecting to the snaps which held it in place. Alicia gave directions while Gray navigated potholes in the road and avoided oncoming traffic.

Leon had called ahead and Eddy was expecting them, having just completed the breakfast shift. He remembered Alicia as the teenager with the spectacles on vacation with her parents and was happy to answer her questions. His recollections of the events surrounding Anastasia's death could have been copied and pasted from the same textbook as read by Carlos, Leon and Violet, however. He was wholly in support of Owen Rapley's innocence and of the fact that it was unlikely that Anastasia would have been meeting with another man on the beach that night. As with the other three, in spite of his insistence that Owen was not the killer, Eddy was unable to offer suggestions as to alternative suspects and had never heard of anyone who went by the name of Omar Prestlock. He was unaware of Owen's whereabouts these days, although his best guess was that he might be found in St. John's. He and Alicia shared a few brief memories of the days of Rock Palm before Eddy announced he needed to return to the restaurant to supervise lunch preparations. Gray and Alicia thanked him and made their way back to the Jeep.

'Where to now?' Gray asked as they climbed in. 'Henroy on the west coast? Rock Palm?'

'St. John's. To the hospital,' Alicia replied.

'The hospital?' Gray asked with a look of surprise.

'Leon's idea,' Alicia said, unfolding a street map of the capital. 'He's good friends with one of the doctors who works there: Dr

Jarrick King. According to Leon, Dr King was a trainee back in ninety-five and worked with the medical examiner who was called to the scene of Anastasia's murder at Rock Palm.'

'The one who never made it back to the hospital morgue?'

'Yeah. Him. A Dr Daryn Miller. Leon called Dr King this morning. He's expecting us.'

It was a short journey south to St. John's, although the late morning traffic in the busy town slowed them considerably. The hospital, a modern-looking building painted yellow and orange with a white roof, was elevated on a grassy mound surrounded by young palm trees and a sweeping tarmac road. It was located close to the somewhat sterile and impersonal cruise ship terminal. Three cruise ships were in port that day, docked at two quays in the heart of Antigua's capital, towering over the Caribbean town with imposing grandeur.

Gray turned onto the road leading to the hospital and they found a parking space close to the main entrance. They walked to the reception area, where they were greeted by an austere-looking receptionist who called Dr King.

'Take a seat, he'll be with you in ten,' she said curtly before returning to her computer screen.

Five minutes later, Dr Jarrick King, a tall man in his late fifties, emerged from a corridor on the opposite side of the reception area with a wide smile. He was dressed in a pale pink shirt and smart navy trousers with a stethoscope and a hospital lanyard around his neck. He introduced himself, insisting they call him by his first name before leading them back to his office, a small, compact room with floor-to-ceiling shelves filled with medical journals and textbooks. In the centre of the room was a large wooden desk, piled high with more journals and papers. Somehow, Jarrick had managed to create just enough space for a computer monitor, a keyboard and a framed photograph of him receiving some kind of award.

'Sit down, sit down,' Jarrick said, waving his hand at two office chairs facing his desk. 'Leon tells me you're looking into the Rock Palm murder from twenty years ago?'

'We are,' Alicia replied. 'Thanks for meeting us at such short notice.'

'Not at all. A pleasure. How can I help?'

'I understand you were a trainee back in ninety-five?'

'I was almost qualified and on one of my final placements back then, yes.'

'And you worked with the doctor who was called to the scene of the murder at Rock Palm? The one who examined the body?'

'Yes, Dr Daryn Miller. I remember him well. He was a first class doctor, one of the best I've ever worked with. An excellent teacher too.'

'Did you know the other hospital employee who went with him to the scene?'

'Not well, but I knew of him. Tyrell Green, his name was. We were sad to lose both of them though, of course.'

'What happened that day?'

'As far as I remember, we got the initial call from the police quite early in the morning; we hadn't been at work for long. With Hurricane Luis on the way, there were additional jobs to be done, as well as our usual ward rounds and so on. We had to plan for the worst and, as you know, the worst happened. Murders were extremely rare on the island back then. They still are. I remember wanting to join Daryn and Tyrell for the experience, but with the hurricane approaching, things were particularly tense that day. I was told to stay at the hospital and help with the preparations for the storm. Were it not for that, I probably would have gone with them, and then I might not be here today… Anyway, they set off in the van, and that's the last we heard from them.'

'Other than their concerns about the approaching hurricane, did you notice anything unusual about either of them that morning?'

'Not really. They had a job to do and that was it. I remember Tyrell moaning about Daryn's driving before they set off. Daryn had a reputation for driving a bit crazy on the roads, we all knew that. Most of us just hung onto the edge of our seats and prayed, but Tyrell was a particularly nervous passenger. Maybe that's what happened. Some people said the hurricane got them, but it's possible Daryn lost control of the van and they came off the road somewhere.'

'Was there any chance of foul play?' Alicia asked, remembering Carlos's remark that it was no accident that the van had gone missing.

'Such as?' Jarrick asked with a frown.

'I don't know, perhaps the van being hijacked and the body stolen? Something like that?'

'I've never heard that theory before,' Jarrick replied. 'It's much more likely that Daryn was in a panic to get back to the hospital and lost it on a corner somewhere.'

'Any idea where that might have happened? Hypothetically, of course.'

'Police asked us the same thing back in ninety-five. Almost impossible to tell. That's another thing about Daryn. He had this obsession with taking shortcuts. Most of them weren't shortcuts at all, but he'd always argue that they were the fastest route. Those were the days before SatNav of course.'

'What did you tell the police?'

'We didn't know what to tell them. As you can imagine, search and rescue was severely hampered for weeks afterwards because of the devastation from the hurricane. If there was ever any hope of finding the van before the storm, there certainly wasn't any after it. It's one of the worst I remember. Leon said you were in Antigua just before it made landfall. I guess you were one of the last tourists to be evacuated.'

'I was,' Alicia replied. 'Jarrick, imagine it was you who went to Rock Palm to examine the body and bring it back to the mortuary here. What road would *you* have taken?'

'I would've gone via Lyons Hill Road and then taken the Sir Sidney Walling Highway. I guess that's the route Daryn took but I can't be certain. There's a road I always dread driving along; it's a mile or two out from Rock Palm, on the way to Lyons Hill Road. Don't know why, I just don't like it.'

Alicia asked Jarrick to mark the road on her map before answering a few more questions about the procedures that were

229

adhered to back in the nineties following a suspicious death, but there was little more to be learned from the doctor. He promised to contact them at The West Beach Club if he remembered anything further. Thanking him for his time, they said goodbye and made their way back to reception and outside to the Jeep. It was almost midday and the sun was high overhead. They drove into the town and bought two bottles of water from a small store before setting off for the boutique hotel where Henroy was employed as a groundsman.

As with every other previous employee of Rock Palm Resort, Leon had forewarned him of Gray and Alicia's visit. The receptionist at the small hotel, set in an idyllic location overlooking a white sand beach, called Henroy on a handheld radio, informing him of their arrival. Within five minutes, he was in the reception area of the hotel, dressed in a sage green shirt and matching trousers. He apologised for his dishevelled and sweaty appearance, informing them he'd just been chopping branches off a row of palm trees. He was subjected to what had become routine questions asked by Alicia and, as expected, the usual textbook answers were given. It was the same every time. Nobody deviated from the script.

'The one thing I find intriguing is that everyone we've spoken to is adamant that Owen Rapley was innocent,' Gray remarked as they set off on a coastal road heading south. 'Without a shadow of a doubt. How can they be so certain when, in reality, the evidence seems to be stacked against him?'

'We need to find him and speak to him ourselves,' Alicia replied. 'Leon's on it; says he'll reach out to some friends in St. John's who work with the homeless. It's a small town, they should be able to locate him fairly easily.'

'And then there's this Omar Prestlock guy,' Gray continued. 'What's he got to do with it all? Nobody's heard of him, no one knows who he is… How's he involved exactly?'

'I have no idea,' Alicia replied. 'He's a mystery. So far.'

'What route are we taking to Rock Palm, by the way?' Gray asked, glancing across at the map Alicia held open on her lap.

'We'll stay on this coastal road for a while and then head inland on Fig Tree Drive, which takes us through Antigua's tropical rainforest. We'll go inland a bit further and then take Lyons Hill Road to the south and east of the island. Don't worry Gray, the map looks a bit spartan, but I think I can remember these roads, they haven't changed much.'

'How long will it take us?'

'Half an hour. Maybe longer. Depends on how much you rag this Jeep.' Alicia gave Gray a sideways glance with a faint smile.

'I'll take it steadily and enjoy the scenery,' Gray laughed. 'I'm thinking about Daryn Miller and his sidekick Tyrell.'

'I wonder what really happened to them.'

'Do you believe in coincidences?'

'You know I don't.'

'Then I think we can rule out an unfortunate accident.'

Alicia fell silent. She thought about the van with its three occupants, on their way back to the hospital in St. John's as storm clouds gathered, wind whipped through the trees, gathering strength, and heavy drops of rain began to fall. It was in stark contrast to the brilliant sunshine and cloudless azure sky above the open-topped Jeep, which rattled and shook as they navigated the uneven tarmac roads. Alicia closed her eyes and felt the warm air on her face. She thought of Rock Palm. It had been twenty-three years since her last visit. It was a different place now. Derelict and abandoned. The once lively resort, throbbing with vibrance and energy, had become a faded memory, a blot on the horizon, an ugly scar along the beach. But it still held the key to a missing diamond necklace and a brutal murder. Nature may have taken over, and the fight against vandals, wild animals and the elements may have been lost, but the forsaken hotel had never given up its darkest secrets.

Until now, Alicia thought to herself. *It's time, Rock Palm. Time for your mysteries to be revealed. What have you been hiding all these years?*

TWENTY-EIGHT

The entrance to the long driveway leading to Rock Palm Resort, where once a majestic sign flanked by tall palm trees had stood, was blocked by a rusting metal barrier reinforced with heavy, linked chains. The sign was no more. Instead, thick foliage wound its way across the barrier and weeds forced themselves through large cracks in the crumbling tarmac.

'Not terribly inviting,' Gray said, glancing beyond Alicia at the narrow access road. 'You're sure this was the entrance?'

'Gray, I came here every year since I was seven. Of course I'm sure.'

'Well, I don't think we're going that way. It looks like there's a road which takes us to the beach just ahead. If we park down there can we still get to the hotel?'

'Yeah, I guess we'll have to do that.'

Gray released the park brake and pressed on the gas pedal. The Jeep moved forward with a roar. As they approached the beach there was a parking area to the left where a few cars — mostly rental vehicles — were parked. Gray swung the Jeep in and came to a stop in a cloud of dust.

'Seems like the bay still attracts a few tourists,' he remarked, nodding at the cars parked further along.

'Snorkelling's meant to be pretty good just off the reef out there,' Alicia replied, 'and the beach is gorgeous. I'm sure it hasn't changed much. You'll see what I mean.'

They got out and slammed the doors of the Jeep shut.

'We'll leave the roof off,' Gray said. 'It fits so badly it'll take us half the afternoon to get it back on.'

'Fine with me,' Alicia replied. 'Let's go Gray.'

A sandy path sloped gently down to the beach, a wide strip of pale white sand which wrapped around a crescent-shaped bay. Close to the shore the sea was a vivid shade of teal, darkening to a deep indigo further out. The beach was deserted, except for a couple walking side by side in the distance. A derelict picnic bench and large pieces of driftwood marked the end of the path.

'Which way?' Gray asked, turning in a circle. 'I don't see the ghostly remains of a five-star resort anywhere.'

'Over there.' Alicia pointed to their right. 'You used to be able to see it from here but it's much more overgrown now.'

Gray followed Alicia along the beach. He glanced towards the shore, but beyond the white sand he could only see thick bushes and palm trees.

'It's further down than I remember,' Alicia said, 'but that's probably because it's obscured by all the trees and foliage these days.'

'The coastline's beautiful,' Gray said. 'So lush and green.'

Suddenly, Alicia stopped.

'There it is,' she said.

Through the rambling undergrowth and palm trees, Gray could just make out the dilapidated white rooftop of a building. They made their way towards it and, as they came closer, the overgrown jungle of tropical brushwood and palm trees cleared to reveal the remains of what had once been the majestic Rock Palm Resort. The two-storey building, set elevated above the beach, stood in what had once been a tropical garden paradise. The front of the building was open and, in some places, the roof had completely caved in, although the supporting pillars, spaced evenly at intervals, were still standing. Alicia led Gray through a patch of dense wild grass to a small track in front of the hotel which had been made by inquisitive explorers over the years.

'This was the restaurant,' she said, pointing to what had once been a large, high-ceilinged room in the centre of the hotel.

Gray looked up at it before turning towards the beach.

'It must've been idyllic, having dinner, with what I'm guessing were once stunning views out to sea and across the bay.'

'It was. Mum, dad and I used to sit at a table right over there. The best seats in the house. Sometimes there were yachts out at sea; you'd see their lights twinkling on the water. And the food was amazing. The lobsters were huge, with the freshest, most delicious salads you've ever tasted. There were tea lights on every table and sometimes there'd be a steel band playing over in that corner. There used to be a grand piano there too. A little guy called used to come and play it sometimes, all popular classics, you know, American show tunes, that kind of thing...' She paused. 'It's funny, it all happened right here, twenty-three years ago. And now, it looks like this...'

'You said you climbed out of the restaurant to get down to the beach to where Anastasia's body was found,' Gray said.

'Further along,' Alicia replied. 'Near the pool bar.'

They made their way along the track to the other end of the restaurant, where a wide, open-air passageway led to the pool bar. Its roof was still intact with surprisingly little damage.

'I stepped out of the restaurant about here,' Alicia said. She looked down towards the beach. The thick weeds and overgrown bushes were a far cry from the manicured gardens and carefully tended palm trees she had once slipped between as a curious teenager.

'It's almost unrecognisable now,' she said with sadness in her voice. 'I don't think we can even retrace my steps to the beach. We won't get through all that undergrowth.'

'Let's go back to where we could access the beach,' Gray suggested. 'We can follow a parallel path until we get to the spot where you think the body was found.'

They doubled back along the track to the patch of wild grass where they returned to the beach. Keeping the broken white roof of the hotel in their sights, they walked along the sand. As they came close to the place where the restaurant merged into the covered pool bar area, Alicia glanced back up towards Rock Palm.

'I'm not sure I can remember the exact location,' she said, slowing to a stop. She stood still and looked around. 'The landscape has changed a lot. I think it was about here, but I can't be certain.'

'Approximately then?' Gray asked, following her gaze towards the white, derelict structure, barely visible through the trees and bushes. Alicia looked back at the beach and fell silent.

'Yes,' she said quietly after a few moments, 'it was about here. The terrain is so different now to how it was, probably due to the hurricanes, and nature taking over, and… everything, but I still remember it. She was lying face up, wearing a short, black dress. Her skin was all blotchy and mottled, and there were gashes over her chest and neck. She was covered in blood. It had dried and congealed. She'd been dead a little while, a few hours perhaps. I remember her face was partially covered by her hair. It was blonde, tied with a black velvet ribbon, the same one she'd worn for the show the night before. The stab wounds were pretty deep. The ones across her neck had almost severed the whole way… Oh Gray, it was awful. Whoever killed her must've been half crazed with violence. Some kind of a monster. To think that whoever it was, was so determined, so vengeful and full of hate, and so intent on a merciless kill. I remember her eyes… they were bloodshot with this horrible, glassy, vacant stare.'

'Are you okay Alicia?' Gray asked, placing a hand on her shoulder.

'Yes, I'm fine. It's just… the memory of it. It's suddenly become so real again. She died a terrible death, Gray. Her murderer made sure of that. If Owen Rapley loved her so much, there's no way he'd have been capable of such a brutal act. But if it wasn't him, then who? And why?'

'Someone seems certain enough that the murderer *wasn't* Owen,' Gray said.

'I wish they'd just come out of the shadows and speak to me directly,' Alicia said with frustration. 'Tell me what they know. It would be so much easier that way.'

'They must have a good reason for choosing to remain anonymous,' Gray replied. 'Perhaps they're protecting themselves, or someone else. I mean, it could be someone like Leon, or one of the other Rock Palm staff. Perhaps they have evidence that the murderer wasn't Owen which might incriminate *them* so they can never come forward, but they still don't know the identity of the real killer.'

'It couldn't be Leon though,' Alicia said.

'Don't rule anyone out. I'm speaking from my own experience here. No one's above suspicion. I'm not saying Leon's *guilty*. All I'm suggesting is that perhaps he knows something but can't tell you because he might be risking his own neck, or someone else's. It might also explain how our mystery vacation was planned. He's in the travel business; he could easily have pulled some strings to get you out here.'

'But he seemed genuinely surprised to see my name on the guest list.'

'Of course he did. And perhaps he really was. Perhaps he knows nothing at all. But let's reserve judgement on that for now, keep an open mind and see where all this takes us.'

'Okay, I'll go with that,' Alicia replied. She glanced up and down the beach before looking back at the abandoned hotel. 'You know what Gray?'

'Mmmm?'

'There's nothing to be learned from the beach now. I don't think there are any answers here. Sure, this is where Anastasia's body was discovered, and probably where she was murdered too. We've got the *where* and we know the *how*. But the questions we really need the answers to are the *who* and the *why*. It's my guess those answers are concealed somewhere within the walls of Rock Palm. We just need to know where to look.'

'I think you might be right,' Gray nodded. 'Come on, let's explore.'

They made their way back to the track which ran along the front of the hotel, through what had once been the magnificently landscaped gardens. Alicia's memory was hazy, but as they walked, she tried to describe to Gray how the place had once looked. It was hard to imagine. A devastating hurricane followed by years of neglect meant that the deserted property was now in a state of repair beyond remedy.

They walked across the thick, wild grass towards the guest rooms, all of which had once boasted a spectacular sea view. The low-rise building stretched along the length of the grass before curling round in an arc, encompassing the gardens. The rooms were on two storeys; the ground floor rooms had once looked out onto their own individual terraces while the upper rooms had their own balconies. The external walls were rendered, the cream-coloured plaster badly flaking and peeling away. Some parts were completely overrun with wild, untamed bushes.

Access to the interior of the property was easy. The slatted doors hung half off their hinges or were completely missing from the ground floor rooms. Gray and Alicia stepped carefully over broken terrace tiles, rubble, tufts of wild grass and unidentified debris into one of the rooms. Inside was a dirty, white tiled floor. A smashed lamp lay on its side and an old mattress was slumped against the wall. Alicia disappeared into a small room just off the main bedroom.

'Gray, come in here and see the bathroom,' she called. He joined her. The room was small for a hotel bathroom, but had probably been generously sized back in the nineties. A white bath tub streaked with rust and dirt stretched across one side of a wall. It was filled with broken tiles, bent and rusted metal rods, a plastic cup and a faded, empty crisp packet. Above the bath, on the faded aquamarine tiles, someone had sprayed a single word in brown paint: "Remember".

'Those tiles,' Alicia said. 'It's all coming back to me.' She turned to Gray. 'Let's take a look at the rest of the hotel.'

As they walked out of the room to the open passageway behind, Gray pointed to the tarnished number on the door, hanging askew on its rusted hinges.

'D'you remember which room you stayed in?' he asked.

'It was further along from here,' Alicia replied. 'A ground floor room with a huge terrace. I had the same one every year.'

They walked along the passageway towards the main section of the hotel.

'This leads to the swimming pool terrace,' Alicia said. Sure enough, through an archway, the corridor opened out onto the pool deck area, bathed in sunshine, with most of the large, terracotta tiles around the pool still intact and unbroken. The swimming pool itself, in a wide circular shape and with peeling pale blue paint, was empty of water. There was a collection of dead palm branches, rubbish and other debris from the hotel scattered across the bottom. The pool deck was elevated above the gardens and the beach, with sweeping views of the bay.

'There were sun loungers all around this area,' Alicia said, pointing, 'and tables and chairs under parasols over there by the pool bar.'

'It must've been a stunning place,' Gray said, 'although it takes a little imagination now to work out what it would've been like.'

'It's heartbreaking to see it in this state,' Alicia replied. 'Let me show you the restaurant.'

They walked around the pool towards the covered pool bar where a wide passageway led through to the large room with the arched ceiling. Sunlight streamed through gaping holes in the roof where rotting, wooden supporting joists had fallen through into the room. Twisted skeletons of broken tables and chairs were strewn around what had once been the restaurant. At one end, mattresses, dirty and covered in mould were piled in an untidy heap, while a golf bag still complete with a set of clubs had been tossed into a corner. More dead palm branches, torn sheets of corrugated roof and rusting metal bars littered the tiled floor. The once spectacular views of the bay from the open side of the restaurant were now partially obscured by thick, overgrown bushes and debris.

Gray and Alicia made their way through an archway to the reception area. Outside, a wide circular driveway swept up to what had once been the grand entrance, the roof of which had fallen in during the storm. Covered in rubbish and overrun with weeds, it was a sorry sight. In a room behind the reception area, probably an office of some kind as Alicia noted it had always been off-limits to hotel guests, a lone office chair stood upright in a pile of papers, resort brochures, payment documents, room reservations and other mail, scattered haphazardly about.

'An office behind the reception,' Alicia murmured.

'Where a safe would've been located to keep guests' valuables secure,' Gray added.

'Yeah. Could it still be here?'

'It's just possible.' Stepping over the papers, Gray peered around the room. On one wall, tall cupboard doors hung partially closed. He pulled them open, but except for a dusty stack of old brochures and an out-of-date telephone directory, it was empty. He moved into a smaller room beyond.

'Anything?' Alicia called out. She was leafing through a bundle of papers which looked to be room reservations for past guests.

'No, nothing,' Gray replied, reappearing in the doorway. 'Nothing resembling a safe, anyway. I'd guess that thing's long gone. If it wasn't removed before the hotel was evacuated, it was probably stolen soon after.'

'You're right. But the staff would've left it emptied and unlocked anyway.'

'It was worth a look.'

They stood staring at each other. The only sound was the waves slapping lazily on the beach in the bay behind them.

'Eerie, isn't it?' Alicia half whispered.

'It's like stepping into Sleeping Beauty's castle,' Gray replied, 'as if everyone just ran away the day before the hurricane struck.'

'A ghost hotel,' Alicia said, 'still holding onto its dark, undiscovered secrets. What really happened that night, I wonder?'

'You were here,' Gray replied, 'you probably saw more than anyone, except the murderer.'

'If only I'd *known* what was happening in front of my eyes,' Alicia replied. 'I've always wondered what I might've seen if I'd got to that beach path just a few minutes earlier.'

'What *were* you doing wandering about at that time of night anyway?' Gray asked suddenly.

Alicia turned to face him.

'I was coming back from the auditorium,' she replied. 'I'd forgotten about it. It's over on the east side of the resort. We may be able to get to it this way…' She stepped gingerly over some planks of wood and a metal corrugated sheet towards the main entrance which led outside. Gray was close behind and together they climbed over an uprooted palm tree to a barely visible path which wound its way between foliage and more guest rooms. Up on the hillside, they could just make out giant water tanks which had once supplied water to the hotel, but were now rusting and toppled. Further behind them and out of sight were the derelict tennis courts, along with the painted white wooden hut which had once been the sports reception where Owen Rapley had worked.

'Half of the auditorium is actually underground,' Alicia said as they picked their way along the path. 'According to Carlos the entrance to the foyer caved in during the hurricane, apparently sealing it off. There was also a stage door, although I've no idea where, but that's impassable too, due to debris and storm damage. I guess our best bet is still the main entrance, although Carlos didn't think anyone had managed to get inside since the hurricane.'

'So no one's been in there for twenty-three years?' Gray asked, holding a broken palm branch out of the way for Alicia.

'No. Not even vandals. We may not even be able to find the entrance.'

'Oh we will.'

Up ahead was a low, flat-roofed wooden structure surrounded by undergrowth and tall palm trees.

'There,' Alicia said.

'That's it?' Gray asked.

'Yeah. The entrance was just… oh, I see what Carlos means.' There was disappointment in her voice. As they reached what had once been the entrance to the foyer of the old auditorium, they could see that the wooden roof had completely fallen in. Twisted metal bars and supporting joists had crashed down in front of the access doors.

'We could hunt for the stage door,' Alicia said doubtfully, peering around the side of the building, 'but I've no idea where it was and it looks pretty overgrown back there.'

'Wait,' Gray said, tugging at a wooden joist. A pile of broken tiles and rubble on top of it shifted.

'Gray, be careful,' Alicia said nervously.

'Help me pull this roof joist out of the way,' Gray said, grabbing another. Alicia took hold of it and together they dragged it to the side, dislodging the debris on top of it. They continued hauling more jagged pieces of wood and metal bars away from the entrance.

'It's hardly surprising nobody bothered to try to get into this place,' Gray said, panting slightly. Their faces were red and streaked with dust and sweat in the hot afternoon sunshine.

'That's what Carlos said,' Alicia agreed, wiping her arm across her forehead. 'Vandals and people who want somewhere private to get high or have sex only go for the easy access places.'

'Which this definitely isn't,' Gray said, standing up to catch his breath.

'D'you think we can do it on our own?' Alicia asked.

Gray examined the pile of debris in front of what he hoped was the entrance door.

'If we're able to shift those two joists and that sheet of corrugated metal, we might be getting somewhere,' he replied.

They tussled some more with the rubble, hauling it to one side, with showers of thick dust and debris falling around them as they worked. As they pulled on a large wooden plank, the frame of a wooden-slatted door came into view.

'Gray, that's it,' Alicia said excitedly. 'That's the door to the main foyer!'

They cleared the remaining pieces of splintered wood and tiles away from the entrance and Gray tried the handle of the door. It still worked. He pulled the door gently towards them. The hinges were rusted and the door was stiff, but, with a loud creak, it opened, revealing the dark foyer behind.

'You first?' Gray asked. 'Go carefully. I'll be right behind you.'

Alicia stepped inside, onto the dirty white-tiled floor. With the exception of the single ray of sunlight streaming through the door behind them, it was dark. She pulled her cell phone out of her pocket and switched on the torch. Gray followed suit. Alicia remembered the foyer well. Shining the light from her phone to the right and left, she saw the wooden-slatted, saloon-style doors at each end, which led to either side of the top of the auditorium. She turned right, just as she had done on the night of the murder.

With Gray close behind, she walked slowly toward the doors at the end. She gave him a brief glance before she pushed them open. For the first time in twenty-three years, she stepped into the old, abandoned auditorium of Rock Palm Resort.

TWENTY-NINE

The doors swung shut slowly behind Gray. He and Alicia stood still and silent, shining the light from their cell phones across the ghostly rows of red velvet seats, covered in cobwebs and dust. The place smelt stale and musty, with a woody scent in the air. Alicia closed her eyes and imagined the scene in front of her as it had been twenty-three years before; the bright lights, dramatic music, the glittering costumes of the performers, the mysterious magical props and the rapturous applause from the spellbound audience.

The wide arc of seats sloped gently downwards towards the stage. Alicia and Gray stood at the top of one of the sets of aisle stairs which descended on either side of the auditorium. As Alicia's light reached the stage, she took a sharp breath.

'Gray,' she said, her voice trembling.

'What's wrong?'

'The props, from the final magic show. They're still there, on the stage.'

Gray's light followed Alicia's to the dark bulky shapes below.

'Let's go down there and take a look,' Gray said, stepping past Alicia.

They made their way slowly down the stairs. As they reached the bottom, they gazed at the shadowy sight on the stage in front of them. The wooden cabinet from which Anastasia had mysteriously vanished in her final act was still there, exactly where it had been at the end of the magic show and hours later, when Alicia had crept into the auditorium. The shades were fully up and it was dusty and draped in cobwebs — real ones — but stood as it had done on that fateful night. To the right of the cabinet were the graveyard props and the coffin, also strewn with cobwebs — real and fake — and the plastic ivy. On the other side of the stage was the rest of the elaborate set design, which resembled a cemetery with its macabre array of Gothic tombs and gravestones, and wrought iron gates.

'I can't believe these props are still here, after all this time,' Alicia gasped. 'The magic team never took them away. It's like we've stepped into a time capsule.'

'It's strange,' Gray said with a puzzled frown.

'I remember the magician asking Leon whether he'd seen Anastasia on that last morning, when her body was found,' Alicia went on. 'The magician said she hadn't showed up and he didn't know where she was, but that they needed all hands on deck to dismantle the stage props, or something like that. I remember thinking it was ironic that one of the magician's assistants had "vanished" and that he couldn't find her. That was before they knew what had happened to her.'

'So the magician had no idea where she was either?'

'He didn't appear to. But these props, all still here… Why?'

'Maybe the magician and his team had only just started to clear away and hadn't got to these ones before they heard about Anastasia,' Gray suggested.

'Yeah, perhaps,' Alicia agreed. 'Dad told me the magician and the other assistants were called to the beach to identify the body. They were pretty cut up about her death apparently. I guess in the chaos that ensued, giving statements to the police and so on, they were too distraught to carry on dismantling everything. Perhaps they thought they'd leave them here and come back after the hurricane to get them.'

'Then why didn't they?'

'They couldn't get in, could they?'

'They could have if they'd tried hard enough. These stage props look as though they're worth quite a bit. You wouldn't just leave them here, would you? Surely they had other performing commitments at other resorts across the island?'

'Gray, the island was devastated after the hurricane. The resorts suffered a lot of damage and Antigua was closed to tourism for some time until they got themselves back on their feet again. The last thing on anyone's mind would've been going to a magic show.'

'Fair point.'

'And another thing: they'd lost their star performer. They were a team of, let's see, I think there were four assistants altogether, including Anastasia, but she was the one who did most of the tricks.'

'What happened to the magic team then?'

'I don't know,' Alicia said. 'We could ask Leon tonight.'

'What were they called? Could we look them up online?'

'I don't know if they called themselves anything or not. I remember the magician's stage name was Mallory Mortimer though. Dad once said that *Mallory* came from a French word meaning ill-fated, and *mort*, from *Mortimer*, meant death. He's right of course.'

'Typical stage name for a magician,' Gray said laughing. 'Very nineteen nineties.'

'I suppose it is,' Alicia agreed. 'When you're fifteen with an overactive imagination, it conjures up all sorts of disturbing thoughts.'

'What about these props though?' Gray said, shining the light from his phone onto the stage. He traced the frame of the cabinet. 'What on earth's that all about? Do you remember which trick this was used for?'

'Like it was performed yesterday.' There was a sudden glint in Alicia's eyes. 'Come with me.' She took Gray's hand and led him to the small set of stairs at the side of the stage. Retracing her steps from twenty-three years before, she stepped onto the stage and shone her light onto the ivy-clad coffin. Next to it was the set of steps that Anastasia had used to climb into the cabinet. Alicia directed her light towards the hollow frame in front of them.

'It was the final act of the evening,' she said softly, as they reached the wooden structure. 'Mallory began with his usual magician's patter to introduce the illusion.'

Gray inspected the vertical frame of the cabinet and the metal base.

'Do you know how it was done?'

'Of course.'

'What was the trick?'

As Alicia began to recall the details of Anastasia's final act, her mind returned to her teenage memories of the illusion. She looked out at the arc of red velvet seats, to somewhere in the middle of the fifth row from the front, where she had sat between her parents. From there she had watched Anastasia's every move, every twist and turn of the elaborate ballgown with the hooped skirt. It had been a full house in the small auditorium that night, yet she remembered the audible hush of tense anticipation. She recalled the hot, clammy air, the sickly scent of dry ice, the mysterious synthesised chords, the purple lights dancing across the darkened stage, and the suspense.

As Anastasia joined the magician on stage, Alicia remembered how he took one of her hands and kissed it gently. Sashaying gracefully in the wide, hooped skirt, Anastasia ascended the steps into the wooden cabinet. Alicia recalled the faint, knowing smile that played on her lips as the other three assistants, in their sequinned playsuits and knee-high boots, took their places. And then the shades came down two-thirds of the way at the front and sides of the cabinet. Anastasia's dress continued to sway gently from side to side, still clearly visible in the bottom third of the cabinet. And now the shades were fully lowered to the floor. Anastasia and her dress were completely concealed from view. But within seconds the shades were released, springing back up to the top of the cabinet. Anastasia and her dress had vanished.

'To where?' Gray asked, incredulously. Alicia pointed to the coffin.

'To there. Just a few moments after the shades went up, the lid began to open and Anastasia, wearing the same dress with the wide, hooped skirt, got out.'

'How did they do it?'

'It's very simple really,' Alicia said with a faint, knowing smile. 'It's like this Gray: sometimes people only see what they want to believe, rather than what is actually there in front of them.'

THIRTY

9:30 pm, Saturday, August 25
The West Beach Club, Antigua

Gray and Alicia drank coffee on the restaurant terrace of The West Beach Club, gazing out to sea. The pale iridescent light of a half moon reflected on the dark water and stars shimmered in the night sky. Alicia wore a dusky pink playsuit which accentuated her sun-kissed olive skin, already beginning to tan from the Caribbean sunshine. Gray was dressed in a navy linen shirt and grey trousers, which masked red lines of sunburn as a result of poorly applied sun lotion. After-dinner cocktails remained off the menu, as they had always been since Gray's release from prison; prior to his life-sentence for a double homicide, he had descended into a toxic spiral of alcohol addiction. He had vowed never to return there.

The warm sea air was infused with the aroma of delicate spices and rich flavours from the restaurant, along with the contented chatter of hotel diners and the clink of cutlery. Occasionally, peals of laughter echoed from one of the larger tables. Looking flustered but cheerful, Leon approached Gray and Alicia, armed with his handkerchief and leather-bound file.

'Good evening to you both,' he said with a beaming smile. 'How was your dinner tonight?'

'Delicious thank you Leon,' Alicia replied. 'We sent our compliments to the chef via Roslyn.'

'Ah Roslyn, yes. I saw her talking with you earlier. Was she able to give you anything useful for your investigations?'

'She told us what she remembered, but as expected, there was nothing we didn't already know.'

'What about Henroy and Eddy, and Jarrick the doctor? Did you catch up with them?'

'Yes, thanks for setting up those meetings at such short notice by the way.'

'My pleasure. Were they productive?'

'A little perhaps, but I guess we didn't really learn anything further.'

'That's just it though,' Leon said, 'none of us knew very much, even back then, and now the memories we did have are all but gone.'

'I realise it was a long time ago,' Alicia said, 'but we do have a couple more questions for you, if you'll permit them?'

'Fire away!'

'The magic team who performed in the auditorium at Rock Palm. What became of them?'

'Ahh, the magic team.' Leon rubbed his forehead with his hand. A troubled expression came over his face. 'Yes, I remember them,' he said with a faint sigh. He appeared to be wrestling with his thoughts. He finally gave in. 'I suppose it won't matter to tell you this now. Maybe you already know. Yes, Mallory Mortimer and his team. They were very talented and popular performers back in the nineties. They did their shows all over the Caribbean, but especially at the few high-end resorts we had in Antigua back then, like Rock Palm. Rock Palm was unusual in that it had a specially adapted auditorium, just for Mallory's illusions. It was one of a kind and the magic team sort of took up unofficial residency there for the season.

'They performed in the auditorium every Friday, Saturday and Sunday nights. Tourists came from all over the island to see them. In fact, people even used to fly in from other nearby islands, just for the show. They'd have dinner in the restaurant at Rock Palm beforehand, which was good for us, and then go watch the show. But in the days before the hurricane struck, there were several rumours bandied around. I've no idea how much truth was in them, but apparently the magic team had been stealing jewellery, money, watches, wallets and so on from wealthy guests at some of the other resorts.'

'Stealing jewellery?' Alicia asked.

'Yes. Apparently they were using their sleight-of-hand skills to take guests' valuables. Of course, their shows were entirely aboveboard. According to the rumours, the thefts were occurring at other times of the evening, when the wine was flowing and the guests unsuspecting.'

'How were they caught?'

'I'm not certain exactly, but I believe after a number of reported thefts at a couple of the other high-end resorts on the island — as you know, there weren't many in those days — the guests who'd been targeted, and the hotel staff, put two and two together and came up with the magic team. We never had any issues with them at Rock Palm I'm grateful to say.'

'But, Vivienne Karleman's diamond necklace...' Alicia interrupted.

'Yes, I wondered that briefly at the time,' Leon said, 'but Mrs Karleman's necklace went missing during the time it was meant to be locked in the hotel safe. The magic team were supposedly stealing directly from guests, not breaking into hotel safes. As a matter of fact, it would've been rather useful to me if we *could* have tied them to the necklace. It would certainly have taken the heat off my staff and me. But Vivienne Karleman denied coming into contact with any member of the magic team and remained adamant that one of my own staff had taken it.'

'What happened to Mallory and his team?' Alicia asked.

'Obviously they weren't able to continue performing at Rock Palm after the hurricane. And as you know, with devastation across the whole island, there were no tourists for some time. But even without the hurricane, I believe their contracts with the other resorts were terminated as a result of the thefts. I don't know what's become of them now. They've probably gone into retirement or maybe they're still cranking out a few cheap gigs in Vegas or somewhere. I couldn't say. They certainly don't perform in Antigua anymore. I haven't heard of them since the nineties. They lost their star performer too, so they would've had to have replaced Anastasia.'

'What did they call themselves?'

Leon paused in thought.

'I honestly can't recall. I just knew them as Mallory and his magic team, but I'm sure they had a better name than that. I'll ask Roslyn and Violet; they might remember.'

'Any ideas as to how I could find them?'

'Online maybe?' Leon suggested doubtfully. 'Your guess is as good as mine. I expect they're long gone now. They most likely disbanded after they lost Anastasia. And after their reputation was tarnished with the allegations of theft. Like I said, the best they can manage now is probably a couple of tawdry shows in a dive bar somewhere. That's usually what happens to these people, sadly. Was there anything else you wanted to ask me?'

'Yes, I still need to find Owen Rapley.'

'I've reached out to a couple of friends who work with the homeless on the streets, as promised. We're not a big island, it's hard to remain anonymous for long, but nobody can tell me of Owen's whereabouts I'm afraid.'

'They can't tell you or they won't tell you?'

'Good question. I can only ask though,' Leon said with an awkward shrug.

'But if he knew we might be able to help him...'

'Like he's going to fall for that one,' Gray interrupted. 'Come on Alicia, you know better than that.'

'Yeah, you're right,' Alicia sighed. 'But I have an idea.' She shot a glance at Gray before turning back to Leon. 'The other two people from Rock Palm I'd like to find are Charles and Vivienne Karleman. Any thoughts?'

'None at all. Sorry.' Leon shook his head. 'As I said, I never heard from them since the day the guests were evacuated from Rock Palm. They certainly haven't stayed here; believe me I'd remember them.'

'I'm sure you would,' Alicia said with a wry smile. 'Thanks Leon.'

'No problem,' Leon replied. He surveyed the restaurant behind him. 'It's busy tonight. Saturdays are always busy. There are two flights from London and a flight from New York. A quick turnaround for the staff and a lot of new guests to welcome. If I think of anything that might help you further, I'll come and find you. Have a wonderful evening.'

'You too, Leon.'

When the general manager had disappeared into the throng of diners, Alicia turned to Gray.

'You think he really doesn't know how to find Owen?'

'I think he knows perfectly well how to find him,' Gray replied. 'You heard him yourself; Antigua's a small island. But he's either been instructed to deny all knowledge, or he's choosing to protect Owen of his own accord. Either way, we're on our own with this.'

'Not quite,' Alicia said. 'I need to make a phone call though. What about the Karlemans? Where do we start looking for them?'

'There is a way,' Gray said slowly. 'It's not so much us looking for them, as them coming to us.'

'How's that?'

'I have an idea. On the subject of the Karlemans, do you think it's possible the magic team *did* steal the diamond necklace from Vivienne Karleman?'

'Anything's possible,' Alicia said with a touch of frustration.

'Take me back to the night you were sneaking around the beach and the auditorium,' Gray said suddenly. 'What, and who, did you see?'

'I walked from my room towards the hotel; it was around midnight and all the guests were leaving the next day so it was unusually deserted for that time of night. The holiday vibe was well and truly dying. The first people I remember seeing were the Karlemans. They were in the restaurant having a heated discussion with Leon about Vivienne's missing necklace. I went down to the beach and on my way back, I passed Owen and Anastasia. When I got to the restaurant Leon was still attempting to pacify Vivienne Karleman.'

'And then what? You went back to your room?'

'No. I went to the auditorium, just out of curiosity. I wasn't expecting the magic props to still be there. That was a surprise. I was exploring the props on the stage, trying to figure out how the magic team had pulled off their final illusion, when someone came into the auditorium: Charles Karleman.'

'*Charles?*'

'Yes. I remember I went and hid between the front two rows of seats. He was alone, seemed quite nervous. He walked all the way down to the stage. I was terrified he'd see me.'

'What was he doing there in the middle of the night? Surely not searching for the necklace?'

'Not at all. As far as I could work out, he seemed to be waiting for someone. He kept looking at his watch and then back up to the top of the stairs.'

'Waiting for who?'

'It's w*hom* Gray,' Alicia corrected him with a mischievous smile. 'Can't believe they let you get away with that in a max security prison.'

'Very funny. Now answer the question.'

'According to the notes I wrote in my journal on that last night at Rock Palm, he — Charles — was waiting for someone called Megan. He kept calling her name. He even climbed onto the stage as if he expected her to emerge from one of the props or something. It was a little strange.'

'Who was Megan?'

'No idea. Probably one of the guests. It certainly wasn't one of the staff; I knew all their names.'

'Did Megan show up?'

'No. He waited around for a bit and then left. I hung around a little longer, just to make sure the coast was clear, and then headed back to my room.'

'See anyone else?'

'There was a member of staff at the reception desk doing some paperwork, and then I passed one of the waiters by the pool. Anton. He was carrying a tray. Late night room service or something.'

'That's it?'

'Yes, that's… No, wait. There was someone else. I remember now.' A strange look came into Alicia's eyes. 'There was one other person I saw that night. He was walking up the steps from the beach, alone. I thought it might be Owen to start with but this man

252

was white and certainly didn't have the toned, muscular physique of a keen tennis player. It was Mallory, the magician.'

'The *magician*?' Gray asked with surprise.

'Yes.' Alicia fell silent.

'He's looking guiltier all the time. Perhaps he *was* appropriately named after all. First he and his team are accused of theft, and then he just happens to be walking away from the scene of a murder. Did no one else see him on the beach that night?'

'Apparently not,' Alicia replied. 'There wasn't really anyone else still about at that time. And the next day all eyes were on Owen as the prime suspect.'

'Did the magician see you?'

'I don't know. Maybe he did. He didn't acknowledge me. It was a bit of a shock to see him there, pale-faced and serious. He wasn't covered in blood or anything though. He seemed pretty cool and calm, not like he'd just stabbed his star performer to death in a violent frenzy.'

'If he had, what would his motive have been?'

'I've no idea, but why murder one of your own team? Surely he had more to lose than to gain?'

'You don't know that,' Gray said. 'There are skeletons lurking in the cupboard of every successful partnership.'

'He certainly had the means and opportunity.'

'Every single person you saw that night had those,' Gray observed. 'And maybe there was someone you *didn't* see.'

'I suppose the biggest question is motive. And that's where we draw a blank. Why would anyone want to kill Anastasia?'

'I think Leon just gave us a very good motive for everyone.'

'The thefts?' Alicia asked.

'Yes. If the rumours were true, then suddenly she's not the sweet, innocent magician's assistant she masqueraded as; she's a scheming, manipulative thief. If she'd stolen from one of the hotel guests and been found out, perhaps she was accosted on the beach and things got out of hand. It gives a decent motive to any of the guests.'

'You've just opened up the suspect pool to an impossible number Gray,' Alicia said. 'So now what? We track down every guest who was staying at Rock Palm in the days leading up to the hurricane?'

'Sorry, but it's entirely possible,' Gray replied. 'Who were the guests who said they "witnessed" Owen and Anastasia alone together on the beach that night? We could start with them. Perhaps they wanted to turn the heat off themselves because one of them was a murderer.'

'Leon might remember who they were,' Alicia said doubtfully.

'There are other options to consider,' Gray went on. 'Let's take Owen. He's still not off the hook. Let's say he saw her with another man. He's in love with her, but he's eaten up with jealousy so he lures her to the beach and stabs her. It would explain why he denied all knowledge of knowing her when her body was discovered.'

'Okay, that's possible,' Alicia agreed. 'What about the magician?'

'Perhaps they'd had a disagreement over something in the show, or what cut of their takings she was — or wasn't — getting.'

'Also entirely plausible.'

'And there's even Leon. He was near the beach that night too. He probably saw Anastasia with Owen. Maybe he knew she was the one who'd taken Vivienne Karleman's necklace. He might even have been in on the whole thing. It's an opportunity for blackmail right there. But then perhaps the agreement went sour somehow…'

'Now you're being ridiculous,' Alicia interrupted.

'Not really. It's conceivable…' Gray replied.

'We're still no further forward with this whole thing though,' Alicia said, looking downcast. 'As a matter of fact, I think we've gone backwards. Oh Gray, why did I *ever* take up this challenge? I should've thrown the travel documents in the trash, along with the guidebook and brochure and ignored Spencer's encounter with Vivienne Karlsson and the fake necklace.'

'I very much doubt that whoever set this thing up would've just left you alone,' Gray said. 'Look at it from their perspective. Whoever's pulling the strings behind the scenes — the puppet master — either has to remain anonymous or chooses to for some reason. Why come to you? Why not go to the police and get them to reopen the case? There must be a reason. And why now, twenty-three years later? He, she, or they, seem pretty determined. No expense has been spared to capture your attention. Let's take the necklace that showed up in Spencer's jewellery store for starters. Sure, it wasn't real diamonds, but the moissanite stones were still valued at around four million pounds.

'And then there's the engraving around the girdle of each stone: Who. Murdered. Anastasia. The reason we're here at all. Whoever orchestrated this must've had access to some highly specialised instruments, including a laser to inscribe the words on the stones. They would've also needed a machine to produce the fake grading reports complete with the distorted holograms. We're talking very expensive, specialised equipment.'

'So we're looking at someone with money,' Alicia said. 'Then it can't be Owen Rapley trying to prove his innocence. He's homeless and destitute and on the breadline.'

'Someone on his behalf, perhaps?'

'I doubt any of his friends or family would have that kind of cash to burn on precious stones, engraving instruments and holographic printers.'

'No, but it almost seems as though we're looking for two motives here: one for the murderer and one for the puppet master. Why is the puppet master so intent on this case being solved?'

'Speaking of the puppet master, there's one other person I keep thinking about,' Alicia said suddenly.

'Who?'

'Omar Prestlock. Who *is* he? Nobody seems to know him. Nobody's even heard of him.'

'I've been thinking about him too,' Gray replied. 'I might be able to answer that one. Do you have a pen and paper?'

Alicia produced a pen from her purse and the napkin from the tray their coffees had arrived on. In a circle on the napkin, Gray wrote the letters: O M A R P R E S T L O C K.

'It was actually Omar *R.* Prestlock,' Alicia corrected.

Gray added an extra R into the circle of letters.

'Take a look,' he said, sliding the napkin across to Alicia. 'What do you see?'

Alicia examined the napkin.

'A bunch of random letters,' she said flatly. 'What am I supposed to be seeing?'

'Start with one of the Rs.'

Alicia wrote an R underneath the circle.

'How about an O?' Gray suggested. 'What's that thing you're always saying? *Sometimes people only see what they want to believe, rather than what is actually there in front of them.* Look at these letters Alicia. What is actually written there in front of you?'

'R, O…' Alicia paused. Suddenly a look of realisation came into her eyes. She wrote a C and then a K, crossing out the letters from the circle above.

'It's an anagram,' she said. She wrote in the final letters: PALM RESORT. 'Gray, it's so simple. Omar Prestlock isn't the name of a person of interest at all. It's an anagram of Rock Palm Resort. How did you figure that out?'

'I'm not sure exactly. It sort of came to me when we were at Rock Palm this afternoon. I saw the letters on the sign that led to the beach: ROCK PALM. If you shuffle them around, you can make the word OMAR out of those. When we got back here, I played with the letters a little more, like you did just now, and realised what they meant.'

'How could I have missed that before?' Alicia asked.

'You wanted to believe it was the name of an actual person. Which is a perfectly reasonable thing to do. But this whole thing is about believing what we want to believe, rather that what's actually in front of us, isn't it? Nothing is as it seems. The magic show, Anastasia's last performance, it was just an illusion, like you showed me in the auditorium this afternoon. The necklace and the grading reports brought into the jewellery store; they were passed off as the real thing, but on closer inspection, were all fakes. Even the name and contact details of the woman who brought them in were false. It was just a very clever illusion to make people see what they wanted to believe.'

'I wonder how she did it,' Alicia said. 'Ronan and Camilla are highly experienced gemologists. They should've spotted those fake gemstones a mile away.'

'Somehow she tricked them into believing the stones were real,' Gray replied. 'She led them to believe what they wanted to believe, rather than what was actually in front of them. And I'm quite sure they really did want to believe those stones were genuine diamonds.'

'I still don't get why she went to all that trouble just to get my attention. There were other ways to capture my interest, surely? And then to pay all that money back to Tobias the following day. It would've taken a considerable amount of time and effort. And planning.'

'Perhaps it was to reinforce the motive for finding Anastasia's killer,' Gray suggested. 'Vivienne Karlsson wanted you to know it's not about the diamond necklace or the money, just about solving the murder. And perhaps it's about making wrongs right and finally clearing Owen's name, if he really is innocent. When I was released from prison, the one thing which mattered to me more than anything was justice. If that's what's important here, we have to be careful we don't fall into the trap of believing only what we want to believe either.'

'You're right,' Alicia said. 'Well, we know now that Omar R. Prestlock is simply an anagram of Rock Palm Resort, but it still doesn't bring us any closer to working out who actually sent that package.'

'Other than that he, or she, is connected to Rock Palm in some way,' Gray added.

Suppressing a yawn, Alicia placed a hand on Gray's knee. 'It's late and we've a lot to do tomorrow. Let's go to bed.'

She picked up her purse and stood up. As she did so, she spotted a man dressed in navy overalls pushing a small trolley along the path beneath the restaurant terrace. Probably one of the staff maintenance team. As she glanced across at him, he looked her straight in the eye before averting his gaze. She frowned. He certainly got around the hotel. He raked sand on the beach, tended the gardens and now he was on maintenance duties. He wasn't the friendliest staff member either. He almost reminded her of... She stopped. Gray, close behind, almost walked into her.

'Alicia?'

'Anton,' Alicia said under her breath. 'He reminds me of Anton, the grumpy waiter from Rock Palm.'

Leaving Gray standing alone on the terrace, she ran to the steps which led to the walkway. She hurried down them and along the path in the direction Anton had been heading, but the only people she saw were a young couple walking towards the restaurant.

'The maintenance man who just walked by you, with the trolley,' she said quickly, 'which way did he go?'

The couple looked at each other in confusion.

'Maintenance man?' the man asked in a puzzled voice.

'Yes,' Alicia replied. 'Where did he go?'

'We haven't seen a maintenance man,' the woman said. 'We've just come from our villa down there,' she pointed behind her. 'We haven't passed anyone.'

'But you must've done,' Alicia said impatiently. 'He was here just now, blue overalls, pushing some kind of trolley with tools and things. He was walking this way just a moment ago. He must've walked right by you.'

'No one's walked by us,' the man said, shaking his head. 'Sorry,' he added, almost apologetically.

'It's okay,' Alicia sighed. 'Enjoy your evening.'

The couple said goodnight and continued their walk, leaving her alone on the pathway as Gray caught up with her.

'What was all that about?' he asked.

'Please tell me you saw that maintenance man on the path in front of the terrace,' Alicia said, turning to him.

'I'm sorry Alicia, I didn't. What about him?'

'I've seen him three times now, raking sand on the beach, working in the gardens and he just walked by the restaurant terrace with a maintenance trolley. Every time he seems to be looking in my direction, almost like he's watching me. And then he averts his gaze.'

'Not just being friendly then?'

'He's the most unfriendly, unsmiling person here,' Alicia replied firmly. 'Almost to the point of rudeness. He reminds me very much of Anton, the waiter from Rock Palm. Unsmiling and rude. He looks older now, as he would do. I need to ask Leon about him.'

They returned to the restaurant and found Leon mingling with a table of eight guests. He broke off from his conversation and turned to Alicia.

'I had a quick word with Roslyn about the name the magic team went by,' he said in a low voice. 'She couldn't remember what they were called either. Sorry.'

'Don't worry Leon. Thanks for asking, all the same,' Alicia replied. 'Your estates team; who's on duty tonight?'

Leon frowned.

'I've got two guys working tonight: Gregory and Roy. They double as security. I've actually just spoken to them,' he nodded to the walkie-talkie radio clipped to his belt. 'They're fixing an air conditioning unit outside one of the villas.'

'Where?'

'The other side of the resort. Why? Do you have a problem in your villa?'

'No, nothing like that. Could one of them have walked past the restaurant just now?'

'I wouldn't have thought so. The villa's on the other side of the property.' Leon pulled the walkie-talkie off his belt and spoke into it: 'Roy, it's Leon here. Do you copy?'

After a few seconds there was a muffled reply.

'Go ahead Leon.'

'You and Gregory both still working on that air con unit outside villa six?'

'Yeah, we're here. You need us somewhere else?'

'Ask him if either of them came to the restaurant just now,' Alicia said.

Leon relayed the message.

'No, we've been here for the last hour. Both of us.'

Leon thanked them and replaced the little radio on his belt.

'Do you have anyone else working tonight wearing blue overalls?' Alicia asked.

'No,' Leon said with a puzzled look, 'and our maintenance guys wear beige, not blue.'

259

Alicia sighed in frustration.

'You sure everything's all right?' Leon asked.

'I just saw a guy dressed in blue overalls, pushing a trolley with tools and things. I've seen him before here, raking sand on the beach and tending to the gardens down there while we were having breakfast this morning. He reminded me of Anton from Rock Palm. Do you remember him Leon? He was one of the waiters. I only remember him from the ninety-five trip; I don't think he was there any other years.'

'Anton?' Leon scratched his neck in thought. 'Yes, I think I know who you mean. He wasn't with us for very long though.'

'What was his background? Can you tell me anything about him?'

'Afraid I can't,' Leon replied. 'He'd only been with us for a couple of weeks. He seemed to fit in okay and do his job. I never heard any complaints about him.'

'Have you seen him since Rock Palm?'

'Can't say I have, no. But it's possible he found work on one of the other islands after the hurricane. I really don't know what happened to him.'

Alicia moved the conversation to the guests at Rock Palm who had witnessed Owen and Anastasia together on the beach. Leon shook his head apologetically. He was sorry, he couldn't remember who had come forward the following morning. They drew another blank. With disappointment, Alicia thanked him again and said goodnight. As they stepped down off the terrace and turned right onto the path which wound through the tropical gardens back to their villa, Alicia slid her hand into Gray's.

'He was here. Anton, I mean,' she said, peering into the shadows as her eyes became accustomed to the dimly lit path lights leading away from the restaurant. 'I knew there was something familiar about him when I saw him raking the sand on the beach last night. He was there, on the night Anastasia was murdered. And now he's here. He's involved somehow, I know it.'

'I believe you,' Gray replied, squeezing her hand. 'We'll find him. He's bound to show up again, whatever he's up to. And don't worry Alicia, I won't let anything happen to you.'

THIRTY-ONE

In a vomit-stained white shirt and crumpled, black pinstripe trousers with one of the knees torn out, a dishevelled-looking Spencer Warne gambolled along the pavement with Otto, his co-worker from the jewellery store. Spencer swung around a lamppost while Otto, close behind, swigged from a glass bottle in a brown paper bag. The dilated pupils in their bloodshot eyes looked like large, black holes. Narrowly missing an elderly lady pulling a shopping trolley on wheels, Spencer attempted a loud, tuneless rendition of Singing In The Rain. Passers-by, giving the two men a wide berth, looked on with expressions of disgust veiled with amusement.

'Last night was the *best*,' Otto said, hanging an arm over Spencer's shoulder and swaying towards him.

'Yeah. It was.' Spencer broke off from the song to reply. 'I love you man. We should do this again.'

'That time they threw us out the club,' Otto giggled.

'You were wasted, man,' Spencer added. 'Off your head.'

'Like you were waaayyyy worse,' Otto said as he took another swig from the concealed bottle. He pulled a face. 'Eughhh. This stuff tastes like shit.'

There was the sound of a cell phone ringing.

'Your phone, Otto,' Spencer said.

'Not mine, mate. Yours.' Otto slurred his words. 'I gave that hot blonde girl in the club your number by the way. You're welcome.'

'You what? You gave her my number? The hell you do that for?' Spencer spoke with a mixture of excitement and dismay.

'She was *so* into you. You lucky sonofabitch.'

'Yeah? You think so?'

The phone continued to ring.

'Answer your phone man. You can thank me later.'

Spencer clumsily patted the pockets of his shirt and trousers in an attempt to locate his cell phone. Finally, he pulled it out of his trouser pocket and looked at the screen. He shielded his eyes in an attempt to focus on the caller ID. Thick grey clouds covered the sky, but his eyes were sensitised to the light from his dilated pupils.

'Well answer it then,' Otto said.

Engulfed in a euphoric high of alcohol and cocaine intoxication, and squinting through the brightness of the daylight, Spencer tried to connect what his eyes were seeing on the screen of the cell phone to his brain. The incoming call was from Alicia. He noticed it was the fifth that morning. He'd missed the other four.

'What you waiting for?' Otto asked.

'It's not her,' Spencer said with a troubled expression. 'It's not the hot blonde girl.'

'Who is it then? Your mum?' Otto said with a sneer.

'Yeah right. My mum hasn't called me in twenty years. It's Alicia.'

'Who the hell's that?'

Spencer's cell phone rang off as the caller was directed to voicemail.

'I probably should've answered,' Spencer said, looking suddenly remorseful.

'She your girlfriend or something?'

'No. Sadly.'

'Well, she'll leave a message or call back if it's that important.'

'She's called me four times already.'

'Meh. Women. They're always so demanding. My ex used to be like that. Got really jealous and suspicious if I didn't answer her calls. Forget it Spence. Look, I've got enough coke left to cut a few more lines each. Let's get high again.' Otto pulled a clear plastic bag containing a small amount of white powder from his shirt pocket.

'I'm already high,' Spencer replied, still looking at his phone.

'Come on man, let's do this.' Otto pulled Spencer to the edge of the pavement, near the doorway of what had once been a fried chicken shop. Obscene graffiti covered the crude wooden boards which had been haphazardly nailed over the windows and door. The stench of stale urine and rancid cooking oil lingered in the air.

'Here'll do,' Otto said, dropping to his knees. With hands still shaking from his previous high, he carefully tipped some of the white powder onto the pavement and, with a plastic gym card, attempted to divide the powder into lines a little over an inch long. Spencer knelt beside him and began frantically checking his pockets.

'I've still got that fiver somewhere,' he said.

'I've got one.' Otto produced a five pound note, already curled at the edges. He rolled it lengthways into a cylinder shape and passed it to Spencer.

'You first,' he said.

'Thanks man,' Spencer said. He leaned down towards the neat lines of powder and brought the rolled-up note to one of his nostrils. Suddenly, his cell phone began ringing loudly again. He jumped and hovered over the cocaine.

'Go for it Spence,' Otto coaxed. 'Forget your phone. She'll call back. The bitches always do.'

Spencer paused before leaning further down to the white powder. With his phone still ringing, he placed the note at the end of one of the lines and was about to inhale deeply when, out of the corner of his eye, he spotted a man shuffling towards them. He was wearing a dirty, blue checked shirt, grey trousers a few sizes too large and a navy baseball cap pulled down low over his eyes. The lower part of his face was mostly obscured by a scruffy beard. Over his shoulder he carried a small backpack. He seemed familiar to Spencer.

'Spare some change?' the man asked as he limped closer. He was accompanied by an unpleasant odour of sweat and alcohol. 'What're you boys doing?'

'Get lost,' Otto snarled.

'*Hey!*' the man said in an offended tone. 'I only asked for a bit o' change.'

'And I only told you to *get lost*,' Otto said again.

'Leave it out Otto,' Spencer said, an eternal advocate for the homeless.

'Don't tell me to get lost,' the man replied savagely to Otto. As he came towards them, he spotted the lines of cocaine on the pavement and gave a sly smile.

'Ohhh, I see what you boys are up to.'

'It's none of your business,' Otto said. 'Move along before I call the police.'

'Like you're really gonna call the cops,' the homeless man said with a knowing look, nodding at the white powder. Suddenly he stepped forward and stamped a foot in the middle of the lines, crushing the powder into the pavement.

'You *bastard*,' Otto yelled at him, standing up and shoving him backwards. The homeless man recovered surprisingly quickly and pushed Otto hard against the boarded windows of the chicken shop. Otto moaned in pain and, before he had time to retaliate, took a hard blow to the stomach from the fist of the homeless man. He bent double, swaying against the wall of the shop, preparing himself for the next round of pain.

Spencer, still kneeling on the pavement, watched in horror as the man and Otto fought. He was reluctant to intervene, especially as the homeless man seemed to be getting the better of his co-worker. He was also beginning to feel dizzy and the light was still so bright. Suddenly, a wave of nausea swept over him. He closed his eyes and steadied himself on the wall, trying to control his breathing, but the light-headedness and nausea seemed to worsen with each breath. Suddenly, he dropped to his knees and wretched violently. What was left of the white powder scattered across the pavement was covered in vomit. His stomach hurt and his head was pounding. A few feet away, the altercation between Otto and the homeless man continued, but Spencer was oblivious. Beside him, his cell phone began ringing again. He glanced down at it. Through the haze of nausea and dizziness, he could see Alicia's smiling face light up the screen. He swore under his breath, picked it up and answered it.

'Spencer, where've you been? I've been calling you all morning.' At that moment, the sound of her voice was bittersweet.

'Sorry Alicia, I've been… I was…'

'Where are you? At church?'

'No. I was… I just popped out… Had to get some milk.'

Without warning, the overwhelming wave of nausea was back. Spencer dropped his phone to the pavement and vomited again.

'Spencer? Are you there? Are you okay?' He closed his eyes in self-reproach and wiped his mouth with the back of his arm.

'Spencer! Are you unwell?' Alicia's voice sounded through the speaker of his phone. He picked it up and cleared his throat.

'Not exactly,' he said ruefully.

'What then? What's wrong with you?' He could hear the realisation in her voice as she spoke.

'It's — it's not what you think,' he said.

'Oh? What *do* I think?' There was a hardness to her tone, a note of disapproval tinged with sadness.

'That I'm drunk, and high, and that I've spent the night in a club, boozing and snorting coke.'

'*Have* you?'

'Alicia, I don't know what the hell happened. I just… It was a busy day at work yesterday, what with Ronan and Camilla gone, we're like, two staff members down. It's damn hard work. We're all stressed. And, well, you know, I'm taking a different route to the store every day, just in case I'm being watched. The whole journey took nearly three hours yesterday morning. It's exhausting. Otto — you know Otto from work? — he asked if I wanted to go for a night out in town with him and some of his mates. I said no at first, but he kind of put pressure on me and, well, I guess I thought it would be harmless, you know, and with all that's going on, I thought it might help take my mind off things a bit. We went to this club. Can't even remember where. Soho maybe. I promised myself I'd only have a couple of drinks and there's no way I'd do drugs, but, well, I just don't know what happened.'

There was silence at the end of the line.

'I'm sorry Alicia.'

'It's okay. Where are you now?'

'I'm… I'm just on my way home.'

'Ten-forty in the morning and you're just on your way *home*?'

'I can tell you're mad at me, Alicia.'

'I'm not exactly over the moon, but no, I'm not mad at you.'

'You sure?'

'We'll talk about it later. In the meantime, I have an assignment for you. Look at it as a chance to redeem yourself.'

'I'll try. What kind of assignment? I don't know if I can…'

'Just hear me out before you start refusing. And I realise you're in no fit state for anything right now. I guess it's lucky I booked your flights for tomorrow morning.'

'My flights? Where am I going?'

'You'll need your passport Spencer. Remember we got one for you when you came out of rehab? You haven't lost it, have you?'

'No, I know where it is.'

'Good. Now go home, drink lots of water, sleep off whatever you've been drinking and inhaling, dig out your passport and call Sandra at Tropical Destinations Travel Company this afternoon.'

'Who?'

'Don't worry, I'll send you her details. She's holding some return flights to Antigua in your name.'

'She's *what?*'

'There's also a room booked for you at a beachside motel close to where I'm staying. You leave tomorrow. There'll be a taxi to collect you from outside your apartment at five-thirty tomorrow morning.'

'*What time?*' Spencer asked in horror.

'Set your alarm, Spencer. Set ten alarms. You need to be at Gatwick Airport checking in by seven-thirty. Your flight leaves at ten twenty-five.'

'But… I've got work.'

'No, I've cleared it with Tobias. He's granted you two weeks' leave. You don't need to call him; he's not expecting you in tomorrow.'

'But we're so short-staffed…'

'It's okay, he says they'll manage. I'll let him know you were concerned though. Now, your taxi will drop you outside the South Terminal at Gatwick tomorrow. Follow the signs and ask for help if you don't know where you're going. Remember to check the gate number for your flight on the screens and don't be late. When you land in Antigua, there'll be a taxi to take you to your motel. I'll meet you there.'

'I'm really going to Antigua?' Spencer asked in disbelief.

'Yes, you are. I need you out here.'

'What for?'

'I've a job for you Spencer. It's a job I think you'll do very well. Let's just say you're perfectly suited to the task.'

'What kind of job?'

'I'll give you the full details when you get here. Oh, by the way, when you pack, make sure you throw in a few old clothes.'

'Why?'

'You're going undercover. Remember your life on the streets? It's time to go back there for a couple of weeks.'

'You're kidding, right? I don't even *look* like a homeless man anymore; I'm clean shaven and I've had my teeth fixed. And you think my scrawny white arse is gonna blend in in *Antigua*? No way, Alicia. Worst plan ever.'

'I disagree,' Alicia replied. 'Sure, there are a few cultural differences, and I'm no expert on the rules of the street, but I know you can do this Spencer.'

'Do what?'

'I need you to find a missing person.'

Spencer sighed. She knew she'd win.

'Okay. I'll do my best.'

'Look, I've got to go, it's still only six am here; I've been up since five making these arrangements for you. Don't let me down Spencer. Go home to bed and then call Sandra and pack your bags. And don't forget your passport. I'll see you tomorrow.'

They said goodbye and hung up. Spencer looked around as he slowly got to his feet. There was no sign of Otto or the homeless man. He hoped Otto was all right. He'd call him later. He thought of the homeless man. He'd seemed so familiar somehow, the navy cap pulled down low over his face, the beard. Suddenly Spencer remembered. He was the man who'd been slumped in the shop doorway opposite the jewellery store earlier that week. Spencer had bought him a coffee and a blueberry muffin. Even then there had been something familiar about him. What was he doing all the way over here in Whitechapel? It was an unusual coincidence that their paths should cross so fortuitously.

Still fighting the dizziness and nausea, and contemplating the odds of an encounter with the same homeless man in two very different parts of London within the space of a few days, Spencer walked slowly back to his apartment. The effects of the alcohol and cocaine would wear off throughout the day, although he wasn't sure he'd be able to sleep. He felt a mixture of excitement at the thought of the trip to Antigua, along with a tinge of fear about what Alicia expected of him, and guilt over what she thought of him at this moment. He didn't want to let her down again. If this was how he could make it up to her, then he'd risk life and limbs and give it his best shot.

THIRTY-TWO

It had been a stressful week and Tobias Moncler was looking forward to a relaxing Sunday morning on the golf course with two fellow Hatton Garden jewellers. They had just teed off for the first hole when Tobias received the long distance telephone call from the Caribbean. He waved his friends on to continue the game, ignoring the look of disapproval from one of them; it was widely accepted club etiquette that there were no cell phone conversations on the course. Retreating to a path that ran around the perimeter, he answered the call. It was Alicia. She had an important assignment for Spencer in Antigua, relating to the diamond necklace and the murdered woman, Anastasia. It was an assignment that only he was suitably qualified for. Would Tobias agree to a fortnight's leave for him at short notice? With Ronan and Camilla gone, the store was already short-staffed, but Tobias said they'd manage and granted Spencer's leave. He was about to hang up and return to the game, when Alicia began speaking again.

'Tobias, there's something else I need your help with. I think it would be helpful to track down the owners of the original diamond necklace, the one that was allegedly stolen in ninety-five. Gray suggested the best way to do this is to attract their attention and get them to come to us. I think he might be right.'

'What d'you need me to do?' Tobias asked.

'Gray thinks we can lure them in with the necklace. The thing is, we've no idea whether the original one was actually stolen at all. According to my source, the general manager of the resort in Antigua from where it supposedly went missing, it never showed up before the owners, Charles and Vivienne Karleman, were evacuated with all the other hotel guests ahead of a hurricane which devastated the island. As far as I can tell, the necklace — which was very valuable, as you know — was never reported stolen. It's possible that this is because it was never *actually* stolen, but merely misplaced by the Karlemans and subsequently found on their return home. Which is why the hotel staff were never contacted again by the Karlemans. Then again, if the necklace *was* stolen, or misplaced, and never recovered, there's a slim chance the Karlemans are still on the lookout for it, even after all this time.'

'I'm not sure I'm following…' Tobias said.

'Ah, no, sorry, it is a bit confusing,' Alicia replied. 'Essentially Tobias, do you think you can put the word out that a diamond necklace, worth over twenty million US dollars, is up for sale for the highest bidder?'

'Officially? Like with an auction house or something?' Tobias queried.

'Yes, spread the word, put it up in lights, make it as conspicuous as possible.'

'Alicia, you do remember that I've only got the moissanite replica of the necklace, don't you? I can hardly pass that off as the real thing. It's known as fraud.'

'I realise that, and I'm certainly not asking you to do anything illegal which would jeopardise your business. Do you have any contacts you could confide in at one of the auction houses? All I'm asking is that we lay some bait for the Karlemans in the hopes that we can reel them in somehow. I don't even know if they're still alive, where they live or what they do for a living, but if the necklace was never found, they probably still have half an eye on the catalogues of the major international auction houses, in the hopes that it might resurface one day.'

'Now I'm with you. Yes, I'm sure something like that could be arranged. I have a contact at one of the international auction houses in London with a prominent global presence. I'm sure he'd be happy to help. How soon do you need this to happen?'

'As soon as possible. Time is of the essence.'

'No problem. I'll reach out to my contact this afternoon. The necklace is sure to attract considerable attention from interested parties…'

'Can you let me have the names of everyone who enquires about it?'

'Of course.'

'Oh and one other thing…'

'Yes?'

'In the general description of the necklace, can you put that it consists of forty-eight flawless, round brilliant cut diamonds?'

'But there were forty-nine.'

'There were in the moissanite necklace. I'm not sure but it's possible that the genuine necklace had only forty-eight.'

'So what, there were only forty-eight round diamonds in total?'

'Either that or there were forty-nine and one of them was different to the others. It seems that whoever commissioned the imitation necklace wasn't aware of this.'

'Understood. I'll be in touch when the word's out.'

'Thanks. We'll talk soon.'

Tobias's golf buddies were nowhere to be seen. There would be little point in attempting to catch up now. He pocketed his golf ball and slid his driver into his golf bag. As he made his way back to the clubhouse he called Rick, his contact at the auction house. The morning on the golf course was abandoned for lunch in Mayfair.

THIRTY-THREE

3:35 pm, Monday, August 27
The Sunset Motel, Antigua

Dressed in a loud Hawaiian shirt with matching shorts, Havaiana flip-flops, a white baseball cap and fake, oversized Ray-Bans, a travel-weary Spencer Warne emerged from the minivan. The taxi driver retrieved a fake Samsonite suitcase from the trunk of the taxi and placed it on the tarmac beside him. Wishing Spencer a pleasant vacation, he jumped back into the driving seat of the minivan where his last two tourist drop-offs of the day, a young honeymoon couple, were seated in the rear. Alicia, who had been waiting in the motel reception, hurried outside.

'Spencer! You made it!' she said excitedly, giving him a bear hug.

'Alicia! Am I glad to see you,' Spencer replied with a wide grin.

'Oh my, you've certainly dressed for the vacation,' Alicia said, stepping back and surveying Spencer's choice of attire.

'Realised I didn't have any clothes for, like, hot countries so I did a bit of airport shopping. What d'you think?' Spencer held his arms out and looked down proudly at the shirt.

'Please tell me this isn't your undercover outfit,' Alicia said with a look of amusement.

'Duh! No! Course not. Don't worry, I've brought some other clothes. Trust me, I know what I'm doing. I've spent half my life on the streets. This ain't my first rodeo.'

'No, but it is your first one in Antigua.' Alicia knew Spencer was putting on a brave front.

'Yeah, it is,' he replied, 'and it's damn hot here too. I feel like I'm in a sauna.'

'You're not in Blighty now,' Alicia said with a smile. 'Let's go inside and get you checked in.'

Spencer picked up his suitcase and followed Alicia into the motel reception. The receptionist, a smartly dressed young man, welcomed him to The Sunset Motel and issued him with a keycard for his room and instructions on how to use the safe.

'You're in room thirty-two, Mr Warne. If you head back out of reception and follow the path around to the left, your room is on the upper level, about half way along,' he said, stretching over the desk and pointing. Spencer thanked him and followed Alicia out of the reception.

'How was your journey?' Alicia asked as they made their way along the path to Spencer's room.

'Not bad. The flight was long. I watched about three movies and we still hadn't got here. Didn't realise this place was so far away. Oh, and I made sure I wasn't followed.' He cast a furtive glance over his shoulder.

'I'm relieved to hear it,' Alicia said. 'You'll be able to take care of yourself on the streets, won't you?'

'Yeah. Course,' Spencer replied with a measure of uncertainty. 'Like I said, I know what I'm doing.'

'Keep your cell phone with you. You can call me any time.'

'I will.'

'You're still okay with this, aren't you?'

'Yeah. Yeah, 'course I am.' The words were forced. 'It's the least I can do to make it up to you anyway.'

'What d'you mean?'

'I let you down on Saturday night. After everything you've done for me. You've been so kind Alicia, and I blew it the other night. Made a big mistake. But if I can make it up to you by helping you here, then I'll do my best.' The words sounded sorrowful and forlorn.

'You don't need to make anything up to me.' Alicia stopped and turned to face him. 'Sure, those weren't your finest hours but we draw a line under it and move on. Agreed?'

'Thanks,' Spencer said with a touch of embarrassment.

Alicia gave him a firm hug before turning back to the path. It led through an avenue of palm trees to a two-storey building with a flat roof. It was painted cream and was studded with alternate doors and windows, all with blinds drawn across. At one end, a small set of balustraded steps led to a row of rooms on the upper level.

'Need a hand with your case?' Alicia asked.

'I'm good,' Spencer said, wrestling with the plastic handle.

'It looks heavy.'

'All holiday essentials,' Spencer replied, panting slightly as the case bumped up the steps behind him.

'How many Hawaiian shirts did you buy at the airport?'

'Three. Maybe four.'

They reached the walkway at the top of the steps. As the receptionist had informed them, room thirty-two was about halfway along. Alicia inserted the keycard into the reader on the door and pushed it open. Spencer followed her inside. The room was small and basic, but looked clean and comfortable, with the decor in various shades of brown.

'I hope you like it,' Alicia said.

'It's very nice,' Spencer said, removing the fake Ray-Bans and looking around.

'Good. I'll let you get settled in. There'll be a taxi to collect you at six-thirty this evening to take you to The West Beach Club where Gray and I are staying. You're having dinner with us tonight.'

'I am?' Spencer asked in surprise.

'You've got three hours to shower, change, have a nap, whatever you need to do before then. And don't forget this.' Alicia threw the keycard onto a small table opposite the double bed.

'I won't,' Spencer replied. 'See you at dinner.'

8:05 pm
Falmouth Harbour Marina, Antigua

The multimillion dollar super-yacht Dark Illusion was docked at Falmouth Harbour Marina, close to the brightly lit Antigua Yacht Club Marina Building. Her sleek, fifty-eight metre hull skulked low in the darkness and the reflection of her white and purple lights shimmered on the black, calm water as waves gently lapped against her side. Small RIBs scurried back and forth between the jetty and other yachts of assorted shapes and sizes, berthed in the harbour, ferrying passengers to and from the bars and restaurants across the marina. Dark Illusion employed no such activity. She remained mysterious and silent, anonymous and detached from the bustle and liveliness surrounding her.

A curious onlooker may have assumed that the affluent passengers onboard the super-yacht, whoever they were, had abandoned ship that evening for one of the restaurants nearby, leaving the crew below deck with their various tasks. The onlooker may also have wondered who the passengers were. Wealthy millennials perhaps? A celebrity with an entourage de rigueur?

Over an after-dinner cocktail at one of the waterfront bars, an onlooker may even have pondered the cost of chartering, or owning, such a palatial vessel. A truly interested observer may yet still have conducted a brief online search for such information, but the internet presence of Dark Illusion was shrouded in as much mystery as the ghostly silhouette currently ensconced in Falmouth Harbour.

With luxury and extravagance at the fore of the design brief, no expense had been spared when the super-yacht was constructed in 2012. The interior boasted the finest of materials including dark oak, white onyx and Lalique crystal, with leather and silk furnishings. The craft accommodated twelve guests and fourteen crew with seven cabins, which included a full-width VIP stateroom and an impressive master suite with a study. On the lower deck there was a fully stocked bar with a wine cellar, a cinema room and a state of the art gym. The main deck was a showcase of opulent dining, entertainment and relaxation areas, while on the sundeck a large jacuzzi was surrounded by sun pads, loungers and another well stocked bar.

In the study adjoining the master suite, a man in his sixties, slightly greying, slightly balding and losing a battle with an expanding waistline, tapped at the keys of a laptop, his piercing blue eyes fixated by the images on the screen. Reclining on a cream leather sofa, he wore a black t-shirt and grey linen shorts. A gold chain hung around his neck, just visible under the collar of his t-shirt. His deeply tanned face had a hardened jawline.

There was a knock on the door of the master suite.

'Come in,' the man said sharply in a clipped British accent. The door opened and a man twenty years younger entered. He was of African American descent with a body to which many hours in a gym had obviously been dedicated.

'Ah Anton. Perfect timing,' the man with the laptop said. 'I trust everything went smoothly with Sarkis this evening?'

'All according to plan, Charles,' the younger man replied in a hybrid accent of British and American. 'The trucks left Sudan two hours ago and are heading north towards the port of Alexandria as we speak. I'm in touch with Assim. The cargo ship is due to arrive in port tomorrow night.'

'Excellent.' Charles nodded with approval but the jawline remained hardened. 'And details of the shipment?'

Anton produced an iPad and tapped on the screen.

'All in order,' he said, passing it to the older man. 'AK-47s, mortar shells, rocket launchers, machine guns, as per the consignment.'

'Very good,' Charles replied, handing the iPad back to Anton.

'There is one other thing you may be interested in,' Anton replied, tapping the screen again. 'You mentioned the other day about a wedding anniversary gift for Vivienne.'

'I did. Well remembered Anton. Have you found anything?'

'I think I just might have. How about this?' He returned the iPad to Charles. There was silence in the cabin as Charles gazed at the screen for a long moment. Anton waited patiently.

'Do you like it?' he asked.

'Where did you find this?' Charles asked, without looking up.

'It's a new addition to the catalogue of one of the major international auction houses.'

'Has Vivienne seen it?'

'I believe she has. She's on the privileged client mailing lists of most of the global auction houses, as you know.'

Charles sighed with a slight grimace.

'Where is she?' he asked.

'I think she's in her stateroom.'

'Ask her to come in here. Immediately.' It was an emotionless command, although Charles appeared visibly moved. His eyes were suddenly wet with tears.

'Of course,' Anton replied. He knew better than to ask if something was wrong.

Ten minutes later, the door to the master suite opened and a woman entered. In spite of extensive cosmetic interventions, botox and fillers, she looked to be roughly the same age as Charles. Her wrinkled, sun-damaged skin was tanned and freckled. Her dark hair, heavily dyed, was streaked with a rainbow of caramel highlights and cut in a short bob. She wore a cobalt blue velour tracksuit on her slender frame with diamond-encrusted sandals on pedicured feet.

'What d'you want Charles? I'm about to head to the gym.'

Charles hadn't moved from his position and still gazed at the iPad on his lap. He handed it to her.

'Anton tells me you've already seen this?'

Vivienne took the iPad from him. As she studied the screen a strange look came into her eyes, one of anger tinged with fear. She swallowed and turned to Charles.

'Yes,' she replied abruptly. 'I was going to speak to you about it. After all this time. And suddenly... there it is. You think it's genuine?'

Charles glanced at Anton with a raised eyebrow.

'What would you say, Anton?'

'I don't see why it shouldn't be,' came the reply. 'The auction house is reputable and if you care to read the description...'

Vivienne looked back down at the iPad screen on which was displayed the image of a necklace; a perfect circle of glittering, colourless diamonds with a dazzling pear-shaped, pink diamond in the centre.

'How many colourless diamonds are there?' Charles asked suddenly.

'It says here there are forty-eight,' Vivienne said, reading the description aloud. She looked at Charles again. 'It's the one, isn't it?' She paused and then said in a low voice: 'I want it. I want it back.'

Charles did not reply.

'Is everything okay?' Anton ventured the question.

'Charles, I want that necklace,' Vivienne said again, more insistently.

'All right then.' Charles nodded slowly. He appeared to be distracted, as if his thoughts were elsewhere. Turning to Anton he spoke deliberately. 'Contact the auction house immediately. Tell them I will pay any price for this necklace.'

'Of course. What name shall I give?'

There was a pause before the reply.

'Karleman. Charles Karleman.'

9:30 pm
The West Beach Club restaurant, Antigua

The Lobster Thermidor, served with a green salad and sautéed potatoes, was washed down with a pint of fruit punch. It was accompanied by the animated conversation of Gray and Alicia, along with the vibrant music and energetic dancing of the Caribo Dancers, a flamboyant group who performed for diners in the restaurant of The West Beach Club.

'I think I'm going to like the Caribbean,' Spencer said with a broad smile as he tapped his feet in time to the reggae beat. 'Those dancers are killing it.' He turned to his dinner companions. 'Thanks for dinner, by the way. Really appreciate it. I think it might even be as good as Chicken Shop.'

'As good as *where*?' Gray asked.

'Chicken Shop and Dirty Burger,' Alicia replied with a laugh. 'It's the place in Whitechapel where Spencer and I used to meet for lunch when he was my informant. It's also become the litmus test against which every other restaurant is measured.'

'Ah. I see,' Gray replied. 'So the food here is of a high standard then?'

'*Very* high,' Spencer said with a serious expression.

'It's become a bit of a trend for Spencer to receive his assignments over gourmet dinners,' Alicia remarked, 'speaking of which, we need to brief you for your next one Spencer.'

'You said you needed me to find somebody,' Spencer said warily. 'A missing person. On the streets.'

'That's correct,' Alicia said. 'His name's Owen Rapley.'

'D'you have a picture of him?'

'As a matter of fact, I do,' Alicia replied. From her purse, she produced a photograph she had removed from her mother's photograph album. It was the one of her parents playing a game of tennis on the courts at Rock Palm Resort. In the top right corner of the picture, slightly out of focus, was a young, well-built man in his early twenties. He was tall, handsome and muscular and dressed in a white t-shirt and shorts.

'He doesn't look like he belongs on the streets to me,' Spencer said, taking the photograph.

'He didn't back then. That photo was taken in nineteen ninety-five. He was the manager of a sports reception and a tennis coach at a very nice five-star resort here on the island, very similar to this place.'

'*Ninety-five?*' Spencer said. 'That's more than twenty years ago. He won't look anything *like* this now.'

'I'll bet he doesn't,' Alicia agreed. 'He was in his early twenties back then. Now he'll be in his forties. And he certainly won't be wearing his tennis whites. But you did ask for a picture, Spencer.'

'All right, what's his story?' Spencer asked, discarding the photograph on the table.

Alicia filled Spencer in on Owen's background from the very beginning. He listened intently and nodded occasionally. A waitress arrived with a fresh round of fruit punches.

'So, just to clarify, there was never enough evidence to convict Owen of Anastasia's murder,' Spencer said, picking up one of the punches and taking a long sip.

'That's correct,' Alicia replied, 'other than the testimony of witnesses who saw them on the beach together.'

'So… Do you think he *is* innocent?'

Alicia paused.

'I'm not certain,' she replied. 'I'd like to think he is, but we don't have any proof of that. He could still be the killer. We can't be sure. Just because everyone says he's innocent, it doesn't mean he is. Be careful Spencer. Keep that in mind.'

'Don't worry. I can take care of myself.'

'I know you can.' Alicia looked at him with a touch of fondness.

'I won't let you down again.'

'I believe you,' Alicia said. 'Anyway, that's all the information I have. It's over to you now to find him.'

'And I will,' Spencer replied. 'I won't fail. I know what it's like to be homeless and I know how to find people who don't want to be found.'

THIRTY-FOUR

The call Alicia had been waiting for came in from Tobias just after eight o'clock the following morning, slightly sooner than she had expected, but welcome, nonetheless. He informed her that Rick, his associate at the London offices of a leading international auction house, had already been contacted by a number of interested buyers for the necklace which had been added to the auction catalogue.

'He knows it's a fake, doesn't he?' Alicia said.

'Yes, don't worry, he's in the loop. We know how we're going to play this, it's fine.'

'Good. I just don't want to cause you any trouble, Tobias. You've been through enough already.'

'Don't worry about me. But speaking of people getting into trouble, I trust Spencer's arrived safely?'

'Complete with a suitcase full of garish Hawaiian shirts. My eyes are only just recovering.'

'Ah. Good. Why doesn't that surprise me? Glad he's okay. I've got a list of names for you of the potential buyers who've registered their interest in the necklace, but I think you'll only be interested in one of them.'

'Oh?'

'Does the name Charles Karleman sound familiar?'

'Wow. That was fast.'

'I thought it would. One of his people made contact with Rick first thing this morning. Asked to speak with him personally. Charles Karleman is desperate for the necklace at — and I quote — any price.'

'That's interesting.'

'It is. Based on the background you've given me, his desire for the necklace at any price tells me two things: one, that he's willing to pay for what he believes is the genuine diamond necklace. He obviously isn't aware that there's an imitation in circulation, ergo, he probably isn't connected with Vivienne Karlsson in any way. And the second thing is that I don't think the Karlemans ever found their lost, or stolen, diamond necklace — whatever happened to it — and they've been looking for it all this time. And now they want it back. Gray's plan worked Alicia. You've found them. And you'll never guess where they're based.'

'London? New York? LA?'

'Antigua.'

'*Here? On the island?*'

'Yes. And what's more, Charles has agreed to meet with you personally.'

'With *me*?' Alicia sounded shocked. 'Tobias, how did you...'

'I hope you don't mind Alicia, I took it upon myself to go one step further. Of course, if it doesn't suit you, Rick and I have a story we can go back to Charles Karleman with so you've lost nothing. I just thought you'd like to meet him...'

'Go on Tobias. I'm listening.'

'When Rick told me the Karlemans were based in Antigua and would pay any price for the necklace, I asked him to relay the message back to them that the vendor — that's you, by the way — also resided in the Caribbean and would like to meet with Charles personally to discuss a price for the necklace without taking it to auction. I believe Rick gave him some spiel about the auction house providing a more personalised service for certain VIP clients. Anyway, Charles agreed to this and, if you are also in agreement, is awaiting your instructions on when and where you'd like to meet. If Gray's happy to pose as an international representative of the auction house, that would make things a little more authentic.'

'Smart work on your part Tobias,' Alicia said. 'I think it would be a very good idea to meet. What about the necklace though?'

'You don't need it. I'll send you lots of professional pictures that you can take to the meeting with you on a laptop or iPad. Interestingly, Spencer's asked for some pictures of the necklace too. What's he up to?'

'I've no idea why he'd need those,' Alicia replied. 'He's probably got some crazy plan going on though. Sometimes it's better to leave him to it.'

'He's okay though, isn't he?'

'He's fine. I won't let anything happen to him.'

'Thanks. He's not a bad employee these days and he's been particularly loyal with this whole necklace fiasco. It's funny, when I took him on at the beginning of the year, some days I asked myself what on earth I was thinking. But he's beginning to show some promise.'

'I'm glad to hear that. Thanks for giving him a chance.'

'Not at all. Now then, about this meeting with Charles Karleman. When and where shall I say? Obviously this is your call.'

'Do you happen to know where in Antigua Charles is based?'

'No, I just have a contact number for him.'

'Fine. There's a café on the second floor of the Antigua Yacht Club Marina Building in English Harbour called Cloggy's. The food is excellent and it has stunning views over Falmouth Harbour if you ever bring your wife out here one day. I can thoroughly recommend it. How about there, tonight, at seven? I'll meet him in the bar for drinks and we'll take it from there.'

'I'll relay the message and get back to you when Charles has confirmed.'

'Thanks.'

'You're welcome. I hope it's productive.'

Surprising even himself, Spencer woke early that morning. He presumed it was due to the five hour time difference between Antigua and the UK. He stretched and rolled across the bed to the nightstand where his cell phone was attached to a charger. He unplugged it and checked his emails. The photos he'd requested from Tobias had been dutifully forwarded and Spencer gazed at them. The necklace had been professionally photographed from a number of angles in clever lighting and looked spectacular, even on the screen of a cell phone. He briefly allowed himself to entertain the image of Alicia wearing nothing but the necklace before he sat up and got out of bed. He showered quickly and dressed in casual clothes: a black, short-sleeved shirt, cargo shorts and the Havaianas. He removed one hundred dollars from his wallet in various notes and placed them in a concealed pocket in his shorts, along with his phone. Smearing a high factor sun lotion across his face, neck, arms and legs, he picked up his room key.

Ensuring the door of his room was securely locked, he trotted down the stairs and followed the path to reception. The sun was already high in the sky and in the distance Spencer could hear the sound of the ocean. There was a different receptionist on duty to the one who had checked Spencer in the previous day. As he handed in the keycard to his room, Spencer asked if the receptionist could call for a cab to St. John's.

'No problem,' she replied amicably. After a brief conversation with a cab company, she assured Spencer he would be collected out front in ten minutes. He thanked her and headed outside to wait.

It was a pleasant drive to St. John's and, as the cab driver chatted about the history of the island, Spencer took in the views and marvelled at the variety of tropical trees and plants along the sides of the roads. He was charmed by the colourful houses that they passed; they were simple yet homely. He thought he'd fit in well with the laidback, outdoor lifestyle of the island.

Twenty minutes later, they reached St. John's. Unsure as to where the best place would be for his assignment to begin, he asked the cab driver to drop him off somewhere near the centre of town. He'd find his way from there. He declined the offer of a return journey later in the day, paid the driver and got out. As the taxi rejoined the line of traffic, Spencer stood on the pavement and looked around. He'd studied a map of St. John's the night before, but aside from enabling him to get his bearings, an encyclopaedic knowledge of the streets was less important than his instincts and gut feelings. As instructed, he made a call to Alicia to inform her he was live on location and that he'd be in touch in due course. Wherever Owen Rapley was hiding, Spencer would find him.

THIRTY-FIVE

7:00 pm

Cloggy's Café, English Harbour, Antigua

Wearing an elegant floor-sweeping dress in navy, teamed with diamanté sandals and a coral necklace from the hotel gift shop, Alicia entered the bar with Gray close behind her. He wore smart grey trousers and a white linen shirt and, with a laptop bag slung over his shoulder, he carried a black leather-bound file — borrowed from Leon — brimming with papers. Understated yet professional. She ordered a large glass of Pinot Noir while he ordered a lemonade. Cloggy's bar was dimly lit in warm hues of orange and gold. Close to the entrance of the café was an area with tables and chairs, beyond which a vaulted wooden ceiling rose above a comfortable lounge area with low sofas and easy chairs in neutral colours. From here, a series of glass doors led through to the gallery outside, which afforded magnificent views of the multimillion dollar yachts moored in the harbour.

'Think you'll recognise the Karlemans?' Gray asked, taking a sip of the lemonade.

'Probably,' Alicia replied, 'but they'll be going some if they recognise me.' She stiffened suddenly. 'They're here. Right on time.'

'Both of them?'

'Yes. Oh my gosh Gray, Vivienne looks even more ghastly than I remember her from the nineties. Help me here, I don't know how I'll keep a straight face.'

Gray turned towards the entrance of the bar as a couple entered. The man, in his sixties and with a dark tan, wore a grey short-sleeved shirt and jeans. His blue eyes were startling and he wore a gold chain around his neck, just visible underneath his shirt. He was accompanied by a woman of roughly the same age, although significant attempts and sums of money had clearly been spent in an effort to disguise this. The art of the subtle application of makeup appeared to have been overlooked. A flowing, leopard-print chiffon dress had been complemented with four inch stiletto sandals, also in leopard.

Alicia stepped towards them.

'Charles Karleman?' she asked.

'Yes,' the man replied without smiling.

'Hello Mr Karleman, I'm Melissa Jones. Please call me Melissa,' she said, selecting a variation of a past alias she had used for previous undercover work, conducted as a freelance journalist. She held out her hand.

'Charles,' the man said abruptly and shook her hand firmly. He turned to the woman in the leopard print. 'My wife, Vivienne.'

The women shook hands and Gray dutifully introduced himself as Jonathan Kendle, associate jewellery specialist from the Private Sales team of the auction house with whom the necklace was listed. There was more official hand-shaking before Gray invited them to an area in the far corner of the bar with low sofas surrounding a glass-topped table. Champagne was ordered and delivered as Gray opened his leather-bound file and set up the laptop on the table in front of him while Alicia made small talk with Charles and Vivienne.

'Have you been in Antigua for long?'

'Many years now,' Charles replied. He glanced at Vivienne. 'Haven't we darling?'

'We love it here,' Vivienne replied. Alicia remembered the clipped British accents from the conversations with Leon in the restaurant at Rock Palm. It was as if no time at all had gone by.

'But you're from England originally?' she asked casually.

'Surrey. We never go back though,' Charles replied.

'Nothing to go back *for*,' Vivienne chipped in. 'Why would we? I mean the weather, for starters; it's always cold and raining in England. I don't do cold and raining, do I Charles?'

'No Vivienne, you don't.'

'It's all far too depressing,' Vivienne went on. 'Give me sunshine and a blue sky and I'm happy.'

'Oh I agree,' Alicia replied eagerly. She shot a glance at Gray who nodded.

'We're all set,' he said. He slid the laptop towards the Karlemans. On the screen was a picture of the diamond necklace against a black velvet background. It was one of the photographs taken by a professional photographer at the auction house in London. As Charles and Vivienne leaned forward to view the image on the screen, Alicia watched them carefully.

Vivienne's eyes narrowed and she took a sharp breath in. She was a hardened, cynical woman, used to getting her own way and having everything she wanted. The necklace had escaped her grasp at Rock Palm Resort when it was lost — or stolen — twenty-three years ago and now, finally, the treasure was within her reach once more. And she wanted it back. At any price. It was there in her eyes, the lust for the diamonds, the passion, the greed.

As Gray slowly advanced the screen to the next few pictures of the necklace, the Karlemans were captivated. Alicia shifted her gaze to Charles and was shocked to see his eyes faintly wet with tears. Did the necklace really mean that much to him? He had seemed so unperturbed by its disappearance twenty years ago, yet now his face was full of emotion; sadness perhaps, regret, anguish, heartache... Guilt? Surely Vivienne should have been the one to be moved by the reappearance of the necklace after all this time. She was the one who had been most visibly upset at its loss. And yet, strangely, it was as if their roles had been reversed and the tables had been turned.

'Have you owned the necklace a long time?' Charles asked in an attempt to recover himself.

'Ten years,' Alicia replied. 'It was a gift.'

'Oh.'

There was a brief silence before he ventured another question.

'Do you know the history of the necklace?'

'Yes, of course. It was a gift to me from a friend. We're no longer in contact now.' The carefully prepared answers were simplistic and straightforward.

'And before that time?' Charles asked curiously.

'This necklace has an interesting provenance,' Gray interrupted. He glanced at Alicia. 'If I may, Melissa?'

'Oh yes, please do,' Alicia replied. They had prepared a story and rehearsed their lines. As far as anyone could tell, the provenance of the real diamond necklace had remained unknown since nineteen ninety-five. Until then, it had belonged to the Karlemans. If the necklace had been stolen, it was anyone's guess as to whose hands it had passed through since that time. Charles's question had been anticipated and they were ready.

'The necklace dates back to the late nineties when it was commissioned by a wealthy diamond trader as a gift for his wife. Each stone was individually graded by the GIA, the Gemological Institute of America, before being placed into the necklace. The original grading reports are all in order for each stone. Of particular note is, of course, the centrepiece of the whole necklace; the pink stone.'

The story was a lie and Charles and Vivienne would know that more than anyone, but if they believed the necklace was the original which had once belonged to them, and chose to redeem it with minimal fuss, they would have no choice but to play along with the fabricated backstory.

'It's breathtaking,' Vivienne said, taking in every word.

'Isn't it?' Gray replied. 'It's a pear-shaped, Fancy Vivid pink diamond, originally mined in western Australia. As I'm sure you're aware, pink diamonds are some of the rarest and most cherished gemstones in the world. Only a few mines in the world produce pink diamonds, and of those diamonds that are cut and polished, only one in roughly ten million will possess a colour pure enough to be graded Fancy Vivid, a somewhat coveted colour grading from the GIA. This particular diamond weighs just over ten carats and has a natural colour origin and even distribution, combined with a balanced saturation, tone and pink hue, which again, is extremely rare. In the Fancy Vivid pink range, diamonds of more than five or six carats are hardly ever encountered. Actually, fewer than ten percent of pink diamonds weigh more than one-fifth of a carat. Let me tell you, this particular diamond is quite spectacular in the flesh.' He had done his homework with the gemology jargon.

'What about the smaller round diamonds?' Charles asked.

'Ah, they're just as special,' Gray said with a confident smile, 'and again, extremely rare. Each stone weighs just over two carats and has a flawless clarity. They all have a colour grade of D which, as you'll no doubt appreciate, means the diamond is completely colourless. The cut grade is excellent. Would you like me to go into more detail?'

'No, that's fine. The necklace is beautiful,' Vivienne replied. She looked across at Charles and placed a hand on his knee. 'Darling? I think we're happy with everything, *aren't* we?' The words were spoken firmly, almost threateningly.

But Charles wasn't listening. He appeared distracted and deep in thought. In her peripheral vision, Alicia could see he was fighting back tears and was struggling to remain composed. Something about the necklace was troubling him.

'*Charles?*' Vivienne said again.

'Yes.' He blinked and shook his head in an attempt to regain control of his emotions. 'Er, how many of those little round diamonds did you say there were, Jonathan?' he asked. 'The two-carat, flawless ones?'

'Forty-eight,' Gray replied in a matter-of-fact tone. Charles nodded. Alicia and Gray had questioned Leon further on his memory of the number of small, round diamonds. He had remained insistent that the number they'd listed in their records for the safe at Rock Palm was forty-eight. Vivienne Karlsson's duplicate necklace had forty-nine. They'd decided to go with Leon's memory; there was no telling where Vivienne Karlsson's version had come from. As to the discrepancy in the number, Gray and Alicia hoped that Charles wouldn't home in on this detail and question them further. The number of the smaller stones on the necklace in the photograph was forty-nine. They were clearly visible. All anyone had to do was count them. Which is what Charles proceeded to do. Gray and Alicia watched him closely and held their breath. They sat silently and patiently as he completed the count and sat gazing at the screen of the laptop for a long moment.

'How many d'you make it babe?' Vivienne asked.

'There are forty-nine of the little ones,' Charles replied.

'That's what I counted.'

Alicia closed her eyes. *What now?*

'It's the one, isn't it?' Vivienne said.

'Yes,' Charles replied soberly. 'It's the one.'

Alicia shot a sideways glance at Gray. They'd explained to the Karlemans that there were forty-eight of the smaller diamonds — which the Karlemans had accepted — and yet the count had confirmed that there were forty-nine. And they were still satisfied. Gray returned Alicia's glance with a warning stare: *keep playing it cool.*

'We are *very* interested,' Vivienne was saying excitedly. '*Aren't* we Charles?'

Tears were welling up in Charles's eyes again. He hastily pulled one of the napkins from the small pile on the table and stood up.

'If you'll excuse me for a moment,' he said, 'I think I've got something in my eye.' He turned quickly and hurried off in the direction of the restrooms.

'Is he okay?' Alicia asked Vivienne, with a concerned expression.

'Oh he'll be fine,' Vivienne replied breezily. 'His eyes are probably watering at the amount he's about to shell out for my anniversary gift. I don't have anything to do with the money side of things — that's his domain — I just like spending it, but what sort of amount are we looking at here? Not that money's an object, obviously. Oh, Charles'd kill me for saying that. He says I could never be a ruthless negotiator like him. Probably a good thing I don't really care about all that anyway, as long as I can spend it I'm happy.'

Alicia took a sip of champagne in an attempt to hide a look of distaste at the woman who sat opposite her. Gray could do the talking. He waffled on for a few minutes about the Rapaport Price List, the international benchmark used by dealers to establish diamond prices in the global diamond markets. He was careful to avoid mentioning any numbers relating to the necklace. Vivienne's eyes quickly glazed over in boredom. Gray was just explaining that the Rapaport Price List was updated weekly every Thursday at one minute before midnight, Eastern Standard Time, when Charles returned to the group and reseated himself. His face was red and blotchy and his eyes slightly bloodshot.

'Is everything okay?' Gray asked.

'Yes, yes thanks Jonathan.' The reply was strained. 'Just a little speck in my eye or something. Bit of grit or sand probably. It's fine.'

'Good.'

'We were just about to talk money,' Vivienne said, placing a fawning hand on his arm. Charles gave her a look of alarm.

'Don't worry darling, I know that's your area of expertise,' Vivienne said quickly, 'but I've said we're *definitely* interested.'

'Of course Vivienne,' Charles replied stiffly, 'if that's what you want.' He looked at Gray and Alicia. 'I suppose we need to talk numbers.'

'Certainly,' Gray replied, 'if you're happy to do that now? If you'd like to go away and think about it, then...'

'No, we'll do it now thanks Jonathan,' Vivienne interrupted quickly, urgently.

'Very well.'

Gray turned the laptop to face him and reduced the image of the necklace to one corner of the screen while he brought up some official-looking documents and reports which Tobias had forwarded from Rick, his auction house buddy, to make the meeting as authentic as possible. With the attention focused away from the necklace and onto sums of money and diamond prices, Charles appeared to recover himself. His jaw reset itself into a hardened line as he negotiated with Gray and Alicia. Vivienne examined her manicured nails and poured herself another glass of champagne. After fifteen minutes, they had agreed on a price of just over twenty-two million US dollars. Gray outlined the terms and conditions of the sale and summarised the particulars of the agreement for each party, guided by extensive notes in an email from Rick, which had been forwarded by Tobias.

'I'll talk to my accountant this evening,' Charles said. The quivering voice had been replaced with a brisk, businesslike tone. 'And I'd like to see the physical necklace myself before any money is transferred.'

'Very good,' Gray replied. 'That can certainly be arranged.' He glanced at Alicia who was scrolling through the calendar on her cell phone.

'Do you know The West Beach Club?' she asked.

'Of course,' Charles nodded. 'Nice place.'

'Would Thursday evening at seven suit you?' Alicia asked. 'I'll book one of the private meeting rooms.'

'Yes, that's fine. We can be there at that time,' Charles replied. Vivienne signalled her agreement.

'Wonderful,' Gray said. 'Then if you'd be so kind as to sign in the boxes marked with a cross, I'll fill out the rest for you and we'll look forward to seeing you both on Thursday evening.' He pushed some papers and a Montblanc fountain pen towards Charles.

With a flourishing signature, Charles obediently signed the forms Gray had produced. The signature of Melissa Jones was equally vigorous and illegible. Gray raised an amused eyebrow towards Alicia before gathering up the documents and placing them in the leather-bound file.

'It's been an absolute pleasure meeting you both,' he said to the Karlemans as the four of them stood up. Vivienne downed the last of her champagne as Gray waited to shake hands with her. He produced a business card which had been hastily produced by a receptionist at The West Beach Club and handed it to Charles.

'My private number,' he said. 'Please don't hesitate to call, day or night, if there's anything else you need.'

'Thanks.' Charles examined the card and slid it into the top pocket of his shirt. He shook Alicia's hand warmly.

'It's been a pleasure, Melissa.'

'Likewise,' Alicia smiled graciously. She turned to Vivienne. 'I hope you enjoy the necklace as much as I have.'

'I'm sure I will,' Vivienne said emphasising each word.

The Karlemans bid Gray and Alicia goodnight and turned to leave, nodding to the barman on their way out.

'Where are they going, Gray?' Alicia asked.

'I'll give them a moment and then follow them out,' Gray replied. Thirty seconds later, he made his way to the entrance by the bar and into the corridor outside. He walked to the balcony which wrapped around the side of the building. Remaining in the shadows, he peered down the steps that led to the ground just in time to observe a large black Mercedes pull up outside the building. A man got out of the driver's seat and opened the rear passenger door. The Karlemans got in. The man shut the door before returning to the driver's seat. The Mercedes sped away down the entrance road to the marina and turned left. Gray took note of the licence plate and returned to Alicia, still seated in Cloggy's lounge.

'See where they went?' she asked.

'A car picked them up and drove away. But I got the licence plate number,' Gray said, scrawling it on a piece of paper. He looked at the half-empty bottle of champagne. 'I feel as though I could down the rest of that, or preferably something stronger.'

Alicia looked at him with alarm.

'Don't worry, I'm just kidding,' Gray laughed. 'Vivienne certainly knocked it back though. I'll settle for a ginger beer instead. And I hope that's the last time Jonathan Kendle has to make an appearance, I'm not sure I'm cut out for the role of associate jewellery specialist.'

'I thought he was impressive,' Alicia said, 'and he definitely managed to convince the Karlemans.'

'So did Melissa Jones.'

'Thanks. What did you think of the Karlemans, by the way?'

'He's a difficult one to figure out, but she's transparent: stupid, spoiled and selfish.'

'I'd say that's a pretty insightful character appraisal,' Alicia replied. 'She's exactly as I remember her from twenty-three years ago. They both are, except Charles's behaviour this evening wasn't what I was expecting at all.'

'He seemed almost... emotional at times,' Gray remarked.

'That's what I thought. Like he had some personal attachment to the necklace.'

'Do you remember him being upset when it was reported stolen at Rock Palm?'

'On the contrary. Vivienne was the one making a scene. Interestingly, Charles seemed unfazed by the whole thing. Which makes it even more puzzling as to why he'd be so moved by it now.'

'Is it possible he knew what happened to the necklace all those years ago?' Gray asked suddenly.

'How could he?' Alicia asked. 'And if he did, why keep it from his wife? And why is he prepared to buy back a necklace which is technically owned by him anyway?'

'Well, that's fairly obvious,' Gray replied, 'Vivienne's desperate for it. He's trying to keep her happy, isn't he? Could he have sold it back then, but didn't tell her? Maybe his business was on the rocks and he was heading for bankruptcy. Perhaps it was the only way out. If he sold the necklace on the quiet, he could save his company, his home, his luxury lifestyle, his marriage… But he couldn't let on to Vivienne that he'd sold her prized piece of jewellery. She'd never have understood. Remember what she said earlier? She never deals with the money, that's Charles's domain.

'Suppose he couldn't explain to her that he had to sell her necklace or they'd face financial ruin? He probably made a deal and sold it, hoping she'd never realise it was gone. We know from Leon she had many other necklaces to choose from. Notice it went missing soon after it was announced that the guests were going to have to evacuate the hotel the following day, before the hurricane made landfall. Maybe Charles had a buyer in Antigua and was leaving it till the end of their vacation to sell the necklace, but he then had to hurry things along.'

'I guess that's logical,' Alicia said thoughtfully, 'and it would explain why he wasn't overly concerned with its disappearance at Rock Palm. But something doesn't quite add up. You saw how cold and calculated he was when you began discussing figures. He certainly didn't get emotional at the sum of twenty-two million dollars. He's a hardened businessman, whatever line of business he's in. Why would he well up at the memory of selling one of his spoiled wife's necklaces?'

'Perhaps she was more upset at its disappearance than he'd imagined she would be,' Gray suggested. 'Maybe he realised how much it meant to her, but there was no way he could get it back for her. Maybe he's been wracked with guilt all these years and now, finally, he can make it right again.'

'The only reason Vivienne was upset that her necklace had gone missing was because she wouldn't be able to flaunt it around the cocktail bar anymore,' Alicia said curtly. 'Believe me Gray, she didn't shed one emotional tear for those diamonds. There's probably not a sentimental, compassionate bone in that botox-ravaged body of hers. She's greedy and self-centred and her superficial personality goes no further than her own little narcissistic world. But Charles, he was deeply moved by the necklace...'

'So if it wasn't lost or stolen, or sold...' Gray began. 'What else could have happened to it?'

'Maybe it was *given* away. As a gift,' Alicia said suddenly.

'By Charles?' Gray asked. 'Who would he give it to?'

Alicia thought for a moment. Another image of Charles Karleman had drifted into her mind. He was standing in the auditorium at Rock Palm, in the shadow of the magic props on the stage. He appeared nervous and uneasy and glanced anxiously towards the top of the stairs. He was waiting for someone. Megan. But Megan never came.

'I think we need to find out who Megan is,' Alicia said, looking at Gray.

'You think he gave the necklace to her?'

'Either that or he was *going* to give it to her in the auditorium, but she never showed.'

'The necklace wouldn't be lost then, would it? And how did he get it out of the hotel safe anyway, without anyone knowing?'

'He probably bribed a receptionist or something,' Alicia replied, 'and you're right, he wasn't *going* to give the necklace to her. He already *had.*'

'Maybe he arranged to meet her to get the necklace back again, in light of the fact that Vivienne was making such a fuss about its disappearance.'

'Megan was hardly going to show up for *that* meeting, was she?'

'That's assuming she knew what it was about.'

'No, I think Megan meant something to him. Perhaps she was a secret lover. Or maybe even…' Alicia stopped mid-sentence. 'Gray, let's get back to The West Beach Club, there's something I need to check.'

'I'll call a cab,' Gray said, picking up his cell phone. There was a message on the screen. It was from Spencer to them both. Three words. It said: Found Owen Rapley.

THIRTY-SIX

It had been a long, hot and tiring day spent wandering the streets of St. John's. Spencer was beginning to feel his bloodhound's nose for finding people who did not want to be found had lost its sense of smell for good. His clean, upright life had leeched it out of him and now his career as an informant was at an end. His casual enquiries around the busy town as to Owen Rapley's whereabouts had led to him being threatened, chased and spat at, and in addition, he'd learned some fine new language, courtesy of the less desirable parts of Antigua's capital.

He'd spoken with various people: shop owners, cab drivers, homeless folk, street vendors and bar tenders, but nobody claimed to know anybody called Owen Rapley, the once disgraced tennis coach from Rock Palm Resort. Spencer had walked every dead end street and roamed every unsavoury alleyway. He'd loitered around dumpsters and shop doorways. The elusive Owen Rapley remained undetected. Spencer was beginning to wonder if he even existed at all. Perhaps he'd died and no one had noticed.

It was late in the afternoon and the sun was beginning to complete its diurnal arc towards the horizon. Spencer was tired, hungry, thirsty and sunburned. His aching feet were throbbing and swollen and covered in dirt from the street. He gazed ruefully at the brand new Havaianas, which were now in a sorry state.

He had reached the western side of the main town and sat down on a low wall opposite one of the cruise ship terminals. Weary cruise ship passengers, in oversized hats and carrying bags emblazoned with cruise line logos, were making their way back to the two giant ships docked at one of the quays after a day spent exploring the island. Spencer marvelled at the vast, multi-storey ships, rising grandly above the dock, dwarfing everything around them. He wondered what they were like close up and joined the throng of passengers heading for the walkway lined with colourful shops and cafés, which led to the ships.

As he neared the ship docked closest to the town, he noticed a commotion next to a small pavilion outside an ice cream shop. A middle-aged couple, dressed in khaki shorts and t-shirts with white sun visors, white socks and white trainers, were shouting angrily at someone. They were each carrying cruise line bags and it was clear to Spencer that they'd spent most of their time on board the ship in the buffet line.

'You're a common thief,' the man from the cruise ship shouted aggressively at another man who stood in the shadow of the pavilion. Dressed in a dirty grey t-shirt and black shorts, which had once been trousers but were cut off at the knees, he stared defiantly at the ground with a sullen expression. He looked to be roughly forty years old, was unkempt and unshaven and his thick hair was in matted dreadlocks.

'I saw you go for my wife's purse.' Cruise ship man continued his rant in what sounded like an American accent to Spencer. 'There's probably video evidence from one of these shops too. And witnesses. I'm getting security over here from the ship. They'll have the police arrest you.'

The other man stood silently, apparently unwilling or unable to defend himself. Spencer suddenly felt an overwhelming desire to stand up for him. He'd been in countless situations like this himself on the streets of London. He sauntered over to the little group and pushed past a small crowd of inquisitive onlookers.

'Hi, is everything okay here?'

The man from the cruise ship looked at him in surprise.

'No it damn well isn't,' he replied fiercely. 'This man just stole from my wife's purse.'

'You sure about that sir?' Spencer asked.

'Course I'm sure. Bunny had a fifty dollar bill in her purse and it ain't there now. This lowlife stole it from her. I'm reporting him to the ship's security officer.'

Glancing at the man who still stood staring at the ground, unmoved, Spencer reached into the concealed pocket of his shorts. He pulled out a fifty dollar note and handed it to the man.

'Here, take it,' he said. 'I'm a friend of this man. I'll vouch for his integrity if you report him to security. You're from one of the ships, right?'

'Yeah,' the man said with a puzzled look as he took the note.

'You're leaving tonight. It'd be a shame for you to let this one incident spoil your vacation. You've got your fifty dollars back. Why don't you leave it there, let me take care of this man and go enjoy the rest of your cruise?'

'But what about *him*? I mean, he could target somebody else. He's a common thief. He should be locked up.'

'I'll deal with him,' Spencer said firmly. 'You go have a wonderful evening.' He glanced at his watch. 'What time does your ship leave port?'

'Five-thirty,' the man replied.

'Better hurry,' Spencer said, 'it's a quarter to five now.'

The man looked at what Spencer perceived to be a fake Rolex, strapped around a thick, freckled wrist.

'Whadda you say, Bunny?' he said, turning to his wife.

'Let's go Floyd. Not worth missing the ship for this.'

'Fine,' Floyd said.

'Have a lovely evening sir,' Spencer said again. Without another word, Floyd and Bunny turned and joined the last stragglers of cruise ship passengers hurrying to board.

Spencer turned to the man and introduced himself.

'I'm Spencer. What's your name?'

With reluctance, the man looked at Spencer.

'Owen.'

'Owen Rapley?' Spencer asked, taken aback.

'Yeah, that's right.' He spoke in a hostile tone. 'Why d'you just do that? Give that man the fifty dollar bill? And who are you anyway? You been sniffing round asking after me all day. Well, you fin'lly found me. What you want with me?'

Spencer took a deep breath in. He could hardly believe it.

'Want a beer or something?' he asked Owen.

'Why not?' Owen replied with a shrug.

In a small bar overlooking the quay, the two men sat sipping chilled beers and gazing at the sunset, which cast a rich orange glow on the dark waves. Silhouettes of small boats and fishing craft bobbed on the water. Reggae tunes drifted from a nearby bar and a gentle breeze whistled through the masts and rigging of sailboats moored closer to the shoreline.

'I was homeless once,' Spencer began, 'on the streets of London, back in England. Went from one hostel to the next. Knew all the highs and lows of drugs. And hope. And despair. The winters in London can get pretty cold. Sometimes we get snow. You ever seen snow, Owen?'

Owen, still with a sullen expression, ignored Spencer and took a long sip of beer. Undeterred, Spencer carried on.

'Sometimes in those freezing temperatures, when there was snow and ice on the ground and a north wind, I got so cold I used to think I'd be better off dead. Not that anybody'd care whether I died or not. But then things changed. I met someone who became a really good friend. She always took an interest in me, gave up her time for me when she didn't have time, encouraged me to do something with my life. Sometimes I helped her with research and stuff. It was nice to feel that somebody actually needed my help, you know? But she's the reason I'm here now, talking to you.'

Owen remained silent, his dark eyes fixed on the last of the sunset in the darkening sky.

'My friend — Alicia's her name — she asked me to find you. I'm good at finding people who don't want to be found. I used to be those people. Antigua's not exactly the streets of London, believe me, but for all the differences, we're the same. People are the same. I've come to realise that since I got here.'

Owen gave Spencer a sideways glance and scowled.

'Maybe you're wondering why Alicia wants to find you,' Spencer went on. He could see his old self in Owen: cynical, untrusting and filled with bitterness, masking the pain of shame and rejection. 'Maybe you're wondering what I'm doing — a reformed addict from the streets of London — talking all this crap about hope and despair and helping people.'

Owen shrugged again and looked straight ahead.

'I'll tell you why, but first let me tell you a true story. I'm not really into love stories, but I s'pose that's what you'd call it. There was this young couple, they were in love. They had an exciting future, filled with hope. I'll call them Ollie and Anna. One tragic morning, Anna's body was found on the beach. She'd been brutally murdered. Stabbed to death.'

Spencer sensed Owen stiffen beside him.

'Ollie was devastated, broken. But worse still, he didn't have an alibi. Witnesses put him at the scene of the murder and he was soon the prime suspect. And then Anna's body was lost on the way to the morgue and all the evidence was destroyed by a hurricane. Anna was a magician's assistant; Ollie was a talented tennis coach at a nice hotel on a tropical island. There was never enough evidence to convict Ollie of Anna's murder. You know why, Owen? He didn't do it. But he couldn't prove he was innocent either. So what happened? Ollie's name was tarnished. He couldn't find another job after the hurricane, he lost his home, his friends, his reputation, but most of all, he'd lost the only woman he'd ever loved. Anna was gone from his life forever.'

Spencer paused. Owen's eyes were wet with tears. He stared at the ground.

'Owen, listen to me,' Spencer said in a softer voice. 'My friend — Alicia — believes you're innocent.'

'Your friend don't know nothing about me,' Owen mumbled.

'Oh but she does,' Spencer replied firmly. 'She was there that night, when it happened. Well, not exactly *there*, on the beach, but she was staying at that hotel where you worked. What was it called? Rock Beach Resort or something?'

Owen was silent.

'Alicia knows you didn't do it,' Spencer went on. A slight stretch of the truth but his own instincts were beginning to convince him that Owen was, indeed, innocent.

'Why didn't she say that *then*?' Owen asked suddenly.

'She and her parents were evacuated from the hotel with all the other guests. They were flown home to the UK before the hurricane made landfall. It was Hurricane Luis, back in ninety-five. But you know that. You were here. Alicia never found out what happened afterwards, at Rock Beach…'

'Rock *Palm*,' Owen corrected.

'Sorry, Rock Palm.' Spencer smiled to himself. Owen was thawing.

'Look, man. The past is the past, whatever happened back then. I don't wan' talk about it. Okay?' Owen said bitterly.

'Sure I get that,' Spencer replied. 'I hate my past too. It sucks. Never want to go back there. Always go forwards, I say. But that's what we're doing, Owen. Moving forwards.'

'Yeah right.'

'Don't you think finding Anastasia's true killer and clearing your name is a step forwards?' Spencer asked.

'It's too late for that.'

'It's never too late.'

Owen shrugged. He didn't reply but fresh tears filled his eyes at the mention of Anastasia's name. He still thought of her every day of his life, but he hadn't heard her name spoken out loud for a long time.

'Why are you doing this now, after all this time?' he asked in a quivering voice.

'Ever seen this?' Spencer asked. He pulled his cell phone out of his pocket and scrolled to a set of photographs. They were the professional images of the necklace that Tobias had sent him. Owen glanced at the screen and frowned.

'No,' he said gruffly.

'What if I told you it belonged to one of the guests who stayed at Rock Palm in ninety-five?'

Owen took another look at the necklace as Spencer scrolled.

'Which guest?'

'Her name was Vivienne Karleman.'

Owen thought for a moment before replying with a shake of his head.

'Never heard of her.'

'Do you remember *anyone* wearing this necklace?'

'I saw a lot of crappy jewell'ry at Rock Palm.'

'Did you know this necklace was reported as stolen?'

'No. Why would I? I was the tennis coach not the lost property man. What's this got to do with me anyway? Being accused of stealing now, am I?'

'This necklace is part of the puzzle,' Spencer said. 'Owen, I'd like you to meet my friend Alicia. You can trust her. She believes in you, that you're innocent, and she wants to find the truth. Who Anastasia's killer really was. She thinks you can help. She said for me to tell you she's good friends with Leon Fayer, Violet and Roslyn. I think you know them.'

'Yeah. I do. They're good people. They stood by me. For what it was worth. How does your friend know I'm innocent?'

'She was there, at Rock Palm, remember? Trust her Owen. I did. She's in Antigua right now. It's time to find out who really killed Anastasia, after all this time. And clear your name. But we need your help.'

'I already told you, I don't know anything.'

'I'll bet you know something. You went for a walk along the beach with Anastasia, around midnight. What happened after that?'

'Nothing.'

'*Nothing*?'

'I suggested we go back to my cabin, like we always did, but she said she was meeting someone so she'd be along later.'

'She was meeting someone? At midnight? Who?'

'She didn't say.'

'So you just said goodnight and see you later?'

'Yeah. But she never came.'

'Did she say the reason for the meeting?'

'No.'

'So that was the last you saw of her?'

'Yeah, apart from when I was asked to go to the beach the next morning. I knew what'd happened before I even got there. I just had this... *feeling* that something was wrong.'

The conversation fell silent as they watched the skipper of a small fishing boat skilfully pick up a mooring buoy in the harbour.

He cut the engine and the boat bobbed gently in the water as he moved around in the yellow glow of the dimly lit cabin.

'How would you feel about meeting Alicia?' Spencer asked suddenly.

Owen shrugged.

'I'll call a cab.' Spencer pulled out a card that the motel receptionist had given him that morning and made the call.

'How do I know this ain't some kind of trap?' Owen asked.

'I didn't just shell out a fifty dollar bill to Bunny and Floyd to lure you into a trap,' Spencer replied. 'What sort of name is Bunny anyway? Sometimes you have to trust people Owen, even if it goes against everything you've been telling yourself the last twenty-three years. You have to trust that I believe in you, because I do. When Alicia told me your story, I always thought you were innocent, but now I've met you, I know for sure.'

He typed three words and pressed send. *Found Owen Rapley.*

THIRTY-SEVEN

It was nearly nine pm by the time Gray and Alicia arrived back at The West Beach Club following their meeting with the Karlemans. They paid the cab driver and made their way into the reception area. Leon, who was talking to one of the receptionists, hurried over to meet them with an amused look on his face.

'How was your evening?' he asked.

'Productive thanks Leon,' Alicia replied.

'Good!' Leon lowered his voice. 'There's someone waiting for you.' He turned and pointed to a corner where two men sat laughing and chatting animatedly. One of them wore a dirty grey t-shirt with black shorts cut off at the knee. He was unshaven with thick, matted dreadlocks. The other man wore a black, short-sleeved shirt with cargo shorts. He looked sweaty, badly sun-burned and in desperate need of a shower.

'*Owen?*' Alicia asked, looking back at Leon.

Leon nodded his head.

'Haven't seen him for years. He'd become bitter and withdrawn and would barely communicate. That's what twenty years of living on the streets does to you, I guess. Hard to believe it's the same man sitting there now. I never thought I'd see that side of him again, that fun, laughing and joking side we used to love about him. What's your friend's story? How'd he get Owen to connect like that?'

'Spencer has special powers,' Alicia said with a smile.

As the three of them approached the two men, the smell of sweat and street grime grew stronger.

'Spencer, you look like you need a bath. Urgently,' Alicia said. Spencer turned at the sound of her voice and sprung up from the sofa.

'Alicia!' he said, throwing his arms around her in a giant bear hug. He caught sight of Gray behind and released his grip.

'Just friends,' he said quickly.

'Spencer, after everything you've done today, you are very welcome to hug Alicia,' Gray replied good-naturedly.

'I would've preferred it if you'd taken a shower first though,' Alicia added.

'Thought you'd be used to that by now,' Spencer replied.

'I suppose I should be.'

'There's someone I'd like you to meet,' Spencer continued. 'A good friend of mine.' He turned to Owen. 'I think you already know his name…'

Owen stood nervously as Alicia held out her hand to him and introduced herself.

'It's a pleasure Owen,' she said warmly. In spite of the dreadlocks and years of living on the streets of St. John's, Alicia remembered him clearly from the tennis courts at Rock Palm. His well-built frame had become slightly emaciated, but he still bore the handsome good looks she remembered as a fifteen year old.

'Thanks for coming,' she said as they shook hands. 'I hope an evening with Spencer hasn't been too much for you?'

'Hey!' Spencer laughed. 'And by the way, you owe me a new pair of flip-flops.'

'I knew there'd be something!' Alicia said. She glanced at her watch. 'We haven't eaten. Have you guys eaten yet?'

Spencer and Owen shook their heads.

'Let's all have dinner together. The food here is excellent.'

'Me as well?' Owen asked apprehensively.

'Of course,' Alicia said. 'You as well. If you'd like to join us?'

'I… Yes, thanks.'

'I'll call Angella — she's the mâitre d'hotel in the restaurant tonight — I'll ask her to have a table for four ready straight away,' Leon said.

'Thanks Leon,' Alicia replied. She turned back to Spencer and Owen who had apparently circumvented all racial and cultural boundaries, and all shadows of the past, to become firm friends.

'Come on you two,' she said. 'Drinks and dinner are on me tonight.'

The four of them sat around a table in the restaurant at The West Beach Club enjoying a sumptuous feast of barbecue glazed chicken, sweet potato fries, steamed vegetables and a bottomless basket of cornbread drenched in butter. This was accompanied by pint glasses of fruit punch and followed by New York cheesecake and coffee.

'This is the best meal I've eaten in years,' Owen said, relishing a spoonful of the cheesecake. Throughout the evening, his air of cynicism and mistrust had softened. A large part of this was thanks to Spencer's amusing tales of his former life on the streets of London, which intrigued Owen greatly. Spencer also regaled the group with anecdotes relating to his longtime companions at the Whitechapel Mission and the Emergency Department of the Royal London Hospital, both of which he frequented most days. Spencer enjoyed being the centre of attention and continued his story to the present day. Owen listened intently as Spencer described how he had checked himself into rehab, got himself clean, had his teeth fixed and how suddenly he had found himself working at a Hatton Garden jewellery store in London.

'Actually, it was all thanks to Alicia,' Spencer said, taking a noisy slurp of coffee, buzzing from the caffeine. 'I wouldn't be here now if it wasn't for her. But enough about me. You wouldn't be here either Owen. And there's a reason you're here now.'

'It's true,' Alicia said. She looked directly at Owen. 'We really do need your help. I know it will be difficult for you to cast your mind back to that night at Rock Palm, the night Anastasia was murdered, but if we're ever going to know the truth — what really happened that night — I need you to tell me everything you can about what you remember.'

'I'll try,' Owen said. 'I don't remember much though. Spencer said you were there that night too. Is that true?'

'Yes, it is. I was a guest at Rock Palm. I used to come with my parents every year. I was fifteen in ninety-five.'

'I think I remember you,' Owen said. 'You wore glasses back then though.'

'Don't remind me!' Alicia laughed. 'Yes, you're right. I did.'

'You weren't bad at tennis either.'

'Thanks. I haven't played in a while now. I could probably use a few lessons.'

'The last time I played was at Rock Palm.' The words were spoken with sadness.

'Bet you'd get your skills back in no time,' Spencer said kindly.

'I bet he would,' Alicia agreed. 'But Owen, take me back to that night at Rock Palm. I remember seeing you and Anastasia walking down to the beach together, on that little beach path.'

'Really?' Owen asked.

'Yes, I couldn't sleep so I went for a walk. I saw the two of you together as I came up from the beach. I wanted to ask Anastasia how she'd pulled off that illusion, you know, the one where she wore that black dress, disappeared from the cabinet and reappeared in the coffin, still wearing the dress…'

'Oh, *that* one.' A faint smile passed across Owen's lips. 'Yeah, I remember that too. I'd always sneak into the back of the auditorium and watch her perform when I could. She was incredible. But I couldn't tell you how that trick was done. She never told me any of her magic secrets.'

'Was she quite a private person?' Alicia asked.

'Yeah, she was.'

'Tell me about that night.'

'We went for a walk along the beach together. Late at night was the only time we had to ourselves. I worked all day and she worked most evenings either at Rock Palm or at other resorts on the island. Anastasia loved the beach, and the sea. We must've come back from the beach at about one am, I don't know, something like that. We'd normally go back to my cabin — it was over by the sports reception — but she said she had to meet someone and she'd be along later. I don't know who she was meeting, or why, but I trusted her, so we said goodnight and that was the last time I saw her alive.'

Owen's voice faltered and he struggled to fight back tears.

'Did you go straight to your cabin?' Alicia asked.

'No. I went to the reception. I had some paperwork to finish up. It was for some sports equipment or something, I can't remember now. I chatted to Leta, the receptionist, for a while and got on with the paperwork. It must've been around two am when I went back to my cabin. I'd expected Anastasia to already be there but she still wasn't back. I waited up for her for a bit but she never came. I fell asleep in the end. The next morning I woke up and… I just had this bad feeling that something wasn't right. I got dressed and was on my way to the main hotel when I heard that somebody'd found a body on the beach. I knew it was her…'

Owen's voice broke and he paused to compose himself.

'And then Leon asked you to join him on the beach to investigate,' Alicia said.

Owen nodded.

'That must've been hard for you,' Alicia said.

'It was, but what could I say?' Owen replied. 'I radioed for security and then went down to the beach with Leon and the woman who found Anastasia. And she was there, lying in the sand…'

'Why did you deny knowing her?' Alicia asked gently.

'Our relationship was a closely guarded secret. Only the magic team and a very few members of the Rock Palm staff knew about it. We preferred to keep it that way. I don't know, I guess I just panicked. I was so shocked to see her, my emotions were just… numb. I knew I'd been seen around the hotel late that night by a few guests and I didn't have an alibi. I was terrified someone would come forward and say they'd seen me with her that night. I just wasn't thinking. But once I'd said I didn't know her, I had to stick to my story. I should've told the truth from the beginning but I just lost it and ended up having to tell more lies. By then it was too late. I was the prime suspect.'

'Do you remember which guests — or staff members — you saw after you'd said goodnight to Anastasia?' Alicia asked.

'Not really.' Owen shook his head. 'It's hard to recall now. I've spent the last twenty-three years trying to block those memories.'

'Try to think back,' Alicia coaxed. 'Anything at all that comes to mind may be significant, even if you think it's nothing.'

'After I left the reception, I passed Leon. He was going in the opposite direction and we said goodnight. I remember seeing one of the hotel staff by the pool with a room service tray and I think there was a group of guests who'd just been dropped off by taxi from somewhere else on the island. That's about it.'

'Nobody else?'

'Not that I remember.'

Alicia changed tack. She trod carefully with the next question.

'Were you aware that Anastasia and her fellow performers were allegedly involved in the theft of valuables from guests at a number of resorts on the island?'

'She mentioned it, yeah, but it wasn't true.'

'So the magic team were wrongly accused?'

'Yeah, they were. It wasn't them.'

Owen was resolute and Alicia knew there was no point pursuing the subject. Slightly disappointed, she realised that they had drawn a blank with the former tennis ace. She had one more question for him.

'Anastasia, that was her stage name, right?'

'Yeah.'

'What was her *real* name?'

Owen hesitated.

'I don't know if I can remember,' he said slowly. 'We all knew her as Anastasia. I never heard her called by anything else in the time we were together. It was always Anastasia.'

'So she never mentioned her real name?'

'Uhhhhh, yeah, maybe she did once. I'm not sure but I think it began with an M or something. It might've been Maria or...'

'Megan perhaps?'

'Megan. That sounds right. Yeah, I think it was Megan.'

11:40 pm
Oasis Beach Bar, The West Beach Club, Antigua

The Oasis Beach Bar was still busy with animated guests drinking after-dinner cocktails and enjoying the warm Caribbean night. In one corner, the barman delighted a young couple with flamboyant mixology skills. In another corner, a woman in a brightly coloured floor-length gown, crooned along to Killing Me Softly, a tinny backing track echoing from a speaker behind her. Gray and Alicia sat on a low sofa, facing the beach. On the table next to them were two cups of coffee and Gray's laptop. Alicia tapped at the keys and stared intently at the screen. Spencer and Owen had said goodnight, Spencer returning to his motel room further along the beach and Owen to one of the staff cabins at The West Beach Club, courtesy of Leon.

'You think Owen's a killer?' Gray asked.

'I don't know, do you?'

'The problem is he just managed to cement our suspicion of his motive for murder. By telling us that Anastasia had said she'd arranged to meet someone, but hadn't told him who, it's possible he went back to find out. He said he trusted her, but if *you* told me you had a midnight meeting with someone on a beach, I'd have a hard time going to bed without being a tiny bit curious as to who it was with.'

'So what, he waited and watched from the shadows, saw her with another man and stabbed her in a fit of jealous rage?'

'It's amazing what people will do out of love, and I think he really was in love with her.'

'I agree. But he just doesn't seem the type to…' Alicia's voice tailed off as a new screen appeared on the laptop. Gray leaned in towards her.

'What is it?' he asked. On the right hand side of the screen were the words HM Passport Office — Her Majesty's Passport Office — and on the left, the words General Register Office, Official Information on Births, Marriages and Deaths.

'I've found her,' Alicia said in a low voice. 'I've found Megan.'

THIRTY-EIGHT

8:45 am, Wednesday, August 29
The West Beach Club restaurant, Antigua

It was another cloudless morning with clear blue skies. Gray, Alicia and Spencer sat around a table on the restaurant terrace, engrossed in deep conversation over breakfast. Alicia had opted for yoghurt and fruit, while Gray and Spencer had exploited the cooked buffet with enthusiasm.

'Leave any sausages for the other guests did you Spencer?' Alicia asked looking at his plate in disbelief.

'Plenty,' Spencer said with a mouthful of fried bread. 'I just hope the other guests leave some for me to have seconds. And thanks for inviting me to breakfast, by the way.'

'It's a working breakfast, Spencer,' Alicia said sternly, 'I warned you about that.'

'Yeah, don't worry, I'd guessed anyway. There's no such thing as a nice, leisurely meal with you, is there? Anyway, what's this all about? Know who the murderer is yet?'

'I'm not sure. Perhaps.'

Spencer stopped chewing and put his knife and fork on the plate.

'*Perhaps*?'

'I can't prove anything yet, but I have an idea, yes. I just need to pull it all together.'

'Well, who is it?' Spencer asked excitedly.

'Not so fast, Spencer, I won't say until I'm sure. In the meantime, I've another job for you.'

'Great.' Spencer rolled his eyes. 'Can't I take today off? I'm exhausted after yesterday, plus Owen and I were planning on hanging out.'

'You'll have time for that later,' Alicia said. 'You, me and Gray are going to take a little trip this morning.'

'Oh yeah? A threesome. That'll be nice. Where to? I wouldn't mind doing a bit of snorkelling. Or one of those party boat cruises. I quite fancy that.'

'Rock Palm Resort.'

'The place where the murder was?' Spencer swallowed his mouthful of fried bread with an alarming gulp.

'Yeah.'

'I'm not going there,' Spencer said firmly. 'It's haunted. Owen was telling me last night. According to the locals, Anastasia's ghost still roams the ruins of the hotel searching for her killer — the real killer — to avenge her death and vindicate Owen.'

'You'd better keep an eye out for her then,' Alicia said, 'she might be able to confirm if I'm right or not.'

'No, I'm serious. You won't get me anywhere near that place. I'd rather spend the day wrecking another pair of flip-flops on the streets of St. John's than go to Rock Palm. Ghosts are real, Alicia. Trust me, I've seen one. I was under a bridge over Regent's Canal in east London. It was the ghost of a man who drowned in the canal in Victorian days.'

'Is there a chance you were high on something when you saw this ghost?' Alicia asked with amusement.

'No,' Spencer insisted. 'I was sober at the time. Promise. Anyway, wild horses won't drag me to that haunted hotel.'

'*I'll* have to then, because you're definitely coming,' Alicia said firmly. 'I need you. Now, keep eating, our taxi will be here at nine-thirty.'

'If anything bad happens to me Alicia…'

'I will take full responsibility,' Alicia said. 'Right. What else? Oh, Gray, any luck with your online search for the magician or his magic team?'

'Nothing. And I've searched extensively: Vegas, Atlantic City, cruise line entertainment programmes and guest speakers, magic forums, magicians for hire, Mallory Mortimer and his flying circus, everything I could possibly think of. I came up with nothing.'

'In which case, I'd like to try something else,' Alicia said. She turned to Spencer. 'You heard from Hattie lately?'

'Yeah, had a message from her this morning. She said she misses seeing me in the coffee shop.'

'Good. I need you to send her a message back.'

'Already did.'

'Another message, Spencer. I want you to ask her to pass on a message to Vivienne Karlsson from Alicia.'

'You *what?*' Spencer looked shocked. 'Hattie's got nothing to do with that fraudster.'

'Don't be so sure,' Alicia replied. 'Do you think it's a coincidence that Hattie came into your life within days of Vivienne Karlsson bringing that fake necklace into the jewellery store? Don't be fooled Spencer.'

'Yeah, but Hattie's not...'

'Got your phone? I want you to write this to Hattie: *Message from Alicia, the puppet, for Vivienne Karlsson, the puppet master: Mission accomplished. Rock Palm Resort auditorium, Antigua, 1800 Atlantic Standard Time, Friday, August 31.*'

'The hell is this about?' Spencer said, typing in the words. 'Hattie'll think I'm crazy.'

'Just send it, Spencer,' Alicia said impatiently, 'and trust me.' She watched as Spencer's finger hovered over the send box on the screen before he pressed it.

'That's done it now,' he mumbled crossly under his breath. 'End of a beautiful relationship.'

Within minutes the screen of his phone lit up. It was a reply from Hattie. It read: *From Vivienne Karlsson to Alicia, the master sleuth: Message received. Invitation accepted. PS: from Hattie to Spencer: dinner when you get back?*

Spencer blinked in astonishment at the words before handing the phone to Alicia.

'Good,' she said in a businesslike tone. 'That's settled then.'

'How did you know to contact Vivienne through Hattie?' Spencer asked in disbelief.

'Just a hunch,' Alicia shrugged. 'Spencer, you really need to keep eating or we'll be late for the taxi.'

'But… Hattie wants to have dinner,' Spencer said, rereading the message on his phone. He looked at Alicia in panic. 'What shall I say? She's friends with Vivienne Karlsson. Which means she's mixed up with a bunch of crooks. She's probably being nice so she can get me into bed and trick me into telling her the code for the night safe at the store. She's not interested in me at all. She just wants to seduce me to get her hands on the jewellery. I've been had, Alicia. Hattie's out to con me. She's nothing but a…'

'Spencer, stop,' Alicia said. 'You have absolutely no evidence of that at all.'

'It's pretty obvious,' Spencer replied. He began furiously typing a reply into his phone. 'I'll tell her what I think of her. She's a common thief. A liar. A cheat. And I won't be…'

'Spencer, leave it for now,' Alicia said firmly. 'Forget the reply. We've a busy day ahead and I need you to focus. The taxi'll be outside reception in five minutes.'

Spencer reluctantly put his phone away and forced half a sausage into his mouth as he pushed back his chair and stood up. Grabbing a slice of fried bread from his plate, he followed Gray and Alicia out of the restaurant.

'There's someone else we need to communicate with and I've no idea how to do that,' Alicia was saying to Gray.

'Who?' Gray asked.

'Anton Shields.'

'The sand-raker, gardener, maintenance guy?'

'Yup. And primarily the waiter. That's what he was back at Rock Palm in ninety-five, although he was a very bad one. I'm not sure he was actually a waiter at all. Except back then he was in the public eye. His work appeared legitimate. This time he's sneaking around under the radar and nobody seems to have heard of him. He was here, Gray. I saw him with my own eyes. And it's no coincidence he's back after all this time.'

'Leon says he hasn't seen him since Rock Palm.'

'Then either he really hasn't, or he's lying and he's covering for Anton.'

'Why?'

'Pick one: money or love.'

'Could be either.'

'But most likely to be money.'

With Spencer following close behind, they reached the hotel entrance where their taxi was already waiting. Leon was at the reception desk patting his forehead with his handkerchief and talking on the telephone. He waved as they walked by. They climbed into the taxi and Alicia leaned towards the driver.

'Rock Palm Beach please.'

'No problem.'

The driver punched some buttons on his radio before pulling away from the entrance. As they made their way along the lane which led from the resort to the main road, Spencer turned to the driver and spoke in an uneasy voice: 'The rumours about the ghost at the old Rock Palm hotel; are they true?'

The day at Rock Palm Resort was tiring but productive. Spencer's personal highlight was the lemon and garlic tilapia with mixed salad and French fries at the open-air beach bar nearby. The three of them sat on a picnic table overlooking the sea as they discussed their morning's work and plans for the afternoon. Spencer, who had so far not experienced any supernatural encounters, remained wary and would not be left on his own. Amused by his nervous questions about ghosts and hauntings, the jovial lady who served them at the beach bar gave him a necklace to wear. It was made from quartz crystal, which she informed him would absorb negative energies, transform them, and amplify positive energies.

'You'll be all right now, Spencer,' Alicia said, as Spencer ceremoniously placed the necklace over his head.

'I'm not taking any risks,' Spencer said, patting the necklace, 'especially after what you're expecting me to do. I never signed up for this, you know. I've had enough of drama. I just want a quiet life.'

'Well, in future keep your mouth shut about fake diamond necklaces and con artists,' Alicia replied.

'Touché,' Spencer said. 'Lesson learned. FYI, this is the very last time I'm ever helping you out with one of your investigations.'

'You're retiring, are you?'

'Something like that,' Spencer mumbled, 'if I make it out of that place alive.' He patted the necklace again and glanced at the abandoned hotel further along the beach before returning to his lunch in meditative silence.

THIRTY-NINE

5:05 pm, Thursday, August 30
V. C. Bird International Airport, Antigua

The Bombardier Learjet 45XR touched down smoothly on the runway and taxied to a gate at the far end of the terminal. A black SUV with black tinted windows made its way swiftly towards the private jet as the door opened and a set of stairs descended towards the tarmac. Four women and a man, smartly dressed and wearing oversized sunglasses, made their way down the steps towards the waiting car, each pulling a small roller case behind them. They were neither relaxed nor in a hurry.

Details of the flight plan for the jet had not been made public and the flight details were scant. At best, a dedicated aviation enthusiast would have been able to deduce that the flight originated from an airport on the outskirts of southeast London. The five fake passports presented to passport control had been issued by Her Majesty's passport office in the United Kingdom six months previously. Outside the terminal, another waiting SUV was parked with instructions to transport the party to a resort in the northwest of the island. The roller cases were loaded into the trunk and the final door of the SUV closed. The taxi sped off as the last of the sun's rays slipped below the horizon and darkness fell.

6:10 pm
Falmouth Harbour Marina, Antigua

There was an air of unease and disquiet onboard the super-yacht Dark Illusion soon after Charles Karleman received the email from Jonathan Kendle, associate jewellery specialist from the auction house. The email was short and to the point and had been sent on behalf of his client, Melissa Jones. It contained revised details of the location where the Karlemans were invited to view and collect the twenty-two million dollar diamond necklace they were about to purchase.

'What d'you mean a *new* location?' Vivienne asked. She was lying prone on her massage therapist's couch, her lower half covered with a towel. She spoke through the breathing slot to her cell phone positioned on the floor beneath her. 'I thought we were meeting in a private room at The West Beach Club.'

'Melissa wants to meet somewhere else,' Charles replied. He was immersed in bubbles as he lazed in the jacuzzi on the sundeck of the yacht.

'Well, *where?*'

'It's…' Charles hesitated. 'You're not going to like this Vivienne.'

'Oh I don't care where we meet, I just want that damn necklace.' Vivienne winced as the massage therapist worked on a knot in the middle of her back.

'Okay then. She wants to meet at Rock Palm Resort. In the auditorium.'

Vivienne fell silent as Charles's words sunk in. She turned to the therapist. 'Give me a minute.' With a nod, the therapist placed a towel across her oiled back and left the room.

'*That* place,' Vivienne said through clenched teeth, pronouncing the "t" at the end of "that". 'Why does she want to meet *there?* Are you *sure*, Charles? Is this some kind of vicious prank? Is the email legitimate?'

'I thought that too,' Charles said, 'so I called Jonathan's private number and spoke to him personally. He confirmed it. Melissa wants to meet in the auditorium at six o'clock tomorrow evening.'

'But it's… that place is a *wreck*,' Vivienne said. 'It can't be safe, surely. It's probably full of squatters and drug dealers. And some people say it's haunted. Tell Melissa, or Jonathan, or whoever, that we're not going there.'

'I've already tried,' Charles replied. There was a note of desperation in his voice. 'Believe me, I don't want to go back to that place any more than you. The very thought fills me with horror, but according to Jonathan, Melissa says it's there or the deal's off.'

'The *what?*' Vivienne was breathing hard. 'The little bitch. How *dare* she? What is this? Some kind of sick game? She's playing games with us Charles and I *won't*…'

'Calm down Vivienne,' Charles said sternly. 'You're already playing her game — whatever it is — by getting all hot and bothered. Melissa's not budging. Do you want the necklace or not?'

'Yes.' Vivienne sounded like a spoilt child who was about to lose a fight.

'Then we've no choice but to play her little game, whatever it is.'

'Did you get Anton to run a background on her?'

'Yes. According to him, she checks out.'

'That's something I suppose.'

'Don't worry, we'll make sure we've got the upper hand here. I've already discussed with Anton how we'll handle this. You and I will go into the auditorium. He'll keep a low profile outside.'

'I'd feel better if he was with us, in the auditorium.'

'Let me take care of how we do this,' Charles said, suddenly bristling with impatience. 'Anton will be outside, armed, but I'll be wired. He'll hear everything that's going on. If there're any threats, or you and I are in any danger, he'll be straight in. We'll be quite safe.'

Vivienne huffed crossly.

'I'm not happy about this at all Charles, but I suppose I'll have to be. Anything to get that necklace. All right then. Six o'clock tomorrow evening. Tell Jonathan we'll be there.'

'Already have,' came the reply. The screen of Vivienne's cell phone went dark as Charles ended the call. He picked up the glass beside him; it contained an eight year old single malt Scotch whisky. He downed the contents before plunging himself beneath the bubbles. It was the only way to hide the fresh tears in his eyes.

FORTY

6:01 pm, Friday, August 31
The auditorium, Rock Palm Resort, Antigua

What had started out as a cloudless, sunny day had turned to a dismal, overcast afternoon as a tropical rainstorm blew in from the Atlantic. Menacing, thick grey clouds, dense and towering, were carried upwards by powerful air currents in the darkened sky. A brisk wind whistled through the carcass of the derelict hotel and, as the first few drops of rain began to fall, the final guests arrived at the auditorium. Each guest had received a personal invitation from Alicia — or Melissa, in the case of the Karlemans — and had been present in the auditorium on the night of Anastasia's final performance in nineteen ninety-five.

Alicia, Gray and Spencer had spent the previous two days clearing the entrance to the auditorium. A generator, on loan from The West Beach Club courtesy of Leon, had been set up backstage by Gray. It would provide electricity for the music and lighting, and the stage props. As the invited guests entered the auditorium through the foyer, just as they had in ninety-five, they were met with a familiar sight. Beyond the arc of dusty, red velvet seats and gently sloping aisle stairs, was the stage. It was set as it had been twenty-three years ago, for the magician's final illusion. The array of Gothic tombs were there, untouched, along with the gravestones and ivy-strewn wrought iron gates.

To the right of the stage was the coffin, draped with cobwebs and illuminated by the glow of a red light. It was positioned side on, with the foot end pointing towards the centre of the stage, just as it had in ninety-five. But it was the large wooden cabinet in the centre of the stage, caught in the beam of a white stage light, which drew gasps from those who entered the auditorium. The foreboding, shadowy frame, elevated on its platform, stood silently and mysteriously. A set of steps led up to it from the right hand side. Through the open sides, the stage behind and beneath the cabinet could be seen clearly from the rows of seats. The cabinet was empty.

Gray had not connected the old air conditioning unit of the auditorium to the generator. Apart from the fact that it would draw too much power, the wiring was frayed and the unit had seized and rusted through. He had, however, mounted two hidden cameras in the foyer over each entrance to the auditorium. These were remotely connected to his laptop, the screen of which he now watched carefully from an area just off stage left. On his right stood Spencer and three members of the restaurant staff from The West Beach Club: Violet, Roslyn and Angella. The three women wore elegant, long black dresses. They had once served guests in the restaurant at Rock Palm Resort. On Gray's left was Alicia. She was tense, yet composed and with a solemn expression on her face. There was a damp, musty smell in the humid air.

The small group of six stood silently watching as the guests entered the auditorium and were greeted by Leon in the foyer. At Alicia's request, he had taken the evening off from his duties at The West Beach Club to assist her with the final part of her investigations. Owen, dressed in a white shirt and blue jeans borrowed from Leon, was already seated in the middle of the second row from the stage.

The next guests to arrive were Charles and Vivienne Karleman. They had been dropped off in a nondescript Ford SUV and had cautiously navigated the path leading to the auditorium. Charles was dressed in a grey cotton shirt and grey trousers, while Vivienne had opted for a silk zebra-print blouse and black trousers. They pushed open the door to the foyer where Leon stood waiting to welcome them.

'Good evening Mr and Mrs Karleman,' he said with a smile. 'How lovely to see you again.'

As he shook their hands, the Karlemans stood dumbstruck.

'*Again?*' Vivienne asked, narrowing her eyes in the dim light in an attempt to identify him. 'I'm sorry, have we met before? Do I know you? Where are Jonathan and Melissa?'

'Oh they're in the auditorium,' Leon replied casually. 'You'll see them in due course. And yes, Mrs Karleman, we have met. Perhaps I might refresh your memory; it was, after all, a long time ago. I'm Leon Fayer. I was once the general manager of this resort. It closed its doors for the final time twenty-three years ago, almost to the day. You were two of the last guests ever to check out.'

'*Leon*? Leon *Fayers*?' Vivienne stood in shock with a look of surprise. '*You*? What are *you* doing here? What's going on?'

'Actually it's Fayer, but you never did get that right, did you?' Leon replied. 'I understand you're here about a necklace though. I'd better show you to your seats. I know Melissa won't want to be kept waiting.'

Leon ushered the Karlemans through the set of saloon-style doors on the right. They entered the auditorium and Vivienne gasped.

'It's… This place… What *is* this? What's going on?' She turned to Leon. There was a note of panic in her voice.

'I'd take a seat near the front,' Leon advised. 'There are plenty to choose from. We're not fully booked this evening.'

'But Mr Fayers,' Vivienne protested, 'this is…'

'Just go and sit down you stupid woman,' Charles hissed from behind.

'How dare…' Vivienne began, but, catching a warning glint in her husband's eyes, she turned obediently and made her way gingerly down the stairs. They chose two seats in the sixth row back, close to the aisle. More whispered protests could be heard from Vivienne followed by another stern reply from Charles after which she fell silent.

At the top of the stairs, Leon was greeting the final guests; a party of five consisting of one man and four women. With the exception of one of the women, who was considerably younger, the rest of the group appeared to be in their late forties. They were dressed in smart casual attire, mostly dark colours, and all but the young woman took their places in the centre section of seats, a few rows behind the Karlemans. Vivienne turned inquisitively to see who the latest arrivals were.

'Who are *they*? What are they doing here?' she whispered noisily to Charles. 'I thought this was a private meeting.'

'Shut the hell up and turn round,' he snapped. With a hurt look, she reluctantly obeyed.

Back in the foyer, Leon closed the entrance doors, mopped his brow with his handkerchief and glanced up at one of the hidden cameras with a nod. As he made his way into the auditorium, there was a loud crack of thunder outside and the rain began to fall heavily. He took a seat a couple of rows back from the Karlemans and waited.

'What's going on Charles? Where's the necklace?' Vivienne whispered. Before Charles could reply, the lights dimmed and the stage darkened. There was an audible hush in the auditorium and an air of anticipation as an enchanting, slightly eerie track began playing through a set of speakers on each side of the stage. It bore a striking resemblance to the synthesised chords which had once sounded through the original speakers in nineteen ninety-five. Over the music, a man's voice spoke.

'Ladies and gentlemen. Thank you for coming this evening. We appreciate some of you have travelled a few thousand miles to be here. Let me assure you though, you won't be disappointed with tonight's entertainment. In a moment, I'll introduce you to your host for the evening, but before I do, let me ask a question that I'd like each one of you to consider personally: *why are you here?*

'Twenty-three years ago, almost to this very night, two things happened here that would change the course of the lives of every one of you. All of you were affected in some way by what took place and all of you have carried dark secrets with you from that night. Now it's time for those secrets to be revealed. And so, without further delay, I'd like to introduce to you Miss Alicia Clayton.'

As Gray finished his carefully rehearsed spiel, he switched off his microphone. Nodding to Alicia, he switched on four of the six purple spotlights hanging above the stage and illuminated the cabinet with the white light once more. He'd changed the bulbs in each of the lamps and had oiled their moving parts, but they were rusted through. The best he'd been able to do was tilt them towards the cabinet and the coffin and leave them there.

Unsmiling, Alicia left the small group and walked onto the stage. Her entrance drew gasps from every member of the small audience. All eyes were fixed on her and the dress that she wore. It was an elaborate ballgown — black in colour — with a tight bodice and a wide, floor-length, hooped skirt with ruffles. Her long dark hair was partially scooped back from her face and tied with a black velvet ribbon. One of Angella's friends, a talented seamstress, had worked all day and all night to complete the dress, from a pattern design roughly sketched by Alicia. It was almost identical to the original dress, once worn by Anastasia.

Alicia wore a small microphone attached to the top of the bodice. She stood just in front of the cabinet, in the glare of the lights, and looked out to the small groups dotted about in their seats, not far from the stage.

'Thanks for coming,' she began. 'Most of you know my real name's Alicia Clayton, not Melissa Jones as I led some of you to believe.' She glanced in the direction of the Karlemans. 'Sorry about that. There's something else I should probably apologise for too; the necklace you saw in the auction house catalogue, that's not real either. It's a cheap fake.'

Vivienne gasped and brought her hand to her mouth.

'Yeah, sorry Vivienne, I realise this is particularly disappointing for you as you were once the owner of the real thing, weren't you?'

Vivienne's sunburned face turned pale.

'How did you know…?' she began, before she quickly stopped herself. Alicia continued.

'But twenty-three years ago your necklace went missing, didn't it? What happened to it? Was it lost? Stolen? Or none of those perhaps. It was never found though. The day before Hurricane Luis made landfall in Antigua, every guest and staff member was evacuated from this resort, myself included. And the real diamond necklace, worth nearly ten million dollars back then, was never recovered. No one knew where it was. Actually, that's not quite true. One person knew, but then she was viciously stabbed to death on the beach. So now we have two mysteries: who murdered Anastasia and what happened to the diamond necklace?'

'This is *preposterous*,' Vivienne said loudly, getting to her feet. She looked down at her husband. He was staring straight ahead at the stage, towards Alicia, with a curious look on his face. It was hard to read.

'*Charles*!' Vivienne said in annoyance.

'Please sit down Vivienne,' Alicia said firmly. Glaring at Charles, Vivienne sank back down into her seat.

'The prime suspect for Anastasia's murder was Owen Rapley,' Alicia continued. She glanced down at him. He had a blank expression on his face. 'You'll all remember he was the manager of the sports reception here, and the tennis coach. He and Anastasia had been seeing each other for a few months. According to him, they were very much in love. Yet why did he lie about knowing her when her body was found, stabbed to death? On the night she died, they'd been seen walking along the beach together. Was he one of the last people to see her alive? Perhaps he was *the* last. He certainly had the opportunity and the means to murder her. But what was his motive? According to him, she'd agreed to meet someone else on the beach later that night. Who? Another man? Did he secretly watch and wait and after he saw her with this other man, stab her in a jealous rage? That's what the police thought anyway, but there wasn't enough evidence to convict him.'

She turned to Leon.

'Leon, you've always been adamant that Owen wasn't the murderer. Why is that? Guilt perhaps? Because you know who the real killer was? Because *you* were the real killer? You knew Anastasia was part of a ring of thieves stealing from guests at high-end resorts throughout Antigua and the Caribbean. She and the magic team had also been stealing from guests at Rock Palm, but you covered it up for a slice of the pie, didn't you? In addition, the magic team brought a lot of business here and you didn't want anything to threaten that.

'Did Anastasia steal the ultimate prize: Vivienne's diamond necklace? Or were you the one who secretly took it from the hotel safe and gave it to her? Did you have an agreement that you'd get a cut of the proceeds in exchange for handing it over and keeping quiet about the thefts? Perhaps the agreement with Anastasia went sour. You were seen in the restaurant and around the pool bar late that night. You could've easily taken a knife from the kitchen and slipped down to the beach. Were you the person Anastasia was meeting after she left Owen?'

Leon sat silently without moving.

'Speaking of the ring of thieves,' Alicia went on, directing her gaze towards the group of four sat directly across from Leon. 'Here you all are. Finally, we meet again. I admit I've been a little slow where you've been concerned. You certainly gave me plenty of clues, but, just like in your magic show, you led me to see what I wanted to believe, rather than what was actually there in front of me. Congratulations, by the way. Cleverly done. I've still a few unanswered questions about how you did it, but we'll get to those.

'What was *your* motive for Anastasia's murder? Was it just one of you or were you all in it together? I'd say you divided the spoils that you'd stolen from the guests fairly evenly. You wouldn't kill one of your own for a couple of Rolex watches, would you? Anastasia was a valuable player in the team. It would take something big to lead to one or all of you to plot and execute her murder. But the diamond necklace *was* big, wasn't it? Ten million dollars back in ninety-five was serious money. You could've retired on that. No more lugging magic props around the Caribbean and trying to secure bookings every season. Hard life, wasn't it? For the hours of practice you put in every day, the pay was pitiful. Is that why you decided to start using your sleight-of-hand skills to steal from guests and supplement your income? How resourceful.

'But then on that fateful night, the night of your final performance, just before you were about to go on stage, Anastasia showed you something which would change your lives forever, didn't she? She had in her possession the most stunning diamond necklace you'd ever set eyes on. It was obvious it was worth millions. But after she'd shown it to you all, what did she do with it? Where did she put it? At the end of the performance, she'd hidden it somewhere and wouldn't reveal its location. Did she tell you she and Owen were planning to run away together? How *dare* she?

You were a team. Like family. How could she let you down like that? How could she just leave with her ten million dollar diamond necklace while the four of you were left struggling to make ends meet with a magic show dwindling in popularity?

'You knew about her and Owen. You knew they'd be meeting on the beach. Once Owen had left her, did the four of you confront her? Were you all lying in wait for her? No. That would've been too obvious. Perhaps just one of you then. Mallory, the man in charge. Did the job fall to you? You were seen returning from the beach in the early hours of the morning that Anastasia was killed.'

Alicia paused for a moment. The whistle of the wind and the faint sound of a crack of thunder could be heard outside as the storm raged. She cast her gaze in the direction of the Karlemans.

'Ah, the necklace. As I said, it was originally yours, wasn't it Vivienne?'

Vivienne sat motionless. She didn't reply.

'Those diamonds,' Alicia went on. 'They were something special, weren't they? They dazzled and sparkled and glittered. It was the most incredible — not to mention costly — piece of jewellery you'd ever owned. I can't imagine how you felt when you went to the hotel safe and it was gone. But where? How? No one seemed to know. It had simply vanished into thin air. But I'm afraid it's true; before you'd even realised it was missing, Anastasia was showing her newest item of jewellery to the magic team, minutes before their final show was about to begin, even as the audience was excitedly filing into this auditorium and taking their seats.'

'If you're right about that — and I don't believe you are — then prove it,' Vivienne said icily. 'Where did she put it?'

'I'm so glad you asked,' Alicia said, with a mock smile. 'It's a question that's been bothering me for some time. But I'm sure it must be a little tedious listening to me going on. With that in mind I've planned some entertainment for tonight. Some of you may remember...'

From backstage, Gray increased the volume of the music.

'Spencer, you're up,' he said, nodding towards the stage. Spencer, dressed in a pair of black trousers two sizes too large for him, and a white shirt borrowed from Leon, stood frozen to the spot. His brown hair had been scraped back from his face and Alicia had applied pale makeup in a rather unsuccessful attempt to cover the sunburn on his nose and cheeks. Around his neck was a black cape, made by Angella's seamstress friend.

'I'm not ready for this,' Spencer whispered in a panic.

'Spencer, you spent all of yesterday rehearsing,' Gray said firmly. 'You *are* ready. Now get out there onto the stage.'

'I *can't*,' Spencer protested.

From behind, Violet, Roslyn and Angella surrounded Spencer.

'Remember that steak on the menu at The West Beach Club this evening?' Roslyn said. Spencer nodded.

'Double portion for you and as much coconut pecan pie and rum 'n' raisin ice cream as you can eat if you pull this off,' Angella added.

Spencer had the greatest respect for the three women. Visions of a thick, juicy steak served with crispy, sweet potato fries, followed by a sweet, sticky, coconut pecan pie drifted into his mind; he could almost taste it. He could do this, he told himself. He swallowed hard and took a deep breath before striding out onto the stage to join Alicia. He looked around at the small group of people seated in front of him. He was supposed to say something. His lines. What were his lines again? He'd forgotten them. He glanced at Alicia in alarm. She mouthed the words: *Ladies and gentlemen, do you believe…*

Spencer nodded quickly. He'd remembered. He tapped on the small microphone clipped to his shirt and began speaking.

'Ladies and gentlemen. Do you believe in magic? Or is it all just clever tricks to make the impossible appear possible and the illogical appear plausible? The aim of a magician is to take the laws of nature and convince his audience that these laws are being broken. It's about smoke and mirrors, sleight-of-hand, misdirection, perceptual manipulation. Or is it?' As he began to get into character, his words became more dramatic.

'Permit me tonight to challenge the very laws of our physical world. What you are about to see, ladies and gentlemen, is an illusion which has thrilled live audiences in theatres from as far back as the late eighteen hundreds. It is an illusion which will astound and astonish, a deception which will delight and disturb!'

The shadows of the ghostly set seemed to come alive in the overhead lights. Gray inched the volume of the music up as Spencer fell silent. He began to walk slowly around the back of the cabinet, making flourishing gestures with his hands, just like a real magician. Yes, the cabinet was well and truly empty. The audience could see that. On reaching the right hand side of the cabinet, Spencer climbed the stairs onto the base of the platform inside the cabinet. Empty. Beyond all doubt. He made his way back down the steps and rejoined Alicia on the stage in front of the cabinet. He took one of her hands and gave it a lingering kiss. It was his favourite part of the whole act and was always over too soon.

Firmly and deliberately pulling her hand out of Spencer's grasp, Alicia ascended the steps into the cabinet. Her wide, hooped skirt completely filled the platform area on which she stood, just as Anastasia's had done. Alicia looked out towards the small group of people who sat facing the stage. Spencer was joined by Violet, Roslyn and Angella. They took their places, as they had carefully rehearsed the previous day. Violet and Roslyn stood at either side of the front of the cabinet; Angella stood behind the steps. Spencer was in front of the cabinet. He reached up and grabbed a cord that hung from the top of it. Violet and Roslyn did the same with the cords hanging at each side. They were the original cords, still intact twenty-three years later.

Spencer let down his shade at the front at the same time as Violet and Roslyn lowered the shades at the sides, but not all the way, just two-thirds down, in order for Alicia's dress to remain visible in the bottom third of the cabinet. The dress swayed gently from side to side. Spencer went on to demonstrate Alicia's continued presence in the cabinet with a variety of more over-the-top hand gestures. As he did so, Angella wheeled the steps away from the cabinet leaving Alicia standing alone inside.

Spencer strolled around the back of the cabinet behind Alicia, whose dress was clearly visible in the lower third of the cabinet not covered by the shades. As he returned to the centre of the stage, Spencer took hold of the shade at the front of the cabinet and lowered it all the way. Violet and Roslyn did the same with the shades at the sides. All three shades were now lowered to the floor of the cabinet. Alicia and the dress were completely obscured from view.

But almost immediately Spencer, Violet and Roslyn released the three shades, which rattled back up to the top of the cabinet almost as smoothly as they had done twenty-three years ago. Alicia had vanished. Backstage, Gray flipped a switch and the beam of another white stage light illuminated the coffin to the right of the stage. Wearing the ornate hooped ballgown, Alicia emerged effortlessly from the coffin, just as Anastasia had done. She walked gracefully towards Spencer who eagerly extended his arm to her with a proud smile.

'We did it!' he whispered excitedly in her ear. 'It worked!'

On cue, Gray lowered the volume of the music.

'Anastasia's final performance,' Alicia said in a low voice. 'It's the key to finding the diamond necklace.'

Vivienne straightened in her seat. The magic team sat motionless. Owen shifted his position. All eyes were on Alicia.

'Suspense is all part of the greatest illusions,' Alicia said, 'and, I apologise, but I'm going to keep you in suspense just a little bit longer as to the location of the real diamond necklace…'

'But you know where it is, right?' Vivienne interrupted quickly.

Alicia glanced across at her with a look of disdain.

'Of course, Vivienne,' she replied. 'I wouldn't have you come all the way over here for a cheap fake now, would I?'

Vivienne fell silent. She had no choice but to be patient.

'First though, we've another mystery to solve,' Alicia continued. As she spoke, Spencer, Roslyn and Violet pulled the shades fully down around the three sides of the cabinet and Angella wheeled the steps into their original position. Between the four of them, as rehearsed the previous afternoon, they busied themselves with resetting the props.

'The mystery of the vanishing assistant,' Alicia continued. 'I'm sure Mallory and his glamorous team will agree,' Alicia glanced to the man and three women sat a few rows back from the stage, 'it's a very simple trick. It all comes down to getting your audience to believe something which isn't really there at all.'

She turned to Spencer, Violet, Roslyn and Angella who stood patiently behind her.

'Ready?'

Her loyal assistants nodded.

'Good,' Alicia replied. 'This is how Mallory and his team pulled the illusion off, back in the nineties, in just the same way as you've seen this evening. You're up Spencer.'

Spencer proceeded to walk around the back of the cabinet as Alicia narrated.

'So here's the magic team's original open-sided cabinet with a set of steps leading up to it. The cabinet's made of wood and elevated on a platform so you can see right though it, underneath it and the stage behind it. The magician demonstrates this further to the audience by walking all the way round the back of it.'

Spencer returned to the front of the cabinet and climbed the steps onto the platform inside. Alicia continued her narration.

'To absolutely prove the cabinet is empty, the magician climbs inside. No illusions here.'

Spencer came back down the steps onto the stage and stood beside Alicia.

'One of his assistants joins him on stage; Anastasia in her elaborate ballgown with the wide, hooped skirt which goes all the way down to the floor.' Alicia held out her hand for Spencer who was more than willing to repeat the lingering kiss.

'Thanks Spencer. So now the magician's assistant ascends the steps into the cabinet.' She turned and made her way up the steps onto the platform as she spoke. 'You can see that the fancy, hooped skirt completely fills the cabinet. At this point, the magician is joined on stage by three other assistants.' Alicia gestured to Violet, Roslyn and Angella who took their positions. 'If the assistant and the skirt completely fill the cabinet, as seen by the audience, then how does the magician make her disappear and reappear on the other side of the stage within a matter of seconds? Where does she go? In order to show you what's really happening, we'll turn the whole cabinet round one-eighty degrees, as if you're watching from backstage.'

Gray had attached four castors to the base of the platform, the only modification they had made to the magic props. Spencer, Roslyn and Violet released the brakes on the castors and, with Alicia still inside the cabinet, slowly turned the platform one hundred and eighty degrees. Angella followed them with the set of steps, positioning them next to the cabinet. Alicia turned to face the audience.

'Now you're viewing the trick from behind.'

Spencer, Violet, Roslyn and Angella took up their new positions, facing the back of the stage.

'The magician, standing in front of the cabinet, reaches up and grabs a cord that's hanging from the top of the cabinet. His two assistants at each side of the cabinet do the same.'

The three of them took their cues from Alicia.

'The three cords control three shades which are lowered, at the same time, on three sides of the cabinet, around the assistant. But to begin with, they're only lowered two-thirds of the way, leaving the dress visible in the bottom third of the cabinet. The dress sways slightly as the girl moves gently. To the audience, this confirms that she's still there. But what's actually happening behind the shades is far from what the audience is imagining. First, this isn't any ordinary dress. Concealed beneath the wide sash around the assistant's waist are four eye hooks: two in the front and two at the back.'

Alicia pulled the wide taffeta sash away from the bodice to reveal the four hooks, turning from side to side as she spoke.

'These hooks are vital to the secret. Remember, the shades are drawn to cover the top half of the assistant. Attached to each corner of the ceiling of the cabinet are four cables which the girl inside now releases, like this, attaching them to the four eye hooks on her dress.'

Alicia pulled down the four cables from the top of the cabinet and secured them to the hooks.

'The audience sees the dress sway slightly as she does this but that's all. She then unfastens the back of the dress, like so...' Alicia unzipped the dress at the back, 'and slides down through the waist of the skirt and out of the opening at the back. She climbs down off the back of the platform of the cabinet onto the stage behind. As she does this, the bottom half of the dress visible to the audience sways back and forth slightly. This hides her movement as she slides out and, importantly, convinces the audience that she's still inside the cabinet.'

Alicia completed this manoeuvre gracefully. She was now wearing only the bodice of the dress and a pair of black leggings, leaving the skirt of the dress hanging in the cabinet by the four cables. She faced her audience. Even Mallory and his team, who had performed the same trick many times, sat spellbound.

'From the front, the escape isn't visible. But how? The magician demonstrated moments ago that you could see right underneath the cabinet. There's a secret here too. A mirror, triggered by the assistant standing by the steps, flips down into place — from the centre of the base of the cabinet to the floor — and reflects the stage beneath the cabinet. This is done seconds before the girl escapes. It also explains why the tombs and gravestones, and wrought iron gates, part of the elaborate set design, are all offset to the side. There's nothing immediately behind the cabinet but the bare stage. So where does the assistant go? Remember the steps? They're not what they seem. They're hollow. From behind the cabinet, the assistant crawls off the platform and into the hollow part of the steps, just before they're wheeled to the right of the stage by the third assistant.'

Alicia climbed into the hollow steps and scrunched herself into a ball on her back with her knees bent. Angella dutifully pushed the steps, on newly oiled castors, across the stage to the coffin.

'The girl climbs out of the steps and into an identical skirt which is concealed behind the coffin, keeping well out of sight of the audience.'

Alicia held up a duplicate hooped skirt and stepped into it, refastening the sash over the bodice. She then knelt down and slid into the coffin from the back. Pushing open the lid, she emerged wearing what looked like the original dress, but which the audience now knew was the same bodice but a replica skirt.

'While this is all happening, what's the audience seeing?'

Alicia moved back to the centre of the stage.

'The magician walks around the back of the cabinet, once again to confirm that you can see right through the platform underneath. Remember, the audience can also see the dress swaying to and fro in the bottom third of the cabinet not covered by the shades. The moment the magician reaches the opposite side of the cabinet, it's safe for the mirror to be triggered. As the magician returns to the front of the cabinet, the girl inside climbs down onto the stage, obscured by the mirror, and into the hollow steps.

'Now, the magician takes hold of the shade at the front and lowers it all the way down to the floor of the cabinet at the same time as his assistants at the sides lower their shades. But within a matter of seconds, the three of them release their shades, sending them rapidly back up to the top of the cabinet. The girl inside has vanished. We already know she's long gone, but what about that wide, hooped skirt? It can't be an easy thing to hide. There's one more secret to be revealed. Hidden in the cabinet is a false ceiling. When the shades are fully down, a stage hand activates a magnetic switch which sends the false ceiling down to the base of the cabinet.'

On cue, Gray activated the switch and, to the surprise of the audience members, with the exception of Mallory and the magic team, the ceiling fell quickly to the base of the platform of the cabinet, crushing the skirt.

'So now, when the shades are raised by the magician and his assistants, the cabinet is empty; both the girl and the dress have vanished. And that, ladies and gentlemen, is how the trick was done.'

Mallory and his three assistants gave a small round of applause.

'It goes back to the very simple fact that sometimes we only see what we want to believe, rather than what's actually there in front of us,' Alicia said. 'Mallory and his assistants led their audiences to believe that Anastasia was still in the cabinet, but in fact she was long gone. When she emerged from the coffin on the other side of the stage, the audience was led to believe she was wearing the same skirt; she was actually wearing a duplicate. And sometimes, the smallest details are the most important ones; a seemingly insignificant part of the illusion — the moving of the steps by the third assistant — holds the key to the whole thing.

'As with every good illusion, it's all about timing. Timing is crucial. The magician walks around the back of the cabinet when the shades are partially lowered so the audience can see right through it and underneath it, but *before* the mirror beneath is activated — when you'd no longer be able to see his legs — and *before* the assistant slides out of the dress onto the stage behind. Timing. If the floor mirror was activated too soon, the magician's legs would suddenly disappear. If it was activated too late, the girl climbing off the platform would be seen.

'But I've kept you all in suspense for too long. There are still two mysteries to be solved. You're each here this evening to find out the answer to at least one of these. Let's start with the diamond necklace, the *real* diamond necklace, originally owned by Vivienne and, on the night of the murder, reported stolen by her. It was never found before the staff and guests were evacuated from Rock Palm Resort and Hurricane Luis made landfall in Antigua. Rock Palm was devastated by the hurricane and never rebuilt. The fact that you're all here tonight tells me that nobody knows what happened to the necklace, or where it's been hidden for twenty-three years. Someone even went to the trouble of having an exact replica made, at no small cost. But suppose I told you that the real diamond necklace is right here in front of you, in this auditorium? It's been here since that night in ninety-five.'

'That's *ridiculous*!' Vivienne sneered.

'Is it?' Alicia asked, raising an eyebrow.

'Of course it is,' Vivienne replied. 'How could it be in here? I never came anywhere near this place on the last day until the evening, for the magic show. And I wasn't wearing the necklace then anyway. It wasn't until *after* the show that I realised it'd been stolen.'

'Stolen? Or intentionally removed from the hotel safe?' Alicia asked. 'And while you didn't discover it missing until after the show, it was actually taken from the safe *before* the show.'

'I don't believe you,' Vivienne snapped. 'That's crazy. You're making this up. How can you possibly know that after all this time?'

'After the necklace was removed from the safe, it was given to someone,' Alicia went on, ignoring Vivienne. 'It was *given* to Anastasia.'

'Yes, it was.' Mallory said suddenly, speaking for the first time. 'She didn't steal it. She showed it to us in her dressing room, said it had been a gift to her but she wouldn't say from whom. She literally showed it to us a few minutes before the magic show was about to begin. But she didn't leave it in her dressing room, or anywhere else backstage. We searched every place we could think of the following morning. We never found it. But from the time she showed us the necklace in her dressing room to the time she went on stage, she never left the auditorium.'

'So it must still be here, right?'

'You'd think, but we looked everywhere,' Mallory shrugged.

'Except the one place — the only place — she had time to hide the necklace,' Alicia said.

There was silence in the auditorium.

'Anastasia was the only person who knew where the necklace was hidden. And she revealed its location to no one. Not her closest allies: the magic team. Not the love of her life: Owen Rapley. She probably intended to retrieve it later that night, but she was murdered before she ever had the chance. And then all knowledge of its location was gone. Until now.'

'So where is it?' Vivienne asked in a low voice.

'We put our own false ceiling into the cabinet for the illusion,' Alicia said. 'The ceiling Mallory used for his show in ninety-five is still on the base of the platform, where it crushed and concealed Anastasia's own hooped skirt.'

As Alicia spoke, Spencer, Violet, Roslyn and Angella carefully lifted the new ceiling off the platform and onto the stage. They then proceeded to remove what had looked like the base of the cabinet, but the metal sheet, dotted with holes to reduce its weight, was in fact the false ceiling used in the original illusion. As it was lifted off the platform, underneath were the four original cables and a hooped skirt, almost identical to the one that Alicia was wearing. It was the original skirt worn by Anastasia.

'Remember, Anastasia's dress had *two* skirts. The second skirt was found hanging in her dressing room, but the first skirt, which everyone had forgotten about, remained hidden under the false ceiling, now on the base of the platform. With no time to hide the diamond necklace before the show, and unwilling to leave it in her dressing room, Anastasia hid it in the only other place where it would be safe: in a secret pocket in the first skirt.'

Violet and Angella detached the skirt from the cables and held it out for Alicia. She slid her hand into a small pocket underneath a ruffle towards the top of the skirt and pulled out a circle of glittering, colourless diamonds with a dazzling pink diamond, cut in a pear-shape, in the centre. A collective gasp echoed around the auditorium. There was no doubt, it was the real thing.

'To think it was here, all this time,' one of Mallory's female assistants murmured.

'So it was that hateful little bitch who stole my necklace,' Vivienne said angrily.

'She may have been a thief, but this was one necklace she *didn't* steal,' Alicia replied. 'Like I said, it was given to her.'

'By *who*?' Vivienne retorted.

'Her father.'

'*Who*?' A look of shock came over Vivienne's face.

'Her father: your husband,' Alicia replied steadily. 'You were Anastasia's father, weren't you Charles? Or should I say you were *Megan's* father?'

The look of shock changed to one of horror as Vivienne turned, open-mouthed towards Charles.

'You're lying,' Vivienne said, looking back at Alicia. 'It's not true.'

'It is. Anastasia's real name was Megan. Nobody called her that except her real father. She was your illegitimate daughter, wasn't she Charles?'

Charles remained silent.

'It can't be true,' Vivienne protested. There was a note of desperation in her voice.

'I'm afraid it is true,' Alicia said. From a pocket in her own skirt she produced a sheet of paper. 'A copy of Anastasia's birth certificate: she was born Megan Genevieve Karleman on December the twenty-third, nineteen seventy-four, to Genevieve Lacroix and *Charles Karleman*.'

'It's *not true*,' Vivienne almost screamed. '*Tell* them Charles. You've *never* had any children.'

'It is true,' Charles said suddenly, his eyes glistening in the lights. 'I was twenty-two. I wanted to travel and see the world. Genevieve was eighteen. She was a dancer, touring with the Paris Opera Ballet company, one of the most distinguished ballet companies in the world. Megan's performing talents came from her mother. It was only a brief fling. We were shocked when we found out that Genevieve was pregnant. Even though it meant her dancing career was over, she was determined to keep the baby.

'I was angry with her. I didn't want to support a child. Not back then. I didn't want any responsibilities. I was young and selfish. We lost touch. I had no idea what happened to her. Then about six years later, I received a letter from her. Somehow she'd tracked me down. I was living in the States at the time. She told me...' Charles struggled to get the words out before he recomposed himself. 'She told me she was dying and that little Megan had gone to live with an aunt in London. She'd enclosed a black and white photograph. Megan was the most beautiful little girl I'd ever seen. She had these wide, innocent eyes and long, blonde hair tied in a ribbon. She was my daughter.' He paused to reach into a pocket. Pulling out his wallet, he produced the photograph of four year old Megan from a small compartment inside. Vivienne glanced at it in horror.

'By that time, I was married to Vivienne. I wrote back to Genevieve straight away, but told her I could never be a good father to Megan and she was better off staying with her aunt. I knew Vivienne didn't want children and by then I was setting up a business and would never have had time to return to London. But I did promise to support Megan financially with whatever she needed. I didn't hear anything back from Genevieve for a few months until her sister, Megan's aunt, contacted me to say that Genevieve had died. She was only twenty-four. Megan's aunt sent details of a bank account in London and every year I deposited a large amount — more than enough — to ensure that Megan would never want for anything. The only thing I asked for in return was an update as to how she was doing, what she was up to. Any little piece of information her aunt could provide, I wanted to know.

'Then on New Year's Day in nineteen ninety-five, I didn't receive the usual update from Megan's aunt. It was from Megan herself. She told me she was a magician's assistant, part of a magic team which performed all over the Caribbean. She said that the team had secured a residency for the year at a five-star hotel in Antigua: Rock Palm Resort. In addition, she mentioned that she would be turning twenty-one in December of that year. She said she'd like to meet and suggested I take a vacation to Antigua. To Rock Palm Resort. Vivienne was more than happy with the idea. We'd moved back to London by then and so we came out here in late August. We'd booked to stay for three weeks, but then the hurricane…'

'A diamond necklace worth nearly ten million dollars was a very generous twenty-first birthday gift,' Alicia said.

'*You gave her my diamond necklace*? I knew it!' Vivienne hissed. 'Didn't you think I'd notice it was missing?'

'Honestly Vivienne?' Charles said, looking at her for the first time. 'No. I didn't. You brought so much other jewellery with you. The receptionist had to make extra space in the hotel safe just to fit all the boxes in.'

'Well, I *did* notice it was missing,' Vivienne retorted.

'I'll say you did,' Leon interrupted from behind. 'You sure made a lot of fuss about it, accusing my staff of stealing.'

'How did you get the necklace out of the safe without anyone knowing?' Vivienne asked her husband.

'Oh I suspect someone *did* know,' Alicia said, looking inquisitively at Charles. 'I suspect one of the receptionists was paid a very generous sum of money to look the other way while you had access to the safe. Nothing was documented and nobody said anything about it afterwards.'

'Pretty much,' Charles said.

'So you removed the necklace from the safe, in order to give it to Anastasia, or Megan, your daughter,' Alicia continued.

'She'd been performing at one of the other resorts on the island during the afternoon. She only got back at Rock Palm with an hour or so to spare before the magic show here.' Charles spoke quietly. 'We met backstage in her dressing room and I gave her the necklace. I told her its value and that it was her twenty-first birthday present from me. I remember we hugged and cried. We didn't know when, or if, we'd see each other again. It was the sweetest — and bitterest — moment of my life. If only things could've been different. But with the hurricane moving closer, and the fact that every tourist was due to be flown off the island the next day, our time together was going to be cut short. We agreed to meet later that night, for the last time, here in the auditorium.'

'*You* were the person she said she was going to meet?' Owen said, turning round in his seat. 'She never said who it was, but I had no idea it was her own father.'

'We arranged to meet in the early hours of the morning, when there'd be hardly anyone about, but she never showed,' Charles said.

Alicia remembered crouching between the two front rows of seats, watching the beam of a flashlight descend the aisle stairs before Charles Karleman came into view. She remembered as he stood on the bottom stair, glancing anxiously at his watch and back towards the door of the auditorium. She remembered the unease with which he appeared to be waiting for someone, the way in which he called her name into the darkness: *Megan? You there? Megan?*

'She never came because she was already dead,' Alicia said.

There was a hush in the auditorium.

'Owen, you said Anastasia told you she was intending to meet someone. But it wasn't Charles; it was somebody else. One of you here tonight is a murderer. You all had means, motive and opportunity. Owen, the jealous lover; Leon, who quite likely knew that Anastasia was in possession of a ten million dollar necklace; the magic team, desperate for a share of the diamonds. Or was there someone *else* on the beach that night?'

'How could you *possibly* know?' Vivienne asked.

'Because, Vivienne, I was *there*,' Alicia replied.

'What d'you mean, you were there?' Vivienne said, mockingly.

'I was also a guest here. I was fifteen at the time, on vacation with my parents. I was in the audience watching Anastasia's final performance. *The one thing the audience believed was happening was quite different to what was actually happening.* It was the same for you, wasn't it Vivienne?'

'Excuse me?'

'Charles never told you he had a daughter, did he? When you found out that Charles and Anastasia were secretly meeting, you thought they were having an affair. *You thought they were lovers.*'

'What? *No!* Of course not.'

'Maybe you even had your own suspicions as to what had happened to your necklace. You probably guessed he'd given it to her.'

'That's ridiculous.'

'You knew time was running out to confront Anastasia about her affair with your husband and the whereabouts of your diamond necklace. What enraged you more? The fact that someone half your age had taken your place as the object of your husband's affection, or that he'd given her *your* diamonds? It was *you* she was meeting on the beach that night.'

'That's *absurd*,' Vivienne protested loudly. '*Charles! Say something.*'

But Charles remained silent.

'Armed with a knife, probably stolen from the kitchens, you arranged to meet Anastasia and confront her, where you stabbed her. It was a ferocious attack. I saw the body myself. You must've been eaten up with jealousy.'

In the stage lights, Vivienne's face had turned pale.

'How *dare* you,' she said menacingly. 'How *dare* you accuse me?'

'But that's not all,' Alicia said. 'Terrified that the evidence would lead back to you, you confessed what you'd done to your husband. You knew he'd go along with you or you'd both be in trouble. You knew he'd cover it up. And he did, didn't he?'

Alicia paused as she remembered the words of Carlos Jaxen, spoken in the Italian restaurant in South Kensington: *You see, I don't believe it's an accident that the van went missing. Something happened to it. Something calculated and cold-blooded. Premeditated.*

'It was no accident that the medical examiner's van with Anastasia's body inside mysteriously disappeared, was it?' Alicia said. 'It was never found and there was never any plausible explanation as to what happened to it. But I think you know. It's my guess that Charles paid someone to ensure the van would never make it back to the hospital morgue for fear that any evidence on the body would link you — or even Charles himself — to Anastasia's murder.'

Alicia paused.

'You little bitch…' Vivienne said in a low, threatening tone. She stood up and looked at Charles. 'We're leaving. Right now. Come on Charles. This is a disgrace. You'll be hearing from my lawyers Miss Jones, or whatever your name is.'

She glanced down at Charles again. He hadn't moved. He was staring straight ahead. His eyes had filled with tears.

'*Charles*,' Vivienne snapped. But Charles wasn't listening.

'It's true,' he said suddenly.

'*What?*' Vivienne looked at him in alarm.

'You killed Megan and then you expected me to cover it all up for you,' he said bitterly. Every eye in the auditorium was on the Karlemans. 'You're right,' he said to Alicia who stood motionless on the stage. 'Once Vivienne told me what she'd done…'

'*Shut up*, Charles,' Vivienne said angrily.

'I can't Vivienne. I can't do this any more.' Charles broke down and suppressed a sob. He quickly composed himself and wiped his eyes with his hands. 'She was my daughter — my only daughter. And you took her from me. You *killed* her.'

'But I thought you were…' Vivienne began.

'You thought we were having an affair. You didn't even let me explain. And then I had to clean up *your* mess.' He looked at Alicia. 'You know the truth now. You may as well hear the rest. Yes, I had someone arrange for the ME's van to be run off the road to ensure it would never make it back to the hospital mortuary. I had the idea that by the time the van was actually found, any evidence which might lead back to us would be long gone. As it happened, Hurricane Luis well and truly took care of that. Any search operations conducted by the police were severely hampered by the storm. I don't believe the van was ever found.'

'So it's still out there,' Alicia said, 'and Megan's body was left to rot in the undergrowth, picked to pieces by wild birds and animals.'

Charles, now stricken with grief, suppressed another sob.

'Where was the van run off the road?' Alicia asked.

'Not far from here,' Charles choked out the words. 'About two or three miles out there's a winding road cut into a steep hillside with thick foliage on either side. It was there. I remember passing the place on the way to the airport, seeing tyre marks on the road and a fresh gap in the undergrowth.'

A distant memory crept into Alicia's mind. It was a memory from twenty-three years ago when she was leaving the hotel with her parents. As she walked to the taxi which was to take them to the airport, she remembered noticing Charles and Vivienne standing side by side, neither looking at nor speaking to each other. They were pale and subdued. Then, Alicia had assumed it was due to the loss of the diamond necklace but now she realised it was because of so much more. Suddenly, there was a horrified gasp from one of the magician's assistants.

Alicia looked up to see Vivienne with a gun in her hand. It was a small handgun, probably a nine millimetre, small enough to fit in her purse. She was pointing it straight at Alicia. She moved slowly into the aisle, away from Charles, and took a step towards the stage.

'Well then. Now you know everything, don't you?' Vivienne said coldly.

'Actually, there's one thing I'm still not clear on,' Alicia said. She held Vivienne's gaze steadily.

'Oh? What's that?'

'The knife you stabbed Anastasia with. What happened to it?'

'Can't remember now,' Vivienne shrugged. 'I think I tossed it into the sea. But who really cares? It doesn't matter now, does it?'

'You let Owen Rapley, an innocent man, take the blame for a murder which *you* committed,' Alicia said. 'Not only did you take Anastasia's life from her, you destroyed Owen's too.'

'*She* ruined *my* life,' Vivienne said bitterly. 'I'm glad she's gone. Charles was never the same after that night. Things changed between us forever.'

Vivienne took another step towards Alicia and released the safety catch on the pistol.

'Vivienne, no!' Charles cried out.

Ignoring her husband, Vivienne lifted the gun to her line of sight and began to squeeze the trigger. The sound of a gunshot echoed loudly around the auditorium. A woman screamed. And Vivienne Karleman collapsed in the aisle. Alicia turned to the direction from where the shot had been fired. To her surprise, she saw a rain-soaked man standing behind her with a gun in his hand.

'*Anton?*' she said in astonishment.

'Sorry to gatecrash the party,' he said, re-holstering the gun in his belt. He ran quickly across the stage and jumped down to where Gray already had Vivienne face down on the floor.

'Nice shot,' Gray said as he secured Vivienne's wrists with a cable tie. There was a small pool of blood on the floor next to Vivienne's shoulder. 'Looks like nothing more than a glancing blow.'

'She'll live,' Anton said, picking up her gun. 'The police are ten minutes out.'

He glanced at Charles.

'Good job we had you wired,' he said with a grin. 'I've recorded everything.'

'Anton, what's going on?' Charles asked. He looked dazed and confused. He peered down at Vivienne with disdain. She was whimpering like a wounded animal but he made no attempt to console her.

'You and your partner in crime are about to go down for murder, that's what's going on,' Anton said.

'But you're…' Charles began.

'Allow me to explain,' Anton interrupted. 'My name's not really Anton Shields, it's Matt Lawrence. I'm an undercover agent for the British government. We've been watching you for years, Charles, along with government agencies from other countries. We know you're involved in all sorts of corrupt business activities, including arms dealing. The problem is, you live a squeaky clean life on the surface. You get someone else to do your dirty work so the trail of evidence never leads back to you. But you've always done that, haven't you?'

It was a reference to the hitman Charles had paid to take out the ME's van carrying Anastasia's body.

'Like most others here, I was also at Rock Palm in ninety-five. I was working undercover as a waiter, although I don't think I was a very good one. Sorry Leon.'

Leon gave a faint smile.

'I came to keep an eye on you Charles, but it was soon clear that you really were here on vacation and to meet someone who was very special to you: your daughter. On the night she was murdered, I was watching your movements, but I guess I should've been watching Vivienne's instead. Although we knew you were involved in some lucrative arms deals, we just couldn't pin anything on you. Short on resources, the government department I worked for moved me on a few months later. Fast forward about fifteen years, we obtained a new lead on your business enterprises and I volunteered to go back undercover.'

'I trusted you Anton,' Charles said quietly. 'I let you into my inner circle. You were my right hand man, when all this time…'

'All this time I was out to get something on you. I knew you'd slip up eventually, I just had no idea it would be for a murder your wife committed twenty-three years ago which you covered up. Funny that in spite of your unethical business deals, which contributed to the deaths of hundreds of thousands of innocent people, the one thing your hardened conscience couldn't take was the fact that you were complicit in concealing evidence from your own daughter's murder.'

Charles looked away. He seemed tired, sad and finally defeated, but perhaps also relieved. In the distance, the whining sound of sirens grew louder. Leon got up and made his way to the exit. Within a few minutes, he returned with four police officers following close behind. Raising their eyebrows at the sight of the cabinet on the stage surrounded by the macabre magic props, they spoke to Anton who had hauled Vivienne to her feet. As they handcuffed the Karlemans, Anton turned to Alicia.

'Great work, by the way,' he said. 'I don't know how you did it, but you'll be sure to tell me one day?'

'Of course,' Alicia replied.

'And sorry about all the spying on you and stuff,' Anton added. 'Mallory and his team were pretty smart; when they tracked down the Karlemans and their inner circle, they recognised me from those days at Rock Palm.' He glanced at the magic team. 'Posing as some kind of diamond trader, Mallory asked me if the diamond necklace was ever recovered. I couldn't break my cover, but I said as far as I knew it had never been found. I'd certainly never seen Vivienne wear it since her time here. Mallory then told me that he'd instructed an investigative journalist — you — to look into the unsolved murder of one of his assistants which had occurred at the same time as the necklace went missing. I remembered the murder too, of course. I wasn't sure where all this would lead, but said I'd cooperate with whatever they needed. I also decided to keep an eye on what you were up to myself, after you arrived in Antigua.'

'So that's how you knew I was here,' Alicia said. 'Mallory and his team tipped you off.'

'Yes,' Anton nodded. 'They'd been monitoring the catalogues of all the major auction houses too, so when the duplicate necklace was listed, which I'm guessing was your way of drawing the Karlemans into your investigations, I thought I'd help you along a bit by bringing it to Charles's attention. I knew he'd recognise it and, of course, Vivienne had already seen it. I was certain they'd take the bait.'

'And they did,' Alicia replied.

The police were ready to leave. Accompanied by Anton, they led the Karlemans back up the aisle stairs.

'One last question,' Alicia called out suddenly.

'Yes?' Anton turned.

'How did you get in just now?'

'I broke in through the old stage door. It's pretty overgrown back there, but I knew Vivienne had a gun on her. After Charles's confession I had a suspicion she might try to use it. Guess I got here just in time.'

'Thank you,' Alicia said again.

'You're welcome,' Anton replied before he disappeared through the door at the top.

There was suddenly a noise from the other side of the auditorium and a figure emerged from the row of seats at the very back. A young woman with long blonde hair ran quickly down the stairs. She jumped onto the stage and gave a startled Spencer a powerful bear hug.

'You were *amazing*!' she gushed in a voice filled with admiration.

Spencer stepped back in surprise.

'*Hattie*?' he said in astonishment. 'What are *you* doing here?'

'I'm here with my father,' Hattie said. She pointed to Mallory. 'And I think you may have met one of his team already.' She nodded to one of the women standing beside the magician. Dazzled from the stage lights, Spencer peered towards the small group on his right where a woman, with short, dark hair and a heavily made-up face smiled. She looked familiar and suddenly he remembered her.

'I know you. You're the con artist,' he said in disbelief. 'Vivienne Karlsson.'

The woman descended the aisle stairs and walked to the stage.

'Ryleigh MacVay,' she said, offering her neatly manicured hand to Spencer. 'I'm sorry I lied to you. I hope Tobias wasn't too distressed? We paid back the money as quickly as we could.'

'It's okay,' Spencer replied, shaking her hand with an understanding nod. 'I see why you did it that way. And I'm glad you did.' He turned back to Hattie.

'I can't believe you're here!' he said excitedly. 'When did you arrive?'

'We flew in on a private jet late yesterday afternoon,' Hattie replied. 'It was sort of under the radar. Dad and his team didn't want to alert any border controls or officials that they were back in the Caribbean. Their record's not great here, as you can probably imagine.'

'Don't worry, I've a few convictions in my past too,' Spencer said with understanding. He hugged Hattie tightly. 'It's so good to see you! I've missed you.'

'I've missed you too Spencer,' Hattie replied, hugging him back.

FORTY-ONE

11:20 pm
Oasis Beach Bar, The West Beach Club, Antigua

The group of ten were seated on the terrace sofas overlooking
the beach. They sipped cocktails and fruit punches having enjoyed
a sumptuous feast of steak with sweet potato fries, followed by
coconut pecan pie and rum 'n' raisin ice cream. There were double
portions for Spencer, as promised by Violet, Roslyn and Angella.
Alicia and Spencer had changed into their own clothes and the
diamond necklace was stowed in the safe in Gray and Alicia's villa.
The storm had cleared to the west and the wind had dropped,
leaving a warm, cloudless night with a gentle breeze. There were
still many unanswered questions, but Mallory had the most burning
one of all.

'How did you do it Alicia?' he asked. 'How did you work out
Vivienne Karleman was the murderer?'

Silence fell around the group and everyone looked at Alicia in
anticipation of her answer.

'I guess it started with the process of elimination before
anything else,' she began hesitantly. 'Each one of you had means
and opportunity; I remembered seeing you all near the beach late
that night. Once I'd realised everyone also had a potential motive
for wanting Anastasia dead, I had to take a step back and look
at the whole picture. After I'd spoken to Leon and Owen, I was
convinced they were telling the truth and that Owen was innocent.
But who else was in the picture?

'The only other major players were Anastasia's fellow
performers: Mallory and his three assistants. You guys were the
missing pieces from the puzzle. You'd been in the original equation
and, ergo, had to be in this equation somehow too. And then there
was the fake necklace with the laser-inscribed words *who murdered
anastasia* on each stone, the cleverly faked grading reports and the

travel plans to Antigua. It was an ambitious plan, which I'm guessing took considerable time and money to pull off, not to mention faith in my investigative abilities. The more I thought about it, the more I knew it wasn't the work of a one man band.

'Surely something as calculated and orchestrated as this would involve a *team* of people to execute. Which got me thinking about teams. Naturally, I came up with you, the magic team. Although you still had motive for wanting Anastasia dead, if you'd gone to the trouble of such a determined — and costly — plan to solve her murder, it was unlikely that you were her killers. Then there was Anton, the mysterious waiter who suddenly and unexpectedly appeared on the scene again. Again, it was obvious he was involved, but I couldn't work out how. And finally, I knew the Karlemans were connected to the necklace and may hold the key to Anastasia's last movements. I'd seen them both near the beach late that night.

'I guess something hit home when Gray and I met them at Cloggy's at English Harbour. Gray was posing as a representative from the auction house which had kindly added the fake necklace to their catalogue for the purpose of this investigation. I was posing as the vendor. Their reactions were surprising, almost shockingly so. Charles appeared visibly moved by the necklace. He was emotional, as if it had meant something much more to him than the fact it was just another piece of his wife's jewellery. He certainly didn't care for her. It was clear that their marriage was a superficial, loveless charade of show and convenience. But the look on his face was one of sadness and regret, guilt perhaps.

'In contrast, Vivienne's eyes were full of what I thought was pure lust for the diamonds, greed, an overwhelming desire for the necklace. But that look in her eyes played on my mind; there was something else. It was almost a look of evil, bitterness, revenge. And then I saw it. If Charles had given the necklace to someone who meant something to him, who was special to him, perhaps even someone he loved, and Vivienne had found out about it, that was a clear motive for murder. Her desperation for the necklace and the look of hate and retribution in her eyes was meant for Charles. She'd killed the woman who had taken her place and now, finally, she would have her diamonds back, at *his* expense. He'd bought them once for her, and given them away to another woman. Now he could buy them back again and, this time, give them to *her*. The opportunity for revenge was almost too good to be true.'

'How did you convince the Karlemans that the necklace placed in the auction house catalogue was the real thing?' Mallory asked.

'We took a bit of a risk with that one,' Alicia replied, 'and relied on Leon's recollection of the description of the necklace, rather than your moissanite imitation. Thankfully, Leon's memory hadn't failed him, even after all this time. There was something very distinct about the real diamond necklace which absolutely convinced the Karlemans that they had found the genuine article, Vivienne's original necklace.'

Leon smiled modestly.

'Your necklace consisted of forty-nine flawless stones,' Alicia said, addressing the magic team, 'but Leon said Vivienne Karleman had been adamant that there were *forty-eight*. It was a seemingly insignificant fact, but one which could be crucial to making the Karlemans believe we had the original necklace. How many flawless diamonds *were* there? Forty-eight or forty-nine? Based on the fact that Vivienne had actually *owned* the necklace whereas you guys had seen it for just a few minutes at best, and if Leon's memory was accurate, we decided to go with forty-eight. But the replica necklace consisted of forty-nine round, colourless stones. When the professional photographs were added to the catalogue, we knew one of three things would happen: if there were only forty-eight diamonds in the original necklace, short of photoshopping the images, we had to hope that Charles and Vivienne would read the description without physically counting the diamonds. If they did count the diamonds, they'd know that the necklace wasn't the genuine article. The third option was that there *were* forty-nine diamonds in the original necklace, but one of them was different somehow.

'Bizarrely, but luckily for us, even though the description read "forty-eight flawless diamonds," the Karlemans were expecting to count forty-nine. The only possible explanation was that one of those round diamonds wasn't flawless, known only to the Karlemans, and perhaps placed in the necklace to ensure that it could always be identified by them should it be lost or stolen.'

'How did you figure out where Anastasia had hidden the necklace?' Owen asked. Clean shaven, and smartly dressed, he was almost unrecognisable as the man Spencer had vouched for at the cruise ship terminal a few days before.

'Once I'd worked out that Charles had given the necklace to Anastasia, or Megan, I thought about that night when he'd waited for her in the auditorium and she didn't show. Which got me thinking that this may not have been the first time they'd met there. It made sense. Most of the time the auditorium was empty. Nobody went there apart from the magic team or the hotel cleaning staff. It was also separate from the main hotel and the perfect place for clandestine meetings between father and daughter. It also seemed a logical place for a valuable necklace to be hidden.

'I guessed the magic team, who clearly knew of the original necklace, would have ransacked the place looking for it, so there was little point in searching the dressing rooms and areas backstage. As a teenager, sneaking around the auditorium that night, I'd worked out how Mallory and his team had pulled off their final illusion. On my return to the auditorium a few days ago, I was surprised to find that the magic props were left exactly as they had been from that night in ninety-five. Which also gave me one other possible idea as to where Anastasia could have hidden the necklace. Sure enough, when we removed the false ceiling from the base of the cabinet, the original skirt from Anastasia's dress was still there, with the diamond necklace concealed in the secret pocket.'

'We never thought of that when we searched for the necklace,' Mallory said. 'To think it was there in front of us the whole time.'

'Why *didn't* you dismantle your magic props before you left Rock Palm?' Alicia asked.

'We were planning on packing everything away on the morning the guests and staff were evacuated from the hotel,' Mallory replied, 'but then Anastasia's body was found. That changed everything for us. We knew we were under investigation for the theft of guests' valuables from various resorts throughout the Caribbean. With that cloud over our heads, it was surely only a matter of time before our residency at Rock Palm would be terminated and future bookings at the other resorts cancelled. The last thing we wanted was to be under suspicion for the murder of one of our own team.

'We decided to abandon our props and make one last search for Anastasia's necklace. If we could find that, we could retire for life and we'd never need to do another show again. Ryleigh went through Anastasia's belongings in the cabin they shared, while Dionne, Jess and I searched every place we could think of in the auditorium. But we never found the necklace. As the last few members of staff left Rock Palm that afternoon, we drove away from the hotel with just our belongings, never to return until tonight.'

'Why did you set me up on the hunt for Anastasia's killer now, twenty-three years later?' Alicia asked.

Mallory took a deep breath before replying. He looked at his three former assistants who nodded. It was time.

'After Anastasia was murdered and we left Rock Palm, we disbanded. How could we ever perform again without her? We'd been a close knit team, but with the ongoing investigations into our… fraudulent activities… and a number of resorts threatening to cancel our performing contracts, we decided we'd go our separate ways and ultimately we lost touch. Three years ago, Ryleigh tracked down each of us and said she wanted to meet. She'd been Anastasia's closest friend when we performed as a team. Exactly twenty years to the day of Anastasia's death, we met in a bar somewhere in the West End of London. Ryleigh told us that Anastasia's case had never been solved and her killer was still out there. Owen had been the prime suspect although there'd never been enough evidence to convict him of her murder. But we knew, without the shadow of a doubt, that he was innocent. Even though he had no alibi, he and Anastasia had been hopelessly in love with each other. There was no way he'd killed her. That night we made a pact to find Anastasia's killer and avenge her death.'

'Why didn't you just investigate yourselves or speak to the Antigua Police Department?' Alicia asked. 'Why get me involved in all this?'

'It was clear the investigations would lead to Antigua, where we'd each been blacklisted with criminal records, so there was no way we were going to the police. Admittedly it was many years ago, but we couldn't run the risk of being caught if we came back here and started asking questions about an unsolved murder from around the same time as our criminal convictions. There was too much at stake.'

'Is that why you didn't initially identify yourselves to me?' Alicia asked. 'The cloak and dagger approach was a little alarming.'

'Sorry about that,' Mallory said with an apologetic smile, 'but yes, we didn't want our involvement to taint your investigations in any way, even though we had no idea where they'd lead. We also didn't want to put ourselves under suspicion.'

'How did you know about me and my connection to Rock Palm in ninety-five?' Alicia asked.

'We didn't at first,' Mallory replied, 'but about a year later, I ran into Carlos Jaxen, the owner of Rock Palm Resort, in a bar. It was completely by accident, or perhaps you could call it fate. As you know, he had his own problems. His wife Sophia was very sick and he was in some kind of ongoing legal dispute with a bunch of planning officials over the restoration of Rock Palm. I mentioned to him about our pact to find Anastasia's killer and he, like us, revealed that he had always believed in Owen's innocence. Carlos has always been incredibly loyal to his employees. He was a friend of your father's I believe, and he therefore knew of your work as an investigative journalist and recommended you. He also told me you'd been a guest at Rock Palm with your parents back in ninety-five. That sealed the deal for us. We just needed to find a way to arouse your curiosity into Anastasia's murder and attract your attention.

'We spent the next year observing you and everyone you associated with in the hope that we could formulate some kind of plan. It was a stroke of luck when Spencer came out of rehab and you landed him a job in a Hatton Garden jewellery store. We knew you were close and that he'd been your informant when he was living on the streets. The idea of a duplicate necklace, identical to the one Vivienne Karleman had worn at Rock Palm, and subsequently reported stolen, was Ryleigh's. It was, of course, still a huge gamble on our part. What if Spencer didn't tell you about the necklace? And if he did, how could we be sure you'd even remember it from twenty-three years ago?

'It took six months of hard work, research and planning, but it was our best shot and possibly our only one, to avenge Anastasia's death. Of course, we had a few other ideas up our sleeves to jog your memory if the necklace and the — hopefully familiar — name Vivienne Karlsson didn't manage to. Thankfully, you were on the ball and Spencer also did his part.' Mallory gave Spencer, who was seated close to Hattie, a grateful smile.

'Why Karl*sson* and not Karle*man*?' Alicia asked.

'We thought Karlsson would be enough,' Mallory said. 'We wanted you to be reminded of Vivienne Karleman, the original owner of the necklace, without implicating her directly. Again, we had to tread carefully. We weren't exactly sure who was involved.'

'So you had a duplicate necklace made. An exact replica — almost — of the one Charles gave to Anastasia,' Alicia said.

'We did our best with that,' Mallory said. 'We'd spent the last couple of years trying to track down the original necklace on both the legitimate and the black markets but there was no trace of it. We therefore had only our memories from when Anastasia showed it to us in her dressing room for no more than a few minutes, but it was a pretty incredible piece of jewellery and hard to forget. Apart from the forty-ninth stone, which we'd never have realised wasn't flawless anyway, I don't think we made too bad a job of it.'

'You made an excellent job,' Alicia said.

'The one thing we had between us was money,' Mallory went on. 'We'd all been pretty successful, financially speaking, over the years, with various careers. When we pooled our fortunes, money wasn't really an object. And anyway, we owed it to Anastasia. Part of the pact we made was that we'd do whatever it took to find the truth, even if it meant we were destitute by the end of it. We couldn't quite stretch to a replica diamond necklace, but we could certainly afford moissanite, which was much easier to come by, too. And so the moissanite copy was commissioned, and made, complete with the laser inscription of the words *who murdered Anastasia* on each stone…'

'A nice touch,' Alicia said, with a smile, 'and leaving me in no doubt as to whom this message was for and what you wanted me to do.'

'Once we'd produced the phoney grading reports to go with the necklace we were ready to put the next part of the plan into motion,' Mallory continued.

'Those grading reports,' Spencer said suddenly. 'They were pretty convincing. They looked…' he paused, '*almost* real, but not quite.'

'It was deliberate, of course,' Mallory explained. 'They were carefully orchestrated so that you could tell there was something wrong with them if you looked closely. The fakes couldn't be too perfect. We *wanted* to arouse your suspicions Spencer. We wanted you to realise there was something not quite right with it all. We knew the first thing you'd do would be to tell Alicia, which was all part of our plan.'

'But this is the bit I don't get,' Spencer said. 'When Ryleigh came into the store posing as Vivienne Karlsson, how is it that *I* spotted something was wrong, but Ronan and Camilla, two experienced gemologists, were totally fooled? How did they miss that the gems were moissanite and not diamonds, and that the grading reports were clever fakes? How did you do that?'

Mallory glanced at Ryleigh who took up the story.

'I'm afraid I hypnotised them,' she said.

'You *what?*' Spencer looked aghast.

'I'm an expert in hypnotism and neurolinguistic programming,' Ryleigh continued. 'When I first came into the store, I made sure your co-workers were gently placed under hypnosis, before they could properly examine the gemstones or the grading reports. The stones are pretty hypnotic in themselves, as you know. I narrowed their focus of attention onto the diamonds, to the exclusion of everything else. At the same time, I directed their subconscious with suggestions and subliminal words which were embedded into my dialogue. I had them right where I wanted them: in a hypnotic trance, conditioned to everything I wanted them to believe.

'Of course, there's more to it than that. To begin with, they were the perfect subjects to be hypnotised. Victims of their own greed with an intense desire to prove themselves in the absence of their boss, they *wanted* those diamonds to be real. They *wanted* to be the ones to secure a deal beyond their wildest dreams and to be the envy of every other trader in Hatton Garden. When someone *wants* something so badly, his or her mind is already preconditioned for hypnosis. An easy target for someone like me. In addition, I'd gained their sympathy and trust with a convincing but emotive story of my husband leaving me for another woman.

'It's also the *way* you say things. If you modulate your voice with a particular tone and rhythm, you can make your words smooth and hypnotic in themselves.' Ryleigh's voice slowed as she spoke, as if to demonstrate. 'Even my perfume was carefully chosen. The sense of smell is highly emotive and can be used powerfully in hypnosis. Fragrances can convey a vast array of emotions and feelings from desire to power, vitality to relaxation. Those are the essentials of what happened, in order to make Ronan and Camilla believe unequivocally that what they had in front of them were real diamonds.'

'I *knew* they were acting strangely,' Spencer said. A sudden look of horror came over his face. 'You didn't hypnotise me too, did you?' he asked in alarm.

'No, of course not,' Ryleigh said laughing. 'That wouldn't have been in our interests at all. We needed *you* to spot that there was something going on. The only thing I had to be careful of was that you didn't notice something wrong and point it out to your co-workers before I'd had a chance to hypnotise them. I guessed you probably wouldn't realise the moissanite stones weren't real diamonds straight away, but when I first presented the grading reports to you in the showroom, I was careful not to let you dwell on them for too long. You'd have been sure to spot that they were all the same and bring it to Ronan and Camilla's attention.'

'But when Ronan and Camilla first checked the grading reports against the information on the GIA database, everything was in order,' Spencer said with a puzzled look. 'Even when *I* checked one of the reports that evening, it was legit.'

'But when Tobias returned from his business trip and you checked the reports again, nothing matched up with the GIA online Report Check anymore, right?' Mallory asked.

'Yeah,' Spencer replied. 'How did that happen?'

'I'm afraid we hacked into the computer system of Tobias Moncler Jewels,' Dionne said. 'That's my speciality. Tobias has a pretty good firewall around his local area network, but it still wasn't that big a challenge. After Ryleigh had delivered the necklace and the grading reports to the store, I hacked into the network and set up a fake GIA website. Whenever anyone logged into what they thought was the legitimate GIA database, they were actually being directed to my pseudo one, where the report numbers from Vivienne Karlsson's grading reports appeared to match those of the diamonds listed in the fake GIA online Report Check. Which is why, Spencer, that even when you checked one yourself, you were also directed to the fake database. For a few hours, I had control of the entire computer system of Tobias Moncler Jewels.'

'We chose a time when we knew Tobias would be away,' Mallory added. 'We had a lot of respect for him and we didn't want him to be mixed up in all this.'

'Plus we thought we'd kill two birds with one stone and get rid of Ronan and Camilla for him,' Ryleigh said.

'But they were two of his most trustworthy employees.' Spencer frowned in puzzlement.

'Except they weren't,' Ryleigh went on. 'We'd been watching your co-workers at the store as well as you, just to make sure we got the lie of the land. The plan took six months to formulate before we could go live with it. It had to be flawless without any hitches. In order to prepare for every eventuality we looked into your pasts and surveilled each one of you. Sure, Otto and Keeley's worst crime was that they were lazy. But Ronan and Camilla were up to something far more degenerate. It didn't take long to discover that they were stealing from Tobias.'

'*Stealing?*' Spencer asked in disbelief. 'But he trusted them with everything.'

'I know,' Ryleigh said soberly, 'and they abused that trust. We decided they had to go. And we worked out that we could make that happen as well as attract your — and hopefully Alicia's — attention. We didn't care about making any money from the necklace. In fact, we were prepared to lose it all. We intended to pay the eight million back straight away, which we did. If we could get Ronan and Camilla to go through with the bank transfer, we knew we had them too.'

'So you hypnotised them to make them believe that the moissanite necklace was real diamonds and the grading reports were genuine?' Spencer asked.

'Exactly,' Ryleigh said. 'The next morning when they went to the bank to transfer the money, the four of us were everywhere, keeping tabs on them, making sure it all went according to the plan.'

'Mallory followed them to the bank,' Dionne said, 'and then Jess took over, posing as a customer. She contacted us as soon as the transaction was authorised. We congratulated ourselves that morning on pulling it off. We almost couldn't believe we'd done it.'

'I met Ronan and Camilla back at the store later that morning and released them from their hypnotic states,' Ryleigh said.

'And then Tobias got back from his business trip, saw that the gems weren't real diamonds and the grading reports were fake and Ronan and Camilla realised their mistake,' Spencer said.

'Yes,' Ryleigh continued. 'Ronan and Camilla must've wondered how on earth they'd been deceived, and obviously Tobias, a highly experienced and knowledgeable gemologist and diamond merchant, noticed straight away that something was wrong. In addition, the computer network for the store was back to normal and no longer under Dionne's control. When Tobias — or anyone else — logged into the GIA database to check the phoney grading reports, nothing matched up.'

'And when we checked the contact details for Vivienne Karlsson that you'd given us...' Spencer began.

'You got the sex chatline,' Ryleigh said with a glint in her eye. 'Sorry about that, but we thought we'd have a bit of fun too!'

'Ronan and Camilla being fired was collateral as far as we were concerned though.' Mallory took up the narration again. 'Most importantly for us, you'd told Alicia everything, Spencer, as we'd hoped you would. The ball had started rolling and our plan was working.'

'The next thing you had to do was get me back here in Antigua,' Alicia said.

'Correct,' Mallory nodded. He adopted a solemn expression. 'More apologies needed here. I'd like to say sorry on Dionne's behalf for hacking into various government databases and websites to retrieve your and Gray's personal details: full names, addresses, dates of births, passport numbers and so on.'

'I am truly sorry for that,' Dionne added. 'I hated invading your privacy, but we just wanted to take care of everything for you. We wanted to do whatever it took to help facilitate your investigations, whether it was providing protection, finance, booking flights, a hotel. Look at it as us watching over you, wherever your investigations took you. We were your guardian angels.'

'The puppet masters,' Alicia said out loud.

'I guess you could call us that too,' Mallory said.

'Now I know why you looked so familiar,' Spencer exclaimed suddenly. 'You were that homeless guy slumped in the doorway opposite the jewellery store.'

'Yeah, that was me,' Mallory said, 'and I owe you for the coffee and muffin, by the way. The muffin was delicious.'

'You're welcome,' Spencer said. His face fell suddenly. 'The homeless man who fought with Otto…'

'Yep, that was me too,' Mallory replied. 'Don't worry though. It's all forgotten. There's no judgement from me. Get back on the wagon and carry on. You're doing great.'

'Thanks,' Spencer said, looking relieved.

'You were also the man dining alone at Mullrose Grill when Spencer first told me about the necklace, weren't you?' Alicia said suddenly.

'Yes.' Mallory nodded.

'Those black-rimmed, retro glasses…'

'Were meant to subliminally remind you of your teenage years. I asked Carlos to tell me as much as he could remember of you back then. Of course, I couldn't recall you but he provided me with a photograph of you and your parents.'

'And to think when Carlos and I had dinner he never mentioned you.'

'I asked him to promise he wouldn't.'

'And he kept his word. That's just like Carlos. And the man at South Kensington station? That was you too?'

'Yes, although I was a little careless that evening. I realised I'd been noticed.'

'And you had,' Alicia said.

'You were spying on me too Hattie,' Spencer said, turning to her.

'I know, I'm sorry. It was kind of fun though,' Hattie said with a smile. 'I'm glad we swapped numbers.'

'Did you just want my number because of all this though?' Spencer asked seriously.

'Probably. At first,' Hattie replied. 'But now I've got to know you better...'

'Yes?'

'Well, I'm still waiting for you to teach me how to tell the difference between a real and a fake diamond.'

'I'd be happy to. Any time.'

'It's been a wonderful evening, but I must head over to reception and check everything's okay,' Leon said, standing up. 'Alicia, thank you. For everything.' He hugged her tightly.

'Thank *you* Leon,' Alicia replied. 'Especially for allowing me to accuse you so harshly in the auditorium. I felt terrible...'

'Please, no apology necessary,' Leon said graciously. 'It was my privilege to be a part of the act. Glad I could be of help.' He turned to Mallory and his three former assistants.

'I don't know how you pulled off that masterplan, but you did it,' he said, shaking Mallory's hand and hugging the women in turn. 'Congratulations. And an excellent choice of investigative journalist.' He winked at Alicia before saying goodnight and disappearing in the direction of the hotel reception.

FORTY-TWO

9:50 am, Saturday, September 1
The West Beach Club, Antigua

They were the last guests to finish breakfast on the restaurant terrace at The West Beach Club, but the waiting staff had received instructions from Roslyn to keep the coffee flowing. Alicia and Gray were joined by Spencer and Hattie, Owen, Mallory, Ryleigh, Jess and Dionne, and a later arrival, Anton, who insisted they call him by his real name: Matt. As he helped himself to hot buttered toast and Violet poured fresh coffee for everyone, he regaled the group with events from the previous evening.

'I'm not sure the Karlemans are having the greatest time right now,' he said, taking a bite of toast. 'Their cell mates haven't exactly taken a liking to them, especially Vivienne, and their cell is about half the size of her ensuite in their super-yacht.'

The remark brought amused smiles from those seated around the table.

'They both admitted to everything of course, but then they didn't have a whole lot of choice as I already had the recording of their confessions in the auditorium. Charles knew he was wired, but he thought it was so he could summon me for protection if things went awry. He had no idea his words would be used against him. And Vivienne's loud voice was picked up perfectly by his microphone. Of course, the police are very happy that one of their cold cases has been solved as well.'

They were interrupted by the ring of a cell phone.

'Excuse me,' Anton said, quickly swallowing his mouthful.

'Neville, hi,' he held the phone to his ear and listened for a few seconds before speaking. 'Oh, you found it? Where? Right. Right. So it was where he said it would be? Oh, I see. Yeah, I'll bet it was. But you got it. Great work. To think, all that time. Oh really? Wow, well that's good. Yeah, you too. We'll talk later. Cheers Neville.'

Anton placed the phone beside him and glanced around the table.

'They found the ME's van,' he said.

'After all this time...' Alicia spoke with excitement in her voice.

'Where was it?' Gray asked.

'Exactly where Charles said it would be, although they took him with them just to save time. He'd remembered the location precisely though. It was a nightmare to get to. The van had been run off the road and down a steep drop through trees and thick foliage. I doubt anyone's ventured down there since Hurricane Luis. It's a lonely piece of road a couple of miles out from Rock Palm. The drop leads to nowhere. The van was quite far down, all busted up and smashed in with its doors ripped off. It must've taken a real battering when it careered off the road. They also found a rusted metal gurney a few feet away.'

'Human remains?' Alicia asked tentatively.

'Yep. A human skull and a couple of long bones so far — certainly enough for a pathologist to work with — and they're still looking. There's plenty to go on to confirm the Karlemans' confessions though.'

'I'm glad they found it,' Alicia said.

'I've got something else for you,' Anton said, reaching into a black bag at his feet. Pulling out a white A4-sized envelope, he opened it and extracted a small bundle of papers. He passed them to Spencer.

'I'm not much good at reading this sort of stuff, but I understand we have an expert gemologist in our midst.' He grinned at Spencer.

'Yeah right,' Spencer said. 'I'm far from that. The real gemologist is back in London but hang on, these are...' He thumbed through the top few pages. 'They're official GIA grading reports.... for individual diamonds... There's one for a pear-shaped, pink diamond weighing just over ten carats... They're...'

'The grading reports for each individual stone from the original necklace, yes,' Anton finished.

Suddenly a puzzled look came over Spencer's face as he examined one of the reports near the bottom of the pile.

'Strange, there's an odd gemstone out here. It can't be part of the necklace. It's for a round diamond weighing two carats, but its colour grade is H — not totally colourless — and the clarity is VS1, which means the stone isn't flawless; it's got a few very minor inclusions. Sure, they're difficult to spot and you'd still need a microscope, but it's different to the other stones.'

'It's the grading report for the forty-ninth stone,' Alicia said suddenly. 'Although there are forty-nine round diamonds set in the necklace, only forty-eight are flawless. It's what convinced the Karlemans that I had the real thing.'

'The reports are from Charles,' Anton said, 'along with this.' He produced another, smaller sheet of paper and slid it across the table to Mallory. It was a handwritten note, signed by Charles Karleman. As Mallory read it aloud, his voice quivered slightly.

Dear Mallory (Mortimer) the Magician. On Megan's behalf, please accept this diamond necklace and the accompanying grading reports as a gift from me. You were much more of a father to her than I ever was. It is right and fitting that you should do with the necklace whatever you feel Megan would have wanted. She always spoke with the greatest fondness of you and the magic team, her true family. Please forgive me for the past. Yours, Charles Karleman.

At the bottom of the note was his flourishing signature. There was silence around the table before Anton spoke.

'The necklace is yours Mallory,' he said solemnly. 'It's up to you what you decide.'

'Well, I — I don't really know,' the magician said, glancing at his three former assistants. 'Any ideas?'

'I have one,' Ryleigh said suddenly. 'Spencer, perhaps you and Tobias could help us out here?'

'Sure,' Spencer nodded eagerly. 'What can we do?'

'Can you sell this necklace on our behalf?'

'Of course,' Spencer replied. 'It would probably be best placed in an auction house catalogue…'

'Whatever you think,' Ryleigh said. 'I'll leave the details to you. Of the money we make from the sale, we can donate a large percentage to a Caribbean hurricane relief fund.'

'And the rest of it?' Mallory asked.

'Anastasia always dreamed of setting up her own magic school for young magicians,' Ryleigh began. 'It's just a thought…'

The suggestion was met with nods of approval.

'She would've loved those ideas,' Owen said with a broad smile. The well-dressed, clean-shaven man checked his watch.

'I should get going,' he said suddenly, standing up.

'Where to?' Spencer asked in surprise.

'My new job,' Owen replied proudly. 'I start today. As a groundsman. Here at The West Beach Club. Leon spoke to me yesterday.'

There was a chorus of delighted congratulations as Owen thanked them for their unwavering belief in his innocence. He said goodbye with a firm promise to stay in touch. As he walked away, there was a lull in the conversation. The remaining members of the group gazed contentedly across the terrace towards the brilliant turquoise sea. A small sailing boat drifted lazily across the horizon. Waves lapped gently on the sun-kissed beach and a soft breeze stirred the leaves of the palm trees nearby. It was another perfect Antiguan day. Suddenly, a voice broke the silence.

'Does anyone want to know how to tell a real diamond from a fake?'

AUTHOR'S NOTE:

Rock Palm Resort is based on a real life abandoned hotel on the Caribbean island of Antigua. It was tragically devastated by Hurricane Luis in September 1995 and provided the inspiration for this book. Early in 2018, after twenty-three years, the real hotel was demolished. A new resort is being built on the same site by an international luxury hotel and resort company. The magic trick which was used to conceal the diamonds is an old classic theatre act from the nineteenth century. I am indebted to many sources for the information on gemmology. Although I have tried to ensure the descriptions are as factual as possible, any inaccuracies in this story are entirely my own. While many places in this book are authentic, the characters are wholly fictitious and bear no resemblance to any person in real life.

Since completing *Diamonds Of Deception*, I discovered an archived photograph online of an old payment document for guests who stayed at the original resort, back in ninety-five. They checked out just days before Hurricane Luis made landfall in Antigua. The document had been at the top of a pile of papers scattered across the floor of the hotel reception. It contained the address of the guests' bank: Hatton Garden, London, England. This is, of course, a remarkable coincidence. Then again, perhaps the truth really is stranger than fiction…

Printed in Great Britain
by Amazon